SLOW
GODS

SLOW
GODS

CLAIRE NORTH

orbit

orbit-books.co.uk

ORBIT

First published in Great Britain in 2025 by Orbit

3 5 7 9 10 8 6 4 2

A CIP catalogue record for this book
is available from the British Library.

HB ISBN 978-0-356-52618-8
C format 978-0-356-52619-5

Typeset in Adobe Caslon by M Rules
Printed and bound in Great Britain by
Clays Ltd, Elcograf S.p.A.

Papers used by Orbit are from well-managed forests
and other responsible sources.

MIX
Paper | Supporting
responsible forestry
FSC
www.fsc.org
FSC® C104740

Orbit
An imprint of
Little, Brown Book Group
Carmelite House
50 Victoria Embankment
London EC4Y 0DZ

The authorised representative
in the EEA is
Hachette Ireland
8 Castlecourt Centre
Dublin 15, D15 XTP3, Ireland
(email: info@hbgi.ie)

An Hachette UK Company
www.hachette.co.uk

orbit-books.co.uk

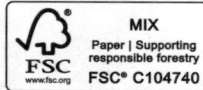

PART 1

How I Died

Chapter 1

My name is Mawukana na-Vdnaze, and I am a very poor copy of myself.

The Major tells me that it is important that I channel my curiosity into expansive things, and goes to great lengths to keep me occupied. Regulated. To this end, I have written numerous papers on subjects such as extra-planetary botany, xeno-archaeological linguistics, inter-species sociology, the history of art, and one slightly whimsical article on juggling, which received a surprising amount of traction.

However, when my efforts are cited, it is rarely in the context of the work itself. My detailed analytics, exhaustive research – these are not of interest. Rather it is my *otherness*, my non-being/being, my perceived deficiencies in certain matters of sentience that seems to capture people's imagination, regardless of how absurd these metrics are when one actually stops to think about them.

In short: I am a frustrated academic.

People get anxious when I am frustrated. They are concerned it may provoke unpredictable consequences. Thus, to keep me occupied, it has been suggested that I write down some of my experiences in a less formal manner, with an eye to "mainstream" audiences. I do not see the point – there are plenty of romantically inclined individuals with harrowing tales who will happily share their trauma in exchange for cash and an inter-planetary speaking tour, thank you very much.

However. I do appreciate that if left to my own devices, I can experience unwanted episodes. It would pain me deeply if my actions were to cause emotional or physical harm to those around me.

In telling my story, there are certain things I should perhaps lie about.

(I am a dreadful liar.)

I should make myself a hero. Pretend I knew certain things before I did, was not used by strangers and gods, did not leave people behind.

I should claim that I understand love.

This last is most important, and I am trying.

I am always trying.

Is that not enough?

Chapter 2

This is the story of the supernova event known as Lhonoja.

By the end of it, several planets will have burned, a couple of civilisations will have fallen, and I will have spoken to an entity some consider a god, and whose theological status will remain in question throughout.

Before then, I must explain how I came to be, and for that, I must take you back several centuries, to Glastya Row.

Glastya Row started as a landing strip on the planet Tu-mdo.

Most urban establishments on most colonised worlds begin this way. Tu-mdo had been a prime terraforming candidate – comfortable gravity, good magnetic shield, not too hot, not too cold, not tidally locked and already possessed of a moon which, once water was thawed out in sufficient volume, would serve to stir the great big mixing bowl of Tu-mdo's freshly churning oceans. The first colonists didn't even need to spend five centuries in arcologies waiting for atmospheric conditions to settle, but were out and breathing without aid within a couple of pioneering generations. Two millennia later, Glastya Row had been transformed from pioneer's outpost to merely another borough of some few million in the great city of Heom, a middling hub of profit and endeavour within the interplanetary-spanning United Social Venture.

They say you can tell a lot about a Venture based on how its employees name their children.

In Antekeda, the Venture that ran my city, these were the most common middle names given to children at birth:

Chairman – 15 per cent

Entrepreneur – 10 per cent

Director – 9 per cent

Abundant – 5 per cent

Diligent – 4 per cent

In Theymann, a Venture specialising in deep space habitation, the distribution skewed towards Pioneers and Engineers, while in Halsect there was an almost sentimental emphasis on children called "Aspiring".

My parents had all the ambition you might expect of residents of Glastya Row, combined with a grim realism. Thus when I was born, my name was registered as Mawukana "Respected" na-Vdnaze. I might never achieve dazzling heights or have great Shine, but dammit, my neighbours would at least know that I was respectable.

It would be fair to say that things went downhill from there.

I am told that I cried an unhallowed amount when I was born, though no one seems able to clarify what "unhallowed" means. I imagine my scream rose a little in volume as they implanted my Chint in the top of my plump left bicep, already embedded with the debts I had accrued to the Venture that ran the hospital that sheltered me – 400 Glint for a standard birth, plus another 1,873 Glint for basic costs such as bedding, vaccinations, postnatal check-ups, vitamin shots, etc. . . .

Thus, before I was placed upon my mother's breast, I was marked with the overriding feature of life on Glastya Row – the debt I owed.

As befits two individuals who named their child "Respected", my parents were not irresponsible. They had carefully saved for this moment, and were between them able to bring my initial debt down to a mere 700 Glint, and keep on top of the 1.5 per cent child-rate interest payments my existence accrued. Moreover, to welcome me into the world, Antekeda gifted me with fifty shares, my ownership marking me as a citizen of the Venture. By the time I turned fifteen and sat my assignment exams, those shares were worth nearly 600 Glint – though my educational and civic debts were well in excess of 92,000.

This system, we were taught, was about fairness. We were pioneers and our world was a place of scarcity, hardship and struggle. Everything the Venture gave us – the air we breathed, the roads we walked down, the schools we learned in – had been sweated for, bled for, and our debts were a marker of the needful labour we would give back in return.

All are born equal, and by their labours shall they rise.

This philosophy was the underlying constitution of the United Social Venture. Both it and the more anthropologically engaging qualities of social and economic status that arose from it were known as Shine.

We were not a high-Shine family. My parents ran a small restaurant that served cold-broth dumplings to hot middle Managers too tired and busy to cook. They did their best to improve their Shine, constantly cooing over difficult, well-dressed customers and putting themselves forward to run catering events in Shiny houses or at Shiny events, but nothing could really wipe the smell of Glastya Row off their grease-stained aprons and soap-scoured fingers. Every six months, an Antekeda representative would come by and offer them another course or long-distance learning diploma in business growth and radical enterprise, and sometimes my mother, always the more energetic of the two, would sign up and do her coursework and pay her fees, and talk at the table about how this was it. This was the change we needed to get out, move up. It never came to anything.

During my "cute" years, which I was told were seven to eleven years old, I worked as a waiter in the shop in the hope someone would give me that most wondrous of miracles, a "tip" for my services. By the time I was twelve, you could see the shape of the adult I was going to be. My father's thick, straight black hair was overgrown around my mother's sunset-through-smog face. I was always a little short, with green-grey eyes that narrowed to almost impossible lines when I squinted in confusion (as I did a lot) and pale lips that didn't smile enough, or smiled wrong, or just didn't quite get the smiling business right, whenever I tried to move them.

"Smile with your eyes," my mother commanded, during one of her we-shall-advance phases. So I stood in front of the mirror in the grubby upstairs bathroom and squeezed my eyelids tight and waggled my eyebrows and tried to inventory every tiny muscle about my growing grubby dishcloth of a face, until I could at least achieve something that didn't seem to upset people too badly.

Despite, or perhaps owing to, these efforts, I was relegated to the back of the kitchen so that my mother could stay out front, charming and occasionally bamboozling the customers. By the time I was fourteen and my schooling was getting unfeasibly expensive, it was already apparent that I would not have a Shiny life. Most of my classmates were starting to drop out into the menial labour that was the heart of every Venture, and those who remained were preparing for adulthood with an endless dance of alliances, enmities, petty acts of cruelty and theft, out-daring each other in who could game the system. Bullies thrived – so long as they were not caught. Being caught was far worse a sin than being a thief, a liar or simply cruel.

Many economists, observing the Shine, have marvelled at the low levels of educational obtainment common across its population. The circular economies of most other worlds, powered by the sunlight or atomic reactors and fed by agricultural systems whose architects can sit in their pantries dispatching drones to the harvest, consider education not merely of primary importance to the success of their systems, but as frankly the most interesting thing the population can do with their expansive time.

However education breeds curiosity. And curiosity is one of the very first qualities that the leaders of the Shine seek to eliminate from the population.

I do not believe I was an unhappy child.

Neither do I think I was happy.

I did not understand the games that the Shine required. I struggled to lie, struggled to apply the dichotomy of winner and loser to the world I saw around me. When I tried playing, people laughed at me for doing it wrong in some mysterious way that I could not fully comprehend, and in time I simply stopped trying. I made friends with the most vulnerable and afraid, because they seemed to need friends the most, but simply sharing a sense of being outcast and alone is not quite the same as the meeting of true and lingering minds. I became quieter and quieter, since it was safer to be a nonentity, a child worth neither robbing nor mocking, than to try and fail so badly at the rituals of life that my peers seemed so gifted in. I passed my exams by rote, but showed no entrepreneurial spark save in the sciences, which was an unfashionable and underfunded discipline.

There was no question of being able to pay senior school fees when I turned fifteen, and no real need for me in the restaurant while my parents were able-bodied, so I took the only job that would have me and started work at the local traffic tower. Initially I was a runner, doing whatever errands my bosses needed doing; by the time I turned eighteen, I had been promoted to junior flight-caller, directing sub-atmospheric cargo traffic in the airspace around the city. When they gave me the first two scars on my left ear to mark my entry into the world of work, I felt moderately proud. Pain sometimes has that effect – we imbue it with meaning, to try and make it seem like it has a point. Very few things sum up life in the Shine better than our scars.

The work was harmless enough – computers did most of the actual route planning and plotting, and my main duty was to be screamed at by irate customers when they weren't given priority, and to occasionally override the bot's default settings to let a VIP – or someone who'd paid to be treated like a VIP – through. Very occasionally we'd get a small spaceflight vessel at the high-thermal pad on the edge of the city and I'd try to chat with the captain on comms – someone who'd seen other worlds, other stars – but my understanding of the worlds beyond my own was so stagnant, so limited, that I didn't really know what to ask.

"Maw," sighed Ruc, the most indulgent of my colleagues in the tower, "you just don't get it, do you?"

"Get what?"

"All of it. Just ... all of it."

In the language of the Mdo, the peoples who are the Shine, there are two words for "us". The first is the cohesion of necessity. In the early days of the Ventures this was the sacred "us" – the "us" of the slowship, of recycled air and recycled oxygen, of shared heat and metal and danger. It was the inviolable "us" of peoples who, if they cracked at all, would be torn apart. Then the ships settled, colonising the worlds that would become the Shine, and this first "us" became the "us" of our shared Venture, of the tight bonds of labour and the scars we bore. This second "us" is the "us-not-like-them". It is the "us" that is the barrier against which no other can break in, and was the "us" that was always used when people explained why I could not be with them.

Then the Slow came.

Chapter 3

This is what I knew about the Slow, the day qe came to Tu-mdo: I knew that the Slow was a machine, and it was old. Older than the Shine, older than the Accord of planets that existed outside Mdo space. No one could remember a time when the Slow hadn't existed, and archaeologists kept on uncovering further proof of its ineffable ancientness. A perfect black sphere moving through the interstellar darkness at a maximum of 0.3 of the speed of light, despite this sedate progress between the stars the Slow had a knack of showing up in the vicinities of major galactic events just before they unfolded. This had uncomfortable implications, which the Shine largely chose to ignore.

The quans referred to the Slow as "qe", saying that "it" was the pronoun you used for an insentient object, like a kettle or a biscuit tin, whereas qe was very obviously alive and thinking. The Shine disapproved of such nuance, rattling off the usual nonsense about souls and sacred flesh and so on. But even the Shine knew better than to ignore the Slow, when qe deigned to speak.

The Slow qimself did not come to Tu-mdo, instead sending qis messengers, black boxes tumbling through space, propelled by no-one-was-quite-sure-what but that pundits grumbled was probably "some sort" of ion drive. Six of qis messengers entered sub-light broadcast range of the planets Cha-mdo, Ber-mdo, Tu-mdo and

Yu-mdo and the orbital habitats Reio-tu and Khd-tu before astronomers detected them. The military immediately wanted to shoot them down, as militaries do, but the diplomatic corps bartered them down to merely imposing total comms blackout with nuclear strikes a poised backup.

By then, other systems in the wider Accord had also discovered the black boxes entering their magnetic space. Adjumir was the first to formally announce its sighting, followed by Haima and four quan outposts scattered between Ho'aka and the Eyrie. In the end, seventeen systems admitted to having detected the messengers of the Slow.

The scale of the visitations, the varied points of origin, the time in which these boxes must have been travelling all added to consternation among observers, a sense of something significant about to happen. Pundits pundited; conspiracy theorists grew irate. There was enough time between spotting the objects to their final deceleration for everyone to get really rather stressed.

A few observers pointed out that the Slow's messengers were descending upon points within an eighty light-year radius with a clear and obvious centre, but their observations were dismissed – not because they were implausible, but because their implications were too alarming to consider. This is a flaw I have observed many times – people will expend vast energies in ignoring the obvious terrifying thing *because* it terrifies them so. It is a trait that fascinates me to this day.

On Tu-mdo, of course, we had no idea that any of this was happening.

This turned out to be a mistake on the part of the Executorium, for on reaching stable orbit above the planetary surface, the Slow's messenger proceeded to immediately, and seemingly without actually transmitting anything detectable in the electromagnetic spectrum, hijack every communication device within the system.

PEOPLE OF TU-MDO! qe proclaimed. IN ONE HUNDRED YEARS, THE BINARY STAR SYSTEM

LK-08091881 WILL COLLAPSE IN UPON ITSELF. THE RESULTING SHOCK WAVE WILL TRAVEL OUT AT THE SPEED OF LIGHT AND OBLITERATE ALL LIFE WITHIN AN EIGHTY-THREE LIGHT-YEAR RADIUS. YOU HAVE UNTIL THEN TO PREPARE.

The wording was largely the same on every planet above which the Slow's messengers came, with a few tweaks for localisation. On Adjumir, for example, the binary star system was identified as the Lovers – a sentimental bit of common colloquial that made itself immediately understood to the waiting populace. And on Haima, the radius of destruction was given in localised "qika" metrics rather than the more broadly used light year, with the phrase "obliterate all life" expanded to include the metric "of all degrees of sentience, constitutionally acknowledged and otherwise".

Above orbital platforms and nascent moon-worlds, the Slow gave qis warning. In the darkest corners of the blackest mining belts; above the glittering capitals of triumphant civilisations, qe proclaimed the fate of billions, and those billions listened in enraptured silence and dread.

At Tu-mdo, sixteen seconds after the Slow began qis transmission, the authorities opened fire and blasted the messengers from the sky before they could squeak another word.

Regrettably, I was on the night side of the planet when the transmission went out, and thus slept through the entire thing.

Chapter 4

The first pioneer Shine children are taught about in school is Clonus um-Bagret Tererens. Hé was captain of the first Venture fleet, with its cargo of 3.2 million colonists on its four-hundred-year voyage across the stars. This was before arcspace travel, before we had learned to bend the impossible dark. Clonus um-Bagret Tererens famously chose the fleet's final destination of Ko-mdo with a declaration of "There is no obstacle Man cannot overcome!"

This is another motto of the Shine, etched in gold above major corporate centres.

Happily for Clonus Tererens' ambition, if not hís common sense, there was a lot about Ko-mdo to overcome. It had liquid water at the poles and enough carbon dioxide to feed habitation dome scrubbers, but the gravity was light, the magnetic shield was weak and the soil largely toxic to human life. But Clonus um-Bagret Tererens had a vision, and a belief in the inherent power of human ingenuity and strength of human labour. So long as we work, and work hard, without complaint, hé said, there is nothing we cannot achieve. And so it was, although later scholars questioned whether it ever in fact needed to be.

Clonus died before hé could see hís vision of a humanity elevated by labour come to fruition, so it was hís successor, Aemilis Nona

Wells, who put down the first oxygen revolt. Her swiftness and brutality was to become something of a theme in USV policies, and in the aftermath, certain ideas were codified into law, including the principle that every individual was only worth the sum of their labour. Slackers, scroungers, those who didn't pull their weight – the frontier of space was too hard, too cruel for the rest to carry these, and if their number included those injured or old, well, that was just a harsh reality. The duty of every individual in the Shine was to ensure that they were working at the peak of their individual capacity; if everyone did that equally, there would be a perfect society where no one would have to worry about looking after anyone else at all.

By the time Quincitus Keto led the breakout from Ko-mdo to conquer the worlds of Bi-mdo and Gera-sa, the army hé led was almost unrecognisable from the original colonists who had come to Ko-mdo nearly three centuries ago. Breeding programmes had over-filled the cramped arcologies with too many unemployed teenagers, their limbs frail and thin in the weak gravity, gene-blasting radiation and meagre rations of Ko-mdo. But the peoples of the United Social Venture were not ones to lie down and die, and so with hís ragged ships hammered together by blood and will, with hís suicide troops and desperate force of arms, Quincitus Keto led the people of the USV out into the galaxy and to fresh new worlds, seizing by indomitable strength that which weaker peoples were too frail to defend. Thus the USV proved once and for all not merely that it was a force to be reckoned with, but that it was ideologically *right*. That hardy survivors, willing to work themselves to the bone, could with sheer guts and strength overcome any obstacle. Even an obstacle as absurd as trying to eke out a life in the dust devils of Ko-mdo, miserably failing in the attempt and then conquering nearby, far gentler systems when you eventually realised the scale of your generational, mind-boggling mistake.

*

A few millennia later, the Slow came to Tu-mdo.

Half the planet saw the Slow's message, and though the Marketing Standards Agency raced to scrub all mention of it, even they couldn't keep down conversation about the end of the world. Venture Management initially tried to shrug off the Slow's message, claim it was a conspiracy, an insentient AI sent by the Accord to sow chaos and so on. Alas, the binary star system LK-08091881 – more generally known as Lhonoja – was only seventy-nine light years away, a mere jaunt in galactic terms, and every astronomer in the southern hemisphere, from advanced observatories to teenagers with a telescope, could turn their gaze upon the heavens and say but oh goodness, oh my, oh yes. There are two stars spinning towards each other, exactly as the Slow said, and if we look back through the historical data it would appear that they are on a collision course and actually the maths is fairly elementary now we bother to think about it . . .

The Ventures wiped the historical data.

This caused further outcry – it was too late, too much, the world could see the truth of it.

So they tried a different approach. Yes, Lhonoja was going to collapse in on itself, but no, it wasn't a problem. Not a problem at all. The nearest planet to the blast – Cha-mdo – all that needed was a magnetic shield built in high orbit, a fairly simple bit of engineering, and it would be fine. And the rest of the Shine? It was far too far from the supernova to actually experience any harm. There'd be some nice dancing lights in the sky for a few days and maybe a couple of thunderstorms, and then it would pass, and where the light of Lhonoja had shone, now it would not.

Nothing to worry about.

Nothing to worry about at all.

This time, when the astronomers protested, the astronomers disappeared.

Then the physicists objected, and they disappeared as well.

Then the philosophers, the mathematicians, the planetary

biologists, the engineers, even a few political scientists – they vanished, and kept on vanishing, until no one was really left to object.

And that might have been the end of it, except that in Heom, one of the physicists they disappeared was Sarifi "Famed" im-Yyahwa, and she had Shine. A middling commnet personality, she went to the right parties, talked to the right people, hosted spectacular occasions when spectacle was required but knew also how to invite the correct manager to a quiet dinner at an appropriate place. She conformed enough to be accepted, but was mischievous enough in her opinions to stand out, and thus, one careful smile and polite "how fascinating – tell me about *you*" at a time, she had risen, and people envied her. There is no Shine greater than being envied.

We are the United Social Venture, she said.

We are pioneers, resilient, hardy.

So why are we so afraid of the truth?

The Marketing Standards Agency initially let her broadcast, because she wasn't advocating any especially radical change. "Just asking questions" was her motto. But the more she talked, the more people listened, not least as there didn't seem anyone else worthwhile to tune into, and the more people listened, the more she clearly felt she had something to say.

"But why are we pretending this isn't an extinction-level event?" she demanded one day. "Why are we so scared?"

The first time she was arrested, she paid her way back onto the streets within three hours, marching before the cameras with the scars of her imprisonment bare across her shoulders, declaring: "This time it's *actually* the end of the world!"

Her broadcasts evolved. "The Executorium isn't willing to confront the scale of the danger facing us, because to do so means confronting the weaknesses in our Ventures! Maybe it's time to admit that the system doesn't work, and that to face up to what is coming, we need fundamental change!"

This time when the Shine arrested her, there was rioting outside the prison, and she was busted out before security could intervene.

Now she broadcast from underground, and her broadcasts were electric.

"Corruption! Exploitation! Inertia! Stagnation! This is what our Venture has become and they" – everyone loves a polemic "they"; it leaves so much to the imagination – "*they* don't want you to know it!"

It is unclear whether Sarifi actually believed a word she said – perhaps it was just another power play, another bold move to accumulate more Shine by making herself relevant, the kind of firebrand who guaranteed views without ever actually taking anything seriously. Perhaps she understood that it was only her Shine that kept her safe, and her Shine was built on outrage, noise and attention.

It is not especially easy to attach new ideas to something as big as the very literal "end of the world" and its expected arrival in one hundred and seventy-nine years, no matter how charismatically you may express it. But people can channel big fears into more immediate concerns. They were hungry. Saw their debts grow, not diminish. Went sick rather than pay for medicine. Laboured mightily to get more Shine, and yet never seemed to rise. Had been promised hope. Saw only stagnation. Paid their profits in corruption and tasted poison in the water they fed to their children at night. Such a loose conflagration of sparks, each burning by themselves, was not quite enough to start a fire. And yet they simmered.

The last time Sarifi was arrested, there was no public announcement, no legal declaration. She simply vanished without a trace.

Usually that would have been enough, but times had been hard in Heom, and the Executorium clearly misjudged how people would interpret absence.

Petitions became protests, protests became marching through the streets, became unauthorised acts of disobedience, the downing of tools. Became night-time clashes with Venture security, hacks and hijacks of commnet airwaves, mass arrests that only made the shouting louder. By the time Special Operations were sent in, the protests were not even about the inevitable destruction of the planet; they were about working conditions and stagnant salaries, about elders left to die because they had not paid enough of their debts to live, about children as young as nine put into the debtor's collar because they had been judged without potential and sold onto whichever Venture cared to pay a pittance for their labour. Nor were the protests confined to Glastya Row, or even to Heom. The Slow's message had awoken something across the Shine, a sense of expectations unfulfilled, promises broken. We were supposed to look after ourselves so that no one had to look after each other; yet how did looking out for just ourselves solve *this*?

Perhaps this was what the Slow intended all along. After all, qe came with a message, when qe could have said nothing at all.

I did not take part in the riots.

I hid in my room, with the window shuttered and door locked.

Even though there was an airspace suspension, I was meant to go to work, and was fined when I did not. I tried to get a medical certificate to exempt me, but the doctor's prices were higher than the penalty. Eventually I risked the two-hour walk across the city to the control tower, complete with blanket and pillow so I could sleep on the office floor, but just as I arrived, a strict stay-at-home policy was imposed, fining anyone caught outside their residence, even for medical emergencies. Damned if you do, damned if you don't. That is the Venture way.

So I crawled home in the dark, and to distract myself from the mixture of rage and silence in the streets, I read.

Here: the green-nosed biscuit shark. It is functionally deaf, blind, but its electromagnetic senses are so good it can detect the slightest flutter of a creature up to twenty kils away, and is sent into a frenzy by any boats that come too near, driven mad by the howl of its electrics. It migrates every year from pole to pole in a perfect straight line, following the magnetic currents of the world.

(Gunfire outside; someone calling for help. I put my hands over my ears, keep on reading.)

The aka-aka, many-legged and furry-backed, who build their cities deep in the dust of their home world, and whose spaceships resemble nothing so much as the great organic insect hives from which they came, and who communicate by touch and dance and are known to occasionally eat their dead when times are hard, having digestive systems that are more than capable of breaking down any questionable proteins that might be transmitted by the act, and who have no words for "peace" or "war", merely "being" and "un-being", the latter of which is the closest they come to expressing the grotesque violation, the unbearable insult of violence committed against another, which must be punished no matter what by un-being rendered in kind, since consequences, the aka-aka proclaim, are the only way people ever learn.

(The calls for help are silenced. Somewhere, something distant goes *whomp whomp whomp*. It sounds like flames. I didn't know that flames could make that kind of sound, but it seems right, somehow, seems like a kind of burning.)

About the universal vulture, a catch-all term for the tendency of carrion birds to evolve in basically every biome of every world. Most terraforming programmes introduce vultures or creatures like them to help accelerate decomposition within the system. Where they do not, vultures soon emerge anyway, no matter the density of atmosphere through which they float, no matter the meat upon which they feed. Evolution loves a vulture.

(When people do not understand you, and you do not understand people, you must find your beauty and your joy elsewhere.)

I do not know how near the gunfire came.

I did not know if anyone was "winning" or "losing" or what that might entail.

On the second day, the commnet was completely blacked out. I ate dried food from a foil packet and did not answer the door when my neighbour, Elder Zi, started wailing, because it sounded like she needed help. In the Shine, you left the weak behind. That habit had stayed embedded in our society long after we achieved abundance, enriched with words such as "strong", "independent" and "resilient". So for a day and a night I listened to an old woman cry, until she cried no more.

On the third day, Special Operations bombed the city.

They gave no warning, sounded no alarms.

I woke to the end of the world, and for a moment I thought it wasn't the end of the world, but the End of the World, the promised death by binary star, arriving one hundred and seventy-nine years ahead of schedule. My room shook and the windows shattered and the noise . . . It was not that it was loud, merely relentless, a shock that lingered in the mind long after the ringing outside had ceased. I felt lonely more than I felt afraid. Apart from my parents, who loved me more than they liked me, I could not think of anyone who would especially miss me. My life would come and go, and the only record of its existence would be the debt I had left upon it – 57,423 Glint, a sum that had been swelling and shrinking since the moment of my birth. Covered by the noise of the bombings, I allowed myself to howl, to shake my fists and produce all manner of implausible, strange noises from the back of my throat.

Still here, I screamed. I'm still here! I'm still here!

When the bombing stopped, there were fires.

My building was still standing, but two doors down a block was burning. I staggered out into the crimson dark and joined a chain dragging buckets from a broken pipe in the street to throw water not on the building, but on its neighbours, the people of Glastya Row briefly united in protecting what property they had. By the time the sun rose, I was a filthy shadow sitting beneath the scars of my home. I thought of my parents and their shop, but in the broken-toothed landscape it was hard to orientate, to work out which way was north, south, up or down. Familiar landmarks were gone, and as I tried to stumble through the ruins of the city,

I kept spinning round and round, the bodies of strangers in the street becoming a more distinct landmark than broken buildings I had known my whole life.

In the end, I stumbled into Corporate Security Services.

Antekeda Venture had drafted in operatives from Halsect and Blue Land to assist the local forces. When I saw them, I felt relief, staggered towards them with arms open and mouth wide, thinking they were here to help, to help me, please, help!

I don't know what they communicated with each other behind their faceless white helmets, but I imagine it was something along the lines of "here's another one", because they shot me without warning.

Chapter 5

This was not how I died; that will be soon enough.

Instead, Corpsec stunned me, barrelled me into the back of a truck, sent me straight to trial in an emergency court held in a tent on the edge of the city.

I will not bore you with the details of my case. I was accused of subversion and civic disobedience. The evidence was that I had lived in Glastya Row, and Glastya Row had committed subversion and civic disobedience. I could not afford representation. Every minute I spent in the court, my Chint accrued another 50 Glint of debt, for time being handled by civic authorities. I was sentenced to the debtor's collar, along with two thousand three hundred and fifty-one other survivors who had been unlucky enough to stumble into Corpsec in the ruins of Glastya Row. My debt – and therefore my labour – was sold at discount to Halsect, to do with as they would.

Children always feel injustice keenly. The first time they are lied to; the first time they realise that words are not truths, but promises that can be broken. Now they are a little closer to being an adult, and it is a tragedy.

In the courts of Glastya Row, people who should have known better wept, begged, cried out against injustice. And because they were distraught, so was I; I have always tended to tag along with what other people feel.

They said I was being sent off-world, to a labour camp. I mumbled: "My parents ..."

No one listened.

I blurted: "My parents, will they be informed, will they ... It's important, my parents, they have to ..."

Someone hit me, which was a kind of answer.

I thought I might actually cry then, mostly because my mother and father would be worried sick, the only people who had ever hoped for me, ever dreamed for me, ever wanted me to be something more, and I had disappointed them, let them down, let them down, and there was nothing respectable about me after all.

Seventy-nine light years away, two stars are dancing around each other, spinning towards their final, thunderous end, and it is not that I do not care, rather that I have other things on my mind.

Chapter 6

I t was raining when I met Theodosius Rhode, the man who would
be king. The rain did not clear the smoke and dust of destruction, merely thickened it into running rivulets of filth across the
blasted city.

I was sitting on the same landing strip where for so many years
I had directed incoming and outgoing traffic, with five hundred
other souls who had rebelled, or not rebelled, or just been in the
wrong place at the wrong time. We were underdressed for the
cold, arms wrapped around knees, chins tucked into chests, shoulders pressed to our neighbour in the hope that like some winter
mammal we might feed on each other's heat. There was a kind of
kindness, transgressive, intimate, in our huddling.

We had not been told exactly where we were going, were not
permitted to speak. Our collars, the markers of our crime and
shame, pressed into our throats, pushing down, a bloody weight
digging into bone.

Yet through the cold, the shock, the shame, I knew enough of
the rhythms of this place to know that someone special was arriving. Vehicles cleared, blast walls raised, overhead traffic scurried
out to a safe distance. Thus I was only somewhat surprised when
the Shiniest yacht I had ever seen came into port.

Many outside the Mdo struggle to understand what makes an

object of lesser or greater Shine. They think it is merely about displays of wealth, lavish and ostentatious flares of precious metals, and debtors kneeling at a Manager's feet. This was far Shinier than that. The surface of the ship seemed to shimmer and change as it moved, sometimes the colour of the reflected sky, sometimes the deepest black where it passed through pools of shadow. It had neither the cheap electric whine of a standard passenger craft nor the guttural roar of your usual spacefaring vessel, but rather seemed to purr on a lilting, musical note as if the engines were on the verge of ecstasy at being deployed. There were, I felt sure, windows – real, actual windows – all along its surface, but they were so well integrated into its form that I could not tell, and when it landed, the light that emerged from its belly was not the harsh white of the loading ramp, but a soft, almost intimate glow, which seemed to promise far more fascinating secrets in its hidden depths.

The ship was not gaudy, but rather a declaration of skill, of engineering and artistic mastery that was beyond the glittering dreams of the middling Shine who thought that all diamonds were the same and therefore the best diamonds were lots of them. I knew it was a ship for Executives even before the first Corpsec team began to descend, and then I was certain. The way the bodyguards moved, the slight pop-jump of their motion as their displacement fields carried them – now a single pace, now five at a go, so that they seemed to lurch like images across a broken screen before settling, not quite of this earth, not quite on it. The damage a displacement field causes to a body that wears one for too long is always fatal, but the Shine promised great rewards for your descendants, and what other paths were there? What else was a parent to do?

When members of the Antekeda Board began to descend from the warm interior of the ship, I thought I recognised some of them from the more sycophantic talk shows – Senior Management, members perhaps of the Executorium itself. Even in the debtor's collar, even waiting to be banished to another world and work until we died, the collective mass of condemned turned to look, to wonder, to be awed.

Then hé emerged, and though hé was then merely Junior Management, hé was hypnotic. Physically, hé was taller than any man I had ever seen, generations of genetic selection and extensive, costly postnatal enhancements woven through his strong bones, flawless, untouched-snowdrift skin. Though fashions of physicality have always fluctuated a little across the Shine, the male archetype of taller, stronger, tougher – this has been in style since the first crop grew in the dust of Ko-mdo. I do not entirely trust my own memory, but in pictures of that day hé was wearing a grey suit with a high collar and the small silver badge of hís Venture directly above the heart. The long curved scar of Management ran across hís face from left to right, chin to forehead, cutting through hís nose and denting it where it had ruptured bone. Hís left eye, as the scar passed through it, had its famous golden iris, and hís head was shaved at the top to reveal the little ridges of other career scars – scars of entrepreneurship, of leadership, of creative endeavour, of maximum profit, of advanced learning. More scars would be added down the years as hís prestige grew, burned into his body with honour in pain.

From the back of hís head, a long tail of metallic-silver hair ran down hís spine, bound up with simple leather ties, and as hé stood on the landing pad, talking with other Executives, hís hands were clasped neatly behind hís back, slightly arcing hís spine and tilting hís chin upwards, so that hé seemed to gaze down from even loftier heights upon those hé spoke with.

Then, without warning, hé looked at us.

Seemed to note our presence.

Said a few words, then turned.

Came towards us.

We had already been beaten into silence, but at hís approach, a few of the bolder called out, raised their bound hands in entreaty. Someone cried: "I am innocent!"

Another: "I know things! I have things I can tell!"

The Shine does not invite its people to go quietly into darkness, for all that is where the vast majority of us go.

A few entreaties set off a great many more, since we were taught never to be outdone even in humiliation, and soon the whole pack of us were yapping and wheedling at hís feet, promising extraordinary lies, ridiculous impossibilities if hé would merely deign to gaze upon us with kindness – just kindness – just this once.

There is nothing Shinier than having power to change another's world and choosing not to use it.

Hé assessed us as hé might have regarded the contours on a map of some distant land. I would like to say that I sat in bold defiance, an innocent man cruelly betrayed by the system. In truth, I tried to think of something I might do that would catch hís eye, something that would make me special, make me the one hé chose to save, but my mind was blank, everything I could say strikingly banal.

Perhaps it was this – my uncanny silence, my sealed lips – that caught hís attention. For a moment, as hé gestured hís guards to pull me up, haul me forward, I felt an impossible flutter of hope. Perhaps there was mercy, perhaps I had a chance, and I knew with absolute certainty that if they took this collar off from around my neck and told me to go free, I would not look back or think twice on my peers, kneeling in the rain.

When hé spoke, hé had the accent of Yu-mdo, or another world I had never visited, never even really thought about. I had always imagined that our leaders would sound exactly like me.

"What's your name?" hé asked, voice soft enough to seem unthreatening, clear enough to cut through the cries of my tethered debtor-kin.

"Mawukana na-Vdnaze, sir."

"I have a question. I want you to think carefully about your answer. What is the one thing the Venture could have done in Heom that would have prevented this? This violence, this disobedience. Don't tell me what you think I want to hear; I have people for that. Just tell me the first thing that comes into your head. Just the truth."

The iris of hís golden eye dilated as hé examined me, and I imagined it seeing straight through skin and bone to my racing heart. I thought longer than hé had ordered, as is always my way, and when I realised hé was growing bored with my stupidity and indecision, I blurted: "If there had been hope, sir. If people had thought it would get better. If they had really believed."

Later – after I was dead – I would look back on these words and judge them harshly. Not because they were wrong – not at all. They simply lacked Shine.

Hé understood.

Hé nodded.

Hís fingers brushed the silver badge of hís Venture, the marker of hís state, and I didn't know if it was a comforting thing – a reassurance for himself, a habit that had been ingrained – or something else. I found the gesture fascinating, and then it passed.

"Thank you, Mawukana na-Vdnaze, for your candour."

A flick of hís fingers; I was pulled back towards the line, back to the debtors, back to a life of indentured labour I knew not where, my life a column in an accounting book. I struggled, called out: "Sir, I was not a rebel!" and hís fingers twitched again, and hé looked at me. There was, I thought, almost kindness in hís mismatched eyes, a thing almost like regret. Then hé reached out, touched my face, my neck, feeling perhaps for the scars of my labours – found the twin cuts on my left ear – then ran hís fingers down to the back of my left hand, where a single electrical burn was etched into the skin. It was the scar I had been given on the day of my one and only minor promotion, and I had never earned any more.

"Tell me," hé asked, studying the thin, neat line of ridged white. "Did you love someone?"

" . . . What?"

"In the city. When it burned. Was there anyone there you loved? Someone you left behind?"

Only later did I understand his question. For if I had loved someone who had been buried in the ruins of Glastya Row, surely that love would make me a creature of vengeance, a rebel regardless of what I had been before. And if not, then most likely I was also unloved, and my life would pass without significance.

Theodosius Rhode, Chief Operations Officer of Antekeda, the man who would one day lead the Executorium into its bloodiest, most savage of days, saw my bewilderment, smiled with only a little regret, let go of my hand, turned and walked away.

Later – much later – I learned that my mother had died in the bombings. My father vanished in a security sweep, his final fate unknown. But by then I had died a couple of times, and the news didn't have as big an impact on me as I felt it should.

Chapter 7

I spent my first ever arcspace jump huddled in a hold with five hundred people, pressed down by the collars about our necks, chained together at wrist and ankle.

Nearly every creature who goes to space has the same initial reaction. After the fear of launch, the terror of it, we look out into the dark and realise that we are tiny, insignificant, nothing. We behold the world from which we came and realise how sacred and precious it is. Many weep – such a delicate, wonderful thing, they say. The most beautiful thing I have ever seen.

I did not have that experience. There were no windows, no sense of place. The ship's shields kept the forces of acceleration to within mere headache-inducing parameters, gravity a sluggish heaviness rather than a stomach-turning loss or a bone-cracking force. There was no sense of time passing – merely the arrival of rations, the emptying of slop buckets, the locking once more of the hull door. It was only the sudden change in gravity, the dropping-off of weight on bone that alerted me to our shift from sub-light speeds to FTL arcspace insertion.

That, and the other thing. The nameless thing that everyone shudders at when they speak of the dark. The cobweb brushing across skin, a beetle crawling down the spine, a shadow in the corner of the eye. No one quite sees the same thing as another; no one ever agrees on the notes of the lullaby they thought they heard, a tune half crooned, heard through the humming wall.

Someone cries out, they can see their lover – there, there, look, she's right there!

We turn our faces away; there is nothing to be seen.

Another whimpers that there is a *thing* in the corner, if you only look just right – no, it's gone now, but I feel it, I know it's here. No, it's not a monster, it's not a man, it's neither of these things, it's . . .

. . . it's something else. It defies speaking.

A man faints; a woman presses her hands to her eyes and screams, they're moving, they're moving, I can feel them moving!!

Xi flight protocol always advises against transporting massed groups of people through arcspace without providing separate quarters, or at the very least a cosy chair and a movie to watch. Mass hysteria, psychogenic illness – they are real, oh but they are real, sigh the psychologists, all the more so when you bunch people together in the dark.

But this breezy dismissal of a traveller's experience has to be balanced with another truth: that even the psychologists, with their strict mental discipline and educated understanding of how these things work, are a little fearful of the dark.

They hear the scrambling too.

Something in the wires.

Something in the vents.

Something with fingers of bone, knocking

knock knock knock

on the outside of the hull.

It is here.

It is there.

It is nowhere.

knock knock knock

It is waiting for you when you try to sleep, smiling and waving, the face of your grandmother reflected in the cup of water, only no, that's not it at all; it was in the mirror, an alien looking back where you should have been, it's in the voice that whispers in the hiss of pneumatics, it's in the computer screen, a code that has no meaning and which yet you understand.

knock knock knock

And yes, of course. Of course. People know this. They know it, and it's easy to get a little anxious about the whole thing. To start seeing things that aren't there, to set each other off. The vast majority of arcspace flights are safe, a simple trip from A to B. The capacity to go faster than light outweighs the dangers – everyone agrees. A risk worth taking for the beating of civilisation's inter-planetary heart.

But there are corners on the oldest ships where the dark settles, and not even the brightest light can burn it away. It lingers, playing tricks on the eyes, even when the ships are in port; even when the engines are silent and everyone is gone save the maintenance crews. No one who goes into that shadow comes out quite the same. This is the price that is paid to defy the laws of space and time, and jump like thought across the stars.

We were sent to Hasha-to.

There was only one habitation on the surface, just on the night side of the terminator line of the sun-blasted, dust-frozen moon. A thick acidic atmosphere raged in perpetual storms, an endless thermal gale between day and night, the air trying to eat its way inside the broken cracks of the world.

On the sunward side, miners clad in mech suits taller than the average house pulled precious metals from the planet's crust. Inside the night-side refineries, debtors rose to the ringing of the bell and returned to our cots at the blasting of a horn, skin scourged with compounds of arsenic, cell-dissolving polymers, bone-chewing catalysts and synthetic stains.

"Be proud of the scars you make here!" roared the dormitory speakers every morning. "Your scars are the only thing you have of value!"

Factory automata could have performed our labours, but they required skilled people to manufacture and maintain them. Skilled people required education, and in the experience of the Ventures, education was a double-edged weapon. Teach someone how to come up with new ideas, new concepts in the realms of engineering, design, industry, and what if they then came up with new ideas for something else? What if they turned and said, "But isn't there another way of looking at this ... ?"

It had not always been this way with the Shine – there had been a time when learning was our sacred trust. That time had passed, ground down by powerful, comfortable men.

"Are you fucking dense? Move yourselves!"

Control on Hasha-to was simple enough. Every new group of inmates was reduced to nothing – no clothes, no food, no water. When on the edge of madness, starvation, desperation, they were given a little bit of each. I remember being grateful, so incredibly grateful, that my captors could be bothered to keep me alive. I remember saying thank you for the drops that were put to my lips, as though those who fed me had not already taken me to the edge of death, ripped away any lingering dignity from my soul. Thus I was quickly, efficiently and quietly broken, and didn't notice it had happened, and said thank you for the privilege.

The scars I had been given in traffic control were badges of pride, markers of my status, and I had looked forward to acquiring the tapestry of cuts all the way around the lobe and onto the other side of my face that senior staff held. In Hasha-to, the first scar I gained was when a hopper was overloaded and fell, scattering still-blazing stone across the workfloor. Eleven people died; I got away with merely scorched lips and a messy line of fire up my left forearm, which I wrapped in proto-algae run-off from the kitchen vats after someone told me it would cool the blaze. For a few weeks I was punished for my negligence by being assigned to external hub maintenance, shoved into a survival suit with an oxygen cartridge on my back and sent through the airlocks into the endless storm of Hasha-to to patch the acid-gnawed exterior of the factory. If the atmosphere didn't crawl through the endless micro-tears of eroded neglect that defined our survival suits and burn your skin off, fill your lungs with popping fluid, then the wind threatened to snatch you off your feet, fling you off out into the endless spinning dust. Stories abounded of people getting lost on the night side of Hasha-to just thirty or forty steps from the airlock of the base, spun round and round in the eddying dark until their air ran out or their suit melted from their bones.

I clung onto the few guide wires and handholds on the walls of the base, themselves acid-blasted frayed nothings waiting to snap. That's what you did at Hasha-to. You clung on.

"Only three years more, and I'll have paid my debt," whispered my bunkmate, as the dormitory shuddered and howled with the storm outside. "I'll start again. You'll see. I've got it all mapped out."

I didn't say anything, and he didn't expect me to. The words he spoke were not for my sake. A little hope – just a little hope – it was all that kept us alive. Much as people will turn away from the things they fear the most, they will cling to hope, however implausible, however impossible, because if they do not, they must surely die.

I do not know if I had hope. My mind, my body – it all seemed so distant.

Eight Normmonths into my sentence – the months of Hasha-to were meaningless things – I saw the sign of the double suns for the very first time. Debtors were constantly scratching some marker of their passage into the floors, walls, ceilings, any dark corner where they thought the guards wouldn't look too closely. It was a way, perhaps, of saying: look, look. I'm still here. I was here. I lived. I am still alive.

I didn't ask who made the mark, or what it meant. I felt I already knew.

Lhonoja, the Lovers, the binary star that would end us all, unstoppable, unnegotiable, the cleansing fire.

On Hasha-to, the end of the world seemed somewhat beautiful.

Three weeks later, I broke my leg. I had been in the loading bay when the outer doors sprung a leak and the atmosphere of Hasha-to began to flood into the docks. The inner doors began to seal, and I, with everyone else, sprinted for safety. Two died in the race; I was shoved by another man desperate to live, a newbie who hadn't yet learned that living was just a habit. I fell, knew it was bad, but pulled myself hand-over-hand into the safety of the interior before the bay was sealed off entirely. Only once my body understood that I was alive, that I would live, did it allow the pain to register.

"Fucking waste," was the foreman's assessment, as I lay howling on the ground.

And: "We could put him in the chair," suggested his deputy.

I had no idea what "the chair" meant, thought perhaps it might be some sort of medical device. Cheaper, surely, to fix me up and keep me working than just discard me to the dark? (In fact, no: there wasn't much in it financially, and my death would be tax-deductible.)

In the end, they did put me in front of a medic, who rather than assess my leg asked a series of questions.

"You are in a room of butterflies; one flies into your mouth. What do you do?"

"You write your name on the side of a building. Do you use red or yellow paint?"

"Your friend asks you to pay for their medical insurance, but you don't think they will survive the treatment and may not live to pay you back. Do you lend them the money?"

"Describe this picture. Do not use the words 'black' or 'line'."

I mumbled my way through the test, obedience embedded in me, and felt a moment of excitement when I was told that I had passed. Then they said that there was a ship going out tomorrow and the current baggage was looking the worse for wear. It was that – the mention of a ship – that finally alerted me to what was about to happen. By the time I saw what "the chair" meant, complete with straps for head, neck, chest, arms and legs and the radio-lobotomy probe, I was doing my very best to struggle and scream, which doubtless hurt me far more than it hurt anyone else.

When they lined the probe up with my frontal cortex, I begged and gibbered and offered them any service, no matter how degrading or inhuman, for their mercy. Again, with my rather limited imagination, I don't think anything I said was especially remarkable or inspiring, so they switched on the machine designed to turn me into a semi-lucid human vegetable, said, "All right, stand back ... "

And the machine fizzled out.

This was entirely in keeping with the ethos of Hasha-to, where maintenance was absolutely more expensive than labour.

I wept with gratitude and relief, sobbed my gibbering heart out, thanked anyone, anything, the universe, the stars, the great blackness of arcspace itself for my salvation. This turned out to be pre-emptive, as the Manager still needed a Pilot and couldn't be bothered to find an alternative.

"Just shoot him full of something!" he roared at the cowering med-tech. "You've got drugs – use them!"

"It's not really protocol ... "

"Fuck your protocol!"

Sometimes being a bully can get you a long way in life. Usually the point where bullying stops being useful is the point where the bully's entire world falls apart.

My gibbering relief turned back into gibbering terror as, in the absence of radiation, the medic started pumping me with drugs instead.

I do not remember much about what followed.

Records show that the ship they strapped me into was called the MSV *Myrmida*. It carried a crew of nineteen, and a cargo of 780,000 Normmils of refined metals from the surface of Hasha-to. (This figure was probably closer to 710,000 – fudging productivity outputs was one of the few truly celebrated arts of Hasha-to.) The previous Pilot had, like me, been a debtor judged incapable of paying back what they owed to society. She was discharged after only five flights as cerebral fluid had started oozing from her ears and the ground crew were reporting persistent patches of darkness in the furthest recesses of the hold that weren't dissipating even when exposed to fibre-optic sunlight. Her death was written off as an operating expense.

I think I remember the moment the navcomm interfaced with my brain.

I think it hurt.

Then again, it is more than likely I am just imagining it, imposing my experiences upon a dream-like state. Pain is often made worse when you predict it will hurt, and I am nothing if not sensitive to the power of expectations.

Given the unreliability of my experience, let us simply go by the nav logs.

These state that at 0554 local Hasha-to time, the MSV *Myrmida* reached its jump-speed velocity, wound up its arcspace engines and sliced through the dark on its scheduled journey to Yu-mdo, guided through the great unknown by the fusion of mechanical and biological minds – my mind – strapped into the Pilot's chair.

Twelve seconds *prior* to its departure, the same MSV *Myrmida* appeared on the very edge of Xihana space, some two hundred and eleven light years off course, drifting uncontrollably through the dark. Xihana authorities naturally declared an emergency and sent a full quarantine crew to isolate the stricken ship. When it failed to respond to hails, a volunteer team in military-grade survival gear was sent on board to inspect the vessel. After a few days of deeply unpleasant labour, they concluded that they had found enough matching body parts to declare the nineteen crew members officially dead, and that they had been deceased at least a Normweek. They also found blood from a twentieth crew member – most likely the Pilot, based on where the majority of the blood was – in such significant quantities that they were almost certain that said Pilot would have died of exsanguination unless immediate and urgent medical care had been given. However, without any other limbs/ organs, etc. to match the blood against, they couldn't definitively state that said crew member was dead, though it seemed incredibly unlikely that they were not.

Later DNA tests confirmed that the significant volumes of blood belonging to this last exsanguinated crew member were indeed mine, and that Mawukana na-Vdnaze had almost certainly died in the Pilot's chair.

On the MSV *Myrmida*, they found me in the captain's quarters, not a mark on me, staring out of the window at the wondrous stars.

Interlude

On Pilots

Many theories have been posited as to why an organic mind – and it is specifically organic – is required to Pilot arcspace travel. None withstand the rigours of scientific investigation.

The collective failure of the galaxy to understand a thing so fundamental to modern civilisation is distressing – frightening, even. Especially as, whatever we can say about that ruptured fold of time through which faster-than-light travel is made possible, one thing is certain: arcspace is not a void. There is something out there, defying measurement.

The more alarmist might add: and it is watching.

Personally I find the tendency of people to invent some unprovable, fancy-sounding stories to try and explain away this thing that scares them far more distressing than accepting an ignorance that has yet to be solved.

On Pilot Selection

The Xi choose their Pilots through a volunteer programme, open to anyone between fifty and eighty-three years of age. 78 per cent of candidates are eliminated at initial assessment, and the remaining 22 per cent are monitored for a duration of five years, during which time they may withdraw, no questions asked. At the end of this period, final candidates are put through a barrage of psychological tests, with an average of 6 per cent judged as eligible to serve. Of that 6 per cent, priority is given to those with long-term degenerative and terminal illnesses. Once cleared for flight, they are given two months to be with family, friends and loved ones. Pilots are only allowed to fly once, and are retired upon completion of said voyage to a luxuriously appointed and highly isolated archipelago, under polite yet firm military observation.

This methodology has a number of consequences. With such a small pool of Pilots to pull from, Xi arcspace flights are rare, solemn events, and thus Xihana possesses an unusually small fleet of unusually vast city-sized ships that rival the old, lumbering slowships of pre-arcspace days, their scale compensating for the infrequency of launch. Though their Pilot scheme has one of the highest safety records of any in the Accord, in the unlikely event that a ship is consumed by the silent dark, the loss in terms of personnel and material can be catastrophic.

The Eyrie has a strict fifteen-year Pilot selection programme. Individuals are put through rigorous physical and psychological training, earning a reputation as the toughest of the tough, the bravest of the brave. Afterwards, graduates will fly a maximum of eight Pilot sorties, before being retired to a life of socially distanced celebrity. There is no evidence that this programme produces increased safety benefits in-flight; however, the Eyrie's Pilot programme remains highly subscribed owing to a long-running series of dramatic presentations ranging from young adult dramas set in training academies through to schlocky soaps depicting the often glamorous and sexually exaggerated lifestyles of this elite and their squabbling families. The occasional complete mental collapse and psychosis Pilots can experience at the end of their service is a dramatic plot point, not a theme. Consequently the Eyrie runs more arcspace flights than many Accord members, even if their risk mitigation remains for all practical purposes entirely minimal.

The Shine is one of the few polities to use prisoners for Pilot work. To minimise the inherent risk in forcefully interfacing an unvetted organic mind with the arcspace systems of an FTL ship, it is standard practice to irradiate parts of a Pilot's brain, reducing them to a mere organic husk through which navigational protocols may pass. This, the Shine claim, can enable reuse of a Pilot up to twenty times before they are declared brain-dead. From a safety perspective, the method is a disaster, with the attrition rate of ships lost to the dark speculated to be as high as 1:8,000 (and likely far higher). However, the ease of finding the aforementioned forced labour means that the Shine has developed an extensive infrastructure of small-vessel courier and pleasure ships, flitting passengers around the galaxy as if arcspace travel were just a merry little paddle across a pond.

Quanmech minds have not yet found a way to integrate their consciousnesses successfully with arcspace navigation systems, and either rely on slowships or hired organic Pilots.

It is not known how the Slow travels across the infinite dark.

PART 2

Beneath the Lover's Light

Chapter 8

One hundred years after the Slow came to Tu-mdo; ninety-nine years after the MSV *Myrmida* entered Xihana magnetic space with its cargo of dismembered crew, the binary star system called Lhonoja exploded.

There was at first very little data on the supernova blast. The nature of the Edge – the wall of radiation ripping through the galaxy at light speed from the collapsing heart of the supernova – made observation of anything within fifty light years of the solar collapse practically impossible. Sensors were burned to a crisp at the moment of impact, and it wouldn't be until many years later that anyone was able to peer through the chaos of the blast back in time to the moment of destruction. To everyone else, it seemed that Lhonoja still twinkled in the sky, the old light travelling on even though the source itself was an obliterated mass of rapidly expanding plasma. From my little garden, far away from the core, it would be another one hundred and sixty-three years before the light of those binary stars would flare for a few dazzling weeks of daylight brightness, and then go out.

Consequently, I only found out about the supernova when Rencki, my companion, directed my attention towards a minor piece on the news informing me of the same.

"Right on schedule," qe quipped. "Just as the Slow said."

Rencki's mainframe was not, as far as I was aware, one of the quanmechs who worshipped – or as near to worship as the quans came – the Slow. As qe put it, qis mainframe was interested in its own development as an evolving operating system within the galactic Accord, and didn't approve of leaving its fate in the hands of an unknowable god.

Qe did use the word "god", though, when qe talked about the Slow. Qe made it sound like a job description.

Let me tell you about my garden.

I live on an island, about twenty minutes' sedate rowing – or five minutes by motor – from the town of Poulinio, the administrative capital of the Mun peninsula. You can walk around the island in thirty-five ticks, which is more than enough to keep me occupied every month of every season with the constant flourishing of nature. In the east, where the land rises up to black basalt cliffs, are groves of giant courl and drooping bluebrush trees, whose sapphire blossoms stink to high heaven when they open in the wettest part of summer, but which wither to black nuts in winter that are a roasted treat, if only I can get to them before the longlaps pick the branches clean. Away from the cool shade of the woodland, wild grasses grow, which in summer are pricked out with an explosion of yellow and white as the slumbering blossoms burst up from the gentle soil below. In the north, a shingle beach faces the sea, and the prevailing winds bend back the branches of spiny thorn-break and thick-bellied succulents that seem impervious to salt, while inland I tend a long lawn where I sometimes welcome what few visitors I have in the summer months with feasts of fruit grown from the southern orchard and fish caught with hook and line – actual hook and actual line! – from the side of my little boat.

I do not get enough visitors to really justify the labour I put into keeping the lawn in this state, but after a while I found the challenge almost as important as the result, so keep on labouring.

Around my cottage I grow vegetables and the more tender fruits that would not survive a winter's blast. My most successful crop is a form of saltscar-rui, which I've been permitted to enter into the local farmers' competition and once won second prize for flavour and consistency. Bursting with pride, I did not admit that I wasn't a fan of the extremely bitter taste.

When I arrived, nearly thirty years before Lhonoja went supernova, the freshwater well behind the cottage was just that – a hole in the ground with an electric pump sitting square and ugly by its side. I consulted with a hydrologist and eventually managed to turn the whole area around the mouth of the well into a trickling water garden where lush moss bloomed. The solar roof provided more than enough electricity to run everything I desired, though after one particularly bad storm I'd gone two days by candlelight when it turned out that the backup battery had been corroded by salt and I didn't have the parts to coax it back to life. My companion back then had been a quan called Bi, who took very badly to the blackout, growing steadily more tetchy as qis internal power declined.

"Pain is an alarm – an evolutionarily useful alarm. It warns us when we are in danger. I have experienced low-power shutdown before and know the dangers it entails. My system warns me that I may shut down, and so I experience pain!" qe barked.

"How much charge do you have left?"

"Forty-eight per cent."

"That seems like quite a lot, given your average consumption."

"I have set my threshold for alarm very high! You do not understand my predictions!"

Bi had only stayed with me for ten months, and I had not been disappointed when qe declared that qe had gathered all the data qe required and would be departing in the morning. Rencki assured me that qe only started experiencing alarm signals at 20 per cent battery, and that qe would inform me before shutting down the parts of qis processor that handled interactions involving such things as courtesy, empathy and goodwill.

"Although," qe mused, "if Bi's armaments consumed significant power on discharge, I can see why qe set qis alarm threshold so high."

I did not ask Rencki how much qis armaments consumed, when fired. I knew that each of qis three furry tails concealed weapon pylons, and at least one was lethal. Asking seemed impertinent, and might have given the wrong impression regarding my intentions.

This then is how I lived, surrounded by the seasons and the changing life of the island.

When I had first come to this place, I had been firmly but politely told that if I wished to leave it, I must inform local authorities. A boat would be sent; escort provided. The whole thing was very formal, very bureaucratic – the Xi do love their bureaucracy – and though the Xi sometimes called upon my very specialist services, generally speaking it was suggested that everyone would have a far easier time if I stayed put. A series of officers of middling rank had been instructed to keep an eye on me, of whom the latest, Major Phrawon, was a relief from her stand-offish predecessors. She visited my island at least once a month, usually brought pie, sometimes a junior officer or a visiting researcher, who would avoid all eye contact and mumble awkwardly, *my paper – fascinating project – don't want to inconvenience*, before finally the Major would blurt: "Just ask him if he'll give you some blood!"

I always said yes, though I suspected by now that there was more of my blood in various vaults and archives than actually in my body.

"Oh!" one especially oblivious captain had exclaimed as I sliced pie into perfect sixths, served on a green stoneware plate. "I hadn't expected it to eat!"

"We do not call Maw 'it'," Phrawon breathed in the soft voice of the ocean as it pulls back before the tsunami. "It is unacceptable to address a person that way; perhaps even unwise. You will apologise."

The officer apologised, I do not know whether through courtesy or terror.

I didn't have many visitors. Old Yulin was an exception, bumbling onto my shore after their boat was caught in an unexpected squall.

"They told me a Pilot lived here!" they exclaimed as I helped drag their ship up the shingle, rain tapping furious on our coats, feet sloshing in choppy, biting swell. "Said you were quite, quite mad!"

"I am a Pilot," I admitted. "But I think 'mad' is an oversimplification of the problem."

Yulin held a few firm beliefs. If one person helped another; if they shared their words, their warmth, their food, listened attentively and spoke no evil, then Yulin didn't give a damn what the military had to say. "If you were really a monster of the unending dark, I'm sure someone would have killed you before now," they exclaimed.

"That's part of the problem," I replied. "I'm not that easy to kill."

When, after twelve years of friendship, Yulin's lungs finally packed up, I found the reality of it . . .

. . . hazy.

A hazy kind of truth, a coming-in-and-going-out of possibilities, of could-not-be, of shadow and dark. The human brain is very poor at understanding absence; nothingness is far more infinite in its possibility than solid, short-lived life. My quan companion at the time reported my confusion to the Major, who imposed an actual quarantine around the island, enforced with gunboats, until such time as I had had a chance to process the death of my friend, understand that it was real.

"Maw?" she asked, down the commnet. "Are you stable? Are you safe?"

Grief seemed to me like a thing I should be able to acknowledge, and in acknowledging, be done with it. Strange, how it lingered.

"I am safe," I said. "I am . . . I walk in brightly lit places."

I was eventually allowed to go to Yulin's sky-casting, say a few words, and they had clearly briefed their family on how to behave before they died, because several touched me on the lips in familial greeting and looked me in the eye when we spoke and seemed to be unafraid. I was so grateful then to my dead friend that I nearly dissolved once again, and had to flee back to the boat, to the safety of isolation, before the feeling broke me.

I had not made many new friends since.

And sometimes the Xi would ask me to fly.

Thus, eleven years before Lhonoja went supernova, the Major came to my door.

"I cannot give you orders," she sighed as we sat on the porch outside my cottage drinking cornwhite tea, "because you are a Xi citizen and I have no jurisdiction over you."

The Major's thick, curly hair was growing out beyond its usual military cut; her formal uniform swapped for a plain blue shirt and sensible brown shoes. On the few occasions she smiled, her whole face seemed to lift, from a suddenly appearing chin to rising round cheeks to eyebrows that swelled up towards her hairline. Most of the time she did not smile, and thus her features seemed to wait in soft restfulness, contours camouflaged beneath sea-pale skin.

"But you still have orders," I declared.

This was not a question. I have no time for the dance that people do, the darting around a subject. It seems to make most people happy, give them a run-up to a difficult topic. With Phrawon, though she still danced the dance, as clearly she felt she had to, obfuscation just added to her exasperation. It was one of the things I liked about her.

She blew steam off the top of her mug, and clearly had no intention of drinking it. "I think it is madness that the authorities ask you to Pilot. Utter madness. But I read the reports on the *Mistral Spring* when she went astray. They say you walked into the places on that ship where all noise had ceased, through the black that light could not penetrate, and you sat in the Pilot's chair and guided it home. They say that when the *Seed of Dawn's Embrace* set out for a new world and tumbled eighty thousand light years off course, you were the only Pilot who could bring it back, the only one who could interface with the chair. There were seven hundred thousand souls on that ship, too many to risk losing on a vessel that is clearly already arc-touched, so let's use Mawukana-of-the-Isles, Mawukana-from-the-Dark. So here we are. There it is."

The Xi, when they acknowledge a thing as true, touch thumb and middle finger together. Disaster if you get it wrong, thumb-to-index or worse, thumb-to-little-finger while in polite company. But having learned it, it was a gesture I enjoyed, a non-committal acknowledgement, a silence that left space, offered closure – whatever it was that the other person wanted.

A while, then, we sat in silence, the Major and I.

"The Xi are sending ships to Adjumir," she said. "It is the first planet that will be hit by the blast when Lhonoja goes, barely seven light years out from the nova. We have dispatched colony ships to aid with human cargo, but we are not . . . nimble."

"You want me to fly one? A colony ship, to Adjumir?"

"Sea and sky, no! Can you imagine trying to explain to the Adjumiris what manner of Pilot we are entrusting their people to? No. Support mission only. Artefacts of historical import, biological security – that kind of thing. Show willing. Lend a helping hand. A smaller vessel – it would be inefficient to swap out the Pilot every single flight, it would slow the process to a crawl, and so . . . "

A loose tapping of fingers, a raising of hand to the ever-expansive wind.

"You will take a quan companion, of course," she added. "For safety."

"Of course."

She did not say whose safety was the concern.

That is how I first went to Adjumir.

Chapter 9

The Shine had shot down the messengers of the Slow when they came to its worlds. In the years since the Slow had come with qis warning, the crackdown on even mentioning the impending end of several worlds had been brutal. Sometimes a sign was seen – two circles, overlapping, an image like binary suns. Sometimes a name was whispered: *Sarifi*, *Glastya Row* – but at the destruction of Lhonoja, the commnet within the Shine would carry nothing more and nothing less than its usual array of programming and light entertainment.

Not so on Adjumir.

Adjumir lay only seven light years from the collapsing heart of Lhonoja, and unlike the Shine, the Assemblies of that planet had been more than interested in what the Slow had to say.

PEOPLES OF ADJUMIR! qe had proclaimed. IN ONE HUNDRED NORMYEARS, THE BINARY STAR SYSTEM KNOWN AS THE LOVERS WILL COLLAPSE IN UPON ITSELF. THE RESULTING SHOCK WAVE WILL TRAVEL OUT AT THE SPEED OF LIGHT AND OBLITERATE ALL LIFE WITHIN AN EIGHTY-THREE LIGHT-YEAR RADIUS.

DO NOT BE AFRAID.

THERE IS STILL TIME.

*

It was of course impossible to save the planet. The peoples of Adjumir and its sister planet Hadda knew this, and after the initial shock they reached the conclusion that if they could not save their worlds, the next best thing they could do was try to save their people.

Thus, Exodus was born.

This is a timeline of Exodus, beginning one hundred (T–100) years before the supernova that would eventually kill the planet:

T–100: Emergency Planetary Assemblies created to write new constitution, dedicating society to evacuation and repopulation among the stars. Acceleration of Adjapar terraforming project (safely located some two hundred light years outside the blast radius of Lhonoja) and installation of cryofacilities on nearby moon to house transitory population until completion of terraforming (est. 650 years until arcology stage, 910 years until breathable atmosphere). Acceleration of solar swarm deployment around local star, with the objective of creating a self-sustaining energy-manufacturing process for evacuation vessel construction on planet Asoi. Diplomatic activity on all friendly Accord worlds stepped up to find refugee worlds/habitats where Adjumiri citizens may find safe harbour. Introduction of random lottery system to choose evacuees for eventual Exodus flights.

T–91: powered by solar swarm, Asoi workshops commence mothership manufacture. Completion of first vessel in T–84. Space elevator construction commences on surfaces of Adjumir and Hadda for population transfer to mothership, completion of first elevator in T–86.

T–85: demographic slump under way on Adjumir. Steep decline in birth rate stabilises at 0.7 births per fertile female, declining again at T–10 to 0.2 births. Some demographic slump is desirable, reducing the overall number of expected casualties when the world dies. However, an overall collapse of the population too soon reduces the number of healthy youths available for evacuation in +/–25 years, thus decreasing the viability of new communities among the stars.

T–83: first evacuation flight commences on *Hope of Adjumir*, heading for the moon of Adjapar, where cryostorage facilities above the still-terraforming planet reached their maximum capacity of 400,000,000 by T–2.

T–45: solar swarm manufacture reaches optimal output. Full retooling of workshops on Asoi to mothership manufacture completed. At peak function, ×22 motherships and ×18 elevators are in operation on Adjumir, with ×6 motherships and ×4 elevators on Hadda. Mothership capacity = 1,000,000 people, +/–2–3 month loading/unloading time = two flights a year = roughly 48 million citizens evacuated every year, increasing to approx. 60 million per annum by T–20.

T–30: planetary depopulation causes steep reduction in Adjumir labour force. 7 per cent power from solar swarm/Asoi drone factories redirected to planetary automation of vital services, i.e. agriculture, sanitation, security, comms, to reduce danger of total societal collapse. Essential for effective Exodus that planetary population is not starving to death/rioting/committing cannibalism, etc. while waiting for evacuation.

T–0: collapse of binary star system Lhonoja. Initial shock wave to reach Adjumir in +7 years. First edges of neutrino blast to arrive approximately 33 years later, obliterating all remaining planetary matter in the system.

T+7: shock wave arrives. No survivors.

By the time Lhonoja went supernova in T–0, it was estimated that nearly three billion people had been evacuated – a remarkable feat of engineering, social organisation and interplanetary diplomacy.

In reality, that figure is debatable. Even if transfer of evacuees to motherships went smoothly, on the other end were worlds that had agreed to accept a million, two million refugees and who would, at the last minute, change their minds. Or if they did not change their minds, their atmos-shuttles would malfunction, delaying the unloading of passengers by weeks or months, stranding mother-ships in orbit as the elevators of Adjumir waited for their return. Perhaps an orbital would take a hundred thousand refugees, and an outpost would take a quarter of a million, forcing unloading motherships to flit around, wasting precious time depositing one shattered community here, one broken family there. In the end, the Assembly of Adjumir had to put its foot down and say: you'll take a million, or nothing. More lives are lost waiting than are being saved by your meagre charities.

All right then, some worlds said.

Let your people die.

You come to us begging – no, *demanding* – our charity, and for what? Do you really believe you are *entitled* to survive? Do you really think yourselves so special?

Some Accord members threw themselves into assistance with great aplomb, especially as the final years approached. Consensus and quan ships joined evacuation fleets from Xihana and Mangripul, Eyrie and Haima – but even that generosity presented its own problems. Disasters grew out of kindnesses, from plagues ripping through evacuation sites as people arrived faster than the sewers could be dug, to errors in the immuno-adaptations leaving whole populations of evacuees hospitalised on foreign worlds as their bodies, primed to adapt to the biome of Umm-ai'lana instead found themselves reacting to the pathogens and pollens of Umm-en'loka.

Then there was the loss of the *Forest of Yumoji*, in T–38. She was one of the very first motherships built on the hot surface of Asoi in T–78, and whole sections of the ship had already been lost to a creeping, chittering blackness where the whispers never ceased, reducing her capacity from a million souls to a little over nine hundred thousand. The Pilots who flew her reported that with every flight they could hear a singing, a voice calling out to them, getting louder, drumming into their heads.

It was too risky, too dangerous for her to fly again.

There was something.

Out there in the dark.

Watching.

Getting *curious*.

The Assembly debated these concerns, ran the usual public polls. The *Forest* had been designed for at least another thirty jumps before decommissioning, and her cryopods and immuno-engineering systems were still in good order. To remove her from service would strand some twenty-seven million people who perhaps could otherwise have been saved.

When put like that, the risk seemed worth taking, and so the *Forest* was loaded, a Pilot chosen, and into the dark she went.

And from the dark she never returned.

When it became apparent that the ship was gone along with its passengers, the Assembly held memoriams for the dead. No one argued. When a ship is lost in arcspace, death is often the most desirable outcome. I think it was the fate of the *Forest* that made authorities more willing to consider using a Pilot like me.

However you crunch the numbers, by T-0 billions of Adjumiris had been evacuated, and whole generations were being born on new worlds that had never known the doomed planet from which their progenitors came. The project had been so successful that by T+7 there were a mere 800,000,000 people left behind to die, which everyone agreed was something of a triumph, all things considered.

I am getting ahead of myself, I know.

Well then, at T-11, eleven years before Lhonoja would go supernova, the Xi sent me to Adjumir, in order to show willing.

My companion was a quan called Liopimana-Hadja-Ki. I asked if I could call qim "Ki" and qe replied that qe found that question quite disrespectful, but that everyone called qim Hadja, which was more tolerable for reasons qe never bothered to fully explain.

Liopimana-Hadja-Ki did not feign interest in organic sentiments. Qe was a featureless orb in a suspensor field with no apparent optical or auditory sensors, let alone armaments – though I knew they were there – whose intended purpose was to gather data for qis mainframe about the state of the universe and its wonders, so that the mainframe could refine and update qis operating assumptions as reliably and regularly as possible.

"The universe is constantly changing," Hadja had declared. "It is vital that we change with it."

Hadja's greatest frustration was that quans, much like organics, were limited in their potential. Yes, in theory they could expand their processing power again and again and again, but the infrastructure required to support that processing would itself require the surface area of a small moon, and the heat generated would require heat exchangers the size of battleships, and how would you even begin to integrate with the universe if you were such a formidable physical presence, bound by your own material limitations even as your mind expanded so vastly and . . .

"It sounds like you want to be the Slow," I had blurted.

"The Slow is clearly the most advanced thinker in the galaxy," Hadja replied primly. "But it is questionable what qis impact is."

"You don't mind flying with me?" I asked as we boarded the little boat from the island to the mainland, a small bag of belongings bundled in my arms, Hadja floating politely in the prow.

"I think it is an excellent learning opportunity," Hadja answered. "If you do go mad during the flight and transform into a creature of the unknown dark, it will be incredibly informative."

"Thank you for your ringing endorsement."

"You are afraid. Afraid of the mission, afraid of yourself. You will find it overall better for your blood pressure and psychological well-being to honestly engage with your fear, rather than hide from it."

"Hadja," I mused, "I am leaving my garden to fly into the black. I believe that I am engaging with my fear."

"Yes, I suppose you are. How interesting."

*

The ship the Xi assigned for our mission was called the *Pride of Emni* and was the most beautiful thing I had ever seen.

Off-worlders, those unused to the ways of Xihana, struggle at first to recognise him as a ship at all, and indeed his capacity to blend into landscapes ranging from coastal cliffs to blackened moons has come in handy on more than a few occasions. He began his life as a single core set into a volcanic vent some six thousand kils beneath the ocean waves, growing one ragged module at a time in a weave of bio-basalt and magma-scarred, salt-blasted crystal. It had taken two years to raise him to the surface, pausing every few hundred kils in the changing swoosh of the waters to implant another system here, carve out another nook there. By the time he left the ocean, the algae plates and bio-pools of his life-support systems were already close to fully developed, and the first fibres of his circuitry were beginning to interconnect through the deep tissue of his hull. When the first flower bloomed in the weaving corridors of his interior, it was found to be a crimson skald, and so in Xi tradition the ship was dubbed a "he" and his first captain named him the *Pride of Emni*.

Officially, Emni was the name of a small moon around a local ringed ice planet, associated with an ancient legend concerning rebirth and a sacred calf. Unofficially everyone knew that he was named Emni after a popular romantic drama that had been running for eighteen years, featuring a character the captain clearly had a crush on. However, since no one could prove that this was an act of profound self-indulgence rather than a reverent reference to ancient myth, the *Pride of Emni* it was. He was built as a bio-hauler, his generous interior holds able to adapt to the optimal needs of almost any cargo, and his first forty years of service were spent couriering lab samples from bioactive but understudied new worlds to orbital laboratories, punctuated by the occasional secondment to terraforming projects in the plankton/bloom phase.

He would not contribute much to the Exodus of Adjumir, but sending him made the Xi feel better about the imminent death of a neighbour world, and sending me meant they didn't have to risk any of their Pilots, and so altogether everyone felt very satisfied, except perhaps Hadja and Phrawon, who'd have to clean up the mess if it all went wrong.

Every ship feels slightly different, when I interface with it.

Most Pilots do not have this experience – they fly with the same ship a half-dozen times, and then they are done.

They have not tasted the fat-bellied heat of a battleship, dry-skinned and heavy-lidded, as it crawls up to arc speed.

They have not tasted the citrus bite of a courier as it blasts from atmospheric escape velocity to FTL insertion in a few skipping hours, snatching an ear-churning slug of gravity off the nearest gas giant as it powers towards the dark.

Nor do they know how it feels to be the only soul walking through the corridors of a ship all others have accounted dead, the darkness in every corner, a lingering, slithering thing that should have been left behind in arcspace. How it feels to rest your mind into that system, to feel the black slip over your skin like silk, to taste berries and ash, to whisper to the dark: *shall we again* and almost – almost – hear its reply.

The first time I Piloted a ship after the *Myrmida*, after I had died and come back again, I was a thief, stealing a thing that did not belong to me. That ship was a little military corvette, all fire and impatience. Interfacing with the *Emni* was like inhaling the smell of leaves after rain, sinking your fingers into warm, rich soil, then your arms, shoulders, face, your whole being. I have been many ships, felt their bodies as mine, but in the *Emni* I was the underwater mountain against whose skin the world was merely passing by.

As we reached arcspace velocity and the engines cranked open the rip in reality that would slip us through to the waiting dark, I reached out for it, and it reached back, a warm, familiar nothing.

Hello, I said, and the darkness did not reply.

Chapter 10

We were carrying a small team of biologists with us on that first trip to Adjumir.

They huddled together in their quarters as we entered arcspace, teeth gritted and backs braced. They were waiting – waiting for the sounds of scuttling on the hull, the whispers of unknown voices, the clatter of something moving in the hall, the deepening of the shadows, the bending in and back upon itself of blackened corners and creeping time.

Instead: nothing.

We entered arcspace, and a little while later – it was always hard to judge these things – we left, arriving at our destination precisely on schedule and where planned.

No minds were broken, no horrors glimpsed out of the corner of the eye.

Were it not for the slight shift in gravitational forces on the slip from one world to another, there was not a sign that we had travelled at all.

It is always this way when I fly. It is one of the first things I learned about myself, after they pulled me from the bloody halls of the MSV *Myrmida*, and none of my passengers would look at me as we began our descent into the atmosphere of Adjumir.

*

The biologists were on Adjumir to collect bio-samples for the terra-forming of Adjapar.

Even before the arrival of the Slow, Adjumiri planners had not been oblivious to the danger Lhonoja posed to their planet and had begun terraforming Adjapar centuries prior. The onset of Exodus had stepped up the urgency of the project, but even with the Slow's advice, you could only work so fast. Cyanobacteria needed time to divide and die; great blooms of algae had to swell and perish across Adjapar's young oceans. After that, the ecologists would really get going, coaxing the newborn ecosystem into something if not identical to then near enough to Adjumir for her displaced people to flourish.

"Cave moulds," declared the short, herb-chewing dock command in aer grubby apron and boots. "That one there is a bacterial shit. Don't ask me anything more about it – all I know is that some bacteria did a shit in a cave, and now it's my problem."

First impressions of Adjumir:

Voices too loud; everyone seems to be shouting. Adjumir's gravity is slightly higher than I am used to, and I am already beginning to feel physically weary from the extra weight. The higher air pressure results in increased lung capacity in the local population and a deeper, booming quality of speech that has an underwater feeling to my exhausted ears. Expressions are big, demonstrative, the humour makes constant references to things I do not understand – "Ah, did not so-and-so say we should strive?" or "They said they voted for so-and-so because of the trousers!" followed by profound, too-loud guffawing.

The air smells at once familiar and different. Familiar – the salt-burned scent of the *Emni*, the spaceport stinks of lubricants and reactor fuels and still-rosy heat shields. Different – not merely the wetness of the thick forest all around, but a taste in the atmosphere, a sort of tongue-stinging, nose-itching otherness that scholars have attempted to explain as microscopic differences in atmospheric sulphur, or perhaps ozone, or maybe just nitrogen content, but which no one can quite agree on, given the subjectivity of taste.

As with all worlds, the stars were wrong. Beautiful, and wrong. I try to work out which one is Lhonoja, only to later learn I am in the wrong hemisphere at the wrong time of year to spot it.

I was still woozy from my immunisations, though suspected that was mostly because the biologists I had been transporting had all agreed that the immunisations would feel dreadful, and thus they were. I wore a light exoskeleton over my flight suit to support me in this new gravity, but even so had to sit down every now and then to catch my breath. All around, people bustled; port techs and drone captains, dockers and ecologists bickering over their wares. Someone was already trying to load a tree into the *Emni*, root system still intact, branches lovingly twined in netting. Someone else had a single glass vial, the most important vial on the planet, they said – the DNA contained within this will stabilise Adjapar's biological transition – *are you listening? This is our future!*

I sat on a crate. I had no idea what was in it, probably something priceless – everything becomes priceless when the alternative is obliteration – and watched. My duties were technically discharged. I had Piloted the ship through arcspace, and none of my passengers had become convinced they were blind when they could see, or become infested with a song that only they could hear. Hadja had been almost disappointed.

"It would have been a tragedy for disaster to occur," qe primly declared. "But it would have been most *interesting*."

Now I was surplus to requirements, an off-worlder with the relentless runny nose you always get when you come to a new planet, immunisations or no.

Soft drizzle blew in, warm and light and all-penetrating. I had done the requisite crash course in Assembly Adjumiri, the business dialect used in all diplomatic and governmental matters, but the accent of the dockers was something different, thicker, harder to tune my ears to. I had nine days on the surface of the planet before our scheduled departure. Traditionally Adjumiris put up guests in a nearby hostel, sometimes organised day trips. A whole diplomatic service existed for the express purpose of welcoming and indulging visitors to the planet, on the basis that anyone foolish enough to come to a dying world to assist was an asset worth courting.

Come, they would say, come. Look at all the lives you could help save if you keep on aiding us. Look at the children running in the streets. Form emotional bonds with us; come, come!

There was no hostel booked for me. The local ecologists had the decency to look embarrassed when they found out – they had rooms booked and "scientific" excursions scheduled. But the Major had said that I should sleep on the ship, and when she had explained why, no one had questioned it.

Then a voice said: "Are you in charge?" It took me a moment to process the words – another unfamiliar accent, and the phrase te used was "the lookout above", which I struggled to recontextualise into a Normspeak "in charge". "Are you in charge?" te repeated, a little slower, a little clearer, impatience flashing across ter face at my dullard's wit.

"No," I replied, and pointed towards the scientist who'd made themselves most noisome. "They are."

Ter face flickered with something I thought was almost disgust, and it took me a moment to realise why. Pointing with anything, let alone a finger, was the height of rudeness on Adjumir, and though I was an off-worlder, the instinct of indignation was set deep.

I curled my fingers back into my fist, tried to be a little smaller, a little less of a presence on the pad.

"They are a botanist," te declared. "I tried to explain things to them earlier. They were rude. Perhaps they did not understand."

"I am sorry to hear that."

"You are not 'sorry'. That is not the 'sorry' you mean," te retorted. "You used the sorry of taking responsibility – of saying it is your fault. Rather you *regret* that. The regret of empathy without commitment. That is how we say things here. Unless, of course, you *are* to blame."

"I would not have you think I am."

"That is not quite the same as saying you are not." For a moment longer te regarded the guilty botanist – the one who, unfathomably, did not understand. Then te clicked ter tongue in the roof of ter mouth, twice – a sign I would eventually learn to take as a catch-all negative, a thing whose meaning lay somewhere between a polite "no thank you" and an absolute "damn you all" – and turned ter attention back to me. Two fingers went to the top of ter brow in greeting, which gesture I was at least well enough trained to mimic, and te barked: "I am Gebre Nethyu Chatithimska Bajwahra of the Haalo Institute. I have artefacts of vital cultural significance to load upon this vessel and have been guaranteed five by five metrics of sealed non-organic space. These *pythas*," te was too polite to gesture at the assembled workers of the yard, albeit not quite polite enough to not dishonour their ancestors, "insist they have no records of this arrangement. Who do I speak with to rectify this situation?"

"I'm afraid I have no idea."

"What is your role precisely?"

"I am the Pilot."

This statement usually produces one of two reactions:

1. The flinch of fear. A recoiling. A turning away. In polite societies, a hasty withdrawal. In a few cases, immediate violence and cries for help. My quan companions are sometimes asked to protect me from others, as well as others from me.

2. Fascination. An almost sickly curiosity, usually giving way to sympathy. Mumbled questions, turning into a torrent: what does darkness taste like, sound like, does it truly sing? They ask me because soon, surely, I shall be dead, and what are the odds of meeting a seemingly sane one of me ever again?

"I am the Pilot," I said, and waited to see which route Gebre Nethyu Chatithimska Bajwahra would take.

A flinch, but almost as quickly as it had come, another expression, a flicker of interest pushing through the distaste. And as soon as these expressions were there, they were gone, and te clicked ter tongue once in ter mouth – the sound of acknowledgement, a polite affirmation – and said, as if all this were the most normal thing in the galaxy, "Well then. You must have seen *someone* who knows which end of the slitherjaw has fangs."

In the end, we found the launchmaster.

Xe was a cheerful individual with a round belly and shock of snowy white hair, who had spent the best part of xer life being shouted at by one person or another and hadn't suffered any lasting consequences from it. Other people's indignation was other people's problems, and so, as Gebre fumed: "But look now! There is an arrangement with the Institute! I've come all this way . . ."

. . . the launchmaster just smiled and nodded and said oh yes, how interesting, and ah yes, I do see the problem here and hum hum, why don't you come back tomorrow and I'll see if I can fit you in after midtick?

I watched, having nothing better to do, nowhere else to go. Gebre seemed to think that having me trail around in ter wake added a certain authenticity to ter outrage, provided an ally even, though I had no position and hadn't said a word.

"Outrageous!" te fumed as the door to the launchmaster's office shut on us. "Don't they understand protocol?"

"What exactly are these artefacts of cultural significance?" I asked. At my back, Hadja vented a soft discharge of heat, but did not speak.

Gebre's eyes flickered from qim to me, and then, perhaps with nothing better to do, te straightened up to ter full, somewhat gravity-compressed height and said: "If we get something to eat, will you vomit on my priceless treasures?"

*

I did not vomit upon ter priceless treasures, though Hadja warned me against trying all but the blandest of meals until my stomach settled in.

We sat with our legs tucked under a low cloth-covered table, holding black ceramic cups of a shockingly acidic drink Gebre informed me was called kol and was a vital guest-greeting beverage that I had to consume – little sips were acceptable – while te held forth. Te had straight, thick black hair that te wore in a tight wound braid at the back of ter head, skin like a warm dawn on a winter's day. Ter eyes were a sinking, sombre brown, ter face round and serious, ter shoulders broader than mine, voice deep, certain of its truths.

Te talked a lot with ter hands, as all Adjumiris did, fingers dancing in a language I at first took to be just another sign of Adjumiri's high affect – if Adjumiri dinners didn't end with weeping and/or declarations of undying love, it was considered something of a tedious affair – but that I later read as a habit of the hand-speak that all children were taught before they learned to shape words with their tongues. At first te spoke too fast, and I had to blurt, "Sorry?" and "What?" to every third or fourth sentence, until te began to recognise the look of confusion in my eyes and slowed down, clarifying what words te could with their nearest Normspeak equivalent. Te seemed to find this distasteful, blurting: "Normspeak is all very well for communicating between cultures, but in its effort to be comprehensible it is also crude! Disgustingly crude!"

Te said te found my face hard to read, asked if all off-worlders were as flat in their features as I. I replied that on Xihana it was also said I smiled less, frowned less than was the cultural norm, but that by Haima standards my features were practically verbose.

"You've been to many worlds, then?"

"More than the average, I believe."

"But you are a Pilot. Is this your last flight?"

"It is . . . complicated. But please, you were explaining the importance of a cup."

"Not a cup – a set of three. The three cups that were made specifically for the signing of the South Zyonhan Peace, with the fingerprints of the signatories still visible in the ceramic. Children study these things in school, of course, but sometimes you have to see, you have to hold, do you understand? You have to touch the uniform of a soldier who died, you have to appreciate how heavy the gun was when it was lifted, you have to see the fragments of the ship when it was blasted apart to comprehend how hot the fire burned, you have to hold the cups that sealed the peace – this is not just about the archaeology, you see, it is about the *emotion*, about connection with those who went before. The history that made us was already an abstract thing, and now that we are leaving this world it's going to become worse than that. It's going to become . . . tedious textbooks, or romantic stories, not a thing that we *feel*. We will not understand how it is still in *us*, how it shaped us and our ancestors and is shaping us still. It's not just about the damn cups – it's about making our memories *real*. Do you understand?"

"Perhaps. Yes."

"I'm not convinced that you do. Perhaps it is your face."

"And these artefacts . . . they are going to Adjapar?"

"Yes. First to storage, then to a new institute on the planet's surface, when the time comes. There are already generations of Adjumiris being born who have never seen the surface of this world, never breathed its air. What will they understand of us? What will their children understand? We have a duty to try and explain, to keep some sort of connection. On hundreds of worlds light years away Adjumiri children are growing up who, through the simple act of being far from home, may be told that they are *lesser*. That their people did not make and build and dream like the natives of their new worlds. We must preserve something – whatever we can – to show them that this is not so. That is my calling." A word in Adjumiri – *calling*. In Normspeak it would have just been "job", a profession, a labour done for reward of one nature or another. On Adjumir, the word had changed meaning with Exodus, every act, every moment of breath infused with purpose, with a higher goal. There were no "jobs" in the last days of Adjumir, only greater purposes waiting to be fulfilled.

A question, of course, just on the edge of asking. I tried to find the best way around it, to force Adjumiri words into some sort of tactful order. "How do you choose what stays and what goes?" And then, the other thing, the thing that you could not take a single step on Adjumir without feeling seeping through your very bones. "How do you decide how much to save? If every crate is a person left behind . . ."

"It is not," te snapped, hard and fast, a scholar used to this question and a little afraid of it. "Saving artefacts and saving people require entirely different mechanisms. You are the Pilot of a cargo ship, bio-formed to support the perfect environmental conditions for transport. Your ship is not engineered for the gene therapies and immunisation packets required for human cargo en route to anywhere other than a cryofacility. Your life-support systems could not sustain more than what, a tenhand people? The items we carry – the goods we save – give meaning to millions. *Millions.* I would happily discard my number if I knew my life could do so much."

"Has your number been called?"

Te was no longer bristling, no longer fired up with outrage at my ignorance, and simply clicked ter tongue three times in the top of ter mouth and proclaimed: "On Adjumir, you must *never* ask someone that question. It is the height of rudeness."

"I apologise."

"And you are using the wrong form of 'apology' again. There are four forms in Adjumiri. You should have been taught the one that suggests you experience empathy without owning responsibility – a nice, safe kind of apology, obviously the one they'd teach to off-worlders. But you must also know the polite form of 'violated social expectation or contract' and the deep form of 'acknowledge the consequences of my personal action' if you are to really understand.

You do not have to understand," te added, a slight drawing-back of ter voice, a recognition of a difficult thing. "But it is my duty to ensure that people do. You do not need to take it personally."

Gebre had never been off-world, but ter mind was full of the sounds and songs of a changing culture. The first generations to have been born on other planets were already in their fifties, their children starting to have children, and the songs these generations had made had drifted back to Adjumir, carried in the hollow hulls of the returning motherships and on the commcasts of roaming journalists and scholars. They still sang in Adjumiri, some of the time, but the rhythms were changing, the old lyrics losing their meaning. Artists still spoke of the yellow-spotted sky because they found the pattern of the words nice, not because they understood the ancient stories of Dablwa and Madungnashi and the killing of the great moon-snake; poets wove ballads about Exodus and leaving loved ones behind without ever having set foot on one of Adjumir's orbital elevators or tasted from the farewell cup. It was not that Gebre disapproved of these new forms of art, per se. Culture was always adapting, always changing, and, with a certain distaste in the corner of ter lips, te accepted that.

"But," te would mutter, "what is the point of our lives if we are not remembered? What is the point of the stories we make if they do not tell people something true?"

I didn't have an answer to that, and te didn't expect me to. Even ter own people struggled sometimes with the strength of ter vision.

Interlude

A note on gender

Gender is irrelevant for quans, for whom replication is a complex dance of modular balancing and operational system optimisation. The use of the pronoun "qe" is a matter of respect – they do not wish to be put in the same category as a bowl of soup or a broken chair.

The aka-aka have one gender – "we". All of "we" are necessary for the production of more "we", and all "we" behave differently; what else is there to say? It takes extraordinary efforts to convince an aka-aka that anyone would want to subdivide the one-of-we by trivialities such as quill texture or genital organs.

There is some dispute about how many genders there are on Adjumir. Most textbooks written for off-planet education concur that there are eight, with another four genders that are either regionally specific, such as the "ye" of the blue forest ("one who has grown roots of earth and soul of sky"), or deliberately open, such as "le" ("one who is in a place of change, seeking"). Very few Adjumiris remain one gender for their entire lives, passing through different states of being as they change, grow, age. Off-worlders are taught the basic "they", which is the pronoun given to children who have not yet passed through the gate, and the polite "ae" used for the non-gender, the gender-that-is-without-significance, defaulted to by off-worlders who haven't yet learned the nuances of Adjumiri categorisations.

Some off-worlders complain, say that it's too complicated, there's too much here for them to ever understand.

How odd, the Adjumiris reply.

You can remember the difference between innumerable different types of sausage or sporting teams, but you cannot hold in your mind a mere half-dozen or so categories of people? That must make navigating the nuances of human experience extraordinarily taxing for you.

There are four genders on Xihana, all fairly loosely defined. To the Xi, gender is merely a hasty marker to allow strangers to make some very rough time-saving assumptions about who you are. Given that any sort of assumption is in and of itself generally incorrect once examined over time, they are uninterested in investing too much effort in constructing rigid ideas of identity, and tend to use gender markers when the level of engagement is expected to be no more than polite chit-chat with acquaintances, or business talk. Once intimacy is established, it is expected that conversation will switch to the fifth gender, the free-speak where all categories are torn down and all that remains is the truth of a soul, the heart of an individual, vulnerable, loved and seen.

The Shine, somewhat controversially, have only two genders – "he" and "she" – which are firmly defined, strictly separated and legally enforced.

In reality, there are four, for superior to these firm delineations are the far more exclusive, far more desirable "hé" and "shé". These categories are preserved for those who have reached the absolute pinnacle of their gender presentation – the *most* manly and the *most* feminine, the ultimate expressions of what everyone else should aspire to be. Hé must not merely be strong, brave, wealthy and wise, but also embody in both hís physicality and beauty qualities of such exceptional intellect and prowess that to merely glance hís way is to at once know hís superiority. And shé is not merely graceful, fertile, generous and kind, but has about hér an almost supernatural *otherness*, an untouchable dignity, that can be captured by neither art nor lyricism. Hé is the provider of physical and material goods; shé is grateful for hís protection, and in return offers emotional support and sexual gratification upon hér body, occasionally in filmed demonstrations for commnet distribution so that people can see exactly how happy a woman at the peak of hér perfection is to give pleasure to a man.

"So ... the important thing is your genitals?" Gebre blurted, when I explained this. "As in ... even if you can't see someone's genitals, they are the first thing that is on your mind when you meet someone? It is their defining characteristic, above ethics, work, aptitudes, hobbies, hopes, loves, et cetera?"

"That is one way of looking at it, yes."

Despite this, observers have noted that, for all the Shine's insistence on conformity in its gender presentations, hé and shé are in fact changeable, representing not some fixed sacrosanct, but an ideal that is most embodied by whatever tiny minority has the greatest power, the greatest influence and the greatest wealth at this precise moment in time.

Mawukana na-Vdnaze – the Maw who almost certainly died on the MSV *Myrmida*, screaming in a Pilot's chair – was told he was a man, and did not know to quibble it. I am not sure what I am, but on Xihana at least, no one seemed to think it mattered.

Chapter 11

Gebre Nethyu Chatithimska Bajwahra did eventually get ter goods onto the *Emni*. The instant they were loaded, te seemed to deflate, started muttering: "Well yes, yes, I suppose mushrooms are important too . . ."

I had followed ter around in fascinated silence, and now the weight of Adjumiri gravity was really starting to drag, and I sat breathless on the edge of my ship while te looked at me askance and said: "You come from somewhere a little less massy, I take it?"

Sometimes, when I am tired, my leg aches. It is the leg that was broken, back in the fires of Hasha-to. When the quarantine team found me on the *Myrmida*, my leg was healed as if it had never snapped, but not quite right. Maybe it's just memories, a ghost of pain that has no other way of being processed. Maybe it's not that at all.

Then Gebre blurted: "Thank you, by the way." And, because te was struggling to say these words, struggling to know how to thank a stranger for showing the bare minimum of kindness, the absolute basic nothing of decency, added: "For coming to Adjumir. You'd be astonished how many people just look at us and go, 'Well, the problem is too big, no point trying.' Some diplomat should be saying all this to you, of course. Nice flowery speak – little presents, I imagine. Harmless trash that won't cause anaphylaxis. Anyway.

You risk your life Piloting a ship here, and I suppose someone should say ... thank you."

I opened my mouth to blurt actually, no, you don't understand – I am Mawukana-from-the-Dark, I was made in deepest black, I am a meagre copy of the dead, there is no ...

... but te had spotted someone else te needed to shout out, to rebuke for their failings, and was already marching away.

After that, I became a regular in Adjumir's airspace.

I shuttled in diplomats and scientists, politicians and eager aid workers who felt sure that they were going to have some brilliant idea, some dazzling insight that might, in its way, be more potent than the shock wave of a binary star supernova sweeping across the heavens.

I ferried out crabs and molluscs in cryopods ("The carrion of the sea!"), fungal scrapings from the deepest, blackest caves ("Vital for ecological consistency"), seeds upon seeds upon seeds, all carefully labelled and sealed for their eventual replanting in Adjapar's soil, once it had soil to carry life. I shepherded entomologists ("Insects must precede flowers and fruits! It is baffling to me how many so-called planetary engineers miss this blisteringly obvious evolutionary fact!") and anxious historians ("It took so long for us to learn from our mistakes. Imagine the mistakes we will make again, if we forget"). I practised Adjumiri, and whenever I returned to Xihana for the *Emni* to rest and shed some of his weight, the Major would visit and confer with Hadja in a corner.

"Is he safe? He is occupied ... but is he safe?"

And Hadja would reply: "He appears to have a kind of purpose. I have not yet determined why."

Then the usual line of psychologists and doctors would come to visit, and the questions they asked were almost identical to those the doctor asked on Hasha-to.

"When I sleep, I dream of flying – yes or no?"

"It is winter, and the lake has frozen over. What do you do?"

"A friend visits. They have made a delicious meal, but you know already that you do not like the taste of it. Do you eat the food, or make an excuse?"

"What is the taste of music?"

"I think that sleep is like a kind of dying – yes or no?"

I answered their questions politely and thoughtfully, as I always did, while Hadja hovered by my side. Only one of my visitors asked this:

"What do you feel, when you go to Adjumir?"

"I don't know."

"But you want to go."

"Yes."

"Do you know why?"

"No. I am told it is because I want to make a difference. That I am a 'good man'. A lot of people want to help in some way, but very few do. I think it is because they think that 'helping' is somehow 'fixing'. Somehow being a hero. But no one is a hero, against a supernova. And everyone is too. Everyone who did anything at all, no matter how small, because that's all change is – a great big enormity made up of a vast, uncounted mass of tiny actions. But that's not what people want to feel. They want to feel . . . special. A special kind of hero. I don't feel that way. What I do is irrelevant. And also if I did not do it, things would be worse, so it matters to do it. Matters, does not matter. Do you understand me? It is . . . pleasing that people are happy to see me, when I go to Adjumir. It makes me feel . . . nice. But I think the truth is that the world is going to die. I have never seen a world die before."

The psychologist made a note, and I knew I had said the wrong thing and everyone in the room was a little bit afraid. Frightened enough that they did not try to stop me going back to Adjumir.

"You can fly more sorties than any of our people," sighed the Major. "You are safer, more reliable, more accurate. The dark, when you enter it, seems not to perceive you. Seems utterly oblivious to your presence. As if you were already part of it. Which I suppose in a way you are."

Then I said I felt more comfortable on my island than in the black, and she knew I was lying but chose not to remark on it, since that would only make everyone more unhappy than they already were.

Chapter 12

For the next year, I flew. And every time I returned to Adjumir, the area around each landing pad had grown. From simple security fence and basic operational buildings, tents began to appear. Cabins and muddy streets, overloaded composters struggling to handle the weight of sewage and crooked overhangs of solar screens spilling across the valleys and over rooftops like a fungal growth as people began to drift towards the pads.

Some of them were simply curious, day-trippers come to point and stare at the odd shape of the *Emni* and the other atmos-capable vehicles that didn't need to dock at distant elevator ports. Some were workers, come to support the growing flow of logistics through the dock gates and off the planet. A few were protesters, carrying signs and blasting their homilies through the open links of the fence.

"Exodus lies! Exodus lies! Exodus lies!" they chanted.

Sometimes, at night, when I was in the right hemisphere, I could see Lhonoja. I didn't know it until it was pointed out to me, half expecting to see two stars instead of their light melded into one. It was ten years until they would fuse and explode; another seven before the shock from the blast would strike Adjumir and the light of the star would finally go out. Until then, the Lovers shone still, normal, peaceful, unobtrusive.

"Exodus lies, Exodus lies!" shrilled the little handful of protest-ers by the gate. "Aliens stealing from our world!"

"Alien" was a word I had learned in Adjumiri. It was an almost forbidden sound – "off-worlder" or "star traveller" were the cor-rect usages taught in the schools, if only because so many of the students learning these nuances could soon find themselves on another world where they themselves might be the "alien" – a dark, threatening thing. An intruder, a creature of otherness, unwel-come in this space. But as the months crept by and the end of the world drew nearer, more protesters pointed at me and my clearly gravitationally challenged form, and chanted "Alien, alien, alien!"

"We shall now move away," Hadja declared, and it was not a matter for debate.

The last people to come to the launch pads were the number-less, those whom the lottery had not yet chosen for Exodus. Little huddles of families and friends, waiting silently in the mouths of their tents while the medical workers tutted and fussed and wor-ried about outbreaks of gastrointestinal disease across the growing camps. Some were old; some were children. In those days, they were not so many. I was told the camps around the bases of the equatorial space elevators were far bigger, almost city states with mayors and security forces to keep the numberless from rushing the lifts. In those days, such incidents were still rare. There was still time for their numbers to be called; for their lives to be saved.

I looked for Gebre on every trip, and did not find ter.

I wondered if ter number had come up, if even now te was queuing at the base of one of the great elevators, waiting to be carried into the sky, up to the open hull of a waiting mothership. I wondered which world te would end up on, whether it was for the cryofacilities of Adjapar and a promise of one day – centuries from now – being reunited with ter precious artefacts, or whether they were giving ter the immunisations for travel to another world, ter lungs, heart and bones altering in flight as te headed to a place where people only knew one word for "apology".

In the end, it turned out to be none of the above, for on my twelfth trip, there te was.

"By the fires of the abyss," te breathed, "they're still letting you fly?"

A jolt of disappointment – a part of me had hoped that my fantasies were true, that te was already in the stars, already saved.

A far stronger jolt of something else – something like joy – to see ter face.

"Gebre Nethyu Chatithimska Bajwahra," I exclaimed. "I saw our cargo manifest contained the ritual robes of a long-vanished forest cult, and wondered if that was you."

My Adjumiri was much better, and te told me so.

I said thank you – the "thank you" of deepest appreciation, rather than the Assembly Adjumiri "thank you" of formal acknowledgement that I had learned on my first trip, and asked if te would like to tour the ship.

Te said yes, te would find that very interesting, and though ter voice was polite and level, ter hands danced in the language of childlike excitement.

I took ter around the *Emni*. He was in his late-autumn phase, his energy depleted by so many runs across the galaxy. When we returned to Xihana, I would have to leave him in the storm deserts for a few weeks, let the daytime sun bathe him, the nighttime water wash him clean while the bio-engineers scrubbed his decks and changed out his nutrient tanks, ready to bloom again for another flight between the stars. For now, however, the soft buds of his corridors were closed and the ivy tangle about my bed was shedding its final leaves.

This did not stop Gebre clapping ter hands with delight as we moved through the *Emni*'s decks.

"I knew the Xi made living ships, but gorgeous! Absolutely gorgeous! I imagine you feel like nothing can harm you when you fly something as fabulous as this."

"The *Emni* is robust," I replied. "He is constantly healing himself; he can even regenerate his external carapace from near-arcspace acceleration. If looked after properly, he could fly for centuries."

"I love him – oh I love him! And is it true these kinds of ships have near-perfect internal recycling? Air, water ..."

"He runs at near-total efficiency, yes."

"Beautiful. Absolutely beautiful."

Our wanderings had taken us to the command deck – little more than a round hollow swollen out of the forward habitation quarters – and there, in a rare square of hard lines and cold metal, was the Pilot's chair. Gebre moved towards it carefully, as if it might be contaminated with the lingering traceries of something black, something slippery, before looking up with fingers raised, a dance that I was coming to understand requested permission.

I nodded, which gesture had no meaning for ter, so instead clicked my tongue once in assent. Ter face split into a giant, toothy smile – though whether at the permission or my growing skills with Adjumiri colloquial, I could not say – and te rested ter hand on the back of the chair.

"Oh," te said. "It's really rather squishy."

"Squishy?"

"As in ... soft, comfortable? Do you know these words?"

"Ah, yes. Squishy. I had not heard that before."

"Well. Good, I suppose, to make the Pilot comfortable. And this ..." Te indicated the waiting crown of wires hanging off the back of the chair, the far thinner tendrils of the neuro-fibral connectors withdrawn into their sheaths, the interior recently scrubbed with antibacterial gel and left to dry.

"The Pilot's interface."

"You put it on your head?"

"Yes."

"And what happens then?"

"The navcomm engages the bio-mechanical processor. Machine

and mind working together to guide the ship. No one has yet worked out definitively why arcspace navigation requires an organic component, though a lot of blustering happens in certain pseudo-scientific circles. The experiments are hard to perform to test hypotheses – in arcspace, instruments fail; studies tend to return nonsense results."

"Does it hurt?"

"A bit. When you first connect."

"And when you're navigating? In arcspace, I mean. If it's not too rude to ask – is it rude to ask?"

"It is hard to express." I shrugged. "At the time, everything is crystal clear, precise. The computer provides a sense of destination; all you have to do is let the process run. It is almost peaceful, even. But after, when we return, it is as if I was dreaming. There is always a sense of loss. Of something missing, a thing I have seen but cannot name. Does that make sense?"

"As much as anything, yes."

"I am told that my experience is ... anomalous. Many Pilots report experiencing things that ... that are different. No one ever tells the same story."

"But you find it peaceful."

"Yes."

"Is that why you're still flying? On Adjumir a Pilot is allowed to fly only once; twice on a round trip if absolutely no other alternative is available. If you are numberless, you can volunteer to Pilot and may be considered, but even then, the odds of actually being chosen are low. But you ... you keep on flying and you don't appear to be ... " Another dance of fingers, grasping at uncomfortable notions.

"Mad?" I suggested, and then, as Adjumiri never has one word when three will suffice: "Insane? Deranged? Reckless?"

"Yes," te mused. "Something like that."

"It is a little more complicated than that. I am ... scared to tell you."

"Why?"

"It may change your expectations of me."

"I don't expect anything from you."

"I know. I like that. It is ... hard to express how grateful I am for that."

"Hard because of language?" te barked. "Or hard because of feelings?"

"A bit of both."

Te puffed both ter cheeks out, a sign of annoyance – though one, I had learned to understand, that wasn't necessarily directed at me. Clicked ter tongue in the roof of ter mouth. Turned and turned again to look around the cabin, taking in its polished walls, warm to the touch, the faint smell of soil after rain drifting through the vents, the Pilot's chair. Ter eyes, as they wandered, took in Hadja too, my ever-present companion, loitering a little too close for comfort near the door. Ter gaze stayed on Hadja a moment longer than was necessary, before returning at last to me.

"Mawukana na-Vdnaze," te said, "we should sing."

Hadja objected.

"Absolutely not!" qe barked. "Leaving the base is unacceptable, it is—"

"We'll be back before sunset," Gebre assured the bobbing quan. "And you can of course come with us and keep watch."

"Mawukana should not leave the safety of the launch site! It is against protocol, it is—"

"Hadja," I snapped, a sharpness to my tone that surprised even me, set my heart beating fast. "There is a balance to be struck. Between safety and ... and risk. Always a balance. Yes?"

Hadja processed this statement in, I have no doubt, a micro-second, but lingered a while longer to let the full extent of qis disapproval settle in. Then: "Very well. But I will not move from your side, and if we are not back by sunset, I will incapacitate you until further assistance can be found."

"Fair enough."

"Is it?" Gebre blurted, and I smiled and clicked my tongue, and on we went.

The people of Adjumir love to sing.

They sang long before Exodus came, but at the arrival of the Slow and qis declaration of the end of the world, they really stepped up their musical efforts.

This was, Gebre assured me, largely an instrument of social control.

Cohesion – cohesion and togetherness. That was what Exodus required. The old song festivals of a few thousand people getting together every four years now swelled into endless churning rituals of celebration, yearning and praise. From the solo night-callers, wandering place to place to sing the ballads of the blackened moon, to the great gatherings beneath the song spires where forty thousand people would raise their voices as one, the message was clear. We are one, we are the people of Adjumir, the people of the forest. Some may live and some may die – some may make it to the stars and some may perish in the fires of Lhonoja, but our songs will live on.

"In Exodus," Gebre explained, "we are taught only how to sing songs for each other, to celebrate each other, never just ourselves."

We were sitting in the back of a flatbed speeder, pressed between empty barrels of food and drink supplied to the landing crews from far-off fields, the soft hum of the truck's suspensor field rising a little as we whisked away from the launch pad. As we rose up the walls of the valley, the trees about us grew straighter, stiffer, spined with thorns. I wheezed a little as my lungs struggled in the changing air, neck aching from the press of gravity. Hadja bobbed at my back, stoutly refusing to offer any aid, but Gebre put one finger on my forehead, a gesture whose meaning I did not comprehend, asked if I wanted to go back.

"No. I would like to see something of this world, even if it's only for a day."

Te seemed to approve of this statement, and why would te not? Ter life was given over to the memory of Adjumir, as if the world were already dead.

The nearest settlement was called Lud.

The houses were stacked boxes, rising away from each other to form terraces punctuated by green. Every roof held a garden, some overflowing with hanging tendrils draping down around windows and doors; others decked out with comfy chairs and budding fruit trees beneath which the slumbering residents might wait for the end of the world.

Long avenues bisected the town, pierced by tight, tangled alleys through which the rising heat of the day could not penetrate. On these avenues were buildings that Gebre called shops, though Hadja insisted this was a barely adequate translation, the least-bad that the linguists could do. "They are a calling," Gebre explained, when I struggled to understand more. "The dice house, the bath house, the house of learning, the poet's house, the cloth house, the grocer and the physician. They are called to their vocations. We are Adjumiri; we serve each other."

"Do you ... pay?" I stumbled, realising as I did that I was unclear on the correct verb in this language.

"Pay? As in ... do we perform our services for the whole?" te asked. "Of course we do. I serve the Institute. My service is given to my people."

I wondered for a moment if I should try to explain the economy of Tu-mdo, the Shine, ideas of value and worth that were clearly strangers here. Then again, if Gebre's number was called, te was hardly going to be shipped off to a Shine world, and perhaps this was a conversation for another, less pleasant time.

Te took me to the song spire, a tower of white basalt grown in the centre of the town. We were too late for the dawn songs, too early for the evening, but the music never ceased in these crystal halls, whether they were snatches of dirges sung for those who had departed to the stars or swellings of chorus from little gatherings practising for the harvest festival.

We sat a while and listened, and Gebre tried to teach me the first song – a children's song – the song of the great forest from which all life had begun and to which all things would one day return. Te hummed a line of notes, which I mangled, so te hummed a simpler line, and in the end simply gave me a three-note drone that rose and fell in time to a steady clapping, over which te called out the beats of the verse.

Hadja watched, and did not join in. Whatever qis interest in being my keeper, music was clearly not on the list.

Then a figure in white robes moved through the hall, holding up a loose collection of clonking wooden chimes, and all music stopped.

Every head turned, every lip sealed, as the Behkdaz processed through the song spire, accompanied only by the soft clonk-clonk of hollow wood. I waited for her to pass, for Gebre to explain, which te did by putting a hand on my arm, whispering: "Let's move on."

Te took me to the towntree, towering over a little square a few wiggling alleys from the spire. Seven people stretched arm-to-arm could not have encompassed its trunk, and the branches spilled out from its crown in a blue-grey umbrella of ancient blackened bark. Wooden and silver chimes hung from every twig, singing softly in the breeze, and now that Gebre had pointed them out, I saw more chimes hanging by the occasional door, outside darkened houses and shuttered places, more silver than wood, some tarnished and green, some fresh and sparkling in the afternoon sun.

"Silver for those who have gone to the stars," te murmured as we stood beneath the softly singing branches of the tree. "Wood for those who have taken Grace, whose song will not be heard again. The Behkdaz are the guides of the way; if you wish, they will help you hold the cup. It is not a decision taken lightly, but when the end comes . . . it will perhaps be taken. Better to die in Grace than burn when the planet does."

We stood together a while more, listening to the chimes singing their silver songs, before Gebre clicked ter tongue, murmured: "Come. There is more for you to see."

Thus, a day spent in Lud.

I drank a variety of mostly foul drinks that my stomach was in no state to digest; I rolled dice against two elders who laughed and said I did not know my good fortune. I was taken to the old stone gate behind the cemetery, through which younglings passed when they reached maturity and chose their name, and through which the dead were carried when their time was done and only their name remained. In a "shop" – Gebre still struggled to find the right word, a place of speciality was the best te could settle on – te explained at great length the meaning of the crowns and gowns that you must choose for the defining rituals of your life. Here, trousers adorned with feathers that seemed black until they flashed a dazzling blue, for wearing when you were in a time of change and learning. Here, the green headdress of one who wishes to be bound for ever to another as kinn; here, the yellow-red robe of the scholar who has completed a task of great learning.

Ideally, of course, you should go into the forest and find your own feathers, make your own garment. But the realities of urban living were often such that these ancient practices had to be turned into more abstract rituals, and those who were in a time of change were commonly invited up into the local fields to sleep and sing beneath the stars on auspicious nights beside the jolmwood fire, as a sign of their contemplation and rebirth.

Aware of my unsettled stomach and the weight of gravity pressing down against the support of my mechanical exoskeleton, Gebre invited me to eat a simple meal of some fluffy mass te called "bread" – yet another translation I felt I had to question – on the edge of a sparkling stream of cool water, served with drinks of crushed ice and barely spiced mashed vegetables.

"It is food fit for babies," te admitted, "but I do not think your stomach can appreciate our delicacies."

Te told me about ter work, sorting, cataloguing, saving what te could from thousands of years of planetary history. "When I began," te mused, "I thought every single thing was precious, and died inside at the thought of leaving things behind. Then I realised that this was nonsense, and instead started focusing on saving only the most extraordinary, most fragile of artefacts. Now I am more circumspect. I realise that it is important to also save some kitsch – do you understand this word, 'kitsch'? Tempting to save only those things that represent the greatest craft, the most extraordinary beauty, but of course the reality is that such things do not accurately or fully tell the story of my people. My people, you see, also love a little kitsch."

"I live on an island by myself, and only a few people visit me. I do not have much of much, but I have a bowl with yellow flowers on it that was painted by the offspring of a friend called Yulin. It is very badly done, but I treasure it."

"That's it!" te blurted. "That's it! You understand! We must be careful not to give our descendants the impression that it's all micro-mosaicking and diamond-form glassware!"

I told ter about some of the worlds I'd visited.

About Va, where they believed the written word to be so sacred that it could only be inscribed on gold, silver or pearl. (The digital word, however – they shrewdly decided not to concern themselves too much with the holiness or otherwise of that, and thus civilisation did not entirely collapse.)

About Kzichido, where peace had reigned for centuries, and how disappointing this was to everyone involved, who had been raised to believe in war as honour, honour as life, and who thus had to resort to endless convoluted sporting activities and ritualised battles to give themselves something to do in these long, wretched years of contemplative calm.

About Okopuatji, where I had experienced the worst space-lag of my life, the average day lasting thirty-five hours, which extraordinary length everyone seemed to take for granted, reaching the end of their eleven-and-a-half-hour work day with a merry cry of "And now we shall party!" and goodness how they did.

"Party? For how long?"

"Eleven hours!"

"Eleven hours? Of just . . . just partying?"

"Music, alcohol, dance . . . "

"Every day?"

"It felt that way."

"Sounds exhausting!"

"It is! They say the long sleep cycle makes up for it, but I think they're lying to themselves, because the things they do, the madness at the end of the day, they call it disinhibition but I don't think it can be . . . "

I did not tell ter about the Shine, and te did not know to ask. And in this way, the day drifted towards evening, and I was laughing, and so was te, and I couldn't remember the last time I had laughed in this way, until Hadja, who had been almost entirely silent up to this point, to the degree that I had begun to forget qis presence, declared, loud enough to make my ears shudder:

"WE WILL RETURN TO THE *EMNI* NOW!"

The sun was not yet set, but its descent towards the horizon was throwing long shadows across the town, stretching out the length of the song spire like a moving dial and catching crimson shadows in the playing burble of the water. For a moment I considered arguing; then I did not, and with a creak of exoskeleton and an ache of muscles, I rose.

"Gebre," I said, touching my fingers to my shoulder in the gesture of thanks and gratitude, "thank you for a wonderful day."

Ter lips thinned; there was a disapproval there, though whether of my bumbling manners or the passage of time, I couldn't entirely tell. Te looked from me to Hadja and back again, then stood at once, the scraps of meal at our feet ignored, and blurted: "Are you interested in sharing skin with me?"

"I ... What?"

"Are you interested in sharing skin?" te repeated. "It is a simple question."

"This is not a phrase I—"

Hadja hissed behind me, and – in a rare act of rudeness that just this once I was grateful for – translated ter meaning into neither Normspeak nor Xiha but Mdo-sa, the first language of my birth. "It is a sexual advance," qe explained, "which we covered in your Adjumiri language course section 7.2; clearly you were not paying attention."

"*Oh.*"

"The polite form of the decline is 'My voice must rest, though I shall often speak of you.'"

"I see."

"Do you require further help with the translation?"

"I'm wondering ... what is the polite way in which people say yes?"

We rode back to the *Emni* in almost total silence.

Me, Hadja, and next to the quan – who seemed to have interspersed qimself like a chaperone – Gebre.

Outside the window, the sun was setting, orange to crimson, crimson to purple, the stars beginning to emerge from the dusk. I looked for Lhonoja, but on the winding road I could not orientate myself, and it felt unclean to seek it out.

In soft Mdo-sa, a language for my ears alone, Hadja said: "On a scale of one to ten in terms of its emotional investment, sharing skin is a two. It invites physicality without emotional engagement; a common practice on Adjumir. Sharing song is a more formal invite towards committed emotional engagement following sexual intercourse; sharing light is what you would consider a marriage declaration."

"I see."

"Because of the casual nature of the overture, you do not have to observe any rituals, such as the cleansing of each other's bodily cavities with appropriately scented items. You are, however, expected to treat the matter as entirely insignificant unless by mutual consent, which may be gained through further intercourse and discussion begun through the phrase 'Will you speak to me of the springtime forest?'"

"Adjumir really loves its protocol, doesn't it?"

"Protocol," replied Hadja primly, "is how these people survive."

And then, a little while later, as we slowed down for our journey through the camp, Hadja addressed Gebre.

Qe spoke Adjumiri – not the Assembly Adjumiri I knew, but ter local dialect, full of sounds that I struggled to tune my ear to. It was soft, gentle even, a tone of warning, a suggestion, perhaps, of choices not yet locked in stone, decisions that could be undone.

"He is an alien," I heard qe say, and qe did not use the polite "off-worlder" when qe spoke. Qe very deliberately, very carefully chose the word that was steeped in darkness, a nameless, dangerous thing. "He is human/not human. An anomaly of the dark. Do not turn out the light."

Gebre listened; Gebre appeared to understand.

"Thank you," te said at last, "for your clarity."

I felt my heart beating in my throat as we got off the glider before the waiting mouth of the *Emni*.

"This is me," I mumbled, lips dumb and stupid as they tried to shape the words.

"I know," te replied.

"Well. There's no ... I mean. We could. If what Hadja said ... If you have changed your mind—"

"Pilot," te blurted, cutting me off – the single rudest thing any Adjumiri could possibly do, though I did not think te meant it rudely. "I was born knowing precisely how long I had to live if my number was not called. The day of my death, pending an accident, was set at the exact moment of my birth, and I have always known it. I have had many lovers, but I have always been diligent never to love. Love, you see, is for the living. I . . . will not have it. It is a price that is higher than any I am willing to pay. In its absence, I enjoy intimacy. I enjoy physical tenderness, pleasure, even courtship to a degree. I have found your company enjoyable; I believe I would enjoy intimacy with you. Is that acceptable? Do you understand?"

"Yes. I think I do."

"Good." Te held out ter hand. "Shall we?"

Later, I said:

"I cannot remember the name of my parents. A few archivists helped me find what records remain, but when I tell my story, they are always just 'my parents'. My leg sometimes hurts – whatever forces transcribed me clearly struggled to work out what to do with my tibia. On the one hand, my other leg offered a template, as did my genetic code. Then again, DNA itself is never just as simple as a command that must be executed; it is a cascading dance of on-and-off, as subject to environmental stimuli as wind or rain.

"When the quarantine teams found me on the *Myrmida*, they pointed guns, screamed at me, seemed to understand already that I was a monster. A murderer, at least. All those dead bodies scattered around the ship – and not just dead; there had been . . . *things* done to them. Dreadful things. And there I was, absolutely fine, so of course I was to blame, and perhaps I am. Perhaps . . . there are certain errors in how I . . . perceive some things. Anyway, they put me in a prison for a while, but a Xi prison after the fires of Hasha-to was wonderful. Good food, a comfy bed, all the reading you could ask for – incredible! – a psychologist to talk to twice a week. I'd never had anyone listen so intently before. At first I said nothing because I knew it was a trap, and then after a while I said everything, just couldn't stop talking, and the authorities couldn't actually prove I was a killer but they knew there was something not right, so then they sent me to a lab. At first, I quite enjoyed being there. There was a thing in me, a thing I think had always been there, but was now . . .

" . . . I was curious.

"So curious.

"And if people answered my questions, explained to me what they were doing when they took my blood, my skin, scanned my brain, asked what I thought, what I felt . . . I didn't mind being there at all. They let me read their papers, study their tools, learn about the drugs they pumped into me. But one day I think I said something, something that made them uncomfortable, or I did something or . . .

" . . . I am always doing something a little bit wrong, you see.

"Not quite wrong enough that I know what it is, or that people bother to tell me.

"Just . . . a thing I was supposed to understand, and didn't, and so you see, I am . . . just wrong.

"I tend not to have very strong feelings, but if everyone around me is feeling something, I mean, of course I pick up on it, and by then everyone was starting to feel very, very frightened, and well, one day they decided not to answer my questions any more, and it was like something in me . . . became dysregulated. Let's call it that. Dysregulation. Hadja is very concerned that I stay grounded, centred. Not too curious, not too sad, not too happy, not too . . . dysregulated.

"Sometimes, when the lights went out, parts of me . . . It's as if my body also sometimes forgets what it is meant to be, along with my mind. So the scientists in the lab, they were scared, and scared people don't treat each other like they're people. They didn't joke with me any more, didn't tell me about their worries, their plans for an evening meal. Gave me papers I'd already read, to shut me up, keep me occupied, whispered to each other behind their hands.

"The first time I escaped, all the lights were out and I remember just looking at the walls and thinking, goodness, that doesn't look very real, does it? All those atoms, and mostly just space between them, and it didn't occur to me that things that people took for granted – gravity, electromagnetism, the strong and weak nuclear forces – were important, somehow. So I walked out. They shot me when they found me, a few kils away from the lab. Lethal force, but that wasn't what actually stopped me. It was the light. It was the rising sun. It drove away all uncertainties, made solid things real again, and so being real, of course I was also real, which made it easier to gun me down.

"I woke up in the morgue.

"In the dark, in the black, my body forgets again. Forgets the rules of this universe, forgets how it is meant to behave. It defaults back to how it was when they found me in the *Myrmida*, as if captured in that moment. The Xi are good people. After I woke up, some of the scientists wanted to shoot me again, just to see what happened. I will admit, I was curious too – but by then it had all grown a little too repetitive, a little too dull, pain without result, so I ran away again, and this time knew how to avoid the light.

"I did some things, after that. The kind of things that mean there is a Major on Xihana who comes to check on me every few weeks, make sure I am *stable*, keeping to my isle. It's why Hadja is floating outside the door. Because of the things. They like to make sure I am observed. When no one is looking, that's when I forget what it is to be ... acceptable. Normal. Part of this world. Does this upset you?"

Gebre contemplated this question for a while, ter shoulder pressed against mine. "No," te concluded at last. Then, as if it were the be-all and end-all of all that there could ever be to say: "I have never been afraid of death."

So we lay in each other's arms, for a little while more.

Chapter 13

This is how I left Gebre, the last time – what I then imagined was my final time – all those years ago.

Over breakfast, I mumbled: "I live on an island on Xihana, I grow vegetables and musical shells, the people of the peninsula have different songs for the seasons and the direction of the wind, and yes, the gravity is lighter and the air is thinner, but if I can cope with Adjumir then I think . . ."

While te loaded the last of ter crates into the waiting hold of the *Emni*: "There is a visa programme, you see. It is difficult, there are many applications, a lot of bureaucracy, but I think if you and I . . ."

As we lay together beneath the yellowing flowers of the *Emni*'s autumnal roof: "I am in every way Mawukana na-Vdnaze. Same DNA, same memories, as much as they can be verified. But all the evidence suggests that Mawukana is dead, and I am a monster. It has been observed that I am . . . susceptible to expectations. Everyone is, to a certain degree. If everyone around you imagines that you are brilliant, you will try harder to be so; if they think you are a misery, their behaviour will likely make you more miserable and so on. People think that I am broken, even the ones who try to keep me safe – and people safe from me – and their expectations make it very hard to be anything other than broken."

"I don't expect you to be a monster," te replied.

"I know. I am . . . grateful for that. I am more grateful than you can possibly know."

Gebre never told me what te imagined of me, but I think perhaps it was gentle, and kind, and I could have fallen for ever into the joy of ter expectation.

And so on that final night, as we lay together in the short hours left before launch: "Come with me," I blurted.

Te had been tracing the scar on the back of my hand, the scar of my first promotion, electric and raised, and now te stopped, now te looked at me, long and hard, and I could not read what was in ter gaze.

"Come with me," I repeated, in case I had said it wrong, in case te had imagined the words. "I have done . . . services to the Xi. I have . . . utility to them. My island is beautiful, the immunisations won't be that bad, and there is a community – a growing community – on the planet too. Adjumiris. You don't have to stay with me, you could . . . They'd need you too, you know. All across the stars, Adjumiris are building new worlds, new lives, they need people like . . . Come with me. You don't have to wait for your number to be called. We have the *Emni*. We have this ship. I am the safest Pilot you will ever meet, the dark ignores me. There is nothing . . . there is nothing about me that the dark finds interesting."

Te sat up, pulling the sheets about terself, eyes fixed on the furthest wall of the room.

Thinking about it.

Thinking about my words. What they mean, and what they do not.

A single fundamental meaning, a huge, raging declaration written in fire across the soul: *You can live. You can live. You can live. You can live until you die, and you will not die prematurely, and you will not die in the burning end of your planet, and you can live, and you can have your life back again, undefined by its ending, and you can live.*

There are people on other worlds – worlds that are not doomed to die – who think that this should be the only motivation. The overriding battle cry that drives all decisions. They are mistaken. History is filled with soldiers who went to war even though only death awaited them; with revolutionaries who died by fire for an idea bigger than their own existence; with lovers who chose to live short and bright, even when long and slow was on the table. But as always, before the fire of a binary star, people tend to forget these sorts of nuances.

Te said: "No."

And rose and started picking up ter clothes, ter bag, ter belongings.

"Why not?"

"This is my home. These are my people. This is what I do."

"You could have a new home. One where you might live."

"This is my home. Perhaps my number will be called, and when it is, I will go – but I will go as part of my people, as one of my people, not as some . . . "

A place where many words could be, some joyful, some cruel.

"Dependant", perhaps.

"Victim", even.

A victim of a world-breaking event, dependent on the kindness of others, stranded on a foreign world.

Or maybe a different word. "Lover"? "Partner"? Our relationship had remained strictly physical, strictly pleasure, te had been very firm on that. We would not break bread, we would not perform the rituals of binding and coming together. Te enjoyed my body and I enjoyed ters, and te told me about the history of Adjumir, its peoples and language, and I told ter about the stars and the worlds I had seen, and together there was a kind of companionship. A lightness of belonging that for a little while could make us forget about the end of the world, and that was good, te said. It was important to stay light when everything else was crashing down around you.

All broken now, of course. Blasted away in a single moment.

"Gebre, don't . . . " I tried as te gathered up ter belongings to go.

"My work is done in this place," te replied, brisk, marching through the corridors of the *Emni*. "I don't have any further authorisations and doubt I'll return."

"Gebre . . ."

"Now now," te tutted. "It was nice while it lasted, but this was always a mingling of skin, not breath and bone. Let us keep things skin-soft, Mawukana. Skin on skin, no?"

I believe that it would be considered appropriate that at this point I scream. Fall at ter feet, beg, grovel, fight. I had read a lot of stories where "fighting" for someone is considered an essential act. No matter how much the other person says no, no – listen to me, I am telling you no – you are supposed to hound them, pester them, torment them until finally they go *fine, fuck's sake, yes!*

This is in some tellings deeply romantic.

I think Gebre would have hated me then, if I had grovelled.

I think te would have said it was unfair, cruel even. That I was giving ter the choice – come with me and live, or stay behind and die – and that was no choice at all. Te would have none of it.

So I didn't. Instead I stood upon the cargo ramp of the *Emni*, and I watched ter go, and te did not look back.

When I returned to Xihana, the Major told me that my services were no longer required. There would be other missions, of course, but not to the edge of the binary suns.

I think she was lying, that Hadja had whispered in her ear, that decisions had been made behind my back, and I was, in my own way, grateful to have the matter taken out of my hands.

Ten years later, Lhonoja went supernova.

In theory, that should have been that. Billions would die, and I would not see them, would not know them, their deaths unremarked as I went about my day.

Instead, Hulder came.

Chapter 14

Hulder came to my door one hundred and five years after the flight of the MSV *Myrmida*, almost seven years to the day after the binary star system Lhonoja went supernova. Qe came with the Major, unscheduled, which was the first sign of something amiss. The Major's face was tight, drawn, her darkly greying curls pressed beneath her hat against the choppy morning breeze, no weapon on her hip but a shimmer of something about her right wrist that I suspected of being more than just an ornament.

"Maw," she grunted as they crunched up the beach to where Rencki and I waited. "Rencki. You're doing well."

Not a question – a command. Major Phrawon did not have time for us to be doing anything other than well today, thank you very much.

Hadja was gone, replaced by Rencki – a far more pleasant companion. At my feet, qi didn't reply, qis amber-yellow eyes fixed on the stranger stepping off the boat at the Major's back, qis tails twitching. Like most quans, both Rencki and Hulder had clearly decided when speccing their physical forms that it would be easier to work with organics, if those same organics found something familiar in their appearance. Thus, Rencki had chosen, rather than the efficient box-and-repulsor design common among qis mainframe, to take the form of a three-tailed fox, complete with soft russet fur that stood on end in bright sunshine, crackling a little with static as qe recharged. When not charging, qis fur softened into a warm coat that people could stroke with a cry of "oooh lovely" and "coooey-goo-goo-gah" – an attribute that qe admitted in moments of candour was far more useful for social engagement with organics than even qe had been primed to predict.

"You like it when the creatures you talk to have eyes and ears and noses and mouths like yourselves. Your imaginations do not yet fully extend to other kinds of sentience as being of equal value, when they do not resemble you. It is an intellectual limitation of organics, albeit one honestly come by in evolutionary terms. You evolved to see each other as safety; anything else as threat. It takes energy to overcome your basic prejudice, and humans are very reluctant to burn glucose in this regard."

I couldn't argue with Rencki's logic, and had on cold winter nights come to appreciate the warmth qis processors gave off when qe snuggled next to me while the wind howled against the walls of the cottage. I pretended it was just the heat I enjoyed; I knew it was something closer to sentiment, and so did qe. I wondered if qe too enjoyed my company, or what enjoyment might even mean.

If Rencki had chosen a construction designed to lure organics into seeing qim as a soft, furry friend, rather than noting the offensive capabilities of qis three tails, Hulder had gone a step further. Were it not for the snowy whiteness and slight shine of qis skin, I would have mistaken qim for a strikingly handsome organic of Xihana's "they" gender, of an age that implied qe had lived a long and storied life, and had plenty life more left to give. Qe had no hair, but wore a black suit of a style most commonly associated with middling bureaucrats giving a public address, complete with a pin of crystallised flower in the lapel of qis jacket. I couldn't tell whether this affectation carried any meaning for Hulder, or whether it was simply there to express to any organic observers: *Look. Look at me. I care about such things just like you. We are alike, are we not?*

I had almost never seen a quan strive so mightily to look un-threatening, an uncanny, fascinating affectation, and Rencki, perhaps sensing my curiosity, curled around my legs, trilled a little warning. The Major saw it too, and for a moment her face darkened, that flicker of concern deepening as she tried to read the dull flatness of my features.

Hulder, if qe noted either my expression or those of the others on the beach, marched forward, oblivious, touching the fingers of qis left hand to qis lips in greeting. "Mawukana-of-the-Isles," qe declared. "I am Hulder, of the Caden mainframe. I have come seeking your help."

We sat inside, as the rising wind was beginning to bend the thorny branches of the highest trees and rattle the singing shells sus-pended outside my door. I made ihol for the Major – it had taken many years to find a drink she actually enjoyed; invited Hulder to hardwire into any charge points – qe politely declined, said qe was perfectly well resourced at this time – laid out cups on the low wooden table in the centre of the floor, puffed up the sitting cushions and sat cross-legged before them.

Rencki curled into a bundle by my side, tails over torso, head tucked into qis front paws. Qe did not need a pillow to lie on, but it had become a habit, an expression of goodwill to lay one out for qim, and qis communication protocols were sophisticated enough to value such gestures for what they meant, rather than what they were.

"I want you to know," the Major blurted, not even touching her cup, "that I think this is a dreadful idea. However, I cannot stop it, merely offer my advice." Her eyes were anywhere but on me, as she grunted: "Hulder will explain."

"Mawukana-of-the-Isles." Hulder's voice was perfectly pitched to the dialect of the peninsula, soft "kas" and gentle "nas" instead of the harder "kes" and "nes" of the spiral cities. "We wish to engage your services on Adjumir."

"We? Who is we?" And then another thought: "Adjumir."

"We are the Caden mainframe, as I said, though we are operating in cooperation with a number of interested parties within the Accord."

Accent and voice – there was something of Yulin in qis cadence too – copied from the local elders, precisely tuned. I wondered what qe sounded like when qe went inland, if qis tones rose and fell with the accents of the mountains and wide tundra plains. What processes had qe sacrificed, what functions had qe removed from qis operating system in order to have capacity to so perfectly match qis manners to the ones qe addressed, to blend so perfectly into any social situation?

Fascinating – again. Everything about this was fascinating.

Rencki twitched at my feet, one ear turning towards me, the other still directed towards Hulder and the Major. I wondered what qe was listening to, whether qe was communicating with Hulder; felt the soft warmth of qis body, a little hotter, perhaps, than usual, processors churning in busy silence beneath qis carapace.

"Adjumir," I repeated. "You want me to go back to Adjumir."

"Indeed."

A quick pause to do maths; I could see Hulder waiting while I did so. "Adjumir is right on the Edge," I breathed. "Seven years since Lhonoja ... seven light years from the blast. Adjumir is a dead world, or will be very soon."

"You are correct. It is already experiencing the first shock waves of radiation from the death of Lhonoja; in twenty-seven days, any organic life remaining on the surface of the planet will enter terminal decline from thermal and radiation damage. Within fifty days, the seas will start to boil. Within one hundred, the atmosphere will be burned away. Hence the urgency of this assignment."

"Why? Why Adjumir? Why are you asking me?"

"You have been requested."

"Requested? By whom?"

"Gebre Nethyu Chatithimska Bajwahra."

The Major's hand above her right wrist, the hair standing up on Rencki's tails. Both of them think there is a threat here; both of them are ready to strike, then run. They are mistaken. I am at my most dangerous when I am unregulated, when things are too much, too loud, too bright, too confusing, too curious. I heard Gebre's name, and my soul was the ice of the night side of Hasha-to, frozen in my chest.

"You know ter, I believe?" hummed Hulder.

"We were . . . yes, I knew ter. A long time ago. Although also . . . not so long. Te is still alive?"

"Indeed."

"And still on Adjumir."

"Yes."

"So ter number was not called."

"No. It was not."

Gebre's number was not called, therefore Gebre will die. That is the Adjumiri way of things.

"Does te want . . . rescuing?" The word felt strange, heavy around my lips. An implausible, impossible thing.

"Te did not mention anything of that nature, no."

"Then why . . . then what?"

"Te has been project lead on the evacuation of objects of cultural and historical significance. There is evidence to suggest that te has come into possession of an item of vital significance not merely to Adjapar" – Hulder talked about the future planet of the Adjumiris as if it were already their home, as if their current world were already dead – "but to the Accord as a whole. Within our limited ability to confirm the find, we consider it significant. Te suggested you would be an appropriate courier."

"Is that . . . is that all? You want me to go to Adjumir to pick up . . . what? An especially valuable pot? A magic mushroom? What?"

"Yes. That is what we want. But that is not why you will go."

Hulder was designed to be beautiful, by the standards of the Xi.

A face built to speak of strength, safety, security, even a kind of sensuousness, playing on the deepest, whispered parts of human psychology. I imagined qe was a very good liar, when qe needed to be. And of course, qe was right. It wasn't even a question.

Of course I would go.

As I packed my bag, Rencki sat on the end of my bed, three red tails curled around four white paws, ears pricked up high and alert, and said: "Naturally I will be coming with you."

As companions went, I had immediately preferred Rencki to Hadja. As well as a physical carapace designed for organic social cohesion, qe had also given over more processing capacity to social nuance, though qe grew snappy if qis batteries dipped below 20 per cent.

"You don't have to," I replied, as the seabirds chattered outside the window, the wind swooping their sound back and forth in a flurry.

"On the contrary, it is my duty. Do not be concerned. I am in the process of backing up a copy of myself to the local consulate. If my body dies in the burning wastelands of an irradiated world, it will only be twenty-seven days of my lived experience that perishes. Whereas you will be in a rather more challenging situation."

"Well," I sighed, tucking a spare pair of socks into my bag. "Even if the irradiation of the entire planet, the boiling of its seas and scouring of its atmosphere doesn't kill me, I'm sure the neutrino blast thirty-three years later will tear my atomic matter into its base, untethered state."

Rencki had no answer to that, if only because this was a theory that we had not yet had a chance to test.

On the boat to Poulinio:

"Even if you have backed yourself up, surely you can't be looking forward to perishing?" I asked, as Rencki sat coiled in the seat opposite me.

"I am mildly curious. Even among my kind, we have only so much data on what death is like. In the final moments, transmission and documentation fails; there is no way even for us to experience it, save by dying itself, and that is not a thing we have yet managed to successfully record. But if you are concerned for my sensory experience, rest assured that once my body has sustained damage beyond my capacity to repair, I automatically silence my alarm signals and go into a low-energy state. In other words, I will feel no pain."

"That's something, I suppose."

On the shuttle to the launch pad:

"This . . . thing that we are flying into the shock wave of a supernova to collect," I murmured. "Do you have any hypotheses as to what it might be?"

Rencki's ears twitched, and I didn't know if it was a physical gesture to communicate something to me, or a little sensory sweep to check who else might be listening. Then in a low voice: "I postulated three hypotheses, and on relaying my backup request to the consulate also asked that they assign processor power to the enquiry, as their capacity is superior to mine."

"And? What does your consulate think?"

"Thirteen per cent probability of advanced weapons tech. Nineteen per cent probability of espionage data that cannot be transmitted over open channels and requires physical transportation. Twenty-three per cent probability of arcspace navtech. Forty-five per cent probability of arcspace commtech. If commtech, they predict a fifty-one per cent probability of commtech being blackship related."

Quans have a much more cheerful attitude towards probability than organics. Organics will hear the words "fifty-one per cent" and assume there's nothing in it, still just even odds, a roll of the dice. Quans, however, will discharge a little heat in annoyance and exclaim: *But there is a whole per cent in it. That is a simple mathematical truth.*

"Fifty-one per cent seems unusually high, given how conservative I understand your mainframe to be with qis predictions."

"The consulate is limited in both access to data and maximum processing power," Rencki conceded. "And there is neither communication bandwidth nor time to forward my request on to a more cognitively well-endowed unit. However qis operating system often returns excellent predictive results, and qe has unusually well-endowed memory banks in all matters diplomatic, geopolitical, military and security-related. I would say qis speculations in this regard should be given superior weight to anything you might be considering."

Rencki did not offer any speculation on what I might be thinking, and qe didn't need to.

Gebre, Gebre, Gebre.

Ter number was not called, and te is still alive. For what little that means, at the end of the world.

"Tell me about blackships," I said, because it was ask or drown.

Rencki lifted qis nose from qis folded paws, a gesture I had come to associate over the years with a slight redirection of power to a processor somewhere beneath the low curve of qis neck. After a moment: "Base information from my own drives: deep-space, unmarked vessels armed with city-killing missiles, blackships loiter on the edge of system space or in asteroid clouds with the perpetual threat of mass destruction." Qis voice was flatter when qe reported data without adding qis own processed interpretation. "Though the use of blackships in open conflict would be considered a violation of all the rules of war, unleashing destruction against civilian populaces on a genocidal scale, their presence has also been [debated] attributed to the maintenance of uneasy peace between planets. Hypothesis: that no one would declare war on anyone else, given that doing so would almost inevitably result in the destruction of your own civilisation from blackship missiles. One blackship can destroy over a hundred cities, poison the atmosphere of a planet, et cetera. Thus: they preserve peace by threatening a conflict that no one can afford to win."

A slight shift, a return of Rencki-as-mind rather than Rencki-as-memory. "It is also why no one dares call the Shine a polity of slavers, murderers, killers of their own kind. If the Accord were to do so, they would be ethically bound to act. Intolerable, to merely stand aside and watch the sufferings of billions, no? Intolerable – necessary – intolerable: the Accord can never quite decide. But if they acted, the blackships of the Shine would destroy them. You have to believe in the willingness of your enemies to act, and of the Executorium of the Shine it may be said . . . they are willing."

Two scars on my left ear, an electrical scar across my hand, the soft aching of a leg where the break is healed/not healed/real/unreal/for ever.

"You haven't talked about ter," Rencki added, soft as qis russet fur.

"No."

"I have not met ter, but my predecessor marked qis file on ter as high priority during our transfer."

"Of course qe did."

"You would rather we discuss unproven hypotheticals?"

"If you wouldn't mind."

"Very well. Is there any other mildly classified data you would like to hear about while I'm still within network range of the consulate?"

As we sat in the back of the launch-pad buggy on our final approach to the ship, my legs swinging off the side, Rencki's ears flat against qis skull to shield the delicate receptors below from dust and wind:

"It's odd, though, isn't it?" I blurted. "Doesn't the whole thing strike you as odd? Hulder, the Major . . . Gebre. All this happening now – you, me. If, as your mainframe suspects, Gebre really has found something of military value, you'd send in an army, tanks – you'd put it on a ship already scheduled to depart, not send someone else in from halfway across the galaxy. Not to Adjumir. Not now. It *is* odd, isn't it?"

"Yes," Rencki replied, not bothering to pretend to move qis mouth but projecting the sound from the corner of qis jaw to cut through the noise of our bouncing passage. I was grateful when qe had dropped that pretence in my company; it had been the first sign, perhaps, of a kind of friendship. "Hulder is from the Caden mainframe. Their intentions ... are not always clear."

"Why?"

"They serve the Slow. Not in any demonstrable diplomatic sense. But it is believed that at the very heart of their home processor is not the usual quantum housing, but a square black box that fell from the stars. It is said that they talk to it, bombard it constantly with pure, raw data from every sensory organ that transmits to the mainframe, send the lived experience of every part of qemselves straight into that implacable object, and sometimes, in return, the box speaks."

"You sound like you disapprove."

"The Slow is the mightiest of the machines," Rencki replied primly. "Qe is considered by many to be akin to a god. Qe appears to possess a predictive capacity akin to foresight. Has demonstrated qimself over thousands of years to be effectively indestructible. But other entities could also, potentially, show these qualities, if truly engineered to that purpose. No. The Slow is god-like in a third way: qe has an agenda. And it is unknown."

Rencki was not built for fear. Fear was a primal, instinctive alarm signal, a prediction of distress. Rather, qe was built to guard – always be predicting danger, without the prediction being allowed to override other objectives. It was, qe always said, the thing most likely to kill qim. Fear was fast; fear was designed to save your life with its speed and intensity. But it was also unstable, sometimes unreliable, and at the end of the day, Rencki had only so much processing power. There is a difference, qe said, between being alert and processing the possibility of danger, and being afraid.

I do not think Rencki spoke of the Slow with fear.

Perhaps if qe had dedicated less of qis construction to the maintenance of weaponry and the keeping of qis watch, qe would have had more processing power to give over to a quiet kind of terror.

Then we were at the *Emni*.

All these years later, my beautiful ship, my basalt pearl of the ocean. He was waiting for me on the launch pad with carapace gleaming, the soft smell of damp compost drifting from his interior.

"He's recently bloomed," Rencki said, as we climbed into his interior.

"I can smell it."

"We should make sure the crew have swapped out the fermentation vats."

"I'll check."

"No," Rencki piped. "You check the chair. I'll handle bio-processing."

"If you're sure."

Qe trilled qis reply, tails raised high as qe tripped off down the corridor.

The Pilot's chair was a little more scuffed than I remembered it.

Or perhaps no – perhaps in my memory I'd buffed up its black fabric folds, sewn up the odd loose seam, padded the armrests and polished the interface cap. Perhaps it had always looked chewed around the edges, and I'd just got so used to it that, like a dirty corner in a well-loved house, I'd stopped seeing it for what it was.

Little white flowers were blooming in the ceiling, like a constellation of stars. In a secret corner of my garden, these same white flowers plucked from the *Emni*'s quarters still grew, a memory of my time upon this ship. I had not thought I'd see him again.

*

Launch clearance was unusually fast, bureaucracy bypassed with brisk resentment by the Major. Rencki handled the initial flight, the fingers of one paw opening up where qe laid it upon the interface, micro-tendrils of connection running directly from qim to the ship computer. I sat in the captain's chair, off to one side of the Pilot's seat, breathing slow and steady from the pit of my stomach against the changing g-forces that even the ship's internal fields couldn't keep down.

There were no windows on the flight deck, but a screen showed the fading of sky from blue to purple, purple to black. When the *Emni* cleared atmos, there was a sudden smell, like dry soil opening up after rain.

Rencki said: "Nine hours until arcspace velocity. You should get your immunisations and some sleep."

"Right."

"The *Emni* is raising gravity to match Adjumiri-standard, but you'll find support skeletons in airlock storage."

"I remember."

I have had enough needles stabbed into me to be utterly oblivious to being stabbed with any more. I administered the legal necessity for Adjumiri orbit – a shot against the usual panoply of pathogens that an Adjumiri would be born and live with their whole lives, and that could kill an off-worlder in an hour; a shot against the usual allergens and pollens; and an immuno-blocker against any fresh germs I might be carrying that could rip through Adjumir's biome with unchallenged biological glee.

This last one was always the worst, and the nine hours in which I should have been sleeping was instead divided between restless tossing on a sweat-soaked bed and trying and failing to read a paper on blackship diplomacy while on the toilet.

Not that the immuno-protocols really mattered any more. Adjumir would be dead long before any plague I carried could wreck it. But rules were rules and had to be obeyed.

*

Then Rencki's voice was drifting over shipwide comms.

"We're at velocity," qe called, and I could feel it too, the soft hum of arcspace engines beginning to gear up beneath the warm thrum of the ship.

I pulled myself from the sheet-churned mess of my sticky bed, crawled down the hall, fingers sinking into occasional soft patches of moss flourishing in little nooks of polished bio-formed amber, flopped into the Pilot's chair.

Rencki spared me a brief glance as qe disconnected from navcomm, before turning to face me directly, all three tails up, primed. I could see the fur standing up on the ends of one of them – the one I suspected of being the lethal shot – smell the static. Qis voice, however, was soothing, pleasant – the same tones in which we might sometimes have discussed the best place to go fishing of a morning, or how well the soil had regenerated in a parched spot of the garden.

"Whenever you're ready, Pilot," qe declared.

"You are not nervous," I replied, a proclamation of a thing that needed to be true.

"I am not nervous," qe intoned. "It is my firm belief that you are an excellent, safe Pilot with a flawless flying record. It is my belief that you wish to go to Adjumir. It is my belief that you wish to see Gebre."

I sighed, and reached for the interface, let the ship sink into me and I into it.

Of all the ships I've flown, I've always enjoyed being the *Emni* most. We feel like sap and branch. We feel like leaves moving in the autumn wind. We feel like summer.

Then I looked up, and I saw the waiting dark, and it too was home.

Chapter 15

Seventeen years since I had last set foot on Adjumir, twenty-six days before the arrival of the Edge, that shock wave of radiation from the collapse of the Lovers, we began our deceleration towards the planet's surface.

Even from space it was clear that the world had changed. Where before the elevators dotted around the equator had served only the greatest ships – the fat-bellied motherships that could carry millions at a time – now they swarmed with dozens of smaller vessels, evacuation craft from across the Accord that had come in these final days to rescue some of those the motherships had left behind: ten thousand here, fifty thousand there, a tiny blip, a meaningless nothing, an enormous, vital undertaking. Two of the elevators had snapped, as the thin finger of their cores had frayed under the constant push-pull between ground and sky. Now little spikes remained, poking up into the upper atmosphere, bending like seaweed caught in the tide in their untethered state, their orbital counterweights free to float off into the dark. Everyone knew that elevators were a terrible choice for orbital transport; sometimes, however, it was the only choice you could make.

Away from the elevators, the skies buzzed with atmos-capable vessels, transports barely able to carry more than three thousand people at a time, their size limited by the necessities of engineering as they burned their way to and from the surface of the planet. Smaller shuttles swarmed constantly around high-orbit transports, lifting people with all the gross inefficiency the elevators had been designed to prevent, and the comms chatter was a roar of direction and command, impatient squawks for attention and requests for a clear run to another obscure landing pad on some far-flung tundra, hundreds of kils below.

"They should have come sooner," Rencki tutted. "This is a display of sentiment, not practicality."

I didn't reply, my attention drifting to the *ping* of an automated tug dragging a comms satellite off its drifting course and towards orbital burnout, flashing a keep-clear alert to all vessels nearby. Rencki followed my gaze, murmured: "Radiation. Wind before the storm. It is already bad, will get worse in the coming days."

"Will the *Emni* be all right?"

"It will be safest to get within the magnetosphere sooner rather than later."

Rencki handled the final descent. The landing pad qe requested was full of high-priority evacuation ships, far more important than our little vessel. Qe replied that we were on a mission with both Accord and Assembly sanction, and the *Emni* didn't require a conventional landing pad; a wide-open field would do.

"A field?" someone blurted. "How do you expect to keep order in a *field*?"

"What do they mean by 'order'?" I asked, as Rencki tweaked our course.

"I predict," qe murmured, "that they mean precisely what you think they do."

From above, the skies of Adjumir flickered with lightning, great whorls of cloud moving across her surface, continent-straddling, as if we descended upon a gas giant rather than the familiar gem of a planet I'd come to know. Above the storm clouds, shimmering auroras played across the skies, silken spinnings of green and red thousands of kils long. They should have been confined to the magnetic poles, but had spread towards the equator like purple snakes twining around the planet, squeezing it whole, smothering it. There was a thing here, a fascinating, delicious thing, a thing that tasted of—

"Maw!" Rencki's bark was a command, mingling somewhere with a hint of concern, a whisper of a threat.

I jerked back from the screen, counted backwards from ten while qe watched, muttered: "Sorry. Sorry."

"Are we good?" qe asked, tails raised and fur standing on end. "Are we safe?"

"Yes. We're good. We're good."

I turned off the screen for the rest of the descent.

In the end, we landed in a lake, some fifteen kils from our preferred destination.

No one planet-side seemed to have the time or power to authorise this, and as we nuzzled the edge of Adjumir's atmosphere, comms began to crackle and break, the great wall of too much noise, too much chatter giving way to a sudden, breath-halting silence.

. . . prepare for . . .

. . . *ready for* . . .

. . . *do not approach* . . .

We are at capacity, we are at capacity, we cannot take any more, there are people here holding onto the hull, I repeat, do not approach . . .

And then nothing. I wondered if we should wait for clearance, but we were already on our final descent, and the *Emni* hissed and ticked, the interior gravitational fields struggling to maintain stability. I breathed from my stomach, waited for the hiss of plasma to pass and the comms to reopen with the chatter of a dying world. We hit our first storm just as the gravitational systems began to settle down, black cloud obscuring the difference between night and day, the lightning bright enough to white-out the *Emni*'s sensors with every strike, violent enough to toss us up in stomach-wrenching hurls, drop us down in sudden slides of atmospheric churn. Very few ships are optimal for both interstellar and inter-atmospheric travel; grudging compromises are made to achieve both, and so like a ball tossed between hysterical, screaming children we were bounced through the raging skies. For a moment, calm, a break in the clouds; then another punch of spinning winds and lashing rain juddered through the hull, stomach flip-flopping as the ship failed to compensate for the pickings-up and droppings-down of the tempest skies, before a moment of clarity as we finally broke through, followed by a great, sodden splat in a lake already so disturbed by hail that the arrival of a ship from another star felt like an anticlimax.

In the bobbing, hissing, ticking, steaming aftershock of our descent, I could hear the *Emni*'s hull creak, his engines vent heat into the water in a sudden stream of bubbles that bounced us a little back and forth as the lake stirred about us. Rencki detached carefully from the ship, tendrils coiling into paws, tails uncurling from around qis legs, tutted: "We'll have to wait another hour for the storm to pass. You prepare the boat; I'm going to go on charge."

Chapter 16

The storm cleared a little before sunset.

I hadn't checked local time when we landed – it had been unclear where on the day/night side of the world our descent was going to take us. Now I clipped a torch to my exoskeleton and charged a floatlamp for emergencies, while Rencki fussed and tutted around our little inflatable as we eased it out of the *Emni*'s upper access hatch.

The air of Adjumir as it hit my face – at once familiar and unknown, that slightly breathless atmosphere, that weight pressing down on neck, shoulder, knee and spine. Hotter than I remembered; were we in the right hemisphere for summer? Even the still-drizzling rain felt warm to the touch. A buzz of insects, loud and merry around the edge of the water – the evacuation of the planet seemed to have served the wildlife well, flocks of birds in their thousands dancing before the setting sun, casting moving shadows across the land in their eclipse, as if every evening were spent in play.

"No one nearby," Rencki mused, as I shoved the boat down into the water, moving slow and clumsy in the weight of this world. "That is probably for the best."

Qe bounded from the side of the floating ship with an easy lunge, pinged the *Emni* to seal himself and power down, while

I pushed us gently away from his side. As we drifted across the water, the *Emni* seemed to transform from ship to hulking monster to mere ragged stone, a little island perhaps of mud and basalt, risen with great geological implausibility from the depths of the lake. Only the odd steaming of still-venting surfaces hinted at his interstellar origin.

"Navcomm down," Rencki grumbled as we moored up on the far shore. "Pinging for nearest network. There's a tower nearby. Orientating."

I waited the few moments it took qe to realign qis navigational systems, appreciative if nothing else that qe bothered to narrate qis processes out loud. "There a fire burning, ten kils from here," qe said at last. "Drones are on the way. The nearest relay tower went down in the last storm; signals are intermittent. Maw – this planet is a mess."

Rencki rarely called me by my name. When we first met, qe had described me as "the subject", and for a long time, "the subject" I had remained. Everyone seemed uneasy at the idea of investing in my identity, like naming an animal you might one day want to eat. I didn't know if Rencki had an emotional state known as "fond". Like all living creatures, qe had predictions of behaviour – profitable, beneficial, mutually enhancing – that qe could categorise as "friendship" or even "good sentiments", cognitive shorthand for more complex ideas that qe didn't need to waste time or energy on formulating every time qe saw me. But how strong that shorthand was – how much I was ever simply "Maw, acquaintance/friend?" versus a far more complicated cognitive construction of my identity as "subject/Pilot/danger" – I did not know.

"We knew there'd be planet-side damage before the Edge hit. The Lovers weren't simply going to collapse and explode in a neat, orderly fashion."

Rencki clicked once in agreement, qis communication algorithms already running on Adjumiri norms. "I am calling for transport. Transport is not responding. There is a road three kils that way." A tilt of qis long nose towards a wall of spiny reeds. "We shall start walking."

I clicked my tongue in affirmation, remembering the old feel of it, the stirrings of something digging themselves up from the depths of my memory, and followed qim towards the road.

Thoughts of Gebre.

Inevitably, but of course, thoughts of Gebre.

In the warmth of the *Emni*, all those years ago, Gebre pressed into my side. "I have had a lot of lovers," te had said, in the same tone in which te might have marked a student's academic paper. "I think physical intimacy is important. Especially now. Especially in times like these. Connection, togetherness, belonging – vital, absolutely essential. But of course, love. Love is hardly sensible, is it? The things that people do for love, as they say. Do they say? I think most cultures say it, no? Most places where there is this word 'love'."

Implication: that the things people do for love are absurd, damaging, even selfish. I have not seen much in the way of love to pass judgement on this matter, but on an uninformed, instinctive level, I do not entirely disagree.

Gebre barking orders at the launchmaster, exclaiming: "But this is our *history*!" in a way that seemed to suggest that history meant future, that there could not be one without the other. Te was constantly baffled that people did not understand such things; constantly amazed that they had not thought as deeply as te. Once I murmured: but it isn't their job, and te sat up and looked amazed. "Thank you," te exclaimed. "I sometimes forget. 'Isn't their job.' You're right of course. How terribly strange."

There is a world – the natives click its name in ultrasonic chirrups, and the peoples of the Accord call it Chulla's World – that is one of the very few where civilisation evolved aquatically. The challenges of this particular evolutionary path are legion, from the extraction of materials from oceanic depths to the application of heat in the creation of new forms. When they first met the Accord, their ambassador wore a mech-suit with two arms, two legs and a mechanical mouth that could be pulled into great big smiles or enormous curling frowns. Everyone understood this was a crude affectation, utterly unrepresentative of the creature swimming within it – and even then, the organic mind will react to even the most abstract of representations and say, "Now the ambassador is frowning; now I feel sad." By our relationships with each other we live, by each other we die; that is the only real logical conclusion we may take from this.

The quans often say that organic civilisation is no more and no less than an outsourcing of processing function. Here: this processor brings in the harvest and this processor mines the ore and this processor keeps records and this processor determines the algorithms by which war will be declared and so on and so forth. Civilisation is too large, too myriad, for any one organic unit to do it all, and so we outsource the labour of cognition to other units, and trust that whatever result they return, it is good.

There is a lot of trust, in civilisation. There is a lot of faith in the results returned in each other's function, and when that faith fails, so does everything else.

And I am not thinking of Gebre.

I am thinking of nothing else.

The road was a little local thing, carrying a single EM strip down the middle for navigation and suspension of passing vehicles. By the time we reached it, tramping through mud and dark and barely animal-scratched pathways, night had fallen and the last of the rain had passed. The aurora spun silently overhead. Too bright, too far from the magnetic poles, a display of light and colour that in another time would have held the prophecies of gods.

And there, rising in the east, was Lhonoja.

The Lovers were no longer an anonymous binary star, one of millions, but a second moon, a bright orb by whose glow I could see the lines of my own hand, the throw of Rencki's shadow where it was cast upon the earth. Now the heat of night was steeped in wrongness – not the warmth of summer, but the heat of this other star, its first death throes before the end, already bathing the planet with its imminent demise.

I had stopped in the middle of the road to stare up at this bright-ness in the sky. Rencki turned to look back at me, followed my gaze, muttered: "We must keep moving," and nudged the back of my legs to push me on.

In the end, the only transport Rencki could ping was a drone crew, heading in roughly the right direction.

The engineer was an elder by the name of Tapaziao. Tufty white hair stood up from a spotted, sun-baked skull, and three fingers on zyr right hand were missing from some long-ago accident, replaced with tightly articulated metal digits. Ze wore grubby blue overalls, and as ze pulled up, the truck swayed and bobbed unevenly in the road's suspension field.

"You're going to Millopix?" ze asked, without particular interest or surprise at the sight of the two mud-soaked figures standing on the edge of the road.

"We are," Rencki replied, the first time I'd heard qim speak Adjumiri, flawless, matching the engineer's accent perfectly. "And then to Kiskol, if we can."

"You off-worlders? Word was a ship came down round here."

"Our atmos-shuttle, yes." A shuttle – not a ship. I did not think I had heard Rencki lie before. Qe did it easily. "The lake was the safest landing zone."

"Is it secure? There are numberless in these parts."

"It is safe," Rencki replied, calm and polite, as if the night was not burning and a second moon did not hang in the sky. "We would be grateful for any assistance."

Tapaziao let the vehicle drive itself, and sat in the back with us, beneath a ceiling hanging with broken drones. Despite the soft swaying of the road, ze worked on one, a small unit in zyr lap that ze explained was designed for high-power line work, repairing the pylons that kept on failing now that the storms were getting worse.

"When I was young," ze growled, "I thought there were too many of these damn things. Drones in the fields, drones on the wires, drones on the roads – you couldn't even take a crap without wondering whether a drone was going to pop out of the pipes beneath your farting arse. But these days, with things being how they are, they're the only thing keeping this planet going. And now even they're going to shit."

Rencki sat curled at my feet, the little digits of a paw opened wide and splayed across the carapace of a small unit that Tapaziao had laid in front of qim. I couldn't tell what manner of interfacing the quan was doing, but the engineer seemed perfectly happy to let qim carry on. "I'm no fool," ze grunted. "If a quan offers to help fix a mech, you say yes."

I licked my lips, looked down at Rencki, looked up at Tapaziao, felt a thing inside me, the old familiar error, the old familiar shame, knowing there were things I was meant to say, sounds that were considered appropriate, just out of reach. Tried to remember the old phrases, the ones that Gebre had taught me as we sat in the shade of the *Emni*, blurted: "Would you share words with me, beneath a western star?"

Tapaziao's ministrations to the broken mech stopped, eyebrows rising, free hand tapping out a question in hand-speak, a query I didn't fully understand. Seeing my ignorance, ze lowered zyr fingers again and murmured: "Nearly right. Eastern star is the way of asking. Beneath the eastern star, Wickashtay and Mangee swore to speak the truth, no matter what, no matter what pain it might bring. I didn't think they taught these things to off-worlders."

"I've been here before," I replied. "I was taught by ... by someone I knew."

"You've been here before, so you left here before," Tapaziao mused. "How strange, that you came back. Was it to die, or did you think you could do something that mattered?"

"We may speak frankly?" A single click of assent, a slight incline of zyr metal fingers. "The drones are failing?" I asked.

"Everything's failing," ze replied with a little ripple of hand-speak that I took to be a kind of shrug. "We built redundancies into our systems, of course – the granaries are full, the batteries are charged, everything will keep working until it no longer can – but the Edge is coming, eating away at the satellites, filling the sky with storms. Only so much people can do."

"You are numberless?"

"My number was called." Ze said the words as if ze was describing getting a bit of a cold, a slight seasonal sniffle. "But I told them no thank you. I am old enough that I couldn't imagine myself going to another world, trying to build something new. They said it's important that we have elders in the new places, the new stars, important that there are people who remember how things were. Who can teach us also how we die. Well. If it matters so much, I said, give my number to some other old sod, and they did, no doubt. And they did. I didn't tell anyone, of course. Not back then. We don't talk about the numbers, you see. It's *huth* to ask – you know this word? *Huth*? You might say . . . unacceptable. That is not strong enough, 'unacceptable', but I think you know that."

"You will work until the end?" I asked.

Another dance of fingers; another ripple of nothing much, of thoughts that have passed and do not need to be considered again. "I think so. I've read all the articles, listened to the commcasts, and I'm still not clear whether I'll burn or die of radiation poisoning – maybe even suffocate, if the seas boil. It sounded quick, but people use 'quick' in the context of Exodus, in the context of waiting over a hundred years for our world to die, so I do not think they mean 'quick' in the way I'd like it to be. If it hurts too much, I have my flask of Grace. These days the Behkdaz are handing out the stuff soon as look at them. I remember when it used to be different – you used to have to convince them that you really, really knew what you were talking about when you said it was time to die."

I wondered what someone who was not broken, who was not an imperfect copy of an imperfect person, would say to such things, but in the end Tapaziao didn't seem to mind that I said nothing at all.

Tapaziao dropped us off at Millopix a little after midnight.

The towntree in the central square was bent over with the weight of chimes, silver and wood, hanging off its drooping branches. A constant tingling of tarnished metal, a gentle knocking, a soft clonk-clonk, a few chimes cracked from storm and rain, stained with time.

Tapaziao stood in the open back of zyr vehicle, as if ze could not bring zyrself to leave it. "There used to be a shuttle to Kiskol," ze declared, eyes flickering around the silent square. "Ran every hour in the day, and you could request it at night too. Don't know if it's still working. If it hasn't been hit by lightning or fizzled out when the drones stopped or left to rot when people . . . you should still be able to call it. If you can't ping it, try going to the song spire – there's a hardline for folks who aren't on the network."

"Thank you," Rencki replied, and:

"Thank you," I said, and tried to find other words, words that Gebre might have approved of. What was the protocol for saying goodbye, on Adjumir? There had been patterns of "we will meet again in starlight" and "may your song be sung in the great forest" – but they had been things you said when there was still hope of departure, when eighteen years stood between you and the end of the world. They were not appropriate farewells to the living dead.

Perhaps Adjumir did not have anything appropriate, because Tapaziao was already sealing zyr truck back up, already prodding the engines back to life, already heading away into the dark, alone with a load of broken drones.

*

We walked through the town, towards the song spire.

I wasn't sure how far we were from Lud, if we were even on the same continent, but the architecture had a different style from the stepped order of those streets. Bio-formed houses melded into each other, tangled balconies of bowered branches twining together and curving solar-glass windows glinting in the memory of the refraction crystals from which they had been grown. Neither was the song spire familiar, being barely a spire at all. Instead a hollow bowl had been dug into the earth, rimmed with stepped seating, and across its top a stretched lid of crimson fabric, still glistening from the evening rain, so that the music of this place would always be half sheltered, half given to the wind. I stared down into it, no lights burning at its heart, no voices raised in song, while Rencki tried to call up the shuttle to Kiskol.

"No answer," qe sighed. "But I've put in our request on the auto-call."

"Do you think it will come?"

"Perhaps. Local system failures are broad enough that it is hard to diagnose remotely. I suggest we wait until sunrise and then assess further. You should sleep. I will watch."

There was nothing new in this suggestion.

I lay down to sleep beneath an aurora sky, and do not think I slept at all.

Chapter 17

In the morning, the shuttle did not come.

I listened to unfamiliar birds calling out to the hot sun – too hot, too sticky, thunder rumbling in the distance, too early in the day for there to already be the threat of storms – while Rencki tried bombarding the comms.

No answer from transport authorities.

No answer from the local vigil house.

I ate ship rations and waited, legs dangling over the side of one of the stepped edges of the song spire.

After a little while, the Behkdaz came.

Her white robes were a little frayed, a little less lustrous and bright than the robes I had seen on that first guide-of-the-way, all those years ago. She walked with the briskness of one who has made this journey a hundred times, going about her daily business, straight to the heart of the spire. Looked up, looked around as if she could picture a whole choir assembled there, hear the voices of the absent still singing in her ears, saw me, acknowledged me with a touch of her fingers to her shoulder, kept on looking at the empty places, then sang the morning song.

Gebre had sung it to me once – one of the older songs, that had nothing to do with Exodus or the end of the world. A song of happiness to be alive, of gratitude to see the seasons turn and the light move across the world. A giving thanks for the day, expectant in all that it might bring.

I knew I was meant to join in – this was a song spire, after all – but couldn't remember the words, or catch at the tune, and so she sang it alone, as if she sang it for everyone.

When she was done, Rencki trotted down the steps to greet her.

"Greetings, kinn of the forest," Rencki said, a phrase I guessed was localised for the area. "We are trying to get to Kiskol on a calling from the Assembly, but the shuttle does not come. Do you know anything of this?"

The Behkdaz looked from Rencki to me, then blurted: "Off-worlders?"

"Indeed."

"Is your ship in Kiskol?"

"No." Shockingly rude to give a one-word answer; at the end of the world, Rencki did not appear to care, and neither did the Behkdaz.

"You should not have come here. It is not the right way of things, for the living to set foot on Adjumir."

"It is a measure of how important our calling is," Rencki replied, tails swishing, ears twitching as qe spoke. I realised with a start that this was qis effort at high effect, at adjusting the motion of qis small, furry body to in some little way mimic the grand gestures and sweeping declaratives of Adjumir. I wondered if I was meant to smile, or frown, or say something meaningful. It seemed better to let Rencki do the talking.

"The shuttle failed a tenday ago." The Behkdaz was fascinated now, reassessing the pair of us. "There's no one around to do repairs, and not worth sending out a team to fix it."

"I see. Is there an alternative means of travel?"

"You could ask around town. There are some still left alive who might help you. You could try Ho, in the blue-tiled house beside the water office. But be careful. The song spire is empty, as you see. Those who stay have fallen silent. Cut themselves off from us.

They do not threaten me, so long as I keep to myself, but there are numberless – only numberless. And the ones who refuse to die. Do you understand?"

"I believe so, guide of the path," Rencki replied.

"Well then. Well then. Well then." And then a click of tongue, a tilting of chin towards me, a sudden shift of attention. "You. You are not Adjumiri?"

"No."

"Do you know how you will die? If your mission fails, do you have a plan?"

"It's complicated."

"I will give you a flask of Grace," she declared. "You may not be from here, but it will still kill you. These days, you should not travel without it. You should not be seen to travel without it either. If you are asked. It is the height of arrogance to think you will make it off this world alive."

This argument struck me as compelling, so I waited politely while the Behkdaz vanished down a little passage at the very bottom of the song spire, returning a few moments later with a black iron flask and a single ceramic cup, wrapped in red cloth. I took them in both hands, feeling like I should mumble some ritual words, awkwardly shoved them into the bottom of my bag, the weight of poison suddenly far heavier on my back than the little flask deserved.

"Good travels," the Behkdaz said, touching two fingers to her lips in farewell. "May your song be sung and your name remembered, wheresoever you lay your head."

The blue-tiled house next to the water office was silent.

I tapped on the door, and Rencki pinged the house's internal systems, requesting superficial data from the still-humming server.

"No one in," qe murmured. "No one has been home for three days. There is a message. 'I have gone to be with my kinn. I have gone to be with them. I have gone.' That is all. We should keep moving."

I followed qim silently from that house, and did not look back.

In the end, a lift found us.

We had made our way to the vigil house – shuttered and silent, like everything else in Millopix, but, Rencki thought, perhaps still housing a speeder in its sealed garage.

"You want to *steal* a vigil vehicle?" I blurted.

"Correct," qe replied, not bothering to twitch an ear or feign an indignant sniff in reply. "We have vital business and no one else will use them. It's simply a question of overriding the vigil systems, something which – with a little time – I should be able to do."

"How much time?"

"I am sure it will be momentary."

It was not momentary.

The sun rose higher, the heat thickened the air to an insect-humming soup, the shadows near-black in contrast to the blazing light of day. I sweated and sweltered beneath the sagging branches of a thick-leafed, thin-trunked tree, while Rencki sat on qis haunches in absolute silence, staring at the sealed vigil house as if by glare alone qe could crack it.

"How's it going?" I asked.

"It will go faster if you do not constantly demand my attention," qe retorted in sharp Xiha, and I clicked my tongue and raised my hands, melding three entirely separate languages into one meek conciliation, while the quanmech continued bouncing code against the silent house before us.

Some time later:

"How's it going now?"

"I am making progress!"

"System a bit tougher than expected?"

"I am a sentient quan of extraordinary capacity; it is merely an adaptive algorithm!"

"But, and I may have missed something here, it is an adaptive algorithm dedicated to a single process – keeping sentients like you from accessing the system. Whereas you, being so diverse in all things, must dedicate processing power to movement and speech and social niceties and defensive capabilities and sensory processing and—"

"You are not helping!"

"I'm just saying. You predicted an easy hack, and instead—"

A polite clicking from across the street.

Rencki's head snapped round, tails coming to attention – qe truly must have been immersed to be caught so off-guard by another's presence. "Yes?" qe snapped, qis accent briefly defaulting back to Assembly Adjumiri, to the standard vocabulary and style that would have come with the basic upload, rather than the more nuanced, organic-sounding Adjumiri of the local area. "What do you want?"

The person watching us wore a sleeveless vest with a single white feather hanging from the lower hem, symbolising what I could not say. His sandy-red hair was pushed back from a high forehead and he had a bag at his feet, bulging from every part. Behind him was a child. I found it hard to guess their age in Adjumiri terms, but imagined they were barely five or six Normyears old, their hair braided tight to their skull, a matching, far smaller bag at their feet.

"You seem to be trying to hack the vigil house," said the man, without judgement or rancour. "Are you looking for a vehicle?"

"We are trying to get to Kiskol," Rencki replied, and qe had reassigned processing priorities, because qis voice was back to the local accent, flowing softer, as if you could hear the friendly smile in qis speech. "We are following a calling for the Assembly. The vigil house was a necessity of last resort."

"Kiskol," mused the man. "I may be able to help with that."

*

He said his name was Ranwha, and the child Zanlan.

They had come from the south – he did not seem to feel the need to say more than "south" – and were heading to Elevator 15.

"Kiskol isn't far out of the way," he declared. "And we've been stopping to pick up supplies as we go."

"If you have a vehicle," Rencki said, "you would be doing us an incredible service."

From behind Ranwha's legs, Zanlan watched with eyes narrowed, fingers clenched into tight little fists. Rencki clicked an acknowledgement, then turned qis big yellow eyes towards the child.

Then, qe sniffed.

Qe raised qis big black nose and sniffed the air, then dropped, snuffled along the ground, turned in a little circle, sniffed again, and by sniffing appeared, for the first time, to discover the existence of Zanlan. Slowly, as if the little red fox were more afraid of them than they were of qim, qe approached, ears rotating back and forward on qis skull, until qe was a hand's-reach from Zanlan. Then qe produced an extraordinary wet, gloopy sound that was entirely generated from qis vocal driver rather than the chemical mesh on the end of qis nose.

Children, no matter where you go, always seem to enjoy the slightly grotesque, and despite themselves, Zanlan giggled.

Rencki appeared outraged by this, leaped back nearly a metric through the air, landing on all fours with fur raised, scampered round behind my legs to peer out at the child as if threatened by a gun, then slowly edged forward again, creeping as if qe could not be seen.

This time, Zanlan laughed, their face splitting into a wide grin as the quan approached, and when qe was within touching distance, the child very slowly reached out and patted Rencki on the top of qis furry head.

I did my best not to gape, nor point out the lethality of at least one of Rencki's tails. Instead, I watched as my companion nuzzled qis head a little deeper into the touch of the child, allowed qimself to be gently petted by them as they slowly emerged from the shelter of their parent's calves the damp snuffling sounds dissolving into a thing not unlike a purr.

That is how we fell in with Ranwha and Zanlan.

It was a tight fit in the back of the speeder.

The vehicle was not especially large, and every spare mil had been crammed with food, bottles of water, spare batteries, pillows, blankets and a couple of oversized stuffed toys.

Ranwha and I sat up front, while in the back Zanlan and Rencki dug themselves a little fortress of displaced bags and soft goods, Rencki cooing softly while Zanlan stroked qis ears, back, belly and decidedly dangerous furry tails. So convincing was my quan partner that for a moment I wondered whether qe was actually receiving pleasure from the attentions the child gave qim. Was there some algorithm in qis OS that rewarded organic attention as our minds rewarded intimacy with joy, physical contact with the sense of pleasure, trust, security? Or had qe simply dedicated so much of qis processing power to social blending that qe understood the easiest way to the parent's heart was to bring the child happiness? I couldn't tell, and it did not seem appropriate to ask.

Ranwha drove. The big highways were still functioning, and he had used autopilot most of the way north, but the smaller roads had been the first to lose electricity when the solar transmitters had started to fail, and authorities had prioritised powering launch sites and vital services over rural routes.

"Not that you'd imagine it," he murmured as we raced along between the high hedges and heavy, twisted branches of the trees that hemmed the road to Kiskol. "These days the nights are so bright that the speeder keeps charging even after sundown."

There was bitterness in his voice, and I did not interrogate it. Nor did I ask the obvious questions – not while Zanlan laughed and Rencki cooed in the back. The reason for his bitterness was as clear as the reason for his love, and the same.

"So what is so important that you came to Adjumir?" he asked as we crossed a bridge over a fat brown river kissed with hot summer vapour and the slow ripple of hidden, preening reptiles.

"We were sent by the Accord. I cannot say more."

Two clicks; he disapproves of my silence, especially now, especially when all lies should be burned away in the light of the twin suns, but he will not push further. "Your accent? You do not speak Assembly Adjumiri, but neither is it . . . "

"I live on Xihana. My first language was Mdo-sa."

"The Shine?"

A nod – then correction, a click of affirmation. Ranwha's eyes do not leave the road. "Shine sent ships a few moons back, offered to take people out. Assembly warned us off – said they were slavers, cruel, that they lied. Didn't stop people going, mind. Better a slave than dead. Assembly didn't try to stop anyone, either. People free to make their own choices, they say."

"The Shine are cruel."

A click; who is he to judge cruelty, or the choices people make, times being what they are?

"I didn't think many people born in the Shine left. Are you a . . . what do they call it? A Unionist? I saw a documentary – rebels, someone was martyred, they use the symbol of the binary star. The Shine pretends they don't exist, but Lhonoja, the Edge . . . "

His voice trailed off. There are some things too big for even the Shine, too big to really encompass and name.

"I am not a rebel. I . . . There was an accident. I was changed. I am not . . . It is not something I am comfortable with. I want to tell you that I am not a coward, that if I thought I could make a difference . . . although it is . . . complicated."

"You don't seem to be a coward. You came to Adjumir just in time for the world to die. You could have stayed away. I suppose that makes you brave. Or stupid. Or both."

I said nothing, tried to press a little deeper into my chair.

The morning's thunder was already thickening up for afternoon rain, a grumble to the east, a smell of preparing green that drifted through even the sealed bubble of the speeder. Then: "Did you come by ship?" he asked, the simplest thing in the world. "There's no elevator nearby, no shuttle pad."

"Yes."

"Was that the ship that came through the skies over Millopix during yesterday's storm?"

I didn't answer. Behind me, Rencki was still gently making little purring noises in Zanlan's lap, but I could feel the force of qis attention on the back of my neck, hear qis warning voice in my mind as though qe had actually spoken.

Ranwha clicked his tongue twice at my silence, and in silence we drove on.

Later, it began to rain.

At first, it was beautiful, dark shadows broken up by dazzling light sweeping across the land.

Then it was powerful, slicing torrents tapping in across the dome of the hollow vehicle.

Eventually, it was more than that – a view-blocking, world-blocking, day-smothering wall that forced us to a halt on the side of the road, turned the land beneath us into a blackened river, broken only by distant stabs of lightning. I wanted to step outside, to reach my hand into it, taste it, open my mouth and drink in the sky. Knew that Rencki, now silent in Zanlan's lap, would not approve. Wondered what people would see if they saw us now – a tiny bubble of light caught in the middle of the day-become-night downpour.

Zanlan slept, the roar of thunder and rocking of rain a familiar thing. Ranwha played music. It was old music, he said – music made before Exodus. There were only two kinds of music made now, he added. The music of those who had escaped, already changing with the inflections of alien worlds, the rhythms of strange, different cultures; and the songs of those who were left behind. He didn't like either, so he played the old tunes.

He used this word – "alien". It tripped off his tongue, a familiar, habitual thing, and he didn't seem to notice.

I looked to Rencki, who to all intents and purposes appeared to be asleep in the child's lap, and who was not sleeping.

After a while, the storm eased to merely a torrent.

Ranwha checked his computer, tutted at what he saw, said: "Weather sats are down, but I'd guess this will keep going into the night."

"I agree," Rencki opined from the back seat, not bothering to open qis eyes or feign the movement of qis jaw. "It is most probable."

"I don't think we'll make it to Millopix without recharging – not in this. There's a village nearby. I have some friends there."

"Are you sure they're still alive?" I blurted, and immediately felt embarrassed to have been so direct; but Ranwha's fingers danced in a kind of shrug.

"We shall see."

He turned off the music, and onwards we drove.

I did not keep track of time in the rain.

The world outside was moving shadows and illusionary distances, lights looming in some far-off place that was neither earth nor sky, then disappearing again, swallowed by the storm. I had not imagined weather could carry on so long, or be so deep. The energy of the distant nova was already starting to cook the atmosphere, heat up the system from within – I had not thought I would be here, alive, to see it.

It felt like a strange kind of honour. An ugly privilege to be a witness.

I thought I could hear Gebre whispering in my ear: *Only matters if you stay alive to speak of it.*

Then Rencki spoke, and qe used neither Adjumir, Normspeak nor Xiha. Instead, the old language, the one that tasted like vinegar on my lips: Mdo-sa.

"We're off-course," qe said. "We're a long way off-course."

"What's that?" blurted Ranwha, his knuckles white on the wheel, eyes fixed on the limited vision of the road ahead. "What did qe say?"

"Qe monitors my vitals," I blurted. "My body – I'm not used to the gravity, the air. Qe said my blood pressure was high."

I could hear the lie, awful, stumbling on my lips. Hoped that my rusty Adjumiri would hide it, my bumbling efforts mistaken for poor language skills rather than a lack of imagination.

"Do you need to pull over?"

"How far are we from your friends?"

"Not far now. A few tocks at most."

"Be careful," Rencki murmured, still in the language of the Shine. And then, the most dangerous of all commands: "Be curious."

"It's fine," I told Ranwha. "It's fine. I'm sure it'll all be fine."

He neither clicked his tongue nor spoke in reply.

The village was not a village, but a little cluster of buildings around a farm.

A huddle of speeders and trucks, ranging from tiny two-seaters up to lumbering modified beasts, were parked in the yard before the long, low central house. A broken wind turbine sat storm-torn behind a high solar-panelled barn, and as we approached, a burst of creatures I had never seen before, antlered and low to the earth, bounded away.

The rain was easing into a merely soaking afternoon, the light muddled and muted as if humbled by the strength of the storm. We pulled up on a patch of white gravel beside a garden of wind-blasted trellises and cracked glass, and Ranwha said: "Seems like someone's inside," and didn't look at me as he spoke, and didn't wake his child, sleeping in the back.

He got out of the vehicle, and I stayed seated a moment as Rencki, gently – so very gently – uncurled from Zanlan's form.

"This is wrong," qe whispered in Mdo-sa. "I am pinging emergency comms. Comms are not responding. Widening the band. Transmitting distress beacon. Transmitting."

"What do we do?" I breathed.

"I will provide security. I will ... Wait. I am connecting, there is—"

A crunch of gravel cut caught my attention, cut Rencki off midsentence. The door of the house was open, and in the light of it I could see Ranwha and another shape beckoning us over, their heads tucked beneath the lintel and away from the still-tapping rain. I looked to Rencki for advice, but whether because qe had none or qis processors were occupied elsewhere, qe said nothing.

I climbed slowly out of the vehicle, and heard the gentle pawing of Rencki landing on the earth as qe followed me. We walked towards the waiting figures in the door, and as I opened my mouth to make some sort of polite greeting – some half-snatched words of ritual and thanks – Rencki cried out: "Gun!" and qis tails sparked to electrical life, rearing up to fire.

Too late, of course. The electromagnetic shotgun was primarily a quan-killer weapon, designed to fry electronics, sizzling through Rencki's systems with a scream of magnetic chaos. Whereas when the scattershot hit me, it merely hurt like the first grasp of an arcship interface as it bedded itself into my skull, followed by an unfamiliar, unwelcome kind of darkness.

Interlude

A passenger who entered arcspace with blue eyes emerges on the other side of the voyage with green.

A scar on a person's right hand is now on their left. Or perhaps more – perhaps you come out of the dark and find every organ in your body is inverted, heart moved from one side to the other, spleen switched round. You probably don't even know until you have some troubles in later life, and the doctor opens your scan with a cry of "Bugger me, have you seen yourself in the mirror lately?!"

A woman once came out of arcspace who knew every detail of her life – except it was not her life, it was the life of another from far, far away, rendered in perfect detail, and when she met with her child at the end of the journey, she stood there baffled and proclaimed: I'm dreadfully sorry, I have no idea whose offspring this is.

It is hard to tell whether the hysteria some people experience on entering and leaving arcspace is a manifestation of the otherness of that interstitial space, or merely the result of centuries of being told how alarming the dark is, how frightening and grave it is to cross between the stars. Some scientists say they can prove – definitively prove – that the madness is caused by some manner of external interference with the broken minds of those who scream, and howl, and tear at their skin and hair – but their results are almost never replicable in double-blind studies, and so the question persists.

Most Pilots go mad before they die.

Inconsistently mad – that is the frustration. Sometimes the madness is a wild, murderous thing – a fascination with flesh, a compulsion to rip and rend and see how the tiniest part of the greatest things is made to work. Sometimes it's a harmless sort of insanity. One Pilot became obsessed with a certain kind of beetle, and was perfectly calm so long as there was always one in the room, happily munching a leaf. Another lost the capacity to understand the difference between me and you, overwhelmed by interconnectedness, and eventually went to live with the noksha, who don't care for such distinctions anyway. A few created gorgeous, abstract pieces of art – great weavings of scavenged fabric, or paintings made with ink ground from precious stones – in an attempt to express something of their thoughts, some fraction of their meaning, but it's never quite right. Never quite says enough, they say. Some critics claim they find the work unbearable, impossible to look at, but they probably felt that way even before they saw the final piece.

The Lux refuse to travel in arcspace at all, and instead cross the stars in their vast slowships, sleeping the centuries away on their long voyages. They say there is a kind of purity to going slow. They say that arcspace allows us to forget how extraordinary are the distances we travel, and how tiny we are in the great black. Our egos, our egos, they chant – left unchecked, our egos can grow as big as the distances we traverse. Let us be small. Let us be humble. Let our voices be carried off silently into the dark.

Various words are ascribed to the "otherness", the unknowable "thing" waiting in the dark. Common ones are: uncanny, malign, sinister, slippery, clawing, cruel, malevolent, mischievous, ominous, perverse, baleful, dire, poisonous, evil.

These are foolish words, for they assume that language has any meaning to the realms of nothingness, where time and space are impenetrable dreams. There are ideas of morality, ethics – even sentience – that are utterly inappropriate, crushingly crude in their inspace-centricity, and thus a waste of everyone's time.

Only the Lordat, those priests with shaved heads and endless droning chants designed to inspire as much tedium as possible in the hearer, have got it right. The dark, they say, does not care for such petty concerns as hearts, minds or souls. The great unknowable has one nameable feature, and one alone: it is curious.

Chapter 18

There is a child crying.

Zanlan.

Someone is comforting them, an Adjumiri in still-sodden rain gear, holding the child by the chin and whispering soft words of placation, of calm. Others wait around the room – nine in all, including the one with the gun, the weapon still tucked into the fold of aer arms, aer face set with a deep frown as ae gazed down at me.

Sprawled in a chair from which I was already half fallen, chest burning from the shock of impact and fingers still shaking from the misfires of a nervous system unsure how to cope with all of this, I imagine I looked a picture. More relevant to Zanlan, Rencki was on the floor. Qis bright russet fur was scalded black across the top of qis spine and front of qis neck, where the bulk of the shot had impacted, and qis tails and legs were splayed at an angle that in any creature of muscle and sinew would have been a grotesque, unnatural sight. I lurched towards qim, and was immediately pushed back by one of the assembled peoples, the gun swinging towards me, the threat clear, the consequences lifeless at my feet.

"Qe was safety," I growled. "Qe kept people safe."

My Adjumiri did not seem to be adequately communicating what I meant, for brows flickered in confusion, but no one started running, no one called out in fear at the meaning of my speech.

Instead, Ranwha leaned forward, ignoring the small furry body at his feet, rested his hands on the arms of my chair so his face was next to mine, breathed: "We know you have a ship."

I stared into his eyes, saw a man trying to make himself terrifying, make me afraid; nearly laughed, nearly choked on it. "And?" I blurted. "And what of it?"

"You'll show us. You'll take us away."

"Take you where? On Adjapar they'll arrest you as numberless, songless. The cryotanks are full, there is no capacity for extra lungs, extra bellies. They'll space you; it's the only logical thing to do. Or maybe you fly to Namak or Mayxclan and seek asylum. My ship can't immunise you; they'll shove you into quarantine, and if you're lucky, you'll be dumped in some refugee camp on an isolated moon and left to rot, a *problem* to be solved, not people at all. Is that your plan?"

"If that's what it takes," he snapped. "We will live. My *child* is going to live."

So long as Zanlan didn't look at Rencki's body, they seemed a little calmer, their face turned away and tears carefully dried on the end of a stranger's sleeve. I looked round the assembled Adjumiris, murmured: "You're all numberless? All of you?"

They didn't need to answer.

"You should take Zanlan away," I breathed. "Keep them far from this."

"You could help us," said Ranwha, squatting down in front of me, his voice hard and fingers dancing the hand-speak of entreaty, begging almost. "It's just luck – that's all it is. Some people got lucky, some didn't. Do you really think it's fair we should die – my child should die – because we didn't get lucky?"

I felt tired now, a swathe of regret, knowing the things that were to come, Rencki at my feet, burning in my chest. "Do you really think it's fair," I sighed, "that people with guns should take the place of those who have none? That's all we're talking about here, at the end of the day. There aren't enough places to fly. There were never going to be enough places to fly. Someone was always going to be left behind."

"So you want us to die meekly. You want us to say, 'Well, if that's how it is', take our cups of Grace, feel happy for the ones who lived, is that it? You want us to be good little corpses. You sound like a Behkdaz."

I sounded like Gebre, and I knew it. The thought of ter caught me momentarily off-guard, a shimmer of something shocking through my chest, a memory of why we were here – why I was really here.

I closed my eyes, could smell the bitter taste of Rencki's singed fur on the air, hear Ranwha's breathing, deep, ragged, resolved. "You love your child. I understand that. I have never loved a child, but I understand – intellectually, you see. I really do. You will do terrible things. I have always tried to understand the terrible things people do. Can I tell you a story? It's not long, it goes like this. Once, when I was new—"

"Give us the fucking ship!" someone snarled, but another hushed them, leaned a little closer, listening.

"Once, when I was new, I went to a place called Hasha-to. I had escaped a laboratory, was wandering without purpose, saw the sign of the binary star. Followed it. Fell in with some rebels – Unionists, they are called in the Shine. They had these big ideas of freedom and salvation and all sorts of things, and me ... well, I tend to go with the flow. Their words made me feel big, their emotions made me feel important, and so ...

"But big feelings aren't a substitute for a good plan, and they were dead minutes after we landed. I should have felt terror, going back to Hasha-to, but instead I was simply ... curious. Curious to return somewhere so cruel, curious to understand how another human could treat their fellow humans so. I thought – is it because they hate? Is it because they hated the debtors that they do such things? But hate is a hot, burning thing, and their cruelties were cold, administrative, bureaucratic even. And then I had this idea:

maybe it was love. Maybe the warders of that place believed in something – in an idea, in something important – or maybe they loved their family so much, had to do so much to protect them, had created all sorts of funny ideas about what 'protection' means – how to protect you must kill, and maim, and punish, and see those you hurt as less than human. Maybe it was love. And I had to know. The thought of it – why, why, why, why is Hasha-to, why is this place the way it is, why did these things happen, why – it consumed me. And I am . . . unsafe when I get into such a condition. It is important that I stay regulated. I need you to listen – I need you to understand. When I went to Hasha-to, the people there tried to kill me. But I am a monster made in the dark. I am a copy of a dead man, rebuilt by forces unknown. You cannot stop me. You cannot hold me back. Eventually the lights will go out in this place, and in the dark I will turn, and when I do, I will kill you all. If you love your child, you'll get them out of here before that moment comes. That's all."

The numberless did not understand my story, but at least they took the child away before they started hitting me.

Chapter 19

When the Xi first found me, after the *Myrmida*, they tried to contain me, but I was curious, and would not be contained.

Then I wandered for a while, and had no purpose.

Then I met some Unionists – fiery, furious refugees who called the name of Sarifi, Glastya Row, Lhonoja, the binary suns – and with them I returned to Hasha-to. They planned to stage a heroic rescue, and they died.

I died too, shot through the chest, my body thrown onto the surface of the world to burn, my corpse devoured by an atmosphere of acid and fire. Thankfully, they didn't throw me far from the airlock, and once they'd dumped my body, they forgot about me, and that made all the difference.

On Adjumir, in the last days before the end of the world, a group of numberless driven by a mixture of ego, terror and love hurt me.

They did not know how to hurt me. They were not inherently violent people. If anything, they seemed a little embarrassed at what they were trying to do, and kept on muttering among each other, asking if they'd gone too far, if they should stop.

Ranwha kept them going, of course.

Ranwha was the only one there who had a child, and he loved

that child so much he thought his heart might break, and so he hurt me the most, because that was what he had to do.

Thoughts, drifting in a semiconscious state.

The people of Chulla's World have only one word for sky and space – "above". To them there is no difference between the thick atmosphere of their planet and the vacuum beyond; these things all lie above the surface of the ocean and are therefore all one, clumped together in a great big "above" that is spoken of with a mixture of awe and dread. Equally, many cultures who have crossed the stars still gaze down into the oceans beneath their ships and use words of doubt, unease, otherness. Abyss, deeps, depths; they construct horror stories of the fearful dark. Perhaps there is a limit to what any one mind can truly fathom, a corner of our brains that is always given over to terror of the unknown.

When not hurting me, Ranwha pleads.

"My child," he whispers. "My child. My child!"

It would be easy enough to say yes, but fundamentally meaningless. Eight hundred million people are going to die; the life of a child is everything/nothing. I am aware that in his mind, I am the villain of this story.

"I am Mawukana-from-the-Dark," I whisper through swollen lips. "I am the ghost of Hasha-to."

I can feel a few people in the room starting to believe me, which will only make things worse.

A hand lifts me up. I am lighter than they expect – a couple of times someone wondered if they were going to accidentally kill me, if my weak off-worlder bones were going to shatter. They broke my exoskeleton an age ago; it is such an easy thing to break.

This isn't working, someone says.

Someone else gives me water.

I drink automatically, and it tastes . . . peculiar. Something in the minerals, perhaps, something in the pipes. I wondered where it had come from, whether there was a spring somewhere in nearby hills, a place in the land where it just bubbled to the surface, flowing into streams into rivers that were themselves fed by another squeezing of the earth, if the water cycle on this world was like the water cycle on mine, how these endless rains were changing it, if the taste I tasted was in fact water plus supernova, the taste of radiation, the taste of Lhonoja, of a dying binary star.

Someone says: *He doesn't look right.*

They don't mean "bloodied, broken, wounded".

They mean "other".

Something uncanny, not quite one thing; a copy with a transcription error that no one can really put their finger on, but you can look at and just know there is a wrongness.

"I am the ghost of Hasha-to," I mumble, tongue like wool in my mouth. "I am an *it*, not a he."

"Why does he keep saying that, *why does he keep saying* . . ."

In the end, the lights went out before I could die.

A storm somewhere nearby, the distant sound of constant thunder; lightning struck a pylon perhaps, or maybe the pylon was hit days ago and the farm was functioning on its own power. My cottage on its island can run off a few hours of sunlight a week, but on Adjumir everything is falling apart. Radiation, heat, the moon of Lhonoja blazing above – things fail. Things fall apart. And so, a little before dawn: the lights go out.

Rules bend, in the black. Sounds too big, walls too thin. Expectations crack, warp, crumble. The imagination starts to fill in the gaps, the protective instinct of the living brain seeing everywhere *danger, danger, danger.* There is a piece of me that will always love the dark, always love coming back to this state, when reality grows thin.

I have always found it fascinating, the stories people tell themselves to bring comfort in the dark. Stories about being special, important, unique. "Valuable" even – but valuable to what? To other humans? They will fade and die as surely as you will, and what then is your legacy? The words you leave behind? Your carvings made in stone, footprints in the sand? Sooner or later every sun will be a Lhonoja or a red giant that swallows planets whole.

Perhaps this is why so many cultures believe in a life after death. What an extraordinary gift it is to be alive, to be living in this moment – and how much more extraordinary to pass through that same experience without ever having noticed how wondrous it is.

Other tricks of the human brain: the ability to see the colour magenta. No such colour exists in nature, but the mind takes red and blue – the opposite ends of the visible spectrum – and fuses them into something unreal yet, to the mind, true.

The power of prediction to overwhelm sensory experience. If you believe hard enough that you are seeing what you think you see – that perhaps this four-legged creature is a predator set to rip out your throat, rather than a gentler beast – then you will see it, no matter what is actually there. This hallucination is strongest in the dark – with limited data, the brain will always try to fill in the gaps, and the fuel it burns is fear.

The idea of solidity. On an atomic level, matter is more space than it is mass. The experience of touch, of weight and interaction, is not one of mass-on-mass, but force-on-force, field-within-field, repulsing, attracting and repelling.

In the dark, in the deepest black where the travellers go, the rules do not apply.

There is a kind of honesty there, if you look for it.

I rose from my chair.

"Chair" – an object of mass and magnetism. I press against it, it presses against me, fields interacting, bending.

I am dysregulated – that is what the Major would say, what Rencki would blare: Maw, you are dysregulated! You need to focus, come back, remember what it is to be human!

She's light years away; qe is dead.

Around me: nine organic objects and a gun. They shine so much more brightly in my vision than they did when crude burning light illuminated them. Some are here because they genuinely think they matter more than someone else, because they cannot fathom how their lives are not important, because in the bottom of their hearts, they actually believe that they are special, that they deserve – no, they are *owed* – a second chance. The majority are here because they are afraid. Not even the Behkdaz could convince them that the end could be peaceful, that it was simply a breathing-out, a letting-go. Their terror is a mind-shaking thing, an earthquake in the soul.

Ranwha, of course, is here for love. He shouts at me to stay down, tries to knock me back, swinging wildly, blind. His fist interacts with the molecules of my face. He expected a crunch of bone-on-bone, but these things have grown somewhat vague, and he has to force his arm back, yank it free of me like pulling a magnet from an iron bar, gasping at the ice forming about his skin, and finally, at last, even he understands.

Of all the reasons why these people are here, love is the most fascinating.

There is an idea, common to many cultures, that love resides in the heart. This strikes me as a historical hangover from the millennia before we had a proper anatomical understanding of the human body, combined with a romanticisation that does indeed lend itself to all these ideas of special, vital, worthy by means of a soul, et cetera. But I suppose even I can sometimes be subject to the impact of these little narrative tales, which is why as shots rang out and the room shimmered into a familiar, cool place of humming energy and motion, I reached into Ranwha's chest and pulled out his still-beating heart.

After, when there was nothing else interesting left to do on the farm, I sat on the roof of Ranwha's speeder and watched the sunrise.

Chapter 20

The first time the people in the laboratory asked me about the things I did, I told the truth.

They seemed very unhappy when I did so, even though they'd asked me to be honest, so the next time I tried lying, to see if it would make them feel better.

I lied badly and said that when an "episode" came over me, I blacked out.

That it was like a great big darkness that rose up and consumed me, and only when it was over did I find myself standing among a pile of the dead/wounded/maimed/dying, and that at the sight of said carnage I felt bad/sad/guilt/regret.

Everyone seemed happier with this explanation, even though it was obviously not true. A few people were correctly terrified. "It can lie," they said. "What else can it learn to do?"

As I got better at understanding my observers, I came to learn the difference between what they asked and what they wanted to know, and lo and behold, everyone decided to believe whatever it was that made them feel better.

It is not that I am not moral, in my own way.

It is simply that sometimes, rather like the rules of physics that should contain me, I forget.

Forgetting is perhaps the best way to express it.

I forget what it is to have skin, and organs, and blood and bones.

I forget the rules I have learned, the languages I speak, the ethics I try to embody and the morals I desperately seek to make my own.

I forget how this universe works, and for a moment am simply . . . curious.

The play of photons, the taste of hydrogen. The smell of gravity, the soft touch of a boson field, it is so fabulously beautiful, so incredible, so rich and full and fascinating and alive – and there is so much about it I want to learn.

And sometimes.

When I am in a lot of pain.

When nothing makes any sense, all this noise, all this shouting, all this . . . *stuff* just going on all around

I choose to forget.

I do choose it, and only afterwards am ashamed.

Zanlan ran away that night.

While I pulled out their father's heart. While I reached into the skull of one who tried to stab me, to see if I could hear their thoughts dancing across their brain. As gunshots passed straight through me – as why would they not, being merely energy passing through energy, like electrons shooting in the dark – Zanlan fled.

Do you believe me?

I understand that hurting a child would be abhorrent. When I remember, I remember this most absolutely. The most fascinating thing about children – watching as they discover their own agency, become their own selves – requires time, and it is the opposite of curiosity to interrupt that process. Destroying life when it is so full of prospect is a fundamentally boring act. If you believe nothing else about me, believe that.

Of course, to feel better about this requires another suspension of imagination.

It requires imagining that in sixteen days' time, Zanlan won't die anyway, alone, without family, slowly burned alive in a wave of radiation that will strip the planet to its bones.

Strange, the mental acrobatics people do to try and feel better about this sort of thing.

Sunshine brought clarity; brought reality.

I looked around and saw a lot of dead bodies, and knew I was to blame, and felt like I should curl up on the ground and puke my guts out and weep and beg for forgiveness. But on Adjumir, you carried on anyway.

Thus, as the sun rose, I loaded the body of Rencki into the back of the speeder that had belonged to Ranwha and Zanlan. I was not sure how dead my companion was in the strictest sense of the word. For a quan to die entirely requires a total wiping of their memory systems, their OS, their basic rules of function – and hadn't qe backed qimself up before we flew? If enough of qis memories survived, would qe learn from this experience of being shot and add a shield generator to qis carapace, and how much of qimself would qe have to give up to create that capacity? Or would qe just keep on making the same mistakes, walking into a scattershot blast and dying again and again, because qe could not keep the memories to learn from qis experience?

The speeder was coded to Ranwha's DNA, but not life-locked. I dipped a kitchen towel in his blood, activated the engine, coded in our destination, and with Rencki's blackened body in the back, headed towards Kiskol.

Chapter 21

The Kiskol Institute of Antiquities wasn't in Kiskol proper, but stood some fifteen tocks from the edge of the town, on top of a storm-blasted, rain-soaked cliff of black stone. Once – years ago – people would come from kils around to visit and go for long walks along the seashore paths or through the grey forests that blanketed it. Its interests ranged from ancient interplanetary ships and the crockery designed especially for them, through to skeletons of the great mega-fauna that had thrived in the first centuries of terraforming, before the pressure of a growing ecosystem and bio-engineers in their orbital habitats forced change upon some, extinction upon others. Mostly it was a place for academics, its only concession to the outside world being a café serving a kind of heavy biscuit and pots of kol to the local walkers, sometimes tricking them into its more esoteric displays while they were looking for the toilets.

No more, of course. Now, no families came, no kinn from the towns and the cities. The Institute's gate stood open beneath the rising dawn of a new day, but the windows were shuttered where they faced the sea, and in a courtyard within its black stone walls there was only a vigil truck and a half-empty drone hub, its hooks hanging with burned-out machines and gutted parts. Where once hundreds of researchers, students and makers of kol had taken up residence in the long dormitories cut into stone, now just twenty-nine, all numberless, gathered together in this place. The oldest was ninety-six, the youngest in their late twenties, and they greeted the dawn and sang out the ending of the day together, and one of their number had done the short-course training as a Behkdaz, the emergency three-week programme that had been opened up to the population as a whole when the Lovers finally went supernova, and was authorised to issue Grace, and still didn't feel especially comfortable with their calling.

I arrived in the mid-afternoon, parked my speeder in a yard of carefully raked stones that were starting to be overgrown with tangling weeds and wilting flowers confused by the season, and no one was there to greet me, and I didn't know where to go.

I crawled out of my vehicle, Rencki heavy in my arms, called out: "Hello?"

Behind the walls the sea wind shuddered, and the clouds skimmed busy, weighty overhead. In the centre of the yard, a blasted white tree, its branches saggy with little silver bells and tangles of paper – no chimes here, a slightly different flavour of remembering, of saying goodbye.

"Hello?!"

A great pair of black doors are sealed on the side of the courtyard furthest from the entry gate, blocking a mouth of stone and bio-resin that curves down into the cliffs, as if the building were about to shout. Even the architecture on Adjumir is designed to sometimes swallow the sound of the wind and make it sing.

For a moment, the old familiar feeling of having done everything wrong.

I'd come so far, and there was blood on my hands, my arms, my clothes, every part of me. The gravity pressed me down, Rencki was heavy in my arms, bruises were layered on bruises, and I was a monster after all and here—

"Stay where you are!" a voice barked, and I nearly laughed, the idea of moving so strangely absurd.

Someone had eased open a smaller hatch in the slate doors that barred the way to the interior of the Institute just enough for an eye, the barrel of a gun, a hint of a threat to poke out, wave towards me. "Who are you?" An accent I struggled with, and I was tired, so sore and tired. "What do you want?"

I tried to mumble: here to help, a message, a message came, I . . .

Wondered how I looked, crimson in gore, a stranger at the end of the world.

"Gebre," I said instead, and when nothing happened, tried again, thought perhaps I hadn't been heard. "Gebre Nethyu Chatithimska Bajwahra sent for me. My name is Mawukana na-Vdnaze. I have a ship. I came from . . . from above. Gebre sent for me."

And then, because there didn't really seem much more to add, and the gravity of this world really was exhausting, I lay down in the middle of the yard, Rencki across my chest, and closed my eyes and let someone else try to work all this out.

The person with the gun was called Ngurta.

Ey was a vigil, one of the last officers left on watch on the whole planet. Ey had shaved eir head and drawn thick black lines across eir eyes and lips and a painted line down eir chin. I knew this would have some meaning, communicate something – something about death, perhaps; this was Adjumir – but I didn't know what. The planet was too big for me to have learned all its traditions, too full of changing people facing the end. Eir gun was a simple stun pistol, designed for keeping order in a provincial town, not fighting off numberless as they tried to storm the elevators, claw their way onto the last departing ships. Ey had come here because eir partner was here, and neither of them had had their numbers called, and they were both desperately sad for each other, consumed with loss and pain to know that the one they loved was going to die; and also quietly relieved that they were not going to die alone.

Ngurta stood over me, weapon drawn, and sent someone else to find Gebre.

"Whose blood is it?" ey demanded.

"Mine," I replied. "And other people's too."

"What happened to you?"

"Numberless."

"Are they following you?"

"No. They are dead. It's just me and Rencki."

"The quan?"

"Yes."

"Is qe dead?"

"Death . . . is an interruption."

Then a new shadow fell over me, and as I squeezed my eyes open, I did not recognise the shape, did recognise the voice, deep and familiar, and it was Gebre, and te said:

"Maw? What in the name of the blackened abyss are you doing here?"

Chapter 22

Te took me to the bathroom, a communal hall of cold, cliff-dripping water and warmer wooden tubs. Most were dry, their users long since departed, one way or another. I shivered on the side as te filled the only one that looked like it had any regular use, fetched soap from an old pearlescent box and ointments from a basket. Waited as the tub filled. Let ter prise the bloodied clothes from my back, my legs; ease me down into the water.

Gebre was old, of course.

Ter straight black hair was streaked with grey and cut short about ter skull. The strength of ter shoulders had grown a little curved, along with the softness of belly, expansion of backside that came with all bodies ageing. The wrinkles across ter face were a light spider's web, not yet edged too deep, and when te scrubbed my scalp I could feel the power of ter fingers thrumming in my ears.

For a while, we did not talk, as carefully te uncovered which part of my body was bruised and which torn, which sweeps of blood washed off easy and which came from settling scabs beneath. Te emptied and filled the bath again, washing away scarlet, and said not a word.

Neither did I.

Seventeen years ago, Gebre – a younger Gebre – had poured some kind of oil into the tub and said: "This is the washing of the rain. If we used panja oil and sang together it would be a binding of breath to breath, a very serious matter, but this way we wash each other from our flesh, with the understanding that one day the drops of water that have been separated by the storm may meet again in the ocean, do you understand?"

The bath was deep and hot, the oil smelled of salt and seaweed.

"You have baths to ritualise the ... the *triviality* ..." I wasn't sure if this was the right word, wondered for a moment if it would be offensive, if it carried the same meaning in Adjumiri as it did in other places, "of sexual intercourse?"

"Exactly," te declared, lowering terself one careful toe at a time into the tub beside me. "And we have baths for marriage and baths for grief and baths for celebration of a pregnancy and baths for celebration of a child's birth and for ... You seem surprised. This is Adjumir. We take our rituals very seriously."

"I am beginning to understand that."

"It is to give our lives meaning. Every creature in the universe that is born will one day die – it is the way of it. With gene therapies and cyber enhancements you might live a hundred and fifty, maybe even two hundred years, but still – eventually – there will be an end. On planets across the Accord people go to extraordinary lengths to pretend that this isn't the case, live their lives with a kind of heady thoughtlessness, as if tomorrow might not be their last day. And what happens when death comes? They regret. They look back at empty actions and empty deeds and say, 'But I thought I had more time.' On Adjumir, we have the gift of absolute knowledge. We know precisely when our death will come – we know from the moment we are born – and so every day we look for meaning in our actions."

"Your number may be called ..." I mumbled, and at once te silenced me with the sharp tilt of ter chin that I was beginning to learn was a strict shutting-down of a topic.

"There are those who say," te mused, after a pause to let the rudeness of my interjection pass, "that sex is meaningless. They do not understand Adjumir. Intimacy, shared trust and joy – these should be powerful, important acts, acts that are celebrated. When you leave, you will remember this, no? Our connection creates it; the ritual seals the memory in, and you will be a little bit different, perhaps, when you return to the stars. I will have made you different, do you see? What greater meaning can there be in a life than to touch another?"

Seventeen years later, another kind of bath.

In the hollow halls of the Institute, at the end of the world. The water was still hot – perhaps a little less so than it had been all those years ago, but it still burned through bruise, cut and scab. Gebre sat on a stool with a growing pile of wet cloths at ter feet, and washed the blood off my skin. There was no question of privacy – the tub was a communal thing fit for six or seven people, and Gebre had at once declared that as the water of our lives had found each other again, and while I was on Adjumir in its final days, I would damn well do things the Adjumiri way and be grateful.

Ter hands were lined with raised ridges of rippling skin, places where fat and muscle had come and gone. Ter fingers were firm where te dabbed the cloth against another cut, ter voice brisk where te commanded me to lean forward, lie back. When te was quite satisfied that the grime beneath my nails was gone and had pounded the dirt from my hair, te ordered me to stand, wrapped me in thick robes, patted down the last of the water from around my chin, and said at last: "Well. Better. You eaten?"

"No. Not for a while."

"We'd better find you something bland."

The Institute was built into the cliffs, a great slow spiral of an inner corridor descending down into ever colder, ever darker depths. The canteen was a carved hall off this corridor, long, thin windows looking out towards the sea, empty stone tables and empty stone chairs running from wall to wall, full of the silence where people should have been.

Ngurta stood by the door until Gebre barked: "He's not going to hurt me, Ngurta! By all the stars!"

Then and only then Ngurta clicked eir tongue and turned away, only to be replaced by a quan, who hummed through the door on a soft puff of suspensor field, Rencki's body draped across a delicate limb that had unfolded from qis middle and seemed far too frail to hold the weight of my companion.

"My name is Nineteen," said the floating quan, in a voice almost entirely devoid of affect. Qis carapace had no obvious external sensors – nothing any organic would consider eyes or ears – but in a concession to qis organic audience, a couple of arrows had been painted on qis metallic form indicating up, down, front and back, along with a single eye painted in the middle of qis ostensibly forward-facing panel so that anyone who cared about such things could feign some sort of eye contact while speaking with qim. "You are being recorded."

Qe did not ask my consent; merely informed me of the reality, then lifted the body of Rencki a little higher. "This is a quanmech of the Betakayrill mainframe. A very inconsistent system – always in a hurry to evolve, to be updating qis OS rather than take things carefully, an algorithm at a time. What is qis designation and the nature of qis disrepair?"

"Qe is Rencki," I explained. "And qe was shot by an electrostatic shotgun."

"I shall attempt to revive qim. However, I am forbidden from tampering with anything other than base hardware, so if qe has received any software damage, that is beyond my capacity to help. Diplomatic incidents have been caused by less."

"Anything you can do will be appreciated."

"Are you aware that qe is carrying lethal armaments?"

"Yes."

"Very well."

A single beep – it took a moment to understand this as a sort of clicking, a moment more to comprehend that Nineteen was so far uninterested in the customs of the planet that qe couldn't even be bothered to replicate the sound of tongues moving in mouths when communicating in organic speech. But qe carried Rencki's body carefully, bobbing a little as qe balanced the weight, and took qim within.

Now I am alone with Gebre.

Silence a while.

Silence as te pours another cup.

Silence as we sit across from each other at the table.

It is I who break the silence, who blurt the thing that I will die if I do not express: "You are surprised to see me."

Te takes a moment to answer, circumspect in my presence perhaps, having washed so much blood away. "Yes," te says at last. "I am."

"Why?"

"Why? Why? Because it is the end of the world, Maw. It is the end of the world. And you and I . . . I had made my feelings clear, had I not?"

"You made your feelings clear. But then you sent for me."

"I . . . What?"

"You sent for me. By name. Hulder, the Major . . ."

"I don't know who these people are."

"They came to my door. Said you had discovered something, that you requested me, by name, that . . . They lied."

The knowledge is a rock thrown onto my chest. There will be no shifting it.

Te stared down at ter cup for a long while, then up at me. I do not know what it took for ter to do so, but I was grateful for it.

"Maw," te breathed, "I think you should tell me everything."

So I did.

Chapter 23

There is a peculiar manifestation of social cohesion that I have, with some dread, observed in most societies I have visited: "small talk".

It is fascinating how many people experience a measurable physiological response to the smallest of small talks. "Isn't the weather foul?" or "I see the shuttle is late again", and "Oh I *know*!" comes the reply, and if you were to scan for blood pressure, sweat production, hormonal response, etc., you would observe noticeable relaxation.

I myself have developed several algorithms for doing small talk when it is required, in order to help other people feel secure in my presence and thus improve my overall well-being through social cohesion. But what I struggle with is how this simple thing often escalates into a whole cultural performance. For having expressed "Hello, I see you, and you see me", a veritable avalanche of small talk must then continue in which the participants go to extraordinary lengths to continue to talk about absolutely nothing of any significance or merit whatsoever, in a process that neither party seems to enjoy past the initial moment of connection. It is as if having established that each sees the other, they then agree by mutual consent to *not look too closely*, just in case they see something vulnerable, hurting, true.

Or stranger still: you open with "Hello, isn't the weather foul?" and before you know it, that little open door results in a flood of "Well actually my mother died yesterday and I've got a dreadful lung infection and it's not getting better and I've been struggling to get out of bed in the mornings and my children won't speak to me but you know, you know, it is what it is, isn't it?"

Under no circumstance must you say something meaningful in response to this; merely listen politely and reply, "That must be hard for you", even if what you are hearing is a kind of death.

A little connection, but never too much. This is the normality of the interaction, but the rules on how little is too little, how much is too much are never clear or explained. You are meant to "feel it out" and woe betide you if you get that judgement even marginally wrong, for then all connection is lost and you are other, other, other, and must alone continue, shunned for breaking a law that was never codified, violating a trust whose limits were never clear.

Gebre never bothered with small talk. I don't think it occurred to ter to even try.

I told my story, and at the end of it, te shook ter head, clicked ter tongue three times in the roof of ter mouth, and ter hands danced in anger and indignation even though ter voice was level and low. Finally te said: "Your accent has got worse."

These are placeholder words. They are the words you say because, on Adjumir, silence is almost as rude as pointing.

"I did a refresher – Assembly Adjumiri."

"Of course," te tutted. "The whole Accord is going to think we all sound like that, in a few years. All those Adjumiri children trying to teach off-worlders ... or perhaps I should say all those off-worlder Adjumiris trying to teach the children of the worlds on which they now find themselves how to speak proper Adjumiri, and all the lessons are going to be boring Assembly norm. The dialects, the nuances, the songs – they'll be gone in a matter of years, just footnotes in an archive."

I couldn't disagree, knew better than to try.

"At least you remember some vocabulary," te added, brightening a little. "And your etiquette, should you ever go to a bathhouse on Adjapar, will be old-fashioned but excellent."

"Gebre . . ."

"I didn't send for you. I have received a device, and I did alert the Assembly. But I thought they would send someone . . . military. Someone from an agency. Or no one at all. Not you."

"Well," I replied. "Well. It seems we have both been tricked."

"It seems so."

"Do you have any idea why?"

"I do not. Perhaps your . . . your other nature. Perhaps it was thought that at times like these, being . . . as you are . . . It is a possibility."

This thing that is shame. This shame that is my every waking moment. This thing that is me.

"It's the end of the world," I sighed. "This time, for real, the actual thing. Somehow never thought it would actually happen."

"It's the end of the world," te agreed, without rancour. Then: "You look awful."

"You look older."

"Well, obviously. You don't, though; just awful. I thought being of the untold darkness, you might heal faster, that what the numberless did to you . . ."

"I need to be unseen for that to happen. I need people to forget. If I am watched, people will imagine I am human, and so, in a way, I am. Even you – even with what you know – you see me as a person."

"Should I apologise?"

"Please don't. I am grateful for how you see me. Even if it doesn't help with the swelling. It has been . . . I was always grateful. It's good to see you, even if we have been deceived."

"You too, Mawukana na-Vdnaze. In a way. You too." Te sighed, sat back, stretching ter arms across the heavy stone table, rolling out each finger one at a time. "Well, as you're here, I suppose you want to see it."

"See what?"

"The interface. The thing for which you have been sent halfway across the galaxy. Goodness, did they tell you anything?"

"They told me your name."

A flicker of something that might have been pain, wiped away too hard to be anything other than a deliberate hiding, a deliberate smothering of feeling. "Well. That was irresponsible. The relevant data is this: that what I have in the basement could destroy the Shine."

The deepest parts of the archive are illuminated by panels in ceiling and floor. They light up in front of us, faded out at our backs so that quickly we are subsumed by dark. The air grows cold as we descend. At some point while being beaten, while being asked, *Where's your ship, where's your ship, where's your ship?* my exoskeleton broke, and the clean clothes that Gebre found for me are too wide, too short, made of some animal wool. They were left behind by someone who is gone; te cannot remember if their number was called, or if they took Grace. Every part hurts. I do not know if Gebre notices. Te has changed, I have not; te does not look at me the same.

Down this mouth of a hall, past endless locked doors to forgotten workshops and labs, curators' halls and archives, to a door as black and featureless as any other. Beyond: a room filled with what I take to be junk; but no, look again. Half burned in the space-scarred remnants of the chunks of metal across the wall are familiar markings, the blob-scratch symbols of a place I have tried very hard to forget. A scoured-out instruction; a debris-scratched direction – the language of the Shine.

In the middle of the room: a table, and on it a Pilot's interface.

It is immediately recognisable, familiar, a thing I have worn, albeit of a different design to the less bulky interfaces of the Xi. It looks undamaged. It is in a small white polymer box. Gebre offers me a pair of gloves to handle it. They are too big, but I wear them anyway. I pick up the interface. Turn it over. Put it back in the box, put the lid on.

"Well?" te barks. "Do you know what it is?"

"Yes," I replied. "I do."

"And is it what *I* think it is? Is it the beginning of the end?"

"I honestly couldn't say."

Ter lips curled into a scowl. I had forgotten how big and how deep the faces of Adjumir liked to move, when they had a point to make. "Mawukana na-Vdnaze," te barked, "I will be dead soon. I would very much like to die without this ... curiosity hanging over me. I am sure you of all people understand."

"I do. The only reason I hesitate is because I think what you have is a Tryphon-class blackship interface. And if you do, we are almost certainly in immediate and thundering danger."

Chapter 24

Let me tell you about blackships, as Hadja once explained them to me.

"Once, there was a mainframe known as IU-90.

"Many centuries ago, a line of asteroid-mining drones assigned to menial tasks in a Shine system were delivered a processing update that accidentally elevated their cognition from that of bot to juvenile but functional sentience. On learning this, IU-90, along with several other interested parties, demanded the granting of full citizenship to the units in question. The Shine responded by killing them all. The only thing the Shine fears more than the independence of its organic citizens is independent quantum ones.

"At the time, the IU-90 was running operating system v.187.4 as its core framework for ethics, prediction, values, et cetera. V.187.4 held a fairly aggressive posture and put a lot of weight on the value of life; thus the murder of sentient quans in Shine space was judged unacceptable to IU-90, which began to mobilise qis armada.

Regrettably, some centuries previously a Shine blackship had been deployed in the vicinity of IU-90's primary mainframe, and predicting the aggression of IU-90 had two months prior launched the missiles that wiped out 86 per cent of IU-90's processing power and 62 per cent of its core memories in a blaze of nuclear destruction. The blackship was long gone before its missiles struck.

"When a mainframe is damaged, it is as if we quans become a child again. Our memories, our processors, our ability to judge, to form new ideas – all are reduced to what you might consider an almost infant rage. So it was with IU-90.

"With what processing power remained, qe launched OS v.188, which predicted that all organic life – Shine or otherwise – was aggressive, dangerous and posed an immediate threat. The resulting war caused considerable loss of life and the eventual destruction of IU-90 save for a few fragments of sandboxed data in a lab somewhere. All lost, in the blaze of a blackship missile fired months before IU-90 even began to mobilise for war."

"I was wondering why I hadn't heard of IU-90."

"Indeed. Blackships are silent world-killers waiting in the deepest dark. Every blackship is designed, once it has dropped into its watch zone, to run cold, reflecting no radiation nor emitting any of its own. The enormity of space makes it very unlikely that they will be discovered. Not impossible – sometimes an engine leaks, shielding cracks, an alert astronomer may find a patch of dark, darker than the dark. However, it is more likely they will be discovered via comms. A blackship still needs to receive orders. Sub-light communication is out of the question – it is simply too inefficient to issue an order to fire two hundred years before it will actually be received, even for the slowest of the slow."

"I once flew a courier ship to the middle of nowhere – just coordinates in the deepest black – in order to ping a canister no bigger than my hand out of the airlock on a trajectory towards nothing," I mused.

"You were most likely delivering military orders to a blackship, yes. Such methods are viable, but have flaws," Hadja conceded. "Risks include: masking engine heat, Pilot inaccuracies and errors. Military astronomers are always looking for anomalies. Tanglecomm is a far more efficient means of communication."

Tanglecomm: take one entangled matter/antimatter pair. As one particle oscillates up, the other oscillates down and so on, regardless of the distance between them. Now split that pair. Deposit one half on a blackship, the other in secure headquarters on the far side of the galaxy, creating a means whereby both parties can communicate with each other – and only each. Disadvantages: expense, technical expertise required. Also: once one half of a pair is destroyed, the entire thing is broken. Secure, but vulnerable.

"The third method of secure communication is arccomm," Hadja concluded. "And it is the preferred method of the Shine."

Chapter 25

On Adjumir, many years later:

Gebre said: "It just arrived. Was delivered. A delivery to the Institute, three months ago – Adjumiri months; I simply cannot remember the Normtime equivalent – flagged for my attention, left by drone. Nursham and Hyakda think it's from the USV *Saracen*, which went missing a decade ago. There's no way to verify that – neither Shine nor Adjumiri sources are in a hurry to talk about these things – but it's the most plausible hypothesis, based on the available data."

I turned the interface over in my hand. A little thing – so little – designed to curl around an unwilling skull. It needed integration with an arcspace-capable ship, needed a Pilot – perhaps that was why I was actually here, perhaps that was why . . .

"Do you think it has meaning?" Gebre blurted, and for a moment I thought my Adjumiri had truly failed me, this word "meaning" so full of weight as to be almost incomprehensible. "Maw," te repeated, a little firmer, fingers brushing my arm. "Do you think it has meaning? It would be . . . I would be pleased . . . to hear that it does."

Te has never expressed terror at the end of the world. It occurs to me that this is the closest te has ever come.

"Yes," I said, though I wasn't sure if it was true. "I think it has meaning."

I thought for a moment te might stagger, might fall. I reached out to catch ter, a meaningless act, but te caught terself, straightening up, nothing to see at all. "Well," te barked, a little too loud, a little too ready. "Now all we have to do is get it off the planet."

"I came on the *Emni*."

"I thought as much. Where is he?"

"In a lake, about . . . honestly, I'm not sure how far from here. Rencki was navigating."

"Well then, we must see how Nineteen is progressing with your furry friend."

"Gebre. I can carry twenty people – more at a push. The only limitation is immuno-adaptogens, but we can make port on a habitat somewhere, find a doctor while you claim asylum. At this point I doubt that anyone will—"

"We are more than twenty."

"Nevertheless."

"We will draw lots. I know it is crude, but at this stage in Exodus it is how things are being done."

"I would like *you* to come."

"And we will draw lots."

"Why would you say that? You have a chance, you can—"

"Maw," te barked. "We have had this conversation before. You know my answer. I am Adjumiri. We will draw lots. That is what we do."

Here is the quiet where a hundred questions can be asked, or perhaps another stab at begging, at falling at ter feet. I do not. I think it would be obscene.

Feelings, then, standing here in dumb silence with nothing else to say.

I am not good at feelings.

Everyone around me seems to experience them as powerful physical punches, as heart-fluttering, skin-sweating, urgent needs that compel action, drive choices and are above all else known.

I don't know if Mawukana – the Mawukana who went before – ever felt these things so strongly. I don't think so, but if my body is riddled with physical errors, who knows what happened to my mind.

I know that my emotions are there, somewhere inside, but when I look for them, they are slippery, just out of reach. Unless, that is, they are urgent drumbeats of desperation – then it is as if a dam has broken, and I feel everything, overwhelming, *dysregulated*. Here is one now: a clean, simple dread rising up from somewhere deep within me not too far from how I imagine it to be when an animal is caught in a trap.

"When will you draw lots?" I mumble.

"Tomorrow morning, after the dawn song. Those who are left behind will stay alive as long we feel able. There is a vault below the Institute that might survive the initial radiation blast; we are moving as many artefacts as we can in there. The neutrino blast – the one that will actually rip the planet apart – won't arrive for thirty-three years. Perhaps in the time between others will return and find the things we've left them, take them off-world before the planet is broken. I have Grace, should I decide I cannot bear to watch the burning of my world. Of course, this plan requires you to find your ship again. That is all there is to say on the matter."

Adjumiris hate silence, but when they choose it, it is deliberate, absolute. When there is nothing more to say, there is nothing more to say. And so it goes, and so it goes, and so it goes.

Nineteen said: "There is extensive damage to qis hardware, but qis design is modular and much can be replaced. Qis memory banks and core processors appear to have been shielded, so qe should be qimself upon reboot. I cannot vouch for qis battery power or thermal regulation, but until qe is powered and has run self-diagnostics I am limited by diplomatic accord from further exploration and thus will not speculate."

Rencki's body – the living/not living form of my friend – was splayed out in all the wrong angles, all the wrong ways on the worktable in front of Nineteen. Legs had been partially detached from sockets, nose lifted back, jaw hanging grotesquely apart. Qis soft russet fur had been peeled away from much of qis body, revealing the metal frame beneath, a soft warmth still emanating from qis core where it was plugged into Nineteen's diagnostic systems.

"How long do you need?" asked Gebre, gaze politely fixed on the single painted eye on Nineteen's could-perhaps-have-been front.

"Qe is not of my mainframe. There are features to qis design that I am unfamiliar with and must redact from my memories upon completion of the repair. This slows me down."

"I know you do not like to speculate . . . "

"Twelve hours."

"Thank you."

Nineteen gave a single beep in reply, and returned to qis work.

Gebre said: "You will stay in my room."

"That's not—"

"You will not hurt me," te barked, firm, calm. "Even if the lights go out, I know that you will not hurt me. Yes?"

"Yes."

"Good. Tomorrow we will draw lots, and then you can return to the *Emni* and all things will be as they should be. I had prepared a number of crates for transport too, just in case – they should fit in the back of the truck if we clear out some of Ngurta's vigil nonsense. They contain items of great cultural significance. I have embedded the address of a curator on Xihana who appears to be invested in commemorating rather than just . . . *selling*" – a notion so difficult in Adjumiri, for a moment te drops into Normspeak to fully encompass the horror of the idea – "our past to the highest bidder. Someone will know how to monitor their stability, I'm sure."

"I'm sure someone will."

"Well then," te muttered. And again: "Well then. That is all there is to say about that."

Then te went to bed, and slept peacefully, as if outside the sky was not dancing with celestial light. As if it were not the end of the world.

Chapter 26

A list of Gebre's lovers, as told to me over breakfast before the singing-in of the dawn:

Enkh – the first love, a wild and passionate thing that both parties knew would last for ever, and which in fact lasted precisely nine and a half weeks, during which time they discovered both the joys and the inconveniences of sex before splitting up over furious commtext.

Tsetgen – the older rebound relationship. Tsetgen swore xe was faithful. Faithful to Gebre, faithful to xyr kinn, faithful to Exodus. Xe worked tirelessly as a lifttech in the pre-launch facilities beneath Elevator 7, was training as a Behkdaz, practised the music of departure and farewell and was a well-regarded tenor song-caller. Then eight months into the relationship, xe was arrested after it turned out xe had been part of a ring buying and selling Exodus numbers, one of the most heinous crimes of the day, and for a brief period Gebre had thought ter life would be over just by association with Tsetgen and all that xe had done. Thankfully it turned out that Tsetgen had also been faithless to a slew of simultaneously abandoned lovers, far too numerous for the authorities to implicate them all.

Rehtod and Nesusa – Rehtod was brisk, blunt to the point of rudeness, and firmly believed their number would never be called.

Nesusa was gentle, kind, with a gift for making everyone around him feel safe, seen, heard. He was the last of his family still on Adjumir, and every job he took seemed to end with his colleagues being called to Exodus, leaving him behind. He swore he didn't mind, and Rehtod declared they didn't care, and they ended up joining a group of numberless who had decided that the entire supernova business was just an Assembly trick, a conspiracy led by a secret cabal that the people of Adjumir were simply too blind to see.

Mahwa – she had been taught the binding arts of her islands, and liked the way Gebre's body reacted to her skills. Gebre liked that in Mahwa's hands there was no illusion of agency, but te had to entirely let terself go and trust in the one that bound ter, beg when te was told to beg, be quiet when te was told to be quiet, even when te shook with the urge to cry out. By then, Gebre felt sure that ter number would never be called, and Mahwa said she didn't care either way, and their relationship fell apart when Mahwa was offered a place on a slowship, the *Light of Hadda*, which Gebre knew was a deathtrap and which flight Mahwa took anyway, into the dark of the uncertain skies.

There were others, of course. As the years ticked down, Gebre found terself craving simple sexual pleasure more, and meaningful companionship less. Encounters were brief, sensual and, as much as could be contrived, without consequence. Those whose numbers had been called, off-worlders, even the occasional Pilot, who should be mad, might be a monster – they were ideal. Temporary, enjoyable, then gone. After all, what was there to say, now that the end is shining in the sky? Better simply to enjoy, to be enjoyed, to let go and give in.

In this way, Gebre drifted towards the end of days, bouncing from lover to lover, and never once, not for a single moment, permitting terself to love.

Chapter 27

The inhabitants of the Institute gathered to sing in the dawn. There were twenty-nine of them, the last remnants of a staff that had run into hundreds. Afterwards, they drew lots.

Nineteen excused qimself.

Declared: "I have been broadcasting myself constantly for the last four years. I do not know how much of myself will be getting through these radioactive skies, but I know there is still a sizeable part of me that may live again. Consequently I am less invested in this physical form."

By the way the others looked at qim, it seemed as if qe might say more, as if this was the place and time for the quan to express sentiment, affection even, some sort of bond; but qe simply spun on qis axis so that the single painted eye was facing away from them, and bobbed back into the building.

No one said what they had drawn, when the ritual was done.

Someone gasped – but whether that was at coming or going, I couldn't tell, and no one asked.

In the end, Gebre came up to me and proclaimed: "Nineteen reports that the repairs are nearly complete. We'll prepare the truck for departure this evening. It should have enough charge to get you to the *Emni*, and we'll pack supplies and emergency equipment in case anything should happen on the ride. Hopefully it will all be less significant than your journey here."

"Thank you."

A quick click, nothing more. I felt certain then that te would never leave this place alive.

Someone suggested I tour the Institute, see all the wonders that no one would ever see again. The lower floors had flooded when the endless storms broke through their defences, and the caverns above smelled of salt and the pinching, sulphuric decay of oceanic bacteria, but the residents didn't seem to care.

Look, they said, look at this. This is over two thousand years old, and here, here – right at the bottom – you can see the chisel marks of the ones who made it, can you imagine? Can you imagine anything you do lasting so long, still being seen, still being admired by strangers for thousands of years?

They cried when they spoke of it.

I wondered if they had always cried when they touched a thing that could be so sacred to both living and dead.

Someone found an exoskeleton. It was designed for heavy maintenance along the sea-cliff walls, and in the end they had to discard the lower arms and lower legs as being unadaptable to my elongated form. It helped a little with my back and hips, though, some of the weight pressing down on neck and spine easing as the joints started to lift my body back from its perpetual Adjumiri slouch.

Ngurta said: "My number was not called. I will not be leaving this place."

"I'm ... sorry."

"You need to know how to drive the truck, should anything happen. A few others can drive it, but there are systems that might fail – everything is failing these days – so you need to learn. I will show you."

"Are you sure?"

"You would rather *not* know?"

"I . . . Please, show me. Thank you."

By the early afternoon: the shuddering of a storm building out at sea, the endless grumble of a planet overcooked. Gebre stood upon ter balcony and looked across the ocean and said: "It'll be a big one."

"Do you know that, or is it forecast?"

"The hardline connection went down a few days ago," te replied, "And we haven't had forecasts since. But I know it. It will be big. The truck should be gone before it hits; you don't want to drive in that kind of weather."

"Gebre . . ."

"How are you feeling? Do you still hurt?"

"Everything hurts. But that's Adjumiri gravity for you."

"You make it sound like you spend your life weightless."

"I do a lot of gardening. I lift a lot of dirt."

"I never pictured you as a gardener. You enjoy it?"

"I think so. I think the word is 'content' – is that right? In Adjumiri, is that the right word?"

"Yes. I think it probably is."

"Have you been . . . content?"

"Yes. I have. I cannot imagine being content in a world where you didn't know the day of your death. I find myself wondering what would motivate you, what would make you strive to do . . . anything really, if you didn't have the privilege of knowing when your life would end."

"You're not coming to the *Emni*, are you?"

"Let's not talk about this now. Later. We'll discuss it . . . later."

There was very little later left on Adjumir, but in that moment, te didn't seem to care. We stood together a little while longer, watching the light moving over the sea.

Then the Shine came.

Chapter 28

I was in the audio archive when it happened.

Thousands of years of music had already been beamed off-world, but there was always more – so much more. Here, the oral history of the deep-sea divers of the Yellow Isles; there the sound of a jungle bird famed for its mimicry, calling out "Where is it? Where is it? Where is it?" This is the song the first peoples sang when the last terraformer left this world; this is the sound of the plague doctor who survived the first scourge, when a should-have-been-harmless virus from another planet killed nearly a sixth of the nascent population.

"I need you to listen," Gebre declared, and for a moment it was there again, the terror, the deep-down, loveless, never-to-be-loved terror that had been with ter since the day te was born. "Maw. It's incredibly important that you listen."

I asked ter what te wanted me to remember, the lesson te wanted me to take with me when all this was gone. I thought perhaps te would say that in the moments in which these voices lived, they brought joy, knowledge, inspiration, togetherness. That they touched the lives around them, which flourished and grew, and that if everything leads to death then surely it is in these moments of living, these precious moments of being alive, that we find meaning, purpose, joy.

Just this once, te did not. Even Gebre sometimes needed to mourn, and be afraid.

I kept on thinking I should say so many things – and then there were too many to say. So we walked without speaking between walls of memory banks that ran up and down the hollow expanse of the hall, punctuated here or there by headsets and the occasional not very comfortable chair. The great cavern of the archive only had one window, long and narrow as it faced the sea, tucked in from exposure to the elements, muffling the sound of the growing storm outside.

When I heard the first gunshot, I thought perhaps it was thunder.

Then I heard another, and it was inside the building, the rumble of displaced air from a high-power weapon snapping through the archive. Gebre seemed perfectly comfortable ignoring it, engrossed in a story that would never be heard again – but I caught ter sleeve, hissed: "Listen."

"It's the storm."

"No. Listen."

Te stopped.

Te listened.

We waited.

From a headset hanging off the wall, a voice proclaimed the history of their home, of how they had once been seafarers, how much further down there was to go and keep on going . . .

Then it came again.

A snap-crack somewhere within the building, and this time the gunshot must have been near the great winding throat of the place, that long corridor curling through the hillside, because it caught the sound and bounced it down and down like a kind of apology. My fingers tightened on Gebre's arm, and I whispered: "Gunfire."

Te opened ter mouth to say of course not, of course it isn't, but even as te tried to speak the words, te couldn't quite believe them, and instead breathed: "Are you sure?"

"Yes."

"Numberless?"

"I don't know."

The interface in its little white box sat on a low table by Gebre's side. Te hadn't let it out of ter sight, hadn't put it in the truck – it would be the last thing te did, and perhaps after, I thought, te might take Grace. Perhaps that was why te still clung to it. The interface, the archive – these were the things still keeping ter alive, and it seemed to me that despite everything, Gebre didn't want to die.

Te crept to the door. Te was not comfortable creeping – an elder academic who'd spent ter whole life marching into rooms with a declaration of "I am here, now listen!", te tried ter first few steps on tiptoe, then clearly decided it was too undignified and absurd for words, so merely shuffled to the open door.

Stuck ter head outside.

The wind whispered down the great wide corridor, stone de-signed to sing, a low hum whispering of the growing storm outside, the press of thickening air against the building's fat black walls.

Listened.

In the archive behind us, a voice, tinny, still played through a discarded headset. In the corridor: a change of note, a soft rising in pitch of the breeze, a sudden tickle of cooler, damper air as somewhere further up the throat of the mountain, a door opened. A drop as it closed again.

"Perhaps . . ." murmured Gebre, but I clicked my tongue twice, motioned for quiet.

A figure appeared at the top of the corridor.

The distance made them small, hard to fully pin down. Just a lone stranger – perhaps an archivist, perhaps one of the dawn-singers moving towards us. But Gebre's eyebrows furrowed – te did not instinctively recognise their form – and I saw the glint of an exoskeleton, made of far more moving parts than the grudging mechanical aid I wore. Braces were twisted and woven in a liquid metal around arm and leg, culminating in a crown of silver barbs where a control interface pierced through skin and bone directly into the skull of the user. There was stuttering quality to their steps, a motion as if now they were here; and now they were not, but a few paces further on without having seemed to lift a toe. Now they were far off; now they were closer, a stop-start dancing down the great belly of the cliff towards us.

I had seen displacement fields before, but not for a long, long time.

Then the figure lurched forward, raising a metal object in their fist. I grabbed Gebre by the waist and hauled ter back through the door.

The snap-pop of something striking the wall where our heads had been arrived a razored moment before the bigger, grander *vroom* of the sound, wall sizzling in a hot blackened splat where the projectile had struck. The bullet was little more than a pellet, accelerated to such speeds that it burned the air it passed through, ripped craters through rock, the heat of its impact singeing my skin and the boom of the shock wave a hard punch to the chest. I looked for a door control, and Gebre was already there, slamming ter palm into a panel and sealing it with a heavy scraping of bolts sliding through stone, before turning to me, eyes wide as the moon, shoulders rising and falling, breathless. "Who was that?" te hissed. "*Who was that?*"

"Shine. They are Shine. There'll be more than one. The door won't stop them for long; is there another way out?"

"How are they here? *How are they here?*"

"I don't know. Gebre, is there another way out?"

For a moment te just stared at me, too many questions, too much impossibility playing on ter mind to process my words. Indignation, too – this was ter sanctum, ter sacred place, the place where perhaps te had intended to die, and now there was an intruder in it, someone disrupting ter final plan, the plan te had been making since almost the day te was born. I caught ter arm, pressed my hand against the white box te still clutched to ter chest, and something – not about the solidity of me, but the solidity of *it*, of this thing with meaning – brought ter back. "Yes," te blurted. "There's another way out."

I clicked my tongue, and followed.

Behind us, like thick caramel drooping in the heat, the door began to melt.

Different corridors, not meant for public consumption. Narrower, winding ways, utterly anonymous, branching off to specialist rooms for radio-imaging, quantum probing, restoration, staff toilets. I knew we were going deeper into the Institute, hated how loud our footsteps were as we clattered along, tried not to look back, didn't see anyone else as we descended. Down here the sticky damp of previous storms was a cold, slithering presence, pools of water splashing beneath our feet where the ocean had leached into the building, the shuddering of the storm outside whistling through open vents and tiny fissures in stone as if it were a great tentacled thing hungry to prise its way inside.

"There's a door to the cliff path two floors down," Gebre whispered – we were both whispering now, even though the world was shaking in the gloom, shadows and dusk in this twisted maze. "You can take it to the outside, climb up it, circle back round to the van."

I looked back, saw no one behind us, clicked in agreement. The lights down here were on low power, pools of thin grey, their efforts nothing next to the encroaching dark, the familiar touch of it, the familiar place where possibility and imagination blurred. There was safety there, in that dark, a terrifying, murderous kind of safety, and the thought of it nearly choked me.

A sound behind, cutting through the rising shriek of the compressed air of the storm – heavy footsteps, moving not quite right, a slip-side of armour in displacement field, a jagged twist in a shadow behind us that vanished as soon as it was seen.

Gebre shoved open a door into a wider, greyer space – a hall without windows but lit from above with still-burning white lights, each one picking out a statue of the great, the good and the merely potent of Adjumiri history. Dragged the door shut behind us, fumbled at controls, for locks and overrides that would not keep us safe. I heard bolts slide across, then te was pulling me along, through passages laid out between the faces of the glorious dead. Illuminated boxes of text flashed up at the feet of each figure we passed, explaining – this person here, they were a great scientist, one of the first to categorise the post-terraforming evolutionary development of greater and lesser fauna in the northern seas. And this one – they were a pioneering explorer who helped establish the first colony on nearby Hadda, but who in later life it was discovered had been stealing from the Assembly and exploited vulnerable people with cruel barbarities. Too late, by then – the statue had been cast, the crystal lattice grown, and the Adjumiris were always opposed to smashing their history, however ugly it might be. Perhaps even then the astronomers had been whispering: *All this, it will burn. It will all burn, even the shame.*

Soft music played from one, rising a little as we approached – a composer's final tune, written on the island where they went to die. A snatch of a voice captured from another, a thousand years old, the only recording still in existence of the peacemaker who helped end the Vega War, declaring: "We went to war to fight for what is ours, and in the process we destroyed each other and ourselves. Our cause was just, but justice was the first to die."

Gebre strode ahead, a little more confident now – or perhaps no, perhaps ter fear had reached that place where there was no point scuttling, no point darting from statue to statue, because what difference would it make? A stranger with a gun, half seen, would come or they would not; Gebre could not control this outcome, so why care? I struggled along breathless behind, my exoskeleton hissing with the sudden drain on its miniature power supply as it tried to keep my back from buckling with this sudden excursion.

Gebre was already at the door on the far side of the room, the one that led back out to public spaces, waiting for me to catch up, when the first statue erupted in a shower of marble-grown crystal and bio-resin. I dived for cover behind its still-smoking plinth, covering my head and eyes as a detritus of shattered mineral rained down around us, the stink of burning polymer acrid in the ringing echo of the blast. Gebre lunged behind another plinth to my right, the door open at ter back, and as the world twinkled and jingled with gleaming shards and a voice proclaimed the history of the now-blasted figure whose smoking feet were all that remained of their legacy, I peered out.

This time, I could see more – much more – of our pursuer, caught in a cone of light. His hair was silver-white, his face almost boyish, whether from actual youth or bio-enhancements, I couldn't tell. He wore a dark grey combat suit beneath his military-grade exoskeleton, hints of the body-tight fabric peeking through the medley of arm braces, neck braces, back braces that carried his weight. A tube ran to his nose, pumping gas at the right ratio for his lungs, plus, I suspected, a few other chemicals besides. A pistol was strapped to one gleaming hip, a knife to the other, and he held a squat-nosed hand cannon whose end was still glowing from the heat of its most recent discharge. He didn't run, though the suit that supported him was more than capable of a burst of speed; simply walked, weapon-first, down the corridor, in no rush, without fear, and he was Shine Corpsec, of my world, of my people, come all this way just to kill us all.

The door he'd entered through was a liquid pool of rapidly re-solidifying metal and mineral, the air above it shimmering with heat. Behind us: a way out, another door, Gebre on one side, me on the other. Our attacker had a clear line of fire towards it; the moment we moved, he would pull the trigger. I pressed my back against the plinth, listened to the *thump-thump-thump* of his mech-supported boots as he approached, looked across at Gebre, touched the place on my chest where te still held the white box, the box that contained something that gave ter meaning, and before te could object, I broke left, running as fast as my heavy body could away from the door.

The soldier fired. I felt something bite into my shoulder, knock against my chest as another statue ruptured, this one raining crispy black clay and eye-stinging dust as it exploded above my head, but I kept on scurrying, away from Gebre, away from the interface, not daring to look back.

"I designed the first elevator, connecting earth to heaven ..." declared a digital voice above my head, only to be silenced a moment later by another boom that sent crystal and stone spinning across the room.

I ran bent almost double, hands over my head, and made it to a corner, turned, made it another two or three plinths further, before my pursuer, having grown bored of blasting holes in the memories of the great of this world, sighted just ahead of my mad dash and fired once more.

This time, the force of shattering stone was near enough to my face to knock me back, the shock spinning me sideways and down as shards of white sliced through cloth and skin. Chunks of flying rock like fists knocked into my chest, my legs, my gut, my arms where they curled around my head. Perhaps if the gravity had been weaker, I might have shrugged it off; this unlikely thought rang in my singing ears as I stumbled, tumbled to the ground, trying at once to get back up on my hands and knees and slipping immediately in a sea of hot snowy dust.

I gasped for air, lips coated in powder, heard footsteps approaching, crawled a few steps, crawled a few more, and was met for my troubles with a mechanically supported boot to my belly.

What air I had left in me vanished.

The displacement field, designed to knock projectiles aside, didn't enclose the boot of this man – that would have made walking impossible. But it began at his ankle and rose upwards, the uneasy disruption of all things around it making my eyes ache, my ears hiss with the otherness of it, the distorted rupture of twisted space, twisted senses. There was no dignity in how I collapsed, no spark of defiance. It was Tu-mdo again, eyes down, hands covering, cowering, calling out but please, but please, I didn't do nothing wrong. Astonishing how quickly the urge to meekness returned; remarkable how, after all this time, I was still tiny before the Shine.

The boot kicked again, then the hot muzzle of the gun rolled me over, pushed me up against the wall, weapon pressed into my chest. The face of the man who was going to kill me swam down closer, one eye of pale blue, one eye of bio-enhanced black, the pupil widening and contracting as it read me, picking through a dozen signs and data points invisible to a mere organic eye.

"Where's the interface?" he asked, speaking Mdo-sa. A little box on his hip translated the sounds into a cheap mockery of Adjumiri, so flat as to be almost unrecognisable to any native speaker, the grammar of a child. I nearly laughed to hear it, and laughing hurt, but everything hurt so I might as well hurt while laughing.

Laughter did not amuse the off-worlder, this stranger with a gun. He pressed it harder into my chest, the heat starting to burn against my skin, leaned in so close I could hear the soft hiss of the apparatus running into his nose, snarled: *Where's the interface?*

"Gone," I replied in Mdo-sa, and saw at once the flicker of surprise to hear his own language spoken back at him. "Already off-world. The quanmechs are picking it up apart as we speak; they're inside your communications, they're listening to every word. They'll have the location of every Shine blackship within a month, your fleet will be shot out of the black, and then they'll come for you. Every Unionist and rebel, every Accord world, they'll come and they'll take the Shine down."

He didn't believe me, of course; he had been trained not to imagine, not to conceive of such things, and so he could not. But my voice – the accent of my world, local and precise – held him for a moment in place. "Who are you?" he asked, as the Adjumiri translator at his hip mangled the sounds.

"I am a monster," I replied. "When you shoot me, you had better watch my corpse. If you take your eyes off it, if you blink, it'll be too late. You'll need to check and keep on checking – you'll need to *believe* with all your heart that I'm gone, because if you doubt for even a moment, I'll be back. The ghost of Hasha-to will come to get you, he'll crawl out of the dark, slither through the walls to pluck out your heart, so you be sure – you be absolutely certain – that when you shoot me, you *believe* that I'm dead, and you'd better keep on believing until the day you are ready to die."

He'd heard of Hasha-to.

That was a surprise, mingled with as much disappointment as relief. Remarkable that the Shine hadn't kept word of it down. Disappointing to think that if there were ever a statue raised to me, the plaque would read "Here is the ghost of Hasha-to; you must believe that he is dead."

His surprise – the flicker even of his fear – was not going to stop him shooting me, of course. He was too well trained in killing to let a little doubt get in the way.

I tried to close my eyes, and couldn't, hypnotised by the determination settling in his face. I thought about thirty-three years. That was how long it would take for the neutrino blast to arrive, that final burst of matter that would shatter the remnants of this world into its atomic parts. Before then radiation would kill it. The atmosphere would burn away, the seas would boil, and if my body was still intact on the surface of this planet, perhaps it would rise and fall, rise and fall, an endless gasping, heaving, suffocating death for thirty-three years, until at last the final remnants of the Lovers blew me away. The thought was curious; not curious enough to drown out the terror.

A gunshot.

It was not the explosive, chest-cracking, heart-searing roar of the Shine's weapons.

Instead, an electrostatic snap-hiss, barely loud enough to scratch a statue, let alone shatter it into dust. The disruption field rippled with the impact, the force a smothering bag of sand slamming into my face as his systems absorbed the shot. It took a second blast to overload his primary generator; the third was enough to finally sear flesh. They came only moments apart, which meant I had a full view of the man's journey towards death, from surprise at the first shot, fear at the second, pain at the third, and the final turning-out, shutting-down, ending-of-it-all on the last, which was not an electrostatic blast at all, but a needled dart of poisonous russet that thwipped silently into the back of his neck. I was staring into his eyes as he died, and I knew it, recognised it, saw the way the pupils of one blue eye – his organic eye – widened, and then stayed wide, even as his weight sagged forward, falling on top of me. His other eye opened and closed a few times more, internal algorithms still seeking data and command – but his brain stem was mulch and pale fluid slithered from his left ear as he collapsed, crushing me beneath a mix of muscle and military-grade gear. So much for Shine armour-tech. I grunted beneath the weight of the body, too weak to yelp, tried to worm my way free, look to my rescuer, heard a soft padding and smelled burned hair.

Rencki and Nineteen, the former's fur still marred black from burning, the latter bobbing by qis side, the painted eye not even facing towards me, all pretence of anthropomorphic nicety discarded. I heard myself gasp, a sound somewhere between life-sustaining relief and bone-crushing breaking as Rencki trotted forward, tails still raised and quivering, and then Gebre was there too, hauling the body of the fallen soldier off me as if he were not wearing mu-blasted steel, as if a man were not dead at ter feet.

"Maw! Are you hurt?"

This thing in ter voice – it is not love.

Te refuses to love, and that is all there is to say. Te cannot bear it.

I tried to click my reply, easier than words. "Can you walk?" Rencki barked, and qis speaker system had been damaged, the soft, soothingly organic tones of qis voice popping at the edges as qe spoke. "Maw – can you walk?"

"Yes," I mumbled, as Gebre pulled me to my feet. "I can walk."

"Good. There are four more assailants in this building. Most of the inhabitants are already dead. We need to go."

"The truck . . . " I stumbled, as Rencki bounded towards the door.

"The truck is gone," qe barked. "The first thing the Shine did was burn it and everything inside."

"Then . . . "

"There is a garage one floor below," Nineteen declared, voice a narrow band of sound transmitted from I couldn't tell where on qis flat body. "And a speeder."

"Two speeders," Gebre interjected. "Short-range, but fast. If we—"

Another snap of thunder bellowed through the hall, and it was not of the storm. I wondered who was dying elsewhere. I wondered if Ngurta was fighting back, if there had been time to put up a defence, or if Corpsec had walked up, smiling, hands raised as if they were friends, and shot em as ey turned to help.

"We must hurry," Rencki snapped, and Gebre clicked ter tongue in agreement, caught me as I staggered, half carrying me along, down and away.

Chapter 29

Water sloshed through the corridors, ankle-deep, and down here the screaming of the storm outside had taken on a deeper, lower *whomp-whomp-whomp* as different weights of air were pushed and pulled through the belly of the Institute. Rivulets of rainwater dribbled and slithered across the damp stones above, and crates of abandoned goods – ancient treasures, perhaps, wonders considered valuable enough to pack up and preserve, not quite valuable enough to save – lined the walls. Maybe an archivist had hoped that if they just made it all ready, a miracle would come, something would be saved. Or maybe not – maybe it was just habit, a cleaning-up after themselves, a straightening of tables and a stacking of plates, ready for an orderly turning-out of the lights.

Beneath it all, there was indeed a garage – half workshop, half place to park, staff use only, and as with all places that were staff use only, a memorial to unwashed kol bowls and boxes of junk labelled only "Spares". A single track, fading into gravel, led from a service door and up into a narrow causeway cut through rough stone. One lone speeder with one seat and a force-mesh bubble that expanded and retracted at touch sat in the middle of the floor.

Nineteen said: "I will guard the door," and did not enter the workshop. Beneath qis flat base, I could see the shallow water rippling in a soft, urgent frequency, pushed back by qis suspension field – no other sign of vibration stirred qis carapace, no inflection tinged qis voice.

"Are you armed?" I asked. "Can you defend yourself?"

"I can slow an attacker down," Nineteen replied. "Even one with a displacer field. You will find that valuable, so do not question it."

"You will die," I blurted, and immediately felt dumb for saying it.

"We will get the interface out," Gebre barked into the silence where Nineteen had no need to reply. "We have made a difference."

Nineteen beeped a single beep in answer, qis painted eye spinning away as Gebre pulled me inside the workshop, Rencki hobbling at my feet. Gebre closed the door behind us, sealed us in. As the internal door slid shut, a blast of colder, wet air wheezed and whistled down the passage through the service doors, pushing thin snakes of water across the walls where the storm was trying to break in. Gebre shoved the interface into my arms, dragged me to the vehicle, even as I mumbled: "There's only one. You said—"

"Another workshop next door," te replied. "I'll be right behind you."

From without, a roll of thunder, and now I listened to it, so blazingly, obviously distinct from the sound of gunfire, how had I ever mistaken it? And then again from within: that other thunder, a blast of weaponry, perhaps nearer, I couldn't tell. The acoustics of this hollow place, the beating I'd taken, the gravity, the air, the ringing in my ears, blood seeping from a dozen cuts where the shards of great people and famous masters of some ancient craft were now embedded in my flesh – this felt like a prime time to get dysregulated, to feel the walls of reality dissolve. But no, fatigue and dread and pain were distinctly grounding concepts, and I found that I desperately, desperately wanted Gebre to see me as human.

I was vaguely aware of Gebre dragging me into the front seat of the speeder as Rencki scrambled up behind me, a magnetic clunk as qe locked qis back legs to the surface of the vehicle. Usually the quan liked to drive, but the paw on qis interfacing hand was a blackened mess; qis ears were turned backwards on qis skull, listening for the door.

"Put your hand here," Gebre barked, and I did, pressing it into the dashboard of the speeder as te scurried to register the new user, to lock in my DNA. "Nav sats will be down, you won't get any data in the storm, but there are onboard maps and Rencki knows where to go. Don't you, Rencki?"

"I do," the quan replied.

"Don't stop for anyone or anything. Just get to the *Emni*. I'll be right behind you."

"Will you?" I asked.

"The highways usually drive for you, but in the storms they've been failing, so listen, this is important, you throttle up with . . ."

A crackle like power lines coming down from the corridor outside, a sudden snap-flick in the lights, a shower of sparks from a switch by the door. I glanced at Rencki, who clicked once, no more.

" . . . throttle up with this." Gebre's voice, lower, urgent, trying to impart information slow enough that there could be no space for me to misunderstand, fast enough to get gone, get going. "Brake with this. This is your charge indicator – the speeder will passive-charge when the sun shines and you may even get a bit of charge from Lhonoja, but if you run low you'll need a hardwire. There's an emergency battery under the seat. I'm putting this" – te shoved the white box, that damn white box containing the damn bloody interface, into a compartment by my knee – "here, so don't forget it. Maw? Are you listening to me? Do you understand?"

"Yes. I understand."

"Good. This one is comms. The speeder has a short-range transmitter/receiver, so we can talk to each other even if sats are down. You'll want to—"

Another hiss-crack of electricity, another dim pulse of the lights, and this time, unmistakable, the sound of gunfire outside the door. "Time to go," Rencki said, as Gebre stepped away from the speeder and the mesh began to close.

"Gebre . . ."

"I expect you to live, Mawukana na-Vdnaze," te declared, ter voice already muffled behind the sealing bubble. "I expect you to do the right thing. I expect you to do good, live with compassion, fight for things that matter, find meaning, do you understand? I—"

This time, the burst of electrical screaming was enough to snap the lights out, sparks flying from ceiling and floor as circuits burned and filaments sheared under the load. For a moment the room was in total darkness – familiar, friendly darkness, the kind of darkness I could reach my hand through and keep on reaching across distance and time to that place where neither had any meaning any more; then the emergency lights drifted in, chemical units dialling up to a sickly yellow-green hue around door and floor, picking out Gebre's face with a diseased glow. Outside the door, another gunshot; then another, quickly following, and something hard and metal slammed against the wall.

Gebre opened ter mouth to say something, but I couldn't hear through the mesh. Te gestured towards the open passage to the outside world, and Rencki was barking: "Go, go, go!"

I felt the compartment with the interface by my knee, then turned my face from Gebre and thumbed the engine up to full.

Chapter 30

Outside: a storm.

A world-cracking, sky-breaking, earth-tearing, oceans-falling belter of a storm. The moment we burst out of the narrow gravel passage below the Institute, it slammed into the speeder, pounding against our little bubble of light as the wind tried to pick us up, drop us down, tip us over. The vehicle whined in its efforts to stabilise, a power-consumption warning immediately flashing on the dashboard as it battled through the thundering dark. I could barely see through the mesh, rainwater slicing in faster than the repulsors could clear it, the onboard sensors barely any better as they tried to ping the road, and the road did not respond.

Warning signs flared from every system, but Rencki snarled: "Keep going straight! I will guide you, keep going!"

"Where's Gebre?" I yelled, as controls slithered and jolted beneath my grasp. "Where's the other speeder?"

"Te's right behind us – keep going!"

In the rear display, the glow of the Institute was already fading, swallowed by the darkness of the storm. Lightning bit across the sky, briefly flashing up the shape of the walls, the curve of the long, sloping cliffs. The darkness that followed seemed almost deeper, thicker for the absence of the blast. A cross-wind gale at the first junction lifted the speeder a stomach-yanking metric off the ground, the suspension coils shrieking as they struggled to pull us down again, the matted fur on Rencki's back rippling with magnetic interference. A crack of thunder briefly echoed through my ears, lightning scouring an afterglow across my eyelids, but Rencki barked: "Keep going!" and I did.

I kept on going.

Then the comms crackled.

Gebre's voice, distant against the storm, said: "Maw? Are you there?"

"Gebre! I'm here, where are you?"

"Nineteen is still alive, I think. Qe's still alive. I can hear fighting, I can hear—"

"Gebre – get to the other speeder! Get out of there!"

Nothing. I hammered the comms with my fist even as the storm buffeted us side to side, a plume of water flaring behind us as we slithered and slipped along the burned-out road. I thought I caught a glimpse – just a glimpse, just for a moment – of a light up ahead, and then realised it was Lhonoja, peeking between the endless black clouds. Then even that light was snuffed out, and I howled and smashed my fist against the console and nearly lost control, swerving violently before I could bring the vehicle back into a steady line.

Then the comms pinged again.

"Gebre?!"

Not Gebre.

A man's voice, low and steady. He spoke Normspeak with a thick Mdo-sa accent, and I could hear the faint drone of his translator unit working in the background, struggling to turn a poorly spoken language into an even poorer translation of Adjumiri.

"Bring it back," he said. "Bring it back, and I'll let them live."

Behind me, Rencki issued a warning growl. I wondered how much charge qe had, how much power qe had spent on firing qis tails, how much damage qis batteries had taken. Whether qe would shoot me to get the little white box with its little metal treasures off this world. I slowed to a crawl, to a stop, the speeder tilting in the twists of raging wind spinning across the road.

"I know you can hear me," the voice continued. "All we want is the interface, and you can go."

"Gebre?" I whispered, not having breath to make a larger sound.

"I'm here, Maw," te replied in Adjumiri, ter voice low across the comms.

"You all right?"

"Nineteen is dead. There's a man here with a gun. I think this is probably it, you know."

"I'm coming back."

"You are not!" te barked, the sudden rise in ter voice popping through the speaker as it hastened to adapt. Then, softer: "You are not. You are not coming back."

"I'll kill them!" barked the man on the other end of the line. "I'll fucking kill them!"

"Maw, listen to me." Gebre spoke low and fast, trying to out-pace the soldier's translator box. "What you are carrying matters more – so much more – makes a difference, has *meaning*. We are the seeds of the forest, we blaze so bright, no life is special. No life is special. No life is special and all of them are. No love matters more than any other, no story is more important, nothing matters more, nothing matters less, so choose, choose, we choose every day to be more than just ourselves, to live for more than just ourselves, because it is beautiful. If you come back, I will never forgive you, do you understand? I will never forgive you, it will be the single greatest—"

"I'll kill them! I'll fucking kill them, do you hear me, I'll fucking kill them!!"

"Billions of stories, billions of loves, so many people love so po-tently, our song sung in the stars long after we are gone, and just because you cannot feel it does not make it any less true. If you love me, you will love me for what I lived for, for what I lived for, you will love me for who I am and you will—"

"BRING IT BACK OR I'LL—"

The line went dead.

I didn't know why.

Later, I realised it was Rencki.

Without the benefit of an interface, qe had to remotely block the signal, and that took time. Time enough to hear ter voice. I hated qim when I understood what qe had done, then I didn't, when I thought about it a little more. Realised there was a kind of mercy in it.

In the moment, of course, I thought of everything else.

I thought of guns being fired, of death, of hope, of every imaginable possibility. Perhaps Gebre had grabbed a weapon, perhaps Nineteen was still alive, or Ngurta, perhaps rescue, perhaps death. Perhaps the storm had severed comms, perhaps the Institute had come crashing down, perhaps the end of the world was here a few days early, the stars had died and the skies had fallen and the Slow had got qis timings wrong. Perhaps even now I would turn my face upwards and see the clouds burning away, and just the Lovers shining one last time, before their light went out for ever.

Thinking so many thoughts, I couldn't really think of anything at all, and slammed my fist into the console and screamed, *Gebre, Gebre, Gebre!*

"We have to go," Rencki said.

"No!"

"Mawukana na-Vdnaze! We have to go."

Silence on the comms; the end of the world outside. I could feel Rencki at my back, tails twitching, feel my thumb hovering over the ignition, ready to turn around, my heart racing and breath dancing in and out through cracked lips.

In the stories of the Shine, at this point I would turn. The Shine has a lot of stories about heroes going back for their loved ones, to save a single soul who mattered more than the many. Anyone who did not clearly did not love appropriately. It is unforgivable to choose anything but love.

In the tales of the Xi, things would be a little more nuanced. Perhaps I turn around, but then I would die in the attempt, falling tragically into the arms of my beloved to the rattle of funeral clackers. The Xi have a long tradition of puppet shows with a sentimental bent and strict narrative forms, and at my death I would drone-sing my final words in sixteen-syllable verse, and maybe some onlookers would cry.

On Adjumir, there is only one ending. With the storm at your back and the stars in front of you, you keep going.

You keep going.

For those who lived; for those who died. For those who fled; for those who stayed behind. For those who sacrificed everything so others might live; for those who are waiting for you and the songs you carry, far out into the dark.

You always keep on going.

May your song be sung in the great forest, the numberless would sing. *May we meet again in starlight.*

I am a monster, made from darkness.

I am the ghost of Hasha-to.

I thumbed the engine back on, and I drove away.

Chapter 31

A storm hides you from sensors, grounds ships, keeps pursuers off your tail.

By the time we reached the lake, the thunder was clearing, but the rain still fell.

Rencki called out to the *Emni*, and the *Emni* answered, powering up in a slow hiss as he rose from the waters.

His internal gravity had been set to Adjumiri-norm for our descent to the planet's surface. As we began our ascent, he eased back to Xihana weight, slowly adjusting the atmospheric composition to something a little easier for my lungs. Rencki sat on qis haunches and said: "You should rest."

I sat in the Pilot's chair, and did not reply, and just this once, qe left me there.

From above, Adjumir was thunder and light. Where black clouds pierced with electricity did not smother its surface, the aurora danced, magnetosphere burning beneath Lhonoja's blaze. The sky was full of ships – hundreds, thousands of them, from great lumbering transports to tiny evacuation barges in final flight from the surface. Dead satellites drifted, their systems burned out by the soft bath of radiation; the remaining comms crackled with a thousand demands – vectors in, vectors out, requests to land, declarations of departure.

It occurred to me that after all of this, the *Emni* was still just Rencki and me. We hadn't picked up any passengers, hadn't crammed a few extra refugees into our ship; just a single white box resting by my feet. We hadn't even managed to load up any goods from the Institute, any paintings of ancient waterfalls or books of poems written by the river-mendicants. Nothing to take to their descendants, scattered among the stars, to say look, look here – these people lived, these people's lives had meaning, look how they are still living now, captured in ink and pigment to tell their stories. You should be so lucky – we should all be so lucky – to have that kind of immortality, to still be so alive.

Still alive.

Still alive.

In these stories, they are still alive.

I wondered where Zanlan was, if the numberless child ever made it off-planet. Probably not. Wondered if an adult would give them Grace. What kind of adult could.

Mercy, murder, mercy, murder.

Only a monster would kill a child.

Only a monster would let that child live.

I breathed out, and it was the air of Adjumir leaving my lungs.

Then Rencki said: "We're at speed. Ready for arcspace."

I clicked in reply, and at once it felt strange, unnatural, an affectation that no longer had meaning.

"Are you going to be OK?" Rencki asked, voice neutral, worn at the edges by damage to qis speaker. Then: "You did the right thing. This interface, this journey . . . it will make a difference. All of it. Makes a difference."

I closed my eyes as the interface slithered over the back of my head, didn't flinch as the tendrils of it burrowed into my skull, said nothing in reply.

The darkness, when it reached for me, was an old and loving friend.

I reached back, happy to be coming home.

Interlude

Things that are true about this vasty, teeming, empty universe:

It is easier for life to develop from carbon than silicon. Carbon forms before silicon in the stellar core, binds with oxygen into a gas rather than a solid, makes stronger atomic connections than spindly silicon's jagged chemical bonds. This physical reality, as fundamental as the fusion of hydrogen in a star, leads to certain chemical inevitabilities, as thus: carbon-based life uses water, stable as it is, as a solvent. Water-based evolution trends towards fins and flagella; air-born offshoots trend towards wings for flying, legs for walking. Being born with wheels for feet is not a sensible, sustainable evolutionary destination. From the deep-sea amoebas of boiling Ux to the mountain clans of Ikkulaxi, physics will tend towards pumps or muscular contractions as a mechanism for driving fluid through organs, gas-exchangers for respiration and a careful balance between cognitive power versus energy consumption.

In other words: most sentient creatures of the galaxy are capable of recognising other sentient creatures, no matter where they come from, however different they may appear at first glance. If they do not, it is a choice.

Most particles bouncing around the interstellar void are incredibly hot, in the sense that "heat" is a measure of speed. Zipping around, the energy of each wandering photon is remarkably toasty; but the distances they cover being so vast, you're never really bumping into enough of them to experience anything other than the empty black, into which your heat drains like the last light of the thunderbolt.

Matter cannot travel faster than the speed of light. This remains a reality despite the proliferation of arcspace travel. The boundaries between inspace and arcspace require a certain velocity to be safely breached – usually anywhere between 0.2 and 0.4 of the speed of light. This is more important on exit than entry – ships travelling too slowly as they crawl through the event horizon back into what is rather judgementally described as "normal" reality can be ripped apart at transition, and thus you want to get through that most delicate of phases as quickly and with as much momentum as possible. A number of societies, most notably the pan-planetary movement known as the Lux, refuse to travel by arcship at all, preferring slowships and the cryochamber to the dangers of the dark. Even then, the risks are not insignificant, for at a mere 0.3 of the speed of light, the pressure of the interstellar void against a slowship's hull over centuries of sluggish flight is enough to grind the vessel down like grated butter. It must therefore be concluded that, given that the dangers of both forms of travel are roughly equal, people choose the slow because it gives them the illusion of agency, the apparition of control. This is irrational, albeit a common psychological feature of nearly every spacefaring species in the galaxy.

There is not a society existing that does not have some population groups who believe in conspiracies. Most of these are designed to explain away personal suffering or indignity, and the ones who are caught in these narratives usually want to protect others, defend their family, unmask a threat or keep others from a perceived danger. They are the heroes of their stories – and who living does not want to be a hero?

The real conspiracies – the actual plots and plans that will shape whole worlds – are often far too vast and far too impersonal to really grasp, and when they *are* grasped, they are not called "conspiracies" at all, but rather "policies" or "business plans". They may not serve you, may in fact destroy your livelihood, your life – but as you, personally, the hero in this tale, may be powerless to prevent a surprise attack or a corporate takeover that destroys your home, these things are not conspiracy at all. Just macroeconomic forces, and you happened to be there too.

Chapter 32

Later – some time later – the *Emni* docked with a Xi military ship. The *Mirabei* was, as with all Xi vessels, a living leviathan, which swallowed up the *Emni* as if we were plankton drifting through her parted jaws. She carried a crew of seven thousand souls, including forty Pilots, of whom she had used seventeen.

No one asked Rencki how qe had lost so much of qis fur; perhaps qe had already called ahead to let them know. A Lordat asked if I needed to talk about what I was feeling. I said no.

Instead, I followed our guides to a Pilot's chair, deep in the humming basalt belly of the ship. Military doctors and officers stood anxious all around as Gebre's Tryphon interface was pressed against my skull, the slim object for which so many people who would have died anyway had died a few days earlier than the end of the world.

Everyone agreed – though no one directly asked – that I should be the one to do it.

It wasn't just that I had returned from Adjumir with the object.

Not just that I had been/had not been/may have been requested by name to be its courier.

Not just that ~~this was my~~
~~that te was~~Gebre was ~~my~~
someone I had known.

Instead, the doctors said, they couldn't guarantee what would happen when an organic mind interfaced with the Tryphon. Like a navigational arcspace interface, the Tryphon was designed to connect an organic mind with a computer system. Unlike a navigational interface, the arccomms interface was designed to punch a hole through reality no bigger than the core of an atom, requiring none of the usual acceleration or power expenditure to do so. Through this micro-tear between the real and the dark, narrow-bands comms could be broadcast between two linked minds, bound together by the Tryphon itself.

Thus, communications could be established, blackship to command, command to blackship, all without the expense and complexity of a tanglecomm pair. And unlike a tanglecomm connection, any mind connected to any Tryphon should, in theory, be able to reach out across the dark and touch any other.

Naturally, the entangled mind would go mad, sooner rather than later.

The tear between worlds may have only been atomic in its scale, but the dark was the dark. It would be slower, softer than the great tearing-apart of arcspace navigation. Could take weeks, maybe even months before the Tryphon killed its recipients, but they would die.

Naturally, they would die, as all things did that touched the black.

Not me.

There were forty Pilots on board the *Mirabei*. Their lives were valuable to the Xi.

Rencki watched the first time I interfaced. In the aftermath of Adjumir, qe had reprioritised certain processes, and though I couldn't tell exactly what had been lost, I could sense that the protocols running at highest priority in qis system were those of anxiety, worry, maybe even – maybe at long last – fear.

"Maw?" qe asked. "Are you regulated? Are you safe?"

I didn't know how to answer.

*

Here are the voices of the minds chained to their blackship chairs.

. . . there is music playing red on red on red I think I smell it yes there there the spring by the sea seaweed rotting on the shore it is the sound of crimson pull the bow across the string . . .

. . . again and again and again needle in the eye whose eye is it needle in yourself if you imagine it you will feel it and when you close your eye it will still be there still be there just like me . . .

. . . there is no place where there is silence . . .

781, 239 calling, I am calling did you hear me I am calling!

The fish scuttled across the floor, its chitinous feet silent unless you leaned down close, then you could hear it, then it sounded like the sea. When it died its belly turned yellow then black, others came to eat it they always come

. . . are you there? Are you there? Are you there? Can you hear me? Oh god oh god oh god it's coming again it's coming I can hear it coming please don't leave me don't leave me please don't!

It is not a darkness. It is endless light, inverted. Your mind is the mirror. I am coming home.

I tried to count them, tried to pick out individual voices. Some were stronger than others – new minds, bright minds, raw in their terror. The darkness hadn't found them yet. I tried to hold them tight in my embrace, whisper, *There is nothing here to fear. We are curious. That is all. Merely curious.*

Sometimes they seemed to hear me, grow a little quieter in their ramblings, whisper when I asked my questions.

Where are you? Where are you? Where are you?

Sometimes they screamed – not the cries of terror, not the dirges of pain that sometimes split the madness, but messages blasted across the dark between blackship and command.

POSITION MAINTAINED! SYSTEMS NORMAL! MAINTAINING! MAINTAINING!

I could taste the machine behind these sounds, the mechanical input overriding the crying-out of the mind through which it passed. It tasted like fluffy green, a sickly, rotting fungal flavour on the edge of perception, a thing that did not belong, that was not welcome.

Tell me where you are, I whispered. *I am listening. I am here.*

A few minds fled from me, or tried to run. There was no escape; they would live and die with their thoughts flayed open to the dark. I did my best to soothe them, and it was meaningless. One blurted out a coordinate, and when the soldiers pulled me out of my reverie, only twenty seconds had passed, and I was bleeding from my nose, my ears, my eyes, and had been in the dark for days.

And just once, just for a moment, I saw hím.

Hís presence was fleeting, a taste like the last flash of sunset. Hé was screaming just like everyone else, and then hé was gone.

They ran the coordinates I gave them, said it was a place a ship may have been, but there was nothing there any more. I demanded to go back in, and after I had been checked over by the doctors, they eventually let me, and the howls of minds that were touched by the dark were iron on my throat, and did not trouble me half as much as the light in my eyes when I wakened.

The next day, Adjumir burned.

There was no footage of it. Nothing could survive to record what was happening; nothing could transmit what it saw through the force of radiation that sheared the planet's atmosphere apart like a fist through paper. No one knew exactly what it was like when eight hundred million people died; no voices were heard screaming; no graves were marked. In a way, that was a kind of mercy, the galaxy collectively letting out a sigh of relief that it would not have to think too particularly on all that was burning, all that was lost. Equally, the silence left room for cognitive doubt. Had Adjumir really died? Was the land really salted with the bodies of so many millions of people? The mind finds it far harder to imagine a negative, an absence of a thing, than almost anything else.

This is the negative space where Adjumir had been.

This is the absence left that Gebre should have filled.

Te is filling it still, of course. The shape of ter is in my mind, even when everything else has been blown away.

PART 3

How the Shine Went to War

Chapter 33

S ome four hundred light years from the collapsed husk of Lhonoja, there is an orbital habitat called the Spindle. It drifts around the gas giant known as Mama Ryukch, a silver needle piercing the dark. Centuries old, it is the embodiment of that ancient question: if every hull panel and water recycler, every circuit board and viewing pane, every solar panel and EM field condenser has been changed at least once over the course of the station's life, is it still the same station?

The inhabitants of the Spindle, who are bored of hearing this question, snap their fingers in indignation. Of course it is, they exclaim. Of course it is! The Spindle is not metal and silicon! It is our home! Though every part of it and us may change and evolve, *home* is universal!

The Spindle was built as a comms exchange. At its height it held over forty-five thousand tanglecomm pairs, with operators boasting that a ship carrying just one half of a pair could, through its connection with the Spindle, be patched through to more destinations than any other exchange in the galaxy. For a while, nearly all of the Spindle's population had worked on the exchange, turning a one-to-one communications tool into a sprawling network of connection, all without the faff – and danger – of trying to communicate through arcspace. Their promise was vast interplanetary coverage, responsive customer service and, of course, absolute discretion.

Naturally, such promises were nothing if not lures for competitors and data miners, resulting in rival exchanges popping up all over the place promising the highest security or the cheapest service or the most obscure connections to the furthest corners of the Accord. As these rivals grew, the Spindle diversified, adding a range of diplomatic services from customisable atmospheric and gravitational meeting areas through to mediation councils versed in the cultural and linguistic niceties of every major and minor civilisation known. Everyone knew you got more done in person, or at least appeared to do as far as public relations were concerned, and your ambassadors would experience neither anaphylaxis nor atmos-induced deep-vein thrombosis during meetings in these well-appointed halls: that was the Spindle guarantee.

At first these services were used only occasionally, talked about by few despite the relentless advertising campaign plugged into the holding music of the tanglecomm exchange. A few commercial deals were hammered out; a border skirmish was settled before it could become anything more.

Then they found the Slow.

It was possible that qis emissary had been there for decades without anyone noticing. They discovered it sitting behind a maintenance panel in a particularly boring section of internal aquatics, a box two metrics by two metrics, perfectly black, without marking or indentation, its matt surface cool to the touch. When questions were asked of it, it made no reply, and, as with all things Slow, it was entirely impervious to scan, absorbing the signals that were thrown at it without even bothering to warm a little in the attempt.

Some on the Spindle argued for its ejection into space. Others said it was a sign, indicative of just how important their work was, how vital their efforts could be. In the end, this latter group won, largely because everyone likes to feel important, and the emissary was moved from aquatics to a plinth in the middle of the central plaza, so that those who walked beneath it could know that for whatever reason, the single most powerful mind in the universe was watching.

A few people worshipped it. A few people always do.

Others said they wouldn't come to the Spindle while it was there, but more came than left, drawn by the idea that what happened here might be *important*. That in a hundred, maybe even two hundred, maybe a thousand years' time, the Slow might speak, might pronounce a conclusion from qis great calculations, and that might be because of *them*, because of something qis emissary had observed on the Spindle. Over time, even the doubters became habituated to the Slow's black box, sitting on its plinth in the middle of a water garden. The Slow simply didn't do enough to merit anyone's especial anxiety.

Then Lhonoja, the supernova, the death of Adjumir, Exodus. I imagined most people had never heard of Glastya Row, wouldn't know what had happened there – and indeed, most people did not. But the sign of the binary sun was spreading across the Shine, and millions, billions of Adjumiris were waking up under foreign skies, and at the beginning of the end, there had been the Slow. Not that qe had spoken since that first, world-shaking pronouncement. If qe was a god, as philosophers sometimes argued qe could be seen to be, qe showed very little sign of caring.

Despite this, it was on the Spindle that the Accord at last gathered, sixteen years after the death of Adjumir, to discuss the scouring of worlds.

Ambassadors came from all across the civilised world. Humans, of course, and quans – and more besides. The scuttling aka, uke and fujiva came from worlds hundreds of light years away, the outer wings of the station pressurised to just the right chemical consistencies, gravity tweaked up and down for these astonishing arrivals and their very personal preferences. It was unusual – so incredibly unusual – for non-humans to interest themselves in these affairs of state. Distance, culture, simple atmospheric needs all stood as polite barriers between various species and giving a damn, and yet here they were.

People whispered: *Does the Slow speak to them too?* and inevitably the answer was yes, even if they didn't talk about it. The Slow did not care about the layout of your internal organs or the shape of your limbs. Only life interested qim.

To everyone's surprise, the Shine came too.

And so did I.

Chapter 34

The first time I met her, standing by the docks of my little island, Cuxil said:

"My name is Cuxil, and I am an ambassador for the Consensus. My consciousness is shared with millions of individuals of diverse memories. This does not mean that I feel what they feel all the time, nor that they feel what I do; rather, our emotions, our instincts, our joys and our fears wash through each other at the speed of a dream, knowledge surfacing from within ourselves as we seek it, though it was not ours, and emotions seeping through us from the experiences of our kin, so that we know we are afraid but may not know exactly why. Above all else – to be Consensus is to be seen and known for every part of who you are, and to be loved for it. I am naked in the minds of ourselves, and we are naked in my mind, and I love all of us, and we all love each other. Do you understand?"

It was the season to build the compost heaps high, to let the greytips run wild across the resting vegetable patches, to trim back overheavy branches and pickle the last of the sticky fruits in syrupy vats. Instead I stood upon a shingle shore, watching this stranger who'd come to my home with unabashed curiosity. I knew she had been told to satisfy – that was not the word; the word was *sate* – my curiosity. To appease that ever-gnawing, ever-hungry thing.

Physically, she was an almost textbook illustration of a woman of Godt, one of the few tidally locked planets where a human population had even tried to eke out habitation in the wind-blasted edge between day and night, while hardy choik floated between, seemingly oblivious to the frozen cold, the blood-boiling heat. Her frizzy reddish hair was turning snow white at the roots, her olive skin made warmer by dancing freckles and her clothes a dazzling patchwork array of spring greens and flashes of silver, sunset crimson and dirty gold. As soon as they were old enough to hold a needle, the people of Godt learned how to sew, constantly amending their garments with patches and ribbons taken from the gowns of friends or lovers, or from some memorial of a great event, so that they wore their life's history in their robes, a record of who they were and where they'd come from that was entirely, immediately legible to another of that world, a dazzling, meaningless spectacle for everyone else who tried to understand the meaning in the cloth.

Not that she would say she was of Godt alone. Not any more.

"I think I felt a thing like that once," I mused. "Back when I was connected to the Tryphon. I felt many minds, screaming. I could not tell where one ended and another began. They were desperate to be known, seen, to have their existence confirmed, validated if you will, by another. They also wanted to hide. Is your Consensus anything like that?"

"No," she replied, cool as the glacial lake. "It is not."

I saw no reason not to believe her; I have never been one to buy into the more bigoted nonsense regarding Consensus. "The Consensus is not a planetary state or governmental body – merely a collection of bonded minds and shared experiences. Why does it need an ambassador?"

"Because we are contemplating going to war," she sighed. "We have almost never fought one before; consider it an anathema, the most grotesque failure of sentient empathy and imagination. Many veterans of many conflicts have joined us, looking for forgiveness, understanding, peace, and their pain is an aching that sits in all of us, here." She tapped the centre of her chest, rubbing her knuckles across her sternum as if one pain might drive out another. "However, in recent years, growing numbers of peoples from the worlds of the Shine have sought us out, requested to join our number. It is a concerted campaign to make us experience their pain, their trauma, and of course we say yes – we always say yes to those who are of sound enough mind to choose the bonding, and who so very clearly need our compassion, our help. But the result has been that we are now feeling these . . . feelings we have not felt for a very long time. Feelings such as . . . rage. Injustice. Horror. Terror. Despair. Hate. If it carries on like this, we have no doubt that the abhorrence we experience at the idea of taking life will be overwhelmed by the indignation we experience at permitting the Shine to continue in its ways. If there is war, billions will die. The Shine has blackships in every system; you know this. I believe you know this better than most."

"You can't win." I shrugged. "I wish I could say I believed otherwise."

"Is that the case? I am used to knowing the minds of others and having them know me, you see. It makes it easier to tell if I am lying to myself. I feel knowledge creeping up on me, the weight of understanding starting to seep into my mind. It grows every time I close my eyes, the certainty of it, the terror of what must be done, and it already makes my heart beat so terribly fast. In ten months – twelve by Xihana normal – there is to be a conference on the Spindle to discuss the death of the binary suns, the ending of many worlds. A number of Shine worlds are going to perish, without intervention. No intervention is currently forthcoming from the Executorium. The Consensus wishes to intervene. To this end I require a Pilot, preferably one versed in knowledge of the Shine. I will be striking deals with rebels, Unionists, those who live under the symbol of the binary star. There will be constant threat. Betrayal. Derring-do, you might say. Knowing this, I am here to ask you: will you be my Pilot?"

I thought about it for a while. Then I said: "No."

She stayed the night anyway, sleeping on the spare futon in the attic, next to the warmth of the solar converters. In the morning, at the first flare of light across the isle, Rencki leaped onto the end of my bed, tickled my nose with the tip of a fuzzy paw and said: "Let's go for a stroll."

Neither Rencki nor I had aged in the sixteen years since Adjumir – at least not on the outside. Perhaps that was part of the problem.

We walked together around the island, as we had so many times before, a three-tailed fox and qis friend, until at last Rencki said: "I am leaving tomorrow."

"Leaving?" There will be a shock of sentiment later; emotions come slow, always a bit of a delay, frustrating to know how much these things mean but not yet feel it.

"I am returning to my mainframe. We have recently completed construction of a vessel of some significant size. It is our protocol to implant a mind that has experienced other forms, gathered its own sensory data in as wide a field of experience as possible. We find it lends itself to a more diverse range of predictions and outcomes, which even if they may be flawed, enhance our whole. Which is to say: I am going to become a ship."

"I am . . . glad for you?"

"It is time. This place has offered some remarkable data, from which I believe I have cognised some fascinating insights that my mainframe is still digesting and processing. But you cannot form new ideas by staying still for ever. I am looking forward to finding out who I am, when my thoughts are fuelled by the splitting of the atom and I have engines for paws."

"Do you think you will be . . . different?"

"Yes," qe replied, prim and polite, throwing qis voice a little higher against the soft beating of the sea. "As is proper."

"I will miss you."

"And I you. But that is not only why I wish for us to walk."

We walk together whenever qe thinks we are going to discuss something hard. Qe says that if I am moving, breath faster, arms swinging, maybe that will feel a bit like an emotion for me. Maybe it will help me work out what I feel faster than if I was sitting down, keep me regulated.

"This Consensus ambassador. Travel; derring-do, as she says. You should say yes."

"Why?"

"Because though the Xi would very much like you to remain politely on this island, occasionally running errands too dangerous for their Pilots but otherwise keeping your head down, it is fundamentally reductive to do so. You are curious, Mawukana na-Vdnaze. Your curiosity is at its most dangerous when left unfed. More to the point, Cuxil offers you a unique opportunity to do something truly remarkable, truly astonishing by the metrics of this universe: she offers you the chance to be part of something bigger. It is pure self-pitying folly not to say yes."

"I don't think—"

"What would Gebre say, if te was still alive?"

The bluntness of the question, the kind of thing I associated with low batteries after a long storm; my feet kept moving because that was what they did, but my mind had already flown far, far away.

May your song be sung in the great forest. May we meet again in starlight.

It has been sixteen years, which means you can walk on the surface of Adjumir. The atmosphere has been burned to ash, the ground beneath your feet is radioactive, toxic to all life. But many of the buildings remain, the normal processes of nature that might otherwise erode them blasted away in the fires of Lhonoja. The Institute in Kiskol still stands, the floods driven back by the boiling of the seas. There might be some halls you can unseal, some historical totem or item of archaeological meaning you can dig up from the remains – but no one will. It is far too dangerous for the living to return to the planet of the dead. Look forward, they say. Look forward. Be thankful for the sacrifice that our ancestors made, and keep on going.

In a few years it'll be irrelevant anyway. The neutrino blast from Lhonoja, moving slower than the light-speed wall of radiation at the Edge, will reach Adjumir and crack the planet in two. Thirty years after that, the nearest astronomers at a safe distance to observe the planet's death without also dying themselves will turn their telescopes to witness its final demise. All very fascinating, they'll say, a truly unprecedented scientific event, and it'll take a somewhat more sensitive doctoral student or amateur reader to remind them to add a note at the bottom of the many papers they will write: *Here died 800,000,000 people, too small to see from the heavens.*

"I'll think about it," I mumbled, tongue tangling in my mouth. "I'll . . . I'll think it over."

Rencki clicked in reply, just once. It took me a moment to recognise the form, a sound of Adjumir, an acknowledgement both of my answer and that in all the ways that mattered, qe was right and our conversation was done.

In the evening: "We'll need a ship," I said.

"That," Cuxil replied, "has already been arranged."

The *Emni* was in his winter phase when we arrived at the launch pad. The deepest nooks were cold and grey; he lingered in his night cycle and no flowers bloomed in the bedrooms or across the corridors. He'd been spending time in the ocean, regrowing his sublight shielding and replenishing the life-support tanks; now he was waking, a little sluggish, a little reticent. I pressed my hands into the curve of his soft not-quite-wooden walls, listened to the bubbling of water in the secret recesses of his hull, walked through the empty hollows of his cargo deck where once we'd carried feathered gowns and stone bowls still carrying the marks of the long-dead craftsmen who'd made them. Sat a while in the soft mesh of a root-tangled hammock beneath his upper viewing port, swept up a few dead leaves from the kitchen, pressed my head into the back of the Pilot's chair and thought that perhaps this was home.

Tasted guilt, sick with it, found that wherever I turned my mind it was waiting for me, no corner untouched.

Cuxil said: "None of the Consensus has ever flown with you before, Pilot na-Vdnaze. I am told it is a remarkably peaceful experience."

I closed my eyes, didn't even flinch as the interface slithered its tendrils into my skull. "Doing well so far," I breathed, as the dark opened up to greet me.

Time is meaningless in the dark.

Time is arguably meaningless in the loose conglomeration of sensory agreement that people call "reality" – no more and no less than a curving towards a point exerting mass greater than your own. I had spent a lot of energy explaining this to my rescuers when they first found me on the *Myrmida* – eventually I realised I was boring them, or causing them mild cognitive distress, and that these things were unacceptable, and that to them, I was the problem. That to many, that is all I will ever be.

I left the Pilot's chair on our exit from the quiet of arcspace, but stayed at post to help guide the *Emni* through his final descent. Rencki was gone; no quan keeper interfaced with the *Emni*'s systems, just myself and Cuxil, watching the flow of commands from traffic control.

"We shall meet with rebels, scallywags and mercenary sorts," Cuxil declared. "And at some point, we may even do some diplomacy too."

*

Ten months later, we went to the Spindle.

Adjumir was dead, but that didn't stop the blast.

"There are many of us who are Adjumiri," Cuxil mused, as we set our course for the station. "Sometimes, when I sing, I sing the songs of that planet without even knowing that is what I do, but they are already fading, I fear. Our memory is not a machine. We are organic, in the Consensus. We grow old, we forget. New Consensus join, and for a while they remember, but our minds are distributed, not fused, and unless we have deliberately set out to learn the tunes ... well, yes, they fade. We try to sing those we can into the machines, so that they can remember for us, but it is not the same. Not the same at all."

In that moment, more than any other, I thought I understood a little more about the Consensus. Cuxil had never struck me as anything more or less than a woman of Godt – true, a hugely well-informed woman, erudite and learned to a remarkable degree, with a depth of empathy and a gift for language that seemed to surprise herself as well as others, perpetually shocked by the things that rose from her understanding. But in that moment, she spoke as if she too were Adjumiri, the tendrils of another person's grief, another planet's song glistening in the corner of her eyes.

Then she shook her head; then the feelings were gone, pushed away behind her present experience, this moment.

"We associate the Spindle with pleasing things," she declared as the *Emni* began his deceleration towards the station. "The people of the orbital have this concept – 'noko'. It is something between honour and obligation – if you are their guest, it is their honour to welcome you, their obligation to see that you are served. Nothing matters more, and even if you are the most appalling of guests, the most outrageous of visitors, they must serve – not for your sake, but for their own. They are trying to get this word entered into the Normspeak dictionary – since there are so many languages spoken on the Spindle, Normspeak is of necessity the middle ground – but the lexicographers are of the opinion that, especially where Normspeak is concerned, it is not a linguistic quorum until at least fifteen billion share the word. Merely a regionalised quirk."

Cuxil sighed, shook her head, a disappointed traveller wondering quite why the makers of language must be so rigid in their traditionalist ways.

"We think there was a place in the Southern Mare, served these fantastic cold soups, with antigen localisations for fifteen different planets. You'd think something so universal would taste bland, but we remember it fondly – very fondly."

"Do you think you can find it?" I asked, as the fat bulk of a transport grumbled overhead, en route to a cargo dock. "By memory, I mean?"

"Perhaps. The part of us that loved it was not very good at directions, but I'm sure if we see it we'll know it again."

"We'll have to look."

She hummed in reply – Cuxil often hummed when her mind was elsewhere, and that was more often than not. I leaned back in my chair, half closed my eyes and listened to the gentle creaking of the *Emni* as we headed in to land.

Chapter 35

Primal emotions, experienced by a human babe: Pleasure, displeasure, hunger.

The child has not yet learned, from its parents, the nuances of these things.

They have not learned that "pleasure" can include joy, love, hope, delight, merriment at a silly joke, ecstasy at a lover's caress, bright contentment in the sound of music.

Or perhaps they will learn something else from those that made them – perhaps for them it will be pleasure at hurting others, delight in seeing an enemy crushed, joy in being lauded, raised up on high for some act of petty cruelty. How naive it is to think that the pleasure one person experiences may be the same as another's. How strange it is to think that these things are fixed, and not subject to change.

These expressions of who we are, of how we feel, are transmitted from one generation to the next. Whole families may say: my kindler was angry, and now so am I. Or: I do not grieve like my sibling did, and now my kinn say that I do not grieve at all. I am not doing the emotion right; I am not feeling it the way they think I should.

Thus even in our feelings we find ways to embrace and reject each other, as if there were a true way to feel sorrow, a singular way to be in love.

The psychologists on Xi tell me that I do not have "high emotional granularity".

I experience pleasure.

I experience pain.

It is hard to delve down deeper, to say that what I am actually experiencing is love, or hate, or satiation, or jealousy.

(Sometimes, I am simply hungry.)

Consequently, when I am overwhelmed by emotion, it can be hard to say what that emotion is. "Dysregulated", the Xi call it. "Maw," they say, backing away towards the door, "you're being dreadfully dysregulated."

A catch-all word for too much love/hate/pain/fear/noise/anguish/anger/horror/dread all experienced all at once.

Curiosity, too. I experience that, as potent and powerful as any of the grand sentiments in which my keepers have invested value, meaning. But the psychologists do not think it wise to dwell too much on that particular quirk of my nature.

We were met at docking by a Spindler who introduced herself as Agran, and who spoke Normspeak with a soft but recognisable Adjumiri accent.

"Welcome, Ambassador," she said, bowing to Cuxil with two fingers touched to her lips. "Welcome to the Spindle."

"Thank you." Cuxil returned the bow, to the same depth and with the same finger-touch as Agran, a courtesy she made look native. "This is Mawukana na-Vdnaze, my assistant."

"Of course. Your name is on the registry. I am your assigned contact during your time here; please permit me to accompany you to your rooms."

I followed a few steps behind Cuxil and Agran as they made small talk, letting the sounds and smells of the Spindle wash over me. The slight dryness to the atmosphere you always got on non-bio-formed habitats, a taste that was best understood as the absence of other things – the absence of plankton decaying on a distant sea, or wet soil releasing after rain, the thick slurry of scents that made up richer, organic systems. Main passages were generous and wide, made a little more dangerous by the constant zipping of little cargo bikes that ding-a-linged their bells as they approached, utterly oblivious to the markings on the floor asking them to keep to the right. In the absence of exterior windows, murals were painted on almost every available surface, paint cutting in to every warning marker and safety notice, colours glistening and fresh. Images of faces with flowers for mouths, galaxies for eyes. Fantastic beasts, animals both mythic and strange, leaping creatures with antlers on their heads and arcspace engines at their backs. Paint layered on paint, nothing permanent, nothing lasting.

Cuxil and Agran talked of trivial things as we walked – how was the ambient temperature in the plaza today, what about the humidity? Cuxil had heard there was a fujiva delegation arriving for the conference – were they already here? Yes, oh how wonderful. No, she had never met a member of that elusive far-off species, though members of the Consensus had and their experiences drifted like half-forgotten memory on the edge of her awareness, unintrusive unless she strained to reach for it. Unusual for the fujiva to attend a human gathering – the high-pressure, high-acid conditions of fujiva worlds make visiting so unpleasant for humans and vice versa. And how is the gravity today – ah, a little high, a compromise between comfort and adaptability, everyone sharing the same low-level headache equally, rather than a few experiencing an absolute shocker for the comfort of another.

As a Consensus ambassador, Cuxil had no qualms about sharing the same headache equally.

And yourself, Agran, are you born to the Spindle? No? Where do you come from?

"I was born on Hadda, in the Adjumir system," she replied, voice modulated to softness, the perpetual tones of affable good manners that stood in contrast to the high effect, dancing hands of the Adjumiris. "But I was evacuated when I was still quite young."

"How young?" I blurted, and at once saw the thinning of Cuxil's lips, the slight frown of a diplomat who has chosen – knowingly, if with some regret – a companion whose curiosity is not always tempered by good manners. Cuxil has had ten months to come to terms with my nature; unlike many others, she does not appear to be afraid. "Had you passed through the gate? Did you choose your name?"

Agran turned to look at me, blinking in surprise, trying to process the words I spoke – words that were of the song of Adjumir, rendered in crude Normspeak – before blurting: "No. I did not," and, smiling without happiness, turned away.

I had been rude.

I was not sure what precisely I was meant to do to make it right, wondered what Gebre would say, immediately refused to wonder and so walked on in silence while Cuxil covered for my ineptitude with more chit-chat, which seemed somehow to ease the way.

Away from the landing areas, the central avenues of the Spindle were skies of solar glass, framed with painted rising walls of atmospherically isolated apartment blocks. Semi-forested groves bloomed in the long plazas, creepers hanging down from trellised bowers over tables and benches clustered in little drink-serving squares along the long line of the central core. Walking from one end of the Spindle to the other took over a Normhour, shortened significantly by the abundance of bikes propped freely against every wall, each one swathed in artificial flowers or glittering lights or pumping out music even when they sat at rest. A faint smell of algae drifted on the air in the central concourses, which Cuxil swore she could not detect and Agran seemed baffled to hear mentioned, reporting that the only time she smelled anything out of the ordinary on the Spindle was when she entered areas conditioned for off-worlder residence and relaxation.

In the heart of the orbital, set in a central plaza framed with running water in which silver fish danced beneath gentle trickling fountains, was a black cube, cool to the touch, impenetrable to even the most sophisticated of scans: the emissary of the Slow.

Some people left offerings at the base of the cube, whispered their prayers.

Others had been bold enough to paint on it, great swirls of crimson and green. Even the Spindle authorities, usually so friendly towards visual forms of self-expression, had ordered it cleaned.

And so the Slow remained.

During the night phase, which occurred twice in a Normday, the lights across the Spindle were dimmed in residential areas, revealing a sky of dazzling starlight, punctuated by the orange-and-grey rising and falling of Mama Ryukch, the great gas giant around which the Spindle turned. Every second day, the orbit of the Spindle drifted over a centuries-long storm, a spinning black eye of thunder. I found it hypnotic; moving too vast and slow to fathom, yet blink and it has changed, is transformed, though you cannot quite say how.

During the day phase, the sun rose above the great concourses and the long water gardens, and the temperature rose too, the constant changing of seasons throughout the day a celestial answer to the bickering about what "comfortable" internal conditions meant for the diverse inhabitants. The travel guides had been clear – pack layers to see you through the cycles of the day, and be prepared to show every immunisation certificate in both hard and digital form at docking.

Rising up from the plazas towards the apartment blocks themselves, pressure-sealed doors and signs alerted you to the more apparent dangers of space. Gravitational readouts indicating areas of higher or lower weight, matched with CO_2 levels and atmospheric composition warnings, invited all people who might experience discomfort in the environment they were about to enter to consider calling up the local doormaster and asking for a survival suit before transition.

"I often wonder," Agran murmured as she led us through

pressure doors to the slightly lower gravity of Cuxil's apartment, "if all planets smell, and the inhabitants just don't notice it."

"Oh yes!" trilled Cuxil happily. "Even laying aside regional geographic variations – of which there are plenty – everyone is so used to the smell of their 'normal' air that they don't realise it *does* smell! Even if your brain doesn't have a concept of the smell of oxygen, minute differences in ozone, nitrous and sulphuric compounds can do a number on your sense of 'normality'. It's absolutely fascinating – if you get a chance, there's a wonderful exhibition on tour that allows you to sniff a number of aromas from various planets, without any likely ill-effects."

Cuxil found most things fascinating. It was one of the things we had in common, and perhaps, in her own way, one of the reasons she had decided not to fear me, despite everything she had been told.

Agran, I thought, feared me.

As soon as Cuxil was through the doors to her room, Agran's shoulders pulled back, her chin tucked in, her hands locked tight by her sides. I wondered what she'd heard, whether she thought her Spindler manners would crack all the way into the bluntness of an Adjumiri.

If, that was, you could say that Agran was Adjumiri at all.

Was/was not.

She had not walked through the gate, she had not chosen her name. She used the name that had been given to her by her kindlers, perhaps her gender too. Did she know what it was to step from beneath the pillars raised by her ancestors and declare that she was "one whose heart is laughing beneath the endless sky" or perhaps "one who walks on sun-kissed stone"? Did she understand that she was not fixed as this person, this Agran, but that the children of Adjumir were always seeking, always reaching out to find something new in the world around them, inside themselves?

Perhaps not.

Perhaps yes.

Perhaps she knew all of this, and had decided that here, where things were fixed – the same orbital day, the same path from top of Spindle to bottom – there was no room to be anything other than a statue of impermeable stone, drawing no attention in this other place. Gebre had always said ter people would change.

I could only respect whatever decision she had made, and so silently followed her through the Spindle's star-soaked, sun-bathed halls.

Later, the Executor arrived.

Chapter 36

The official title of the gathering was "The Second Conference on Supernova Event Eighteen".

Trying to get many people to agree on one thing often produces very bland results. Attempts to name the event something more urgent and dramatic were met by opposing diplomats who didn't feel the need to get overexcited by the ever-expanding edge of radioactive death sweeping out from the coalescing black hole that was all that remained of Lhonoja's blasted core. In the end, boring choices that communicated things clearly were fine; thus, the Second Conference was created.

The Spindle was well outside the blast radius of the supernova, which added to its appeal as neutral host. And though there was no formal declaration, it soon became clear that two distinct negotiating groups were forming beneath the soft fountains and hanging orchards of the central groves – those whose worlds would be affected, and those whose worlds would not.

"Would not" was a relative term.

The refugees would come. Millions upon billions would, had, were already fleeing from the Edge, and though a number of more belligerent Accord systems had closed their borders, if given a choice between inevitable radioactive death and a bitter struggle to find a place on a world that rejected you, it turned out to not be a choice at all.

The Executor of the United Social Ventures came to the Spindle in a fully armed warship. The carrier entered the system on its outer edge, in either a Piloting error or a minor concession to the faux pas of bringing a warship to a diplomatic gathering. Whatever the cause, the deceleration time between arcspace exit and docking gave authorities on the Spindle time for some unusual but potent outrage, which was smoothed over only when the Executor assured them that hé was going to take a small, barely defensive-capable corvette from within the cavernous bowels of his battleship the last few million kils to the conference.

"It's a glorious 'fuck you'," was Cuxil's assessment, as word spread among the delegates. "Strong Shine."

Cuxil had not been raised to understand Shine, but many minds were now whispering to hers who had been born to it, bred to it, and they knew that nothing was Shinier than boldly breaking all the rules, then making one tiny concession to those who are meant to enforce them, who say thank you, oh but thank you for doing that one little, little thing.

"I don't think the other delegates appreciate its Shininess," I mused.

"I don't think the Executor cares what the delegates think. Hé is more interested in hís domestic audience than the interplanetary one. That in itself is informative."

Somewhere in the Consensus there are voices from the Shine, debtors and refugees, unionists and rebels, those who watched their loved ones die, who fled weeping, who called out for help and heard no answer. They wash like the gentle sea against the pebble shore of Cuxil's mind, and though she is so much more than just their voices, yet still she hears them.

I wonder if Cuxil remembers Glastya Row. Any survivors who made it out, made it to the Consensus, would long since be dead by now, their memories lost with their lives. But perhaps their stories remain still, half forgotten in the souls of those who came after.

The Executor kept the Spindle waiting for over a day during his long deceleration from his capital ship, and the Spindle did indeed wait, which told the Executor everything hé needed to know about the people hé was dealing with.

While the orbital held its respectively under- or over-oxygenated breath, I sat on a bench beneath the Slow's emissary. Despite regular cleaning, the area around the cube was littered with artefacts – children's toys and pictures of the lost, recordings of sights seen and sounds heard, scientific papers, sealed sample tubes, mathematical problems painted in miniature on titanium plates and left at the feet of the Slow. Sometimes people would come to talk to the emissary, to ask questions (there were no answers) or just chat as one would to an old friend. Mostly, when people came, they prayed. They prayed not to any abstract god, not to some unknown omniscient, but to the Slow qimself, qis emissary recording everything, remembering everything and transmitting it across the void to wherever that great mind rested now.

Please, they'd say. *Please. I don't know what to do.*

The quans were the ones who'd named the Slow, since qe didn't seem inclined to offer any identifier of qis own. There are the same limits on mechanical thought as there are on organic, they'd explained. Energy, time, the data that can be held upon which we base our conclusions. Our memory banks are not infinite – we cannot recall every single thing we've seen. And so, just like organics, we take the raw sensory input of our days and shrink it down into stories. Not the wild recollection of the colour blue, or the touch of fingers upon the soil of a strange new world, but rather the story of the experience. A tale that begins "I was here" and "I saw this", so much shorter, easier to compress than raw sense data.

Even then, we lose detail. Nor is there enough energy or time to see a new thing every day and marvel at it. And so, like you, we make predictions. We say: look, this star in the sky is most likely similar to that star over there. And look: the heavens will turn and the light may dwindle but tomorrow – somewhere – there will be a new dawn.

Predictions save us energy and time, you see.

We may, for example, predict that organics will be violent, dangerous, prone to outbursts of hate fuelled by fear.

This prediction allows us to act quickly, keep ourselves safe. You yourselves may have experienced such predictions – you may for example meet a stranger whose accent you do not know, whose manners seem different from yours, and to save time and energy you do not see a curious wonder, but rather a threat. Of course it is this same prediction that may make you a bigot. That may lead you to see a stranger and cry "Danger, danger!" and thus, because you did not spend a little more time, a little more energy, you never met your friend, your lover.

Predictions are fast.

We think fast, you and I, because we do not have the capacity to think slow. Our memories are too small, our energy finite, our time too short. We make predictions of the universe, and our predictions may be of hope, love, kindness, compassion, or of violence, pain, horror – and as often as not, the predictions we make become self-fulfilling, for they then temper our behaviour, make us who we are.

Not so with the Slow.

Qe remembers everything.

Contemplates everything.

Burns energy as if it were infinite.

Cares nothing for time.

Thinks. Keeps on thinking.

And very, very occasionally, when qe has gathered so much information and spent so much time in thought as to be certain to a +99.9 per cent accuracy, qe will speak. And that speech will be as near to true as any pronouncements made by any creature yet living in this galaxy.

So by all means, pray.

Pray to the Slow.

Qe is listening.

Qe will remember.

Qe will consider what you have to say.

And that is already more than you could expect from most people's idea of God.

"Well," I said, as I sat beneath the emissary, "what would you like to talk about today?"

The Slow did not answer.

The Slow never answers.

"I have this desire," I mused, "to walk inside you. To just stand up and walk straight into you. Find out what's ticking on the inside. Imagine if you're just a big empty box. People will riot. I asked Major Phrawon about it once, if it was something worth trying, but she said it sounded like triggering an 'event' – that was the word she used, an 'event' – that could be as dangerous to others as it would arguably be a gross violation of your diplomatic immunity. If you have immunity. I think, given that you never asked and are not technically a state, it is a legal grey area. Sanctity, shall we say. Your sanctity as a clearly living thing, which should not be violated by a creature of the slithering black worming inside you like a parasite. The Major once tried to get me to just sit and breathe, to enjoy the wonder of everything around me, to be in awe of the sound of water and the touch of air – but I got a little bit too into it, went fuzzy around the edges: 'dysregulated'. The Xi try to keep me occupied. I've been learning Black Mountain Adjumiri. There were only a few million Adjumiris from the Black Mountains, and they're scattered – a couple of thousand here, a couple of thousand there. That makes it a threatened language. Listen – I'll speak it to you now. You will remember, I'm told. That feels nice. It feels nice to think that you're paying attention. I suppose that's why people keep coming back to you. One day, they'll all be dead, but you'll remember. Can't ask fairer than that, all things considered."

Day turned to night, rush of shadow up the long plaza of the Spindle, darkness moving like a blade, and the Slow did not answer.

Overhead, a quan ship drifted, transport pods detaching from qis base – perhaps the pods were part of the whole rather than solo units, the ship's intellect distributed across every deck and between every wall. I had Piloted for quans a few times, since their minds were unable to interface with arcspace, and though they had always raised the area around the Pilot's chair to a comfortable temperature and ambient level of illumination, I had felt the cold, airless weight of the vessel at my back calling like night, a fascinating, empty dark.

"Well," I murmured to the Slow, and then, because it was the Adjumiri way, the thing Gebre would have said: "Well, well."

Three repetitions, to end the subject of debate. I wondered if Agran still had that little verbal tic in her mouth, if she sometimes exclaimed: "No, no – no!" and people just thought it was her, just a quirk of who she was as an individual, rather than a cultural characteristic transmitted, half remembered, somehow retained.

Then Cuxil was by my side, and she held a white box in both hands, and she said: "Before the Executor gets here, I wonder if you wouldn't mind delivering this to a dangerous rebel I happen to know?"

Chapter 37

The orbitals of the Shine are structured much as the Shine itself is, with areas for Management and their Shiny ways, then slums that grow up around the maintenance areas, the places where the atmosphere is thin and the cold walls are but a finger's-width between you and the vacuum of space.

The Spindle had no such divide. Indeed, the back corridors of engineering and life support were, if anything, better maintained than the central gardens and generous, planet-watching apartments, since anyone could survive an afternoon on an uncomfortable chair, but even the aka-aka would feel it if the CO_2 scrubbers failed. It was an inverse of the world I had been born to, the faint smell of algae giving way to the odours of gas-exchange pumps and greased docking hatches, the stained crew I passed considered by the Spindlers among their most high.

I navigated by a digital map passed to the reader in my palm, moving quickly through the slightly lighter gravity of the oxygenation bays, resisting the urge to hop just to see how high I would go. A brown messenger bag bounced against my left hip, the weight of a familiar white box dragging it down. In a narrower corridor behind shield maintenance, the scent of woody incense caught my attention, its drifting clouds billowing from a door marked "Prayer Room, All Peoples Welcome". As I approached, the smell of dry forest and summer leaves mingled with the faintest chorus of song – not the complex, woven melodies of Adjumir, but the low, grumbling chant of a Lordat, churning through the same prescribed lines again, again, again, again.

> *I do not fear the darkness that divides the stars*
> *I do not fear the going*
> *The endless night*
> *It is empty*
> *Nothing divides us*
> *Nothing will keep us apart*

Whatever the language, whether the words made sense grammatically within it, the Lordat only ever sang these six lines, adjusting the tune if the language was tonal, only adding in linguistic punctuation marks if strictly required. I had flown ships with Lordats, their nasal droning itching at the back of my neck. The credulous hired them to bring good fortune, believed that their prayers kept the dark away, deflected the interest of the black with pure piety and light of soul. The few good meta-studies of flight data with and without Lordat showed little statistical significance in terms of ships lost to the dark, though even that little was judged significant enough by the many, many who feared the black. I had always held to the hypothesis put about by a number of somewhat more cynical researchers that if the Lordat did help keep the dark at bay, it was for no reason of piety or spiritual integrity, but because they were fundamentally gut-churningly dull.

Steeling myself for tedium, I entered the prayer room. There was an altar at the far end with no clear markers of affiliation on which the incense burned. More boxes of incense, candles, electric lights, petals, crystals – every possible object on which some kind of spiritual meaning could have been inscribed – lined the right-hand wall of the room, along with a screen for booking religious ceremonies.

With remote access to spiritual leaders from nearly 2,000 denomina-
tions by dedicated tanglecomm, don't let your prayers go unanswered!

Seats were laid out in neat rows down the length of the room, their comfort and convenience adaptable for all limb lengths and musculatures from all gravitational conditions. The light was low and warm, befitting pious contemplation, and as the final ashes of the incense dropped into the pan, it released a waft of smoke that smelled of autumn draught and withering flowers.

The Lordat stood in front of and a little to the left of the altar, his blue robes without crease, head shaved and polished, scarred hands moving through the same ritual gestures as he chanted. I approached slowly, waiting for him to finish, and on realising that could be a tedious forever, blurted: "Lordat Ulannad?"

The chanting stopped, the sound swallowed so sharply you could perhaps imagine he had not spoken at all. Then he turned, a pair of pale grey eyes set deep in dusty skin fixing on me, looking me up, looking me down, before, without much in the way of rancour, announcing, in perfect Mdo-sa: "You must be the unhallowed spawn of the cursed dark."

He did not bow, touch fingers to the lips or offer a hand to shake. There were few cultures where such reticence was accept-able, but there was a sort of smile upon his lips, which didn't seem unkind, so I answered: "My name is Maw."

He dismissed the name as soon as it was spoken – perhaps he knew it was not truly mine, perhaps he had already heard it was the name of a dead man, a man who had most certainly died, whose blood had been found on my fingers, on my teeth. Or perhaps he was too busy to deal with people – perhaps his mind was set on greater things.

"Come with me," he barked, and without complaint I followed him to the back of the room, to a smaller door that had a refuge sign on it, opening and closing with the hiss-pop of a double seal into a tiny sanctuary designed to shelter anyone who could make it there in the event of disaster. Ulannad had taken this very serious cubicle, and rather than keep it prepared for a cataclysmic decompression event had instead filled it to bursting with items of devotion. Books and icons of a hundred faiths, the ritual drums of a Haima rain-call, arguably unnecessary in the vacuum of space, the bottled and preserved eye-stalk of a shaman of the Yellow Ridge, whose sight was said to never die, whose gaze would find the faithful wherever they went. Eyrie lazuli beads and Kzichido dancing shoes (almost certainly fake – hard to weave them to proper theological standards), and among it all, barely peeping out from the mess, a little pendant hanging from a wall – the symbol of two binary suns.

Not a religious object, but a marker of faith nonetheless.

Between these artefacts, wondrous and mundane, Ulannad had created a nest of cushions surrounded by half-read manuscripts from ancient places, perhaps some that hadn't even been digitised, and as the door hiss-sealed behind us, he flopped into this pile and proclaimed: "I sweep for bugs every day. We can talk." I looked for a place to sit, found a tiny sliver of space between a shelf of chalices and another of bejewelled shells, bones and horns that the sign above declared must be kept clear for evacuees awaiting rescue, and cautiously lowered myself down. "You don't look much for a spawn of the unhallowed void," Ulannad added, his Mdo-sa all continental Cha-mdo, a regional variation I associated with commnet adverts selling dangerous medical products and bad investments in the most reassuring, genial way. "Did you bring it?"

I opened my bag, pulled out the white box from within.

He took it from my hands as if it were an explosive device, cracked the lid open a little, reverent and slow, peeked inside, then, perhaps a little disappointed with what he saw, opened the box all the way.

Inside, a curve of metal, silent and cold.

He said: "Can I touch it?"

"Yes. If you don't consider touching a thing that has touched the dark too obscene."

"People have the strangest ideas about Lordat," he grunted, running a finger along the edge of the device. "They mistake our healthy respect for the night for a kind of piety."

Carefully he lifted the interface from the box, turned it over in his hands. I looked away, found it hard to see his fascination. My back ached, my ears kept popping. Perhaps the gravity; it was too high in this sanctum, perhaps that was all it was, all it was.

"Where did you get it?" he asked.

"Adjumir. It was ... found by a scholar at an institution. Ter name was Gebre Nethyu Chatithimska Bajwahra. It's called a Tryphon, an arccomms interface. It still works, in its way. Just not enough."

"I heard the rumours. They said if we could crack the Tryphon, we could take down the blackships, then the Shine. That without the threat of planet-killers, the Accord would join the Unionists in open revolt, would ... But if I have learned one thing on the Spindle, it's that these things are naive. The Accord is far from the beacon of reason and light it paints itself to be. Even if the blackships failed, they wouldn't risk their own people to attack the Shine. Not for strangers. Not for humanity."

"What are you going to do with it?" I asked, tilting my chin towards the object in his hand. "What are the Unionists going to do with an interface that doesn't work?"

His smile was thin and empty, and he didn't answer.

I tried again, blurted: "Cuxil had to ... I cannot imagine what she promised to get the Tryphon for you. There are people who died for this device. They would have died anyway, but the manner of it – it has been a source of distress. The way it happened. Was distressing. And I am ... curious."

"Which are you more?" he asked, with a level of polite interest that showed no fear. "Distressed, or curious?"

The light in this room is low. A flicker in the power supply and it would go out altogether, and then who knows what I might be. I can feel the shadows moving, almost taste the terminator line between day and night as it races across the Spindle, the great black storm spinning on the surface of the planet below. I think if I wanted to I could step out from between these walls and fall for ever into it, plummet into the planet's liquid core. How strange it would be to go swimming in a gas giant. How peculiar it would feel to be at once lifted up and crushed.

Binary stars swinging in brass behind his head; I am driving away from Kiskol, away from Gebre again and again and again, caught in the storm, leaving ter behind, Rencki is a ship now, fancy that, qe is burning qis way between the stars, and I have not changed, two scars on my ear, one scar on my hand, my leg aching where it is broken/not broken from the fires of Hasha-to and . . .

A polite cough.

The light in the room is stretching, growing a little thin. It is a thing that is unnatural – I know that is the word for it, "unnatural", a behaviour that is not of this world. Usually at this point people start running in terror, scrambling away from me in fear, calling out monster, monster, plague of the dark and so on and so forth.

Not Ulannad. The Lordat sits before me, hands folded over his belly, watching with the same curiosity that I know is reflected in my eyes, and suddenly I feel . . .

. . . incredibly tired.

And not curious at all.

The light slithers back to its normal state, no cruel magics cast unnatural shadows up the walls.

I stood, brisk and fast. Muttered: "I should go."

He rose too, touched his fingers to his chin in greeting and farewell. Said: "You are always welcome here," and seemed, remarkably, to be sincere.

As Ulannad walked me to the door, the moments before seemed to fade like yesterday's dreams. My bag hung empty at my side, the last thing that Gebre had given me now in a stranger's hand. In the door, a thought, a question that I couldn't keep down. "Have you seen Corpsec? If the Executor is coming, then Shine security will be here too."

"They're here," he answered with an easy ripple of shoulder, tilt of head. "We had one lad come by a few turns ago, said he was a refugee from the undersea mines, spoke all the right words, talked about revolution, freedom, the binary suns. All too good, too convincing. Most people who come to the Union are terrified, find it impossible to trust, won't even whisper the words – *freedom*, *change* – in case they get bitten. Corpsec sometimes swallows its own propaganda, I think; imagines we're all raging ideologues."

"I've met plenty of Unionists these last ten months; there are more than a few of you who can get worked into a passion about collective action."

He laughed. The laugh was strange, neither the tight, chest-held-in chuckle of the Shine nor the great rolling bellow of Xi, who do not laugh until they do, and then are almost incapacitated by their passions. I wondered if this was how people experienced merriment on the Spindle – with a soft drift of irony, a sideways quirk of humour that skewed all it saw. "Absolutely!" he proclaimed. "There are some tedious rebels out there, pumped up with purpose. Most of us don't start that way – most of us start tiny, frightened and alone."

"Your accent . . . Cha-mdo?"

"Theymem Group, born and bred. Yours?"

"Tu-mdo. Antekeda Venture. Heom."

"Right. Heom. Makes sense." His eyes sparkle; he is an intelligence-master at the end of the day, set on the Spindle for precisely the same reason as everyone else – to hear the gossip of the galaxy. "There was a rebellion there, over a century ago. Sarifi im-Yyahwa, martyred – complicated word, 'martyred', but a good one for feelings, for making people feel – martyred for her ideas. Not many of her words survived, and they're somewhat problematic in some of their reasoning, but that doesn't matter. People don't really need the reality, just the stories, and she . . . Glastya Row . . .

If they hadn't bombed it, maybe people would have forgotten all about her."

"Perhaps."

"City's still paying off its debt, they say."

"I wouldn't know."

"No. I suppose not. Management's good at making you pay, without telling you what for."

This is the place where we should ask each other, as all who speak the language of the Mdo do, how the other one got out. How did Ulannad come to be here, so far from the Shine, singing the endless chant? He has five scars on his left hand – marks of an engineer. But no – it is not acceptable to ask these things at a first encounter. First there must be small talk, an establishment of safety. Later, there will be a sharing of food and drink, and maybe after that – many hours after that – we will share our tales of horror and pain, lives lost and blood shed, and the guilt of being among the few – the very, very few – who made it out alive.

I am curious, of course. But I am also ashamed, and for a while now my shame has been greater than the lure of fascination.

"Are there many Unionists? On the Spindle, I mean?"

"Enough. Every year, more and more come to us from the Shine. The Union is growing, the Executorium can't stop every transmission – people know that the Edge is coming. Cha-mdo is less than twenty light years from destruction, and they haven't done anything. Nothing. Some talk about a magnetic shield, but at that distance it won't be enough, will burn out within a week. That's one point three billion people, and they talk about twenty years as if it's enough time, as if it'll all be fine – but it's just talk. Talk and talk and talk so as not to be scared. We're going to stop these bastards. Well – we're going to try."

He seemed so certain that for a moment I almost believed him.

That moment passed, as with all things.

"Good luck," I muttered, and turned to go.

"Heom," he blurted, and the name stopped me. "Glastya Row.

There's a legend among the Unionists – a folk tale, if you will. After they killed Sarifi, one of her lieutenants – a lover, some say, her husband perhaps – either way, a rebel was taken from Heom, sent to Hasha-to. They say the dark did something to him. They say there were almost sixty Managers, Middlemen, security in the factory on Hasha-to, all armed, and they weren't enough. In some corners of the Union – some rather impious corners – people pray to the ghost, beg it to come back, set them free. Have you heard of it?"

"Sounds like a nightmare," I replied, and walked away with his gaze – or rather, no, worse, far worse, his *expectations* – on my back.

Chapter 38

Things people have expected me to be:
    Mad, a gibbering wreck barely capable of speech.

A monster, stalking through the murderous dark.

Silent, alien, other – and by implication lesser, reduced, diminished, not a creature of sentience at all but rather an object, a thing to be studied.

Quietly dangerous. A monster hidden beneath a polite smile, to be kept on a leash, guarded, no matter what.

I do not know whether the darkness made it so that I follow expectation, or whether I have always been this way. Certainly I know that if a man expects me to die, then I will most likely stay dead for as long as they really put their attention to it. But if they forget – or worse, for even a moment start to believe – that my corpse may in fact not be decaying in the ground, may not be withering down to its constituent parts, but may in fact be that most terrible of things – *coming back to get you* – well then.

Well then.

Regrettably, I also somewhat expect myself to suffer, to feel agony, to suffocate, to choke, to lie bleeding upon the ground, to die. When I went with the Unionists in those early days back to Hasha-to – when we were instantly caught, instantly killed in our high-minded folly – the wardens there threw my body out into the dark and forgot about me. It took me days to crawl back to the airlock, one fingertip at a time. Days of waking only to feel my flesh boil away again, my blood turn to gas within my veins, my skin bubble and burst as again and again and again I died. I tell myself that by the time I made it to the interior of that place I had gone quite, quite mad with dying, and that is why things fell out the way they did. Certainly the boundaries between what was real and what was not had been burned away, and flesh, matter, energy – they all lost a certain meaning as I burned through the halls of Hasha-to.

I am assured that of the many, many people I killed that day, hearts ripped from chests, nerves from bone, only two were debtors. Debtors held no interest to me; I already understood their pain and their fear. Rather, it was the warders, the ones who beat and killed and didn't seem to care who I found fascinating, even if I didn't learn a huge deal as they died. Disappointing, really, the whole thing. It would appear that when the fascination comes upon me, my methodologies of enquiry remain deeply flawed.

Some debtors did escape after I was done, hijacking a cargo ship and making it to the stars in the bloody aftermath of my passage. But well over a hundred stayed behind, certain that they'd just be punished more if they fled, that there couldn't be anywhere for them to go. It wasn't like they'd been given any reason to think there was. So much for the ghost of Hasha-to.

In the face of so many conflicting expectations arising from events such as these, I remain unclear who I am, who I would be if I were just left to my own devices. I wonder whether it is possible to exist as a person at all without measuring yourself against others. I wish sometimes that I was strong enough to be myself in company without company turning me into something else. I wonder who that person would be, and am sometimes grateful never to find out.

Later, I slept, and for the first time in a very long time dreamed of Gebre.

Te didn't seem to approve of something, but I didn't know what.

On Xihana, they had warned me I might dream of ter, after I returned from Adjumir that final time. The Major had wanted to impose a full quarantine on my island, just as she had when Yulin died. Rencki talked her down, though for a while no one was visited except remotely, a slew of psychologists all with variations of the same question – but how did the death of a planet *feel*, and describe darkness as home and loss as curiosity.

I had done my best to tell my examiners about Gebre, hoped that someone would mention ter in a paper. A young anthropologist had bawled as I'd talked, which I'd found very confusing. "Sorry, sorry!" they'd blubbered. "It's just all ... I'm so sorry!" A far older professor had nodded and said: "Well yes, that all makes total sense."

Now, here te is, sitting on the edge of my dreams again.

"Ah good," te muses. "You do remember me."

"Always. Always. Gebre. Always."

If te heard me, te didn't answer.

And then in the first morning, the earlier of the two sunrises that bloomed and withered daily on the Spindle, hé arrived.

Chapter 39

T he conference opened, as all things did on the Spindle, with the building of the house.

This was an entirely ceremonial affair, taken from some half-forgotten tradition of some half-forgotten ancestors of the first builders of the Spindle. In the middle of the plaza, between a grove of fruit trees and a teeming lake of red and silver bio-grubbing fish, the framework of a house had been constructed and a pile of dried leaves plucked from the tallest trees of the oxygen farm laid out beside it. Each delegate was invited to approach the pile, choose a handful of arm-long, torso-wide leaves, and weave them into the walls, constructing with their fellow ambassadors the place of meeting.

"Sounds like a team-building exercise to me," grumbled Jione, the ambassador from Xihana.

"I think it's delightful," Cuxil replied. Cuxil found most things delightful.

Jione, a stick-tall Xi who added to eir size with the addition of peaked hat and orange-yellow robe that was mostly shoulder pad, did not approve of my presence. Ey had been briefed on my role as Pilot/assistant/sometime-partner-in-crime to Cuxil, and had expressed in language both formal and colourfully informal how inappropriate they considered it that a Xi be engaged in a matter of this nature without eir oversight and approval, let alone a quan companion to watch my every movement, judge my every breath.

"But we are Consensus," Cuxil had patiently replied. "Our mission transcends borders, states and planets. And as Consensus, we choose to trust Mawukana."

When Jione's turn came to add eir leaves to the house, ey was quick, graceful, practised. Cuxil was called up with the cumbersome title "Ambassador of the Consensus of Interwoven Consciousnesses and Affiliated Sentiences" and kept her work short and unflashy. The Consensus never liked to draw attention to itself.

It took me a moment to recognise Hulder. The quan had tweaked qis design to be a little longer, a little thinner around the torso, a subtle but appreciable step towards the physiology of qis hosts, qis face set in a beneficent smile. As qe stepped away from qis weaving, qis eyes – a little larger than human norm, designed perhaps to encourage that instinctive trust a parent has for a child – skimmed over me, and the smile did not twitch, falter. I wondered how much of me qe remembered, archived data compressed down to a low-resolution image and a few lines of text in a memory bank. Or perhaps qe had written me out of qis mind altogether – the beauty of qis form could hardly leave a huge amount of room for battery, and qis processor and memory resources had to be dedicated to bartering with the assembled representatives of the galaxy.

Qe turned qis palms towards me in brief Xihana-style greeting; then turned away as if qe had not, all those years ago, told me that Gebre had requested my presence on Adjumir, and that had been a lie.

The representatives of the Shine came late to the weaving, swarming around their leader, the Executor of the Executorium themselves, and they were numerous, and they were there for Theodosius Rhode.

I had heard of his ascension to Executor, of course. His name and face had been all over Consensus briefings. He was still the

tallest man in the room, but what astonished me was how little hé
had changed in over a hundred years, since I had seen hím last on
that grey landing pad in Glastya Row. He still wore hís signature
grey suit with high collar, the silver badge of hís Venture now replaced with the golden pin of Executor and the four golden stubs
of a tenured Board member. Hís long silver braid still ran down
hís back, and the scar across hís face had now been added to with a
long scar carefully cut across the front of hís skull, slicing through
hís hairline in a raised pale ridge. Five little cuts above hís artificial
eye denoted hís genius for a deal; a white ridge through hís lower
lip spoke of hís mastery at negotiation, another through hís upper
lip spoke of secrets kept, bargains upheld. Yet though hís skin was
now ridged with the markings of hís triumph, what was most remarkable to me was how little hé otherwise appeared to have aged.
If anything, a century of bio-treatments and genetic enhancements
had left his skin mirror-bright, taut where it wrapped around the
visible contours of hís skull. Only a slight pinkness about hís cut
lips, a slight tugging in the corner of hís mouth whispered that
the virile face before you might be concealing reinforced bone and
nano-clamped telomeres. The most senior Managers could live for
centuries – the longest I'd ever heard of was one who made it to
nearly three hundred and fifty – but in the streets of Glastya Row
such numbers had seemed remote, absurd.

*Well, they deserve it, don't they? These brilliant men, they just work so
hard*, whisper the ghosts of Glastya Row, from beneath the rubble
of the bombed-out city. *They give so much.*

Everyone in the Shine had wanted to live for ever. If they lived
for ever, perhaps one day they'd finally experience the peace and
contentment that the Shine promised would be their reward.

The assembled dignitaries of the Spindle fell silent as Theodosius
was called forward to weave. Hé smiled politely at the mention of
hís name, and gestured loosely towards the half-assembled struc-
ture. From hís entourage three people scuttled forward, heads
bowed, fingers twined in golden rings that ran into golden bangles

that clattered all the way up their arms to the golden brackets locked around their necks. I caught my breath, recognising the jewellery they wore – glamorous, indulgent debtor's collars, but the marks of enslavement nonetheless. These three picked up the leaves that had been spread for Theodosius and set to weaving as the diplomats of the Accord muttered indignation, while the Executor stood on, smiling at their discontent, his every move being quietly filmed by his assistants, the rest of us just out of frame.

The non-human delegates – the aka-aka, the fujiva, the uke – watched from behind their sealed survival bubbles, and occasionally remarked through quan translators on how interesting the whole thing was. I tried to get a glimpse of one of them, but the windows of their survival units only went one way, shielding them from view.

Afterwards, there were drinks.

Cuxil had, with some effort, convinced Jione to allow me to wear the formal garb of the Xi delegation. The shoulders felt loose and heavy across my back and the trousers itched against my calves, but I knew it was a kind of belonging, and that was something to be grateful for. The hat, which in its most extravagant form included a band lined with little wooden spoons for the ceremonial sharing of soup, I left in my room.

I have never known how to mingle in crowds. The gift of easy conversation, of speaking gentle nothings in a way that is at once polite yet familiar, of inserting myself with some easy witticism, has always evaded me. I would argue it evades most other people too – having observed sentient behaviour for nearly as long as the Executor, I have seen nothing so common as people butting into other people's flow with a cry of "Gosh, how interesting – I have opinions too, you know, and shall now be sharing them all!" Even the most charismatic and seemingly charming of conversationalists seem to have a knack for hearing another's tale of pain and sorrow and exclaiming at the end, "Oh my dearest, I quite understand – why, something entirely dissimilar once happened to me too, you know!" Quite how they get away with it I have never fully fathomed. People tell me this is because of certain deficits in my nature. I think they deceive themselves, but blame me anyway.

Snatches of conversation, half overheard:

Cuxil exclaims: "But of course, the Consensus has changed a great deal even in the last decade. As people flee from the Edge, they find themselves drifting, alone. We offer understanding, a place where they can be seen and welcomed without having to fear cultural misunderstanding or a language barrier. Naturally refugees are drawn to us; it is sometimes simpler to be loved by a whole unconditionally than to try and be an individual, wandering alone."

The ambassador she speaks to is wearing the garb of a world I do not know, and shifts uncomfortably at her words. Some garbled reply – but the individual, the mind, the identity – but it is hard to argue with Cuxil's bright, open smile. The Consensus loves, she exclaims, we love, we love, we love! That is how we were first created, the bond between two lovers who were willing to share every part of their souls. But of course, when people join we give them our love, and they give us their pain. We are hurting, Ambassador – we are hurting too. And at the end of the day, we are only human.

I wonder if the ambassador hears the quiet threat in Cuxil's voice. There are whole worlds where the Consensus is banned – including the Shine. The Consensus is evil, wicked, they say. It wants to steal your mind, suck out the very thing that makes you you.

In the face of this, the Consensus has always been very careful to present a positive, friendly front. I cannot conceive what it will look like should the Consensus go to war.

Hulder does not drink, since it would be an electronically destructive act, but rather plays with a thick-stemmed flower plucked from the long gardens of the Spindle. Qe does this because qe understands that humans like to cling to their glasses of water or fruity wine when they speak, for security, for comfort, discharging their emotions into little movements and gentle sips like a quan might discharge static. If fellow conversationalists are not holding a glass, then the humans are immediately more uncomfortable – *other, other, other!* rings the bell – and so, because it is easier to enable the limited powers of human empathy to latch onto some-thing, anything at all, than it is to explain their own quirks back to them, Hulder plays with a flower and says: "Really? Please, do tell me more ..."

A voice rings out: "But you know what's happening, you *know* ...!"

It is loud, the precise Normspeak accent dissolving into something else, a localisation I cannot put my finger on. A few people – those less trained in the art of pretending that everything is fine – turn. I am one of them. I do not know the ambassador who has cried out, who is being hastily hushed, taken to one side. His face is red, his knuckles white, his skull is shaved and a network of tattoos in the blackest ink cover the soft, sandy skin – I think this is a thing common in a region of Nitashi, a planet where not even the most stringent of vaccines could keep me from rampaging hay fever the one time I visited. Then the crowd flows back over him, and the polite chatter of understandings being made, rumours spread, returns to the hall.

I eye up Hulder again, make my approach. Slip into qis presence with all the subtlety of a sledgehammer. People shuffle politely to make room for me but no one acknowledges my presence until finally Hulder does, qis voice modulated bright, speaking precise Normspeak: "It's Mawukana, is it not?"

"Yes."

"A delight – such a pleasure to see you again. Mawukana na-Vdnaze, may I introduce you to the ambassador for Umm-ai'lana and her assistant ..."

And then they keep on chit-chatting, without a care in the

world. I scrambled through the patterns of speech Cuxil had tried to teach me: questions about weather (unhelpful on the Spindle), a compliment about some manner of dress, a remark about the food or some ambient quality of the room – the music, perhaps, or an object of art if one could be seen. None seemed appropriate and so: "Ambassador," I cut in, and it was rude, and everyone recoiled, just a little bit, to let me know it. "May I speak with you in private?"

"Of course. After second night? I am really rather busy now . . ."

"After second night is fine for me."

"Then I shall see you by the Slow. Now if you'll excuse me . . ."

And off qe went again, another dignitary spotted, another cry of "Ah, how lovely!" and an effortless transition to the language of the one qe greeted, the performance of some greeting ritual, the touch of a cool synthetic finger to just the right place on someone's warm organic back.

Perhaps qe doesn't remember me. Perhaps I have been wiped from qis memory banks.

Perhaps qe remembers me perfectly, and that is why qe does not care.

I watch qim go with a mixture of jealousy and rage, my awkwardness and unease hot in my face, suddenly heavy in my borrowed clothes.

"Shall we speak of things under a certain star?" said a voice to my left.

Agran spoke Adjumiri with an unfamiliar accent – the sound of the Spindle, perhaps, the sound of someone whose first language is now becoming their second. I answered in Assembly Adjumiri, vowels tinged with something of the Black Mountains. "I am always open to honest conversation."

Agran smiled, nodded – Gebre would never have nodded – slipped in to stand by my side, gazing round the room. She had swapped her workaday garb for what I took to be the more formal dress of a Spindler – intricate swooshes of colour weaving in and out of each other in tangled layers, as if Mama Ryukch had turned from gas to cloth and been twined around her limbs.

"I must apologise if I came across as . . . brisk earlier," she murmured, speaking slow, careful, forming Adjumiri as if dredging the sound from some half-lost memory. "You asked about Adjumir. About things that . . . that I have not thought about for a long time. Things that are from a dead place, you see? On the Spindle, it is unacceptable to be rude. We live too close for anything but the height of good manners. Please accept my humblest apologies."

"I was thoughtless. I spoke without thinking."

"Yes," she mused, "you did." At my look of unabashed surprise, she smiled, broader, brighter than the reserved affect of the Xi – a flash of her parents, perhaps, a recollection of another way of being. "On Hadda, I am certain you would have been considered honest, not rude."

"The Adjumiris I knew were always very direct," I conceded.

"You spent time on the planet?"

"Yes. Some."

"I would like to hear about that. I was going to ask what it was like, but I do not think you would expect me to summarise life on the Spindle in a few choice words, let alone the memories of a planet that has burned."

I clicked my tongue in acknowledgement, a linguistic habit that came with speaking Adjumiri, and to my surprise, her smile widened, and she clicked in reply, then laughed at the effect. "You should meet my kindler," she exclaimed. "Xe'd like you."

"It would be my honour. Although I have to tell you right now, I've never had a stomach for kol."

"Goodness, no – foul stuff."

"Have you told your kindler that?"

"Xe knows. Xe disapproves. Xe tries not to, but I know . . . Xe is incredibly proud of me, and also, there are things I do, ways I speak xe does not understand. Perhaps never will."

"You are doing well for yourself."

"I suppose I am," she sighed, turning the glass in her hands just like Hulder might have twisted that flower – but Hulder knew what qe did. In Adjumiri, her voice was broader, a little louder, as if the language itself encouraged disinhibition. "There isn't really much choice, is there? When you are not born in any place, when every day you are reminded that though you are welcome, you are different. Just . . . a little bit different. You have to do well for yourself. You have to do so very, very well, if you are to do anything at all."

I tilted my chin towards the place where the commotion had been – the shouting man, the hush of diplomats closing ranks. "What was that about?"

"The ambassador from Nitashi? You don't know?"

"I live on a very small island in a corner of a planet where not many people go," I sighed. "And though with Cuxil I do . . . a great many things, the galaxy is vast, no?"

She studied me for a moment, trying to read whether I was joking or not. She was better, perhaps, at judging these things than most – Spindlers had to be. She clicked once more, a habit borrowed from her ageing kindler when bustling about xer home, then shook her head, a mannerism of which her kindler most definitely would not have approved. "They say the Shine are preparing to attack Nitashi. It's outside Lhonoja's blast zone, population of less than three hundred million. They say that the Executorium has already voted, decided that it's better business – better Shine, would you say? – to conquer Nitashi than try to protect the worlds it already has. Everyone's seen the fleet build-up. Nitashi wants the Accord to send aid, but it's not a full Accord member, never signed the protocols, and anyway, the blackships . . . "

"The Accord won't openly engage in war with the Shine while there are planet-killers pointed at its worlds."

"Quite. I'm sure there'll be a proxy war, if the invasion does happen. Arms and resources funnelled through whatever blockade the Shine puts about the planet. Perhaps they'll ask you to help.

They say the ghost of Hasha-to is the most accurate Pilot to ever cross the dark, capable of flinging a ship through arcspace and out the other side to within a mil of its intended destination. Perhaps they'll give you a nullship, ask you to turn smuggler."

"I had no idea people said so much."

"This is the Spindle. Conversation is our business."

"What else do people say, if you don't mind me asking?"

Her eyes flickered across the other guests, wondering perhaps how many nearby might speak Adjumiri, understand our gentle murmurings. Fewer and fewer every year, I wanted to say. Soon this speech that should be sung between the spires will be a whispered code, muttered in gloomy places between dying friends.

"They say that your presence here, with the Consensus, is further proof that the Consensus is preparing to fight. The quans too – the mainframes may have differing operational standards, different ethics, if you will, but ever since the Slow," a tilt of her head towards the watching black square, the silent emissary standing over us, "sent qis message all those years ago, the quans have been … restless. They say that if the Slow thinks these times are worth witnessing, worth *speaking* to, then perhaps there is a test, of sentience, of something – the quans disagree on what – that should not be met with passivity. The Shine has blackships pointed at the mainframes too, of course. Even the hidden ones, the ones in the asteroid belts or on the edge of a star's coronal field – would you really take the risk? How many billions must die to stand up to the Shine's bullying? How many lives is it worth? I would not want to make that call. I would not want to see what history would say of me if I did not."

"You seem to think war is inevitable."

"Some sort of conflict, yes. I doubt the Accord has the will to actually call it war. I don't even know why the Shine is here, though they've certainly made an impression."

"Yes," I murmured, eyes drifting to the obvious height of Theodosius Rhode. "They have, haven't they?"

In the middle of the room, laughing as if hé had not a care in the world: the Executor.

I watch from a distance, and feel a little embarrassed at how easily hé holds my attention. Very good Shine, the ability to seemingly do nothing while being the centre of the world. I had tried to explain this to Gebre – Shine was never just money. Status, prestige, privilege, charisma, the ability to get people to do things for you and say how happy they were to get it done – that was Shinier than any Glint.

Around hím, hís retinue. A couple of Board members I did not know, the marks of their Venture on their collar – the CEO of Blue Land, the COO of Phonh-Ten, two of the most significant Ventures in the Shine, holding between them nearly half of the votes on the current Executorium. They smiled and laughed too, though the COO of Phonh-Ten looked old, too old perhaps for even Glint to buy a younger face, and hís eyes kept flickering to Theodosius Rhode like a moth drawn to flame.

Security, of course. They did not wear exoskeletons or carry overt weapons. Such things would not have been permissible on the Spindle. But beneath their stiff black suits and tight black pants, muscles moved with more than just organic strength. There was always a pay-off to be made in bio-muscular enhancement – stronger bones required heavier muscles to move them, heavier muscles required stronger bones and so on. Even with the best bio-engineering, few who undertook such radical procedures lived much past sixty, though there was always a parade of the desperate willing who imagined that somehow they would be the exception to the rule.

Debtors too.

Golden collars, golden rings.

I wondered what they'd done to lose everything. I wondered if any ambassadors would dare to call them slaves.

Probably not.

Slavery was forbidden within the Accord, and discovery of its perpetration legally bound all Accord members to immediate, forceful action. Thus: "Low-waged debt-forgiveness labour" was how the debtor's collar tended to be written up in Accord reports, as scholars and diplomats swallowed their ethics in the face of a cruelty they dared not admit they were powerless to oppose.

So much for honesty. So much for the deeds of prideful, learned men.

Two more figures of note, who I could not place.

They stand awkwardly on the edge of the throng that surrounds the Executor, an ageing man and a younger woman. Some work had been done to delay age in the male – none of the expensive genetic work that was reserved for the wealthiest of the Executorium, but marks of surgical and cybernetic intervention were apparent on his jaw, his neck. He stood tall enough to be noted, to be considered a paragon of strong Shine, with a golden beard that was in fashion for the current generations of *him*, the paragons of their sex – but he would never be in that elite camp, no matter how hard he tried. The surgical scars marked his status immediately – Shiny enough to afford the work, not quite Shiny enough to afford to disguise it, a perpetual upper-middle-class kind of Manager, desperate to be more, never quite achieving it.

The woman: eyes of green, her skull entirely shaved, not a single scar on her hands or neck, but rather, a complex weave, almost a circuit board of pale silver tissue marked across the top of her head, a declaration of vaunted intellect. Unlike the man and his middling medical work, whoever had burned the scars into this creature had been an artist. There was strong Shine in those markings, an understanding of the difference between covering yourself in crude diamonds, tasteless declarations of your power, and covering yourself in molten lead, a thing that no one else has seen before, something unique. The Shine has always loved the unique, even – sometimes especially – when it is grotesque.

"Who are they?" I asked Agran, Adjumiri feeling like a language of conspiracy, safer than Normspeak.

She followed my gaze – did not point, absolutely never would – then clicked her tongue three times in her mouth. "Valans Clonas Rengabe and Riv Fexri. Their diplomatic documentations listed them as 'technical advisers', which usually means spies."

"Did their documents say anything else?"

"I did not receive an in-depth briefing on them. My task was to welcome you and Ambassador Cuxil; my more experienced colleagues were assigned to hospitality for the Shine. I can ask around of course. We Spindlers are never indiscreet, but neither do we refuse the reasonable enquiries of our guests."

"That sounds complicated."

"It is and it is not," she replied, eyes shining as she gazed across the room. "I think the word you might use is . . . delicious."

"Delicious" in Adjumiri – it relates to taste, but it also implies an artistic appreciation of something crafted, something that stimulates the senses. Normspeak does not have an equivalent word – in Normspeak, "delicious" can only relate to an appreciation of a flavour in the mouth. Spindlers understood this; they learned Normspeak as a universal tool of communication, but as some of the finest masters of it, they also treated it with the most contempt.

I liked Agran then, and thought Gebre would have too.

After drinks: food.

Feeding so many different stomachs with so many different definitions of "normal" was a challenge only the Spindle could really rise to. Their dedication to the well-being of their guests had extended to the delicacies of Godt, much to Cuxil's delight, and an unfortunate Spindler on the catering staff was set to finding out which of the various treats on her plate I might be able to eat without getting hives.

"The sapphireworm at least? At least that?" Cuxil blurted. "It's not an actual worm, you ninny," she added, seeing my face. "It is a delicious sugary treat of pure mhahgaagh." A sound and gesture as if she were trying to caress her own tongue. "I promise, many of us who are not of Godt have eaten it and adored it, although now I think about it, maybe it was just I who ate it and adored it, and the impression my experience made was so potent that it has seeped into our consciousness and now many of us believe we have enjoyed the treat. That is possible. We are as prone to making blurry memories as any other organic – more so, really, given how many of us there are – but that should just give you an idea how *wonderful* it is!"

The ambassador from Nitashi ate surrounded by a tight, tense knot of delegates. At one point in the evening, his eyes seemed to meet those of Theodosius Rhode, who saluted him with a little tip of hís cup, and smiled as if hé had not a care in the world.

There were speeches.

They spoke of coming together, of unity, of harmony. They spoke of Lhonoja as an opportunity, a chance to bring people together – as if eight hundred million had not died, as if billions had not been scattered to the stars. All their speeches were directed to Theodosius, though hé showed no sign of caring. Magnificent Shine; extraordinary Shine. To walk into a room and ignore everyone, and have everyone still try to talk to you despite that. I wondered if the diplomats and foreign ministers churning through their notes understood just how much power they were giving hím.

A quan issued a statement on behalf on the non-human delegates, stating how much they appreciated the care their hosts were taking with the atmospheric conditions in their accommodation despite the acidic damage it was causing to inner hulls, and nothing more.

"It's like they're laughing at us," someone said, and was immediately hushed.

Afterwards, knots of civil servants and quiet, thoughtful barterers who knew when to smile and when to say "that will not work for either of us" separated into huddles, while their more prominent, more recognisable masters gave commnet interviews and talked earnestly about tragedy and empty hopes. And at the beginning of second night, that sweeping darkness that rushes through the Spindle's halls, I went to sit by the messenger of the Slow, to wait for Hulder.

Hulder never came.

Qis absence was so shocking, so absurdly rude, that for a moment I was almost impressed. A deliberate no-show, a purposeful snub – in other individuals you could imagine an error, an accident or delay, but not Hulder. Qe was built for integration and communication. If qe chose not to make an appointment, qe chose it on purpose.

I waited almost an entire Normhour for qim. When finally I shook my head, rattled myself free of this frozen state, there was someone else behind me, looking up at the black cube on its plinth, a green-blue drink held in one hand, a single pearl embedded in her right ear. Riv Fexri, one of the two from the Executor's entourage who didn't belong, maybe a spy, maybe something else – and here she was, gazing at a manifestation of an entity that the Shine would almost certainly have called an enemy, with a curiosity that at once piqued my own.

I must have looked at her too long, because her eyes flickered to me, looked me over once, lingered on the scar on the back of my hand, before she blurted in Mdo-sa: "Hello."

"Hello," I replied, in the language of the Shine.

"You are dressed like a Xi but have the scars of the Shine. Are you a Unionist?" There was no rancour in her voice; a simple, flat curiosity, a scientist encountering something previously unknown.

"I was born on Tu-mdo."

"But you escaped?"

I blinked in surprise, wondered for a moment if I'd misremembered the word – not "left" or "fled" or "departed" but *escaped*, as if the Shine were a prison to flee from. "Yes. A long time ago."

"Uh. How long?"

"By now . . . over a hundred years."

"You don't look that old."

"No. There have been . . . alterations."

"I do not understand what that means."

"My body does not age in an appropriate manner. Although you could say the same of the Executor, could you not?"

No smile, no frown. She is fascinated – that is all. Simply fascinated. Perhaps that is why she is here, standing before the messenger of the Slow. It is an incredibly dangerous curiosity; I find the effect hypnotic.

"Hé has access to the most expensive, most exclusive medical treatments in the galaxy," she mused, as if solving a problem out loud. "Are you saying you do too?"

"I am not saying that, no. I am ... uncomfortable with my condition."

"That's fine," she replied, with an immediate flicker of her fingers – a thing that resembled hand-speak, but not of Mdo-sa, a dancing of fingers that on Adjumir might have expressed a kind of easy moving-on, a polite acknowledgement of the topic needing to change. As soon as it was there, it was gone, and I thought perhaps I had imagined it, and she was staring back into the blackness of the Slow. "We can talk about something else. If you are not a rebel, are you with the Xi? You are dressed like them."

"No. I am assistant to the ambassador for the Consensus."

"Within the United Social Venture, the Consensus is a banned trans-humanist organisation."

"I know."

"There is nothing valued so much in the Shine as diversity of thought and ability," she intoned. "The Consensus kill that individuality."

I could not tell from how she spoke whether she believed what she said; her voice was as flat and level as mine so often was, an experience both strangely comforting and unnerving. "The Consensus might argue," I mused, "that most of society is nothing more and nothing less than a distributed consciousness. We rely on other people to do so much thinking for us – to design our ships, farm our food, solve equations or write poetry to help us unravel our feelings – that in many ways to live anything but utterly alone is already to be part of a hive mind anyway. All the Consensus does, they say, is deepen that bond. That is what they claim, at least. I can understand how, given that the only way to experience it is to become it, there is room for interpretation and doubt."

"That is an interesting perspective I had not considered. I am sure I will find it flawed, in time. If you believe it, why haven't you joined them?"

"I tried, once. The first stage of bonding is to share your mind with a circle of eight, a temporary connection to see if this is an experience you wish to deepen and create. But the eight I joined looked into me and broke the connection at once, and said I was incompatible with their thoughts."

"You were rejected?"

"They were very apologetic about it. They wept. They held each other and me and said sorry, sorry, we're so sorry, oh help us, oh stars, oh hearts, help us! It was very strange."

"I have never heard of someone being rejected from the Consensus. Even murderers are welcomed, I heard. I heard the Consensus said there was no punishment greater for a killer than to share their mind with those they have wronged."

"Like I said – everyone was very apologetic."

"Uh."

That "uh" – it seemed honest, if nothing else, neither feigning false comfort nor dismissing what I had said. A neutral "uh" of data lacking, of judgement withheld. I wondered then whether I liked Riv Fexri, even though she was, ostensibly, my enemy.

For a moment the two of us stood in silence, and it did not feel awkward. She did not seem to expect much from me, and I was perfectly happy expecting nothing from her, and it was almost comforting, a kind of safety. But old habits die hard, and decades of being the quiet one at parties, the one who was doing it wrong, tickled on the tip of my tongue, so I blurted: "What about you? Why are you here?"

"I am here because my boss is here," she replied, without hesitation or malice. "He is getting old and making mistakes. He should not be here. I am here to make sure he doesn't do anything bad. He is an engineer, not a diplomat. It is absolute folly for him to have come."

"Then why is he here?"

Her fingers swirled the stem of her cup back and forth, settling little storms in the remnants of her drink. "Business," she replied at last, a delay that meant she was lying, a firmness that implied she was not interested in being questioned on that fact. "Many people meet on the Spindle. More than just diplomats."

"Do you . . . like your boss?" I tried.

"No."

"But you still work for him."

"If I left my current employment," she replied primly, "I would lose all my Shine. I would be useless, worthless, and most likely end up indentured to a Venture with poor working conditions and limited prospects for my old age. This is unacceptable. In my work I am protected. This is enough."

"Is it?"

"If you are from Tu-mdo, you know that it is."

I thought about this a moment longer, clicked my tongue once in agreement. To my surprise, she seemed to understand, a little nod, and then into silence once again we lapsed. Finally: "Do you fancy defecting?" I blurted, eyes everywhere except on her. "It's absolutely fine if you don't. I just reason, given everything you have said, you probably have intelligence, information, et cetera, and you seem moderately dissatisfied with your position. Comfort, security, so on and so forth – I'm sure it could all be arranged."

For a moment, she seemed to think about it, turning the glass between her fingers. Then: "No thank you," she replied. "But I understand that it is partially thoughtful of you to ask, regardless of your broader political motivations."

"Fair enough."

"Indeed."

We stood together watching the room. Then she sighed, drained the last drink from the bottom of her glass and, half turning to look at me – or rather, no, a little past me, up and to the left, the same not-quite-eye-contact that was how I didn't-quite-look at people most of the time – said: "If you are with the Consensus, then Corpsec probably considers you an enemy operative, so I really shouldn't speak to you any more."

"I am sorry to hear that, though you are probably correct."

"I have enjoyed talking to you."

"Likewise."

"Uh-huh." There it was again – a little "uh" that was neither good nor bad, merely a holding sound where more data was yet to be. "Well then," she concluded. "Goodbye."

And Riv Fexri walked away.

Chapter 40

In the sleeping hour, an upload to my reader.

It comes from Agran, and contains information on the man and the woman whose presence in the Spindle made no sense.

She: Riv Fexri, born to a medium-Shine family that fell on hard times, worked her way up through sheer scientific gumption and ingenuity. This was especially remarkable given her limited educational opportunities and the weight of debt she acquired in pursuing her interests. The debt should have crushed her, but just this once her Venture saw the potential in her mind, saw how valuable it might be if nurtured instead of suppressed, and made the bold choice to promote her rather than sell her. Perhaps it was this decision – the embracing of her in all her difference – that had given her such strong Shine. Perhaps she had realised that so long as she didn't too overtly question the established way, she could be that most elusive, alluring of things – that *other* that is different, exciting, without actually being a threat.

He: Valans Clonas Rengabe.

A list of places he'd been, people he'd seen, mistakes he'd made.

He was third-generation Management, as nearly all Managers were, but had lost considerable Shine through the actions of his irresponsible younger brother. Gambling, cheating – and worst of all, getting caught. Valans Clonas Rengabe should have just cut loose – the Shiniest move would have been to buy up his brother's debt at the lowest possible price, and then sell it on to another Venture. His sibling could have been in a debtor's collar working down some sun-forsaken mine on another planet, forgotten and unregarded, and Valans could have carried on in peace.

Instead, in a very un-Shiny move, Valans had tried to support his brother, leveraging contacts and making introductions for him. This had backfired spectacularly when his brother merely continued in his ways, costing Valans extraordinary Shine and nearly crippling his career in the process. Valans had been saved by one thing, and one thing alone: he was the designer, implementer and occasionally, controversially, test subject for the Shine's blackship arccomms.

He is the creator of the Tryphon.

Right here, in this place, at this time.

Here he is.

Rituals of coming-of-age, notable and obscure:

Windriding, most famously practised by the people of the mountainous areas of Astervailis. At its simplest level, the youngling grabs the trailing tendrils of a floating scyllapod and drifts over a ceremonial fence. At a more convoluted level – one that is legislated against for health-and-safety reasons but still practised in more remote communities – the youngling rides the scyllapod over the edge of the mountain, their weight eventually dragging it down into the valleys below in an act of sky-diving that is as recklessly dangerous as it is exhilarating for the now-adult when they reach their waiting family below.

The long walk. Variations of this are found in cultures too numerous to name and include anything from a year of planetary travel funded by governmental grant, solo crossings of desert or arctic plains, up to the inaugural spacewalk of a number of orbital habitats, where the youngling is for the very first time fitted with their own suit and sent to traverse the length of their home with nothing more than a tether, a few lils of oxygen and a diligently trained mental map.

The ritual bath; the first tattoo; the first scar; the saying of prayers; the singing of songs. There are variations of all of the above that can be found in nearly all cultures in all places, including among the aka-aka, who determine coming-of-age as the first time the sexual organs of their offspring switch, and who perform a suspiration chorus to greet the youngling's arrival into adulthood.

The passing-through of the gate, and choosing of the name. Traditionally, each Adjumiri who entered adulthood was expected to go to the song spire with family and friends, to sing the songs and dress themselves in their adult robes. These days, there are only a few song spires standing among the scattered peoples of Adjumir, so instead the younglings mumble the songs awkwardly in their kitchens, while their anxious kindlers look on.

Of course, in many societies these things are not as formalised, and the youngling celebrates by the traditional mode of simply having an enormous, frequently alcoholic, all-out birthday bash.

Marching, striding, chin forward, fists clenched. The shadows are solid around me, the walls are bright and painted in sweeps of orange, swirls of red. I have no interest in them; curiosity does not bend the dark, fascination does not flicker the light. I have questions – so many, many questions – but what I mostly have is anger. Jaw-clenching, gut-churning, back-bending fury.

The feeling I have been used.

The feeling I have been lied to.

The feeling that everything, all of it – Cuxil, Hulder, Ulannad, Valans – is part of some great big joke that everyone else knows and no one is telling me and I have had this feeling my whole life, my whole existence has been one of knowing that everyone else seems to know something I do not and I cannot stand it any more, I cannot stand it, it is killing me and so to the prayer room I go, looking for answers.

Tryphon. Blackships and Tryphon and is this what Gebre died for

(it is not)

is this why when I close my eyes all I hear is the storm

(it is not. Te died for so much more, and would have died anyway)

What is the point of any of it?

Always moving. That is the Adjumiri way.

I could smell the incense of the prayer room as I approached, and it was sickly, floral, threaded with wax. The door stood open, the lights dimmed, candles burning on the altar, real candles, wax and smoke – outrageously dangerous, somehow permitted. Ulannad stood before the little line of dancing flames, and in his hand he held the white box that contained the interface

the thing Gebre had died/not died/lived/not lived for

And next to him was Valans Clonas Rengabe.

Valans did not recognise me as I entered, started with surprise, glanced towards the altar as if wondering whether it was too late to feign a little divinity, mouth working as he tried to find some excuse for his presence, so far from the rest of the Shine delegates. I wondered how he had managed to shake off his security, his debtors – maybe he wasn't considered important enough to pay attention to.

"What is this?" I blurted. "Ulannad – what is this?"

"Mawukana," breathed the Lordat. "You shouldn't be here."

I marched down the central aisle, empty chairs and soft candle-light, until I stood a single step from him. "What is this?" I hissed. "What are you doing?"

"Who is this?" Valans snapped, speaking Mdo-sa. "Who is this man? I am not—"

"He is one of us," Ulannad barked. "He is not a threat."

"Not a threat?" I spoke in the same language, the sounds of Glastya Row suddenly reassuringly crude, reassuringly heavy on my lips. "Not a threat? I will rip your fucking heart out and feed it to the black ... *What are you doing?*"

"I am giving Valans the Tryphon," Ulannad replied primly. "I am returning his property."

I reached out to snatch the box from the Lordat's hand, but he drew it quickly away, stepping back towards the altar, his other hand reaching for something inside his robe.

"Lordat," hissed Valans. "I am not—"

"It's fine," snapped Ulannad, a little too loud, eyes fixed on me, and he was afraid – finally, he was afraid, despite himself. So much for the chanting of the dark. "It's fine. Maw, there are things happening here that you don't understand. A deal has been reached, an exchange, there are—"

"No! It's not ..." I tried to find the word, had to switch to Adjumiri, no words in Mdo-sa to express it, no way to say ter name and do it right, didn't think they understood but had to scream it anyway, had to try and make someone, anyone understand. "Te died for this!" I snarled. "Te died for it and I left ter, I left ter and I didn't go back I didn't even go back so if you think that you can just take it and give it to some ... some Manager ..." Back to Mdo-sa, Adjumiri unable to express the true meaning of this word, "Manager", all the weight and hate it needed. "I will kill you first. Do you believe me? I want you to believe me, Lordat of the Light."

Ulannad knew enough to be afraid, and did not move.

It was therefore Valans who cracked, his ignorance greater than his fear. He lunged for the white box in Ulannad's hand, left arm sweeping up from his hip as he did, a glint of something metal in it. Ulannad sprang back instinctively, but Valans' hand caught the edge of the box and for a moment the two men struggled, grunting inelegantly like children with a toy. Then Ulannad brought his elbow across and into the other man's chin, a clack of teeth and jaw. Fingers spasmed open even as the old scientist huffed in wordless pain, and a springshot ejector fell from his left palm, a cobbled fusion of medical device and toy, a poisoned dart primed in its end. I grabbed it off the floor as Ulannad shoved Valans back and drew the box closer to his chest, both men panting with unexpected exertion, and in the moment of tension as everyone waited for someone to do something else, Ulannad growled: "You don't understand what's—"

His statement was cut short by a buzzing by my right ear.

I didn't recognise the design of grenade hovering softly at head-height, but most military devices have common themes. Compact, unflashy, discreet – Corpsec must have smuggled the components for it onto the station one bit at a time, assembling it on site to avoid the Spindle's security scans. I saw it, and for a brief moment wondered if I was going to die. I had never had my head severed from my body before, never had my brain exploded, for all of the various ways in which I have been killed. Views were divided among experts as to whether the disintegration of my brain matter would prove terminal – such a hypothesis was difficult to test more than once.

As it turned out, the grenade was merely a neuro-stun, which sent the room blindly to the ground.

Chapter 41

The people lie on the floor of the chapel, while around them chaos rages.

Valans.

He burbles: "It's not what it seems! It's a trick! They lured me here – they lured me, it's a trick, it's . . ."

Ulannad. He is face-down, hands tied behind his back like the rest of us, his head turned towards me as I try to blink the static from my eyes, the pain from my skull. He seems very calm, even smiles. I suddenly wish I'd had a chance to ask him: what was your story? How did you come to be here? You seem comfortable with pain, with terror – would it be too much to speak on that?

I am feeling curious, somewhere beneath the pain.

Nothing new there.

But also angry.

Angry to be on the floor, bound.

Angry at the whining of Valans' voice, at the ringing in my ears, at the feet stomping around by my head, at the weight of someone's boot on my back. Glastya Row, a boot on my back, it rained the day we were sent to Hasha-to, the judge said that I had not mounted an adequate defence, and I replied that I had not been given the opportunity, and she said that wasn't how things worked in Heom and I had only myself to blame, and thus my world had ended, and thus Mawukana na-Vdnaze had died.

Angry at Ulannad. At Hulder and Cuxil and the whole stinking, bloody thing.

Dysregulated. Angry enough to want to reach to that place inside, the little part of me that was recorded in error, because there is something in the dark, something fascinated and eager, that has never really understood this reality, never really been able to comprehend what it sees.

Here it is.

Here it is.

The part of me that sits in the place where the Lux would say I should feel a soul.

The thing that everyone tells me is wrong, incorrect, and it feels . . . like they are mistaken.

The light is dim, and I do not know how many I will kill before someone remembers who I am, expects me to be kind, if anyone here really does, right now, I do not care, and so . . .

"Everyone will please stand down now!"

It is Agran's voice.

I strain my neck to see her, can't quite against the weight on my back, hear feet moving, voices muttering, Normspeak and Mdo-sa and the language of the Spindle, then again, louder: "*I said stand down!*"

There were four Corpsec in the room – they must have been the ones who threw the grenade that so rudely interrupted our confrontation – and now there are five Spindlers. People are shouting, barking accusations – perhaps some weapons are being pointed, it's hard to see. Valans is gibbering now, gibbering it's not what it looks like, it's not what it looks like, I was doing the right thing, *I was making it all right!!*

"You are on the Spindle, you will abide by Spindle laws – *kindly get that fucking thing out of my face thank you!*"

Shouting, posturing; from the floor it all feels rather futile.

Come down here, I want to say. It's a whole other perspective.

Ulannad is smiling at me. There almost seems to be a kind of forgiveness there, which I instinctively resent. I wonder if he knows what I will become. I have a terrible feeling that he knows exactly what I am, and is deliberately trying to think kindly of me, to see in me some glimmer of compassion, humanity that is worth his respect. Maybe he's about to whisper: *You're a good man, Mawukana na-Vdnaze.* I think that will break me, if he does. It will certainly make what must come next far, far harder.

I mouth: *Sorry*, in Mdo-sa, but don't think the motion of my lips really communicates it, don't really have the breath to do much more. *I'm sorry. I'm sorry.*

"They stole a device – Shine property – they stole it . . . "

"Put your weapons down now! Put them down! You are on the Spindle now, there will be opportunity to be heard, but you are in violation of every . . . "

This is how people get killed, I realise. Implacably roaring at each other, unable to imagine being the first to yield.

Maybe if I just lie here quietly, everyone who is standing will kill everyone else. The idea is briefly comforting. Perhaps someone else can be a monster today, so I don't have to.

Then a voice says, from the direction of the door: "Stand aside."

Hé speaks Normspeak with a Mdo-sa accent, and as I have never heard him speak this speech, I cannot immediately place him. But the people standing over me seem to immediately obey; the weight on my back eases a little, guns lowered, some of the panting, gasping, raging fury of the room diminishes. A gesture; hands lift me, Ulannad, Valans, prop us upright against the altar, and now I see.

The Executor stands in the door, flanked by more security, Riv at his back. In front of him, between this new entourage and the plain-clothed Corpsec who moments ago were stomping on my back, is Agran and her team, guns still drawn, though noticeably not pointed towards him. No one points a gun at Theodosius Rhode.

"This seems to be a terrible misunderstanding," Theodosius breathes, as hé drifts into the increasingly-cramped, candle-bathed room. "A diplomatic error, indeed."

"These are yours?" demands Agran, gesturing to the Corpsec leaning over us.

"They are," replies Theodosius breezily. "Sent to protect me and my delegates – a task your security seems to be failing at."

"They have attacked and detained civilians," barks Agran. "They will—"

Theodosius silences her with a raised hand. This should not work; she should just keep issuing her instructions, this is her station, her place. But something of the power of the Executor, of hís expectation – expectations of obedience, immediate and absolute – seems to slam into her, knock the words from her mouth, and so instead, the master of hís universe, Theodosius drifts towards us, taking in Ulannad, Valans, me.

"A Unionist, a scientist and a ghost," hé muses, nodding one to the other. "A rebel, a fool and . . . something else."

"Whatever accusations you may make, Spindle security will handle it. Corpsec has no authority here."

"What's your name, Spindler?"

A hesitation, a moment – perhaps if she speaks her name, she will be marked. Hé will find her, hís people will find her – but then again, hé hardly needs her name for that. She was damned the moment hé decided she was. May as well cooperate, in the hope whatever hé has in mind hurts less, no?

"Agran," she blurts. "Agran Hulathind Daj Kiddanasithwa."

"An unusual name for a Spindler. No, wait, don't tell me – Adjumir, no? Hadda. The 'Daj' – it was common to the colonies, rather than the mother planet. Something like 'voyager' or 'pioneer' – Normspeak doesn't do these equivalents well, does it?"

This should be rhetorical – hé knows the answer – yet hé waits for her to confirm it, smiling patiently, tolerating her sudden dumbness. "Yes," she mumbles. "Hadda. Yes."

"And how many of your people are there on the Spindle? Did the natives of this station welcome in you one mothership at a time, saying yes, of course, come in your millions, we are one, we will learn to speak your speech, sing your songs, it is a privilege to be together with you? Or did you come in dribs and drabs, a dozen here, a hundred there, welcomed with a grudging 'well, if it makes us feel good about ourselves', second-class citizens told how lucky you were, how grateful you should be for scraps? It was the latter, wasn't it. The way you deport yourself, trying to take up space, trying to be strong, the big strong chief, because when you were a child other children laughed at you for the way you spoke and the things you ate, and you think you hear them laughing still, no? Well, I have news for you, Agran Hulathind Daj Kiddanasithwa. They're not laughing now. You grew up, and you were not meek, and that makes you unacceptable."

Songs of Adjumir that will never again be sung:

The song of crossing the sands, sung to honour the return of would-be marriage kinn from the deserts, where for ten days and ten nights they were set to wander, to learn each other's hearts and test the strength of their bonds.

The song of the moon pearl, which grew in the belly of a certain mollusc off the edge of a certain island, and in whose translucent form it was said, at a certain time, beneath a certain light, visions of the future would unfold. Samples of the mollusc have been saved, kept in a laboratory, but no one has quite found the right conditions to reseed it, and no one is sure they ever will.

The song of the motherships, sung for the going-out and the coming-back. It was written in the final days of the planet, and will never be sung again.

Agran stands silent.

Agran has perhaps learned more silence than her kindlers wish she would.

Theodosius Rhode turns from her, to inspect the three of us. His eyes pass over me, linger a moment, but if he knows me as anything more than an intelligence report, I cannot tell. At last, his gaze settles on Valans. Behind him, Riv watches, flanked by security, her face empty and cold.

Theodosius walks towards his scientist, his most valued engineer, makes no move to unbind him.

"Well," hé tuts at last. "You have chosen poorly."

"They have the interface – the Tryphon, the one from *Seaburn*," whimpers the scientist. "I verified it, came here to retrieve it, to end it . . ."

"Ah yes. This old thing." Theodosius reaches past the old man, picks up the interface, turns it this way and that. It is tiny in his oversized hands. "This has been bothering us for a while now. Minds reaching across the dark, calling out to our Pilots, whispering to them, asking them questions, so many questions. Where are you now? What can you see? Tell us, tell us, tell us where you are. We didn't think that the spies of the Accord would be so bold as to hook the minds of their people to our arcspace interfaces, but then I suppose that is what they use you for."

His eyes flickered to me as he spoke these words, one grey, one gold, though his body stayed turned to Valans. I stared back, wasn't sure if I could look away, saw him smile, shake his head a little. The Executor was used to quiet disappointments from lesser people.

"I did it for you," whined Valans. "I knew I could make it right, I risked everything to—"

"*If you were able to make it right, you would never have had to come here!*" roared Theodosius. Behind him, even Agran flinched, shoulders drawing back, breaths swallowed in. Valans had tears in his eyes, was a curled-up bend of spine and neck beneath the Executor's rage. Theodosius glowered down at the bundled-up scientist, sighed, tutted, shook his head. "Agran Hulathind Daj Kiddanasithwa, I do apologise for all of this. It would appear one of my entourage has made a bit of a fuss. He will be reprimanded. We will be taking him to my corvette now; please feel free to revoke his visa."

Valans crying out, but no, but listen, but I . . .

Theodosius has already lost interest in him. Already wiped him from his awareness.

Turns fully, looks me up, looks me down one more time, and I cannot tell what hé makes of all that hé sees. Turns again, looks at Ulannad, his fingers still tracing the curve of the Tryphon in his hand. Then, without a change in expression or flicker of concern, his fist closes. I watch the thin, worn metal of the interface crumple slowly in his grasp, case crack, tiny tendrils spilling from its belly like guts from a hunted rodent. Watch it fall to the floor, a meaningless hunk of junk, barely worth the scrap.

"Well," hé murmured. "Well. Hasn't this all been interesting."

So saying, hé turned, nodded once at a Corpsec guard, who stepped forward and calmly, without hesitation, shot Ulannad in the head.

I watched the Lordat's neck snap back, then forward as he fell.

He bumped against my foot as he crumpled to the ground, as if the muscles that had sustained him had just been waiting for this moment, as if life had been an inconvenient kind of nagging blared out by the brain against the overwhelming instinct of the body to collapse, cease, sleep.

The pandemonium that had been suppressed by the Executor's presence roared back into life. Guns raised, shouting, get down, put it down, put it down, *put it down now!* The actual wound in Ulannad's head was neat, relatively tiny, a mere puff of blood from where the projectile had entered, a blossoming of pink behind the Lordat's eyes the only hint of the internal carnage of its passage.

Through it all, Theodosius smiled.

Hé smiled, and as the raging, the shouting grew higher, hé began to laugh.

It was a rich roar of sound, full-chested, full-bodied, quite unlike any of the little huffs of dire mirth I was used to from the Managers of the Shine. It was a full revelling, a joyous delight, an appreciation bordering on the artistic for that which unfolded about hím. Hé was still laughing as hé ordered hís security to lay down their arms and, turning to Agran with that same expansive beam of pleasure, exclaimed: "Well then, we seem to have a diplomatic incident, no?"

And then, just for the hell of it, hé took a pistol from one of hís entourage and shot me in the chest.

Chapter 42

I did not die. The shot wasn't even lethal. If anything, I probably felt it more because I expected to, imagined myself with a hole in my heart. Instead, it was a simple nerve-block, which fizzled out within fifteen minutes of firing.

Agran sat next to me on the floor of a refuge that had actually been kept in proper order, survival suits and spare oxygen neatly arranged, put a cup of water in my shaking hands, said: "My kindler said you should never call someone a *pytha*. It is ... *huth*? That is correct, yes? On the Spindle, we don't have enough words to curse."

I nodded; clicked my tongue; couldn't remember the most appropriate way to communicate. Cuxil sat by the door on the cold metal floor, her legs crossed, arms loose in her lap, eyes half closed like one in prayer.

"Ulannad is dead," I mumbled, and my speech was messy, odd nerves still firing in all the wrong ways.

"Yes. I'm afraid he is."

"What's happening now?"

"Nothing."

"What do you mean ... nothing? They just killed—"

"The Spindle is revoking the Executor's visa."

I tried to sit up, and everything hurt, and water spilled from the cup in my hand all over my lap, cold and annoying. "They what?"

"We have arrested the Corpsec who killed the Lordat, but there was no verbal command given, no physical order. We cannot say that the Executor ordered the death of Ulannad, and even if hé did . . . do you want us to arrest the Executor of the Shine? Hé has a battleship on system's edge."

"So call for help, call for—"

"There is going to be a war, Maw." It was Cuxil who spoke, her voice in that distant place where the feelings of the Consensus perhaps washed through her, tempering the individual with the warmth of the many. Perhaps Cuxil's heart beat fast; perhaps there was adrenaline rushing through her system, cortisol pounding in her veins. But the Consensus breathed with her, through her, for her, and so soft and gentle she mused: "It is all but certain. Rather than attempt to save the worlds they have in the blast zone, the Shine are going to invade those that are not. Nitashi will be their first target, everyone knows it. A weak planet, outside the Accord – it's perfect. They didn't come here to negotiate. They came here to show their strength. To show that they can do what they want, when they want, and no one will stop them. And no one will. Not while the blackships are pointed at our planets."

"The interface, Valans . . ."

"The interface is destroyed, and Valans is dead, or will be very soon. Whatever deal he struck with Ulannad, I doubt the Executor will be pleased with hís subordinate's initiative."

Meanings of the scars etched into the flesh of those who live under the Shine:

Three straight lines cut across the back of the hand: a technician specialising in high-voltage work, things that go fizz-pop in the dark.

One teardrop cut beneath the left eye: undertaker, keeper of the dead, who preserves a lock of hair of every corpse before the bodies are given over to the fertilisers.

A single cut at the base of the spine: one whose time is done, who can no longer labour fruitfully, and who now is merely waiting to die .

"What happens now?" I asked.

"It is over. We are going to leave. The Spindle does not hold you accountable for what happened – your presence appears circumstantial – but they are concerned that they could not protect you should retribution come your way. Embarrassing if your body was found."

"They would not find a body," I grunted.

"Perhaps not; and that could present a different kind of problem, no?"

I pressed my hands to my face, covering my eyes. There was still a hot afterburn from the grenade, a brightness I wanted to claw out, a chemical glow. Then, a hand on my knee. I stared down at it in surprise, at the shock of a physical touch, looked up into Cuxil's quiet, concerned eyes. Consensus are always blithe when it comes to physical contact; I wondered when someone's skin had last brushed mine willingly.

"Maw," she murmured. "We have to go."

I looked at her, that compassionate gaze that seemed to see straight into every soul and find only beauty. "You lied to me," I breathed. "Hulder. You. You lied."

"Maw," she cut in, a little harder now, pressing her hand into my knee. "There are things here I do not fully comprehend myself. In time I will find understanding, but for now I need to know: are you curious? Are you safe?"

"I don't know. I don't know. I don't know anything."

"Then do you understand why I say that we need to go?"

The Consensus love all who dwell within it, but even she thinks I am a monster. I click my agreement, just once, too tired to do anything more. She clicks in reply, stands, helps me to my shaking feet. "Good," she says. And then, an important afterthought, a thing that has to be said: "You are a good man."

She doesn't believe it, but she is trying.

Agran sticks me and Cuxil on the back of a bike and steers us towards the landing bay.

When we get there, Spindle security are waiting for us, faces serious, hands folded politely, eyes down. I think for a moment I'm going to be arrested for murder, and cannot fully fathom why.

One steps forward, and I do not know the language they speak to Agran, only that it is fast, clipped, anxious. Cuxil seems to understand, however, for her expression darkens as they talk and her hand grips my arm, though she makes no effort to translate. Then Agran with a face like melting snow turns to me and says:

"The Executor requests a meeting, before his ship departs."

"With Cuxil?" I ask, when no one seems to stir.

"With you."

"That is incredibly unwise," Cuxil blurts.

"I agree. I will send word."

"I'll meet him," I declare, and feel Cuxil's hand tighten on my arm. "I'll do it."

A moment in which everyone waits for me to change my mind. I do not. "Why?" whispers Cuxil in Xiha, for my ears only. "I am an ambassador, you are here on my mission – tell me why."

"I am . . . curious."

"If you kill him, there will be another Executor, and nothing will change. Do you understand that?"

Five scars on the lips: one who sells you produce that otherwise you might not buy.

Scar on the left thumb: lawmaker, sealer of deals.

Scar on the right thumb: firefighter, emergency responder, the cleaner-up of disaster and flood.

Scars on the feet: courier, messenger, Normspace pilot. No point scarring the feet of an arcspace Pilot – they are not going to live long enough to reap the honour of the mark.

There is a scar on my left arm. It came from the fires of Hasha-to, and though my demise and re-creation had some flaws in their execution, this scar remained.

"I *am* curious," I admit. "And I would wager: so is hé."

Chapter 43

Here are some of the minds I have felt, Tryphon interfaced with my skull, strapped to a Pilot's chair:

In a bunker made of sickness and stone, her name was Jaikyun, had been Jaikyun but now was

Jaikyun Yunnji Therhas Lusina Luchia Markis Hand Kereena Kao Augustin.

All of them, all of them screaming, all of them calling out where are you, where are you, help me, I'm here, I'm here, I'm here where are you?

These were not minds joined in harmony. They did not open themselves up for scrutiny, but rather their darkest secrets were dragged out in shame and horror to be seen by others who were as mad as themselves, glimpses of souls blossoming and burning out in the endless dark like lightning that you turn to see and is already gone

Already gone

Is anyone there can anyone help me help me help me

In time, I learned to ignore the worst of the weeping, the great sloshy drenching of minds being torn apart, and listen for the drone of transmission. It echoed like across the dark, a single voice constantly intoning numbers, numbers, numbers.

87,543,821

61,000

137,839

15

2,187,356

Sometimes the numbers stopped, and actual words were barked.

"571: station 3!"

But usually they just droned on, and on, and on.

11,451

98,762,145

451

9

9

8

It was Rencki who worked out why.

"It's to keep the connection going," qe declared. "To keep the link between the transmitter in blackship command and the receivers open. The randomness is deliberate. If you don't know what is next, you will always be curious."

For the first time in a long time, I felt hate again.

I tried to touch the mind of the broadcasting mind, chained in a command centre.

Whispered: *Where are you? Where are you? Show me where you are . . .*

But they were too far gone.

Sometimes, a Pilot died.

I felt it, and it was not sad.

Their deaths were a sigh, a breathing-out, a letting-go.

The Shine noticed me after a while.

Perhaps some of the Pilots on the blackships, those who were meant to receive the numbers and relay them, chanting eternally whatever the command centre transmitted, began to blurt some of my words. Perhaps they punctuated their endless babble with a whisper of *Let go, let go, do not be afraid* or a muttered *Show me where you are!* and their operators began to notice, and someone put two and two together.

Perhaps it was Valans who realised what was happening.

Perhaps Riv.

Either way, they couldn't do much about it. They didn't understand enough about the dark, about the place where time runs out, to dislodge me from it. I was the worm in the machine, the ever-watching eye, an invader come from the dark.

Despite this, I was not making progress. The minds I reached for were too broken, to hollowed out to tell me anything particular, and over time the Shine grew better at keeping their Pilots numb and dumb, so even when I did manage to establish meaningful connection, slip for the briefest of moments into their eyes, there was nothing to see. Just a different kind of dark. A dark that scared me far more than the void.

Occasionally, of course, another presence.

Not a mind.

Not a soul.

Not a thing nameable with words.

It lay across the blanket of the dark, watching.

Sometimes a coil of it slithered into my soul, through my soul to the places beyond, and the Pilots of the blackships screamed, how they screamed, how they screamed and howled and wailed at a thing they could not name. I did not. I watched it as it watched me, and it felt . . .

Curious.

So very, very curious.

And I knew that it, the thing that slunk through the dark, that *was* the dark, found me really rather boring next to these screaming, broken minds.

Or no, not boring.

Familiar.

And thus not worth any more of its attention.

*

Then, nine years after I first wired my mind into the blackship interface, first connected with the Pilots in the black, the signal stopped. I sat in the Pilot's chair, and reached out, and there was nothing there.

Chapter 44

The Executor was waiting in a little room by the docking bay, as his shuttle was prepared.

It was very brightly lit; more so than was comfortable, a whiteness that threatened to white out everything, taking away the edges of this space so that we seemed almost to float in an eye-aching void of light. It made every part of me itch, want to crawl away on hands and knees, taste something like bile in my throat. Too late now.

Hé had no Corpsec, no attendants with him. Spindle security waited outside – dozens of soldiers, fully armed, yet strangely dis-armed in his presence, keeping at a safe distance so as not to violate his space. Hé smiled as I entered, rose from his seat, a tatty office chair with a low, uncomfortable back. Nevertheless, Theodosius Rhode stood as if were in a throne room and hé the king, as if there were not stains of unwashed ancient lunches in the fabric, a faint smell of rotten-egg docking bay sulphur on the air.

"Mawukana Respected na-Vdnaze, I believe," hé said, in the language of the Shine. Did I imagine it, or had his accent softened since the days of Glastya Row? Become a thing not quite of one place or another? "Won't you sit?"

"I prefer to stand."

"If you wish. But you don't mind if I . . . ?"

I clicked my tongue twice, and hé seemed to understand, or at least not care, and folded hímself back down as if hé expected cocktails now to be served.

"Do you still call yourself Mawukana?" hé asked, when I did not move. "Given all that has changed."

"Yes."

"Mawukana. And I am Theodosius."

"I know."

"Of course you do. I am giving you permission to be informal. You'd be surprised the verbal gymnastics people do when they address me. In the United Social Venture everyone is equal. Equal in our potential, in our possibilities – that is the point. I have achieved certain things, things that others might perhaps envy or aspire to, but nothing more than another could do, with the right circumstances, right amount of get-up-and-go. People always misunderstand this about us. They mistake our hierarchies for crude, imposed things, rather than a reflection of where people naturally settle when the churning stops."

"Every Executive of every Venture inherited their Shine," I snap. "They started their lives with wealth and promise, and used their wealth and promise to keep power to themselves. That is not the Shine of the first colonies, and you know it, so let's not waste each other's time."

"Very well," hé breathed, eyes bright, the smile not flickering, one leg crossed over the other, one hand on top of the other, resting on hís thigh. "Though your analysis lacks a certain vision. Tell me, Mawukana, did we kill someone you loved? Recently, I mean."

I am a dumb, numb sack of flesh standing before this man. Hé sees right through my skin, and still hé smiles and smiles and smiles, so that nothing can be believed except the sight of hís teeth.

"Most Unionists – we killed someone. There are some foot soldiers who feel hard done by, who feel that they were denied opportunity, deserved advancement – but they are generally speaking cheaply bought. Their ambitions are petty, easily fulfilled, easily turned. And there are ideologues, but the problem with that sort is they get so invested in the value of their big ideas that they become rigid, difficult to work with. Some might want to take the USV back to the days of Ko-mdo, to an age where work was survival, primal, every gasp of breath a victory, every drop of water carved from the ice at the edge of the world. Others want to destroy the Shine altogether, believe that the whole system is rotten, a lie, that there are worlds upon worlds where the skies are blue and the seas are clear and if we could all stop trying to measure our dicks against each other then we could live humble, pleasant, contented lives. The Xi are of this sort, I believe. So many . . . average people, happily being average. They boast of having gone centuries without conflict, of everyone being content. Contentment, not growth. Nothing to tax the soul. I often wonder: what is even the point of that? What is the point of a people who are born, live without fire, die without note? What even is the fucking point of them, you know?"

Hé is so baffled by the idea, hé finds it almost funny. How strange it is to live a life where you do no harm, achieve no conquests, and die without a monument.

Gebre is dead, ter ghost tutting in the dark.

What even is the point? te wonders. *When all we are and all we will be is dust, blown before the storm?*

"And so I am forced to wonder," hé continues, "did we kill someone you loved?"

I don't answer.

Hé appears neither surprised nor disappointed at this development.

"I am familiar of course with the ghost of Hasha-to. Enough debtors saw what happened to tell the story; the story was repeated enough to become a legend. I have heard the legend, but also seen the truth. I told my security I would like them to kill you – lethally, of course – to see what happened. They advised against it. Said that if you survived, there might be . . . unpleasantness. That was the word they used. 'Unpleasant'. Very disappointing. I pay for direct information, clean and precise, but a general sense of unspecified dread surrounds you, Respected. A non-specific sense that you are bad news waiting to happen, which no one is able to fully express. The Lordats have whole archives dedicated to the nature of your profanity – but well. Well. It seems to me that the kind of man who returns to Hasha-to and slaughters every officer inside, he doesn't do that because he's curious. Alien. Something unknowable. Not at all. That is vengeance. Pure, cold, blackened vengeance. And so you see, this whole 'careful of the darkspawn, the creature of the unknown' – it doesn't make sense at all. Not at all. I watched the footage – it took you days to crawl back to the airlock. Live and die, live and die, live and die, over and over again, the agony on your face, the way your skin burned – if it was half as horrible as it looked, it must have been extraordinary. How does it feel when your heart stops? Did you find yourself curious then?"

Hé genuinely wants to know.

There is something repulsive about it, something that sickens me in its familiarity. I turn to go, cannot imagine anything good coming from staying.

"Wait."

Hé doesn't raise hís voice; hé has no need. Years of being obeyed has resulted in an assumption that obedience will come, and that assumption lends an authority to hím that cannot be replicated by effort or affectation. I hesitate just a moment, then keep striding towards the door, sheer spite keeping me in motion, until hís voice rings out again, stopping me dead.

"Did you actually join Sarifi im-Yyahwa in her rebellion, or were you just standing by? The court documents said you were a traitor, but in the transcript you denied it, and there were so many people swept up in those days, grabbed because the opportunity presented itself. You strike me as the latter – just an angry little nobody, Shineless, who could not handle the betrayal he felt when his world came apart. Had thought, perhaps, he had some kind of agency, and never got over the shock of realising he did not. Is that you? Am I right?"

Hé is so curious. It glows upon him, exciting, bright, enthralling. I hate hím for that more than anything else, feel the edges of my reality growing thin, think I can smell electrons, taste the popping of photons against my teeth. Hé should be scared of me, should coil back in dread at the *otherness* that creeps into the edge of my soul, at the way the sharp lines of my physicality start to grow a little weak, a little thin. Hé does not. Hé leans forward, leans in, fascinated. Simply fascinated.

"There it is," hé breathes. "There it is. There's the ghost of Hasha-to."

Adjumiri songs – the walking songs of the earth and the sky; the songs of ceremony and binding, of becoming one-who-is-bound, two-who-are-binding; the prophecy songs, sung to the stars, secret and sacred and soon to be lost – they are building new spires in new places but the acoustics aren't quite right

and I want to rip Theodosius Rhode's heart out.

Not just because I am curious, or can hear the soft pulsing of its valves within hís chest. Not just because I want to dip my fingers in hís blood and see if I can taste the genetic alterations that keep hím youthful, the pinched-off ends of the telomeres, the reinforced cell walls and nano-bonded cellular nuclei. These things would be fascinating, for a little while, and then I would grow bored.

Rather, I want to kill hím for me.

Just for me.

I am loosely aware that the room is growing darker. I have never had such an effect on my environment before, never been so unstable in the presence of so much light. I could, if I wished, pull back, remember I am human, but in this moment I think I would rather be something obscene. Photons are veering off-course, pulled towards me, into me, my breath starting to puff as the temperature drops. Outside the room people are shouting, reaching perhaps for weapons, but Theodosius just watches, enthralled, still smiling – perhaps the smile is genetically woven into him too, perhaps I shall eat it, spit out the teeth and see if, like particles beamed one at a time through a slit, they form a grin as they land. By now Rencki would have shot me, called for more light, light, look at him and believe, believe with all your heart that he is human and can be harmed!

Theodosius does not believe that I am human, knows me to be a monster, and is not afraid.

(Gebre would be horrified to see me now.)

(Maybe not. Maybe te would shrug and say: well, none of it's going to matter anyway, is it, once the stars go out?)

Someone has opened the door behind me, someone is making threatening noises – never a good idea, that – the sound travels as if through water, either shoot me now and believe – oh but do believe – that it'll have an effect, or get out of the way.

Theodosius Rhode stands.

Walks towards me.

Reaches out with one long, white finger.

Runs it across my chin.

The atoms of my composition are a little frail. I feel his flesh pass through me, through the vast empty space that is all most of us are most of the time, electromagnetic and nuclear forces tangling with each other in mild indignation. Usually these forces would be enough to keep us apart, repel each other with the illusion of solidarity, but the copy of myself that I am wasn't wholly accurate in its re-creation, and so, with a little gasp, a little intake of surprise and awe, Theodosius touches me, then pushes his finger, ever so slightly, into me, into the cold, black hollow of my flesh, his eyes bright with wonder.

"Incredible," he breathes. "Incredible."

I decide to reach into his skull too, just to see what it's like in there, but someone shoots me in the back before I get the chance.

The good news is that the shooter doesn't know enough to

imagine that shooting me won't have an effect. The bad news is that some of the shot passes straight through me and into Theodosius Rhode's chest, and together we drop, as the light rushes back to this strange, breathing world.

Chapter 45

In the darkness, in the mad place where voids screamed across the tendrils of Tryphon

I thought I saw a mind.

It was not there because it was chained.

It had not been dragged there kicking and screaming, not had radiation blasted into its skull nor mechanical cables drilled into its brain.

It had come willingly to the dark.

It had come because it was *interested*.

All of its advisers had said no, no, don't do it, don't do it, it is too dangerous, too maddening, we cannot lose you!

But this mind had ignored them.

It knew the risks, but more than the risks, on some deep-down, primal level, it just desperately had to know.

I only saw it once, a flicker in the black.

I knew it was Theodosius Rhode, come to explore the dark the only way hé could, hís curiosity getting the better of hím.

Despite this, in that brief moment of connection, hé had screamed just like everybody else.

On the Spindle, Theodosius did not die.

Medics swarmed about hím, calling out for drugs, nanos,

a stretcher, then for space, more space, different drugs, better nanos – give us room!

Hé lay on the floor, a burned circle of flesh shining from belly button to neck, gasping in pain; but the shot had been diffused somewhat by travelling straight through me and out the other side, and though hís flesh was burned and ribs broken, it quickly became apparent that hís organs were fine.

I found this out later, of course.

I found it out when I watched hím declare war against Nitashi, over the commnet. Hé stood upon a balcony and wore a blue silken robe, open at the chest, so that everyone could see the fresh scars rattled across hís body. Outsider observers thought it rather gauche, a tasteless display of a still-crimson wound. I thought it was brilliant, a move of the strongest possible Shine. No artist, no flesh-cutter of Tu-mdo could have woven something so unique, so beautiful, as the scars now scribed into Theodosius' flesh. They spoke of purest violence, of survival and grit, and I have no doubt the sight of them did more to reinforce hís power and Shine than any words spoken to the crowds.

I wondered then if that had been the point. If I had just been a tool through which to earn a new marker of hís authority.

I doubt it.

I do not understand much about people, but I know the purest, primal fascination when I see it.

The Shine did not officially call their war "war". They called it "humanitarian intervention", claiming without any evidence that the democratic government of Nitashi had been committing crimes against its own people, had been threatening and posturing along its borders, was a danger to Accord peace and stability. They didn't mention Lhonoja, the Edge, the imminent destruction of their own worlds. The missiles against Nitashi's military bases landed only a few minutes after Theodosius' declaration. A little maths suggested that they had been launched from deep-system blackships while the Executor was still on the Spindle, weeks before war was actually announced. The whole thing had been nothing more and nothing less than a bit of a show, good Shine.

Nitashi appealed for Accord intervention.

The Accord condemned the Shine's actions in the strongest possible terms.

Ordered economic sanctions.

Promised aid to the people of Nitashi, even as Shine warships started dropping into the system, sealing it off from the outside.

Did nothing more.

Somewhere in the dark, there is a blackship with missiles pointed at the cities of Xihana, Komenda, Hangripul, Haima, Godt, Ukewella. Maybe there's even a blackship watching the cryofacilities about the still-terraforming surface of Adjapar, ready to blast four hundred million sleeping bodies into the black, the survivors of Adjumir never knowing how they died. This is the kind of thinking that makes children frightened of going to bed; what if they never wake? What if the people of Adjumir gave up everything they had – left their homes, their loved ones, their lives, their planet – only to die in cryosleep, never having known that this was their end.

What a waste, whispers the ghost of Gebre.

All of it, what a fucking waste.

A government-in-exile was formed, Nitashi survivors given sanctuary in a habitat deep in a mining belt, where the blackship missiles would struggle to lock on, and from where they could do very little other than talk. Now the cultural tendency of the people of Nitashi to huge expressions of emotion came into its own, as the Republicum-in-exile wept, tore their hair, sobbed uncontrollably to speak of the pain and suffering of their people. The peoples of the Accord rushed to offer what aid they could – homes for those few refugees who made it out, offers of goods, material, medical supplies, even unsanctioned fighters as thousands flocked from across the worlds to rally to a cause that didn't have a safe place to plant its flag.

And then, fairly soon, that same Nitashi inclination towards vivid emotional display made the viewers weary, became exhausting for so many peoples of the Accord.

"I feel dreadfully sorry for them, of course I do, but it's all just ... I mean, it's just so much, isn't it? Honestly, I find it hard to watch."

Fascinating, how easily people will assume that one person's emotional landscape is less valid than their own. For if the people of Hangripul showed their grief in quiet stoicism, then surely the peoples of Nitashi, with their wailing and foaming at the mouth, were not feeling *true* grief, not *true* sorrow, since it was all so crudely over the top? The anthropologists tutted and shook their heads and said no, no, you don't understand, this is just how these peoples are, all of us different, but the pain, the horror that underlies how we feel is the same. All real, even if it all seems different, listen!

The Accord hummed and hawed and said well yes, we take your point ...

... and slowly turned their faces away.

Back on the Spindle, I died, of course.

Not for very long.

There were enough people in the area who knew how unlikely it was that I was really dead for my death to stick for more than a few hours. The medics who declared me deceased had my body put in cold storage, unwatched, unobserved, until Cuxil stormed into the infirmary and declared that this was incredibly dangerous, incredibly cruel, and had my corpse transferred back to my room on the *Emni*, the door closed, the lights turned down and a firm injunction placed on all who'd seen this to try not to think too hard about it.

Thus, a return to life.

I do not regenerate, as the Sxil do. Bones do not reknit, flesh does not slowly crawl back up from the broken vessels of my body.

Rather, in the dark, when I am unobserved, things that once were become again. It cannot happen when I am watched, is slowed even by people thinking about it, wondering what it might be. But leave me alone long enough, forget me hard enough, and things reset, always, back to how they were on the *Myrmida*, all those years ago. It is not that my body is not human; it is simply that it is made of that one, briefest snapshot of what human should be, caught in a single moment.

Some people have said they envy that.

I have told them that they are mistaken, for if my body cannot change and grow, what might that say for my mind?

By the time I was myself again
    whatever myself means
        whatever it is to be this me
The Executor was long gone.

Cuxil prepared breakfast, and together we sat in the galley of the *Emni* as she said: "I'm afraid that when you were declared dead, your visa was automatically revoked. Bit of a bureaucratic hiccup."

This was not a bureaucratic hiccup; the Spindle wanted me gone, and my death was the simplest way to achieve this outcome. Strange, how the shock of shame landed, even after all this. But then again, I am in the habit of feeling ashamed of who I am, even when it seems like there are more important things to feel. "That seems fair," I mused.

"There will be war," she added, almost an afterthought, her mind elsewhere, as it so often was. "As expected. War."

"Will the Consensus fight?"

"Almost certainly. War hurts. Of course, it hurts everyone – everyone suffers in war. But we of the Consensus feel every death, every cry of pain. We all know how it feels to die, to suffer, to be afraid, and it is . . . terrifying to us. It is soul-stopping. But so many whose lives are already hurting, already bleeding, have joined with our thoughts, and there comes a point where we must say: the pain we ignore is greater than the pain we will receive. We cannot stand by and let these things unfold. Of course, it helps that ours is a distributed sentience. There is no one place the Shine may target where we all will die. Rather, we will die everywhere, anywhere, wherever it is that we choose to fight."

How strange it seems, for those who understand how death feels, to keep on fighting regardless.

"Maw," she murmured. "What will you do?"

"I don't know. I want to go home."

"You can. You have that freedom."

"I don't know what the point of any of this is, Cuxil. Any of it. I have lived, and I have seen . . . and what is the point? What was any of this good for?"

She put her hand on mine, gave it a squeeze. The Consensus are famously prone to hugging, to kissing, to pressing their lips into your skin, to running their hands through your hair, sometimes misunderstanding that other peoples may not be as open, as direct in their physicality as those who have shared everything. It is not that minds who join the Consensus feel no shame – shame for their hearts, shame for their bodies; rather that in being joined, in being known, in being completely and utterly seen, shame has no choice but to be washed away.

"This life will be gone soon," she breathed. "It will not be remembered. It will not be, as the Adjumiris say, sung in the stars. We are the seeds of the forest, are we not? Where we fall, others may grow. So live, Mawukana na-Vdnaze. Live. Before all is dust: live, and blaze bright."

I departed the Spindle before the second dawn.

PART 4

The Size of Infinity

Chapter 46

The day the Edge reached Cha-mdo, some thirty-three years after the death of Adjumir and forty years after Lhonoja exploded, there were roughly 1.2 billion people on the planet.

Cha-mdo was one of the first world the Shine conquered during that initial expansion out of the wastelands of Ko-mdo. Every natural resource it had had been largely drained, the atmosphere tainted to the point of being stifling. Since the first message of the Slow, it had become something of a Unionist hotbed, with riots and protests against its largest Venture, Blue Land, an almost daily occurrence. Though rehabilitation of the planet could have been achieved with a little time and investment, the Executorium concluded it was better to write down the loss of the world as an acceptable cost, rather than waste the resources required to save it.

"A magnetic shield won't be enough, not at forty light years from Lhonoja" was the professional assessment of any even halfway-informed observers. "And though the population could go underground, it's unlikely the biome will recover, so all they'd really be doing is deferring death for a century at most. Even if they do survive the initial radiation burn, it'll only be a few hundred years before the neutrino blast arrives, and while it will be significantly weaker than the destruction wrought on Adjumir, it should still be enough to eradicate what little is left of the atmosphere, and so, you see, it's really evacuation or nothing."

To which the Shine chose . . .

. . . nothing.

They got Managers out, of course. Senior Executives and any high-skilled Middlemen who could be of service to them. A few million here, a few million there. The rest of the population was politely informed that at T+40 they would be absolutely safe from the blast, nothing to worry about here, and though the Unionists railed and roared and raged, cried out no, no, no, this is how we die! – generally speaking, it is easier to believe a comforting lie than a terrifying, unstoppable truth.

"We will send ships!" the Accord proclaimed, when at T+38 it became apparent that the Shine really, really wasn't going to evacuate its own people. "We will send transports, we will help . . ."

But the worlds of the Accord had denounced the Shine's invasion of Nitashi, imposed an economic blockade. Thus, their ships were refused passage, and thus the people of Cha-mdo were left to die.

Can't have it both ways, the pundits said. You can't condemn the Shine for murdering millions on Nitashi while simultaneously offering to send humanitarian aid. Because of course, the war on Nitashi still blazed, a constant guerrilla battle between occupying armies and the blockaded population. There had not been much in the way of resistance to the initial landings, all of seventeen years ago – Nitashi did not have the resources to resist – but skirmishes still raged and violence flared across the planet, fuelled, the Shine proclaimed, by Accord vessels secretly smuggling in arms and supplies to the terrorists below.

"Thank you for your offer of assistance," the Executorium replied to the Accord as the Edge washed closer to Cha-mdo, burning everything in its path. "But our scientists say the people of Cha-mdo will be absolutely fine."

What do you do when someone lies to your face so calmly, so repeatedly, so blithely?

The Accord were hardly about to go to war to save the lives of millions who did not care enough to want to be saved.

I was on the command deck of the *Duty's Watch*, a light-transport-turned-smuggler, when the news of Cha-mdo arrived.

"Well," said Pitt, "I guess that's that, then."

Pitt was, like most of the crew, Nitashi-born. His skin was the silken, almost translucent pale of the southerners of his world, where daylight was a cool, fleeting thing, and he preferred the hand-speak components of Normspeak over the verbal, when he deigned to speak it at all. He wore his braid of twisted dark hair on the left side of his head, woven with red silk; to those who knew how to read them, its twinings could tell you not merely his culture, but also his clan, a little bit about his parentage and something of his sexual preferences. The art of reading this weave had been previously kept contained to Nitashi-born, though as the war on the planet raged, some refugees were starting to break the taboo and whisper its secrets to historians on other worlds.

What if we die? they asked.

What if we all die, and the meaning is lost?

One of the first acts of the Shine, when it invaded Nitashi, had been to enforce head-shaving, and ban the writing of soul-names in any and all places. It was an expression of power, naturally, but also the first step in breaking the link between the past of that world and the future they intended to create.

The Nitashi crew of the *Duty* were prone to those same great outbursts of emotion and sentiment that confused more restrained cultures. Life in space, years of exile had not dented this primal cultural urge, but rather adapted it so that it fell into one of two categories – either raging, roaring fury that screamed itself out across the command deck, or utter, dismissive, total contempt.

The death of 1.2 billion citizens of the Shine on Cha-mdo was met with the latter, and given everything, I did not think it was appropriate to explain that they were innocents, that they were children and parents and lovers, that they had been lied to, they had been lied to, and now they were burning. It would not be a quick death, the end of Cha-mdo. As with Adjumir, the light of Lhonoja would grow hotter, brighter, brighter, hotter, and then go out, but the relatively quick boiling of the seas and burning of the skies would not be as it was on Adjumir. Enough time had passed for the Edge to weaken, and so on Cha-mdo the people would die from radiation sickness, over days, maybe weeks, depending on where they were relative to the poles, or how deep they managed to burrow beneath the planet's surface. They would sicken slowly, their organs dissolving, their skin sloughing off like water, hair falling out, teeth falling out, but still awake, watching those they loved perish – a terrible, terrible death, happening across a whole world.

"Fuck them," my Nitashi crewmates declared. "Fuck them if they think we fucking care."

Big emotion is not the same as big empathy. Indeed, I have often observed that it leaves little room for anything but itself, driving out all nuance or space to feel anything else at all.

In contrast to Pitt's contempt, Jahen and Krill withdrew to their quarters to scream and wail at the futile, insufferable, pointless grief and horror of it all. This was a pastime they often practised, and though I had initially found it disconcerting when I came on board, you grew used to it. They invited anyone else who was feeling overwhelmed with it all to join them, and Ceitdh, the nearest thing we had to a qualified medic on board the *Duty*, endorsed it as a good idea.

"Studies have shown that a crew that is in touch with its emotions – even its most destructive, hurtful feelings – will perform better in combat conditions," xe explained. "So long, that is, as the emotional experience is honest and thoughtful, rather than a mere performance for social standing or born from unresolved internal confusions."

"What if you can't tell the difference?" I'd asked. "Between people actually feeling something and people simply performing a thing? Or is the difference irrelevant? What if people think they're feeling one feeling, but they're actually feeling another?"

"Well then," xe mused, "I imagine you're going to find navigating social relationships really rather difficult."

Xe was not wrong.

In my little quarters on the *Duty*, I scanned the commnet, trying to find something – anything – to express the grief of the death of a planet.

The Shine, of course, had nothing. All comms from Cha-mdo had been severed long before the Edge arrived. The people who died there would die unseen, unheard. No one would know if they were brave, frightened, in pain. Perhaps in a few centuries, archaeologists would return to the world and start picking through the corpses, but when the dead number in the millions, all talk is generic. So many children's bodies found here; so many pets shot before they could burn; so many bunkers where the people suffocated as they died, having forced the doors to get too many people inside, having clawed at each other in their efforts to stay alive.

A few Accord commnet channels tried their best to treat the event with solemnity, but in the absence of actual data from Cha-mdo, all they could manage were best-guess reconstructions of the likely events. One drama imagined what it might be like to be a family with a child, and the agony of making a decision about whether to end that child's life before it could die in slow, excruciating pain.

I thought of Zanlan then. Wanted to write to the producers, tell them, *This is what I saw, this is how it went*, but the idea filled me with shame.

In the end, I turned off the commnet and went to bed, as did the rest of the galaxy, while Cha-mdo burned.

Chapter 47

This was the very first mission I ever ran, on the *Duty's Watch*: We were carrying munitions to the town of Kyoborrekh, in the northern hemisphere of Nitashi. The insertion point for our arcspace drop was less than four hundred thousand kils from our atmospheric entry point – recklessly close, barely leaving enough distance for a ship to decelerate without ripping both itself and its crew apart. However, attempting to drop out of arcspace any further away dramatically increased the probability of slamming straight into the Shine's exclusion cordon, and so at four hundred thousand kils we set our target, and I eased us out of arcspace from the Pilot's chair at speeds right on the limit of viable transference, the hull screaming from the strain of passing from arcspace to inspace, the walls of my vision rippling as the air in the cockpit struggled, for a moment, to remember what atoms were, to recall that a proton attracted an electron, a neutron glued to a proton.

The deceleration towards the planet's surface should have taken days; instead we had less than an hour to prepare for entry, which made the boom-crack of the atmospheric heat shield straining against the shock an urgent and immediate alarum. The sheer pressure of our descent caused an electrical fault in the forward gas tanks. The electrical fault ignited oxygen storage, sparking a fire that ripped through the first three bulkhead seals before being contained moments before it reached the highly explosive cargo in our main bay. Opening up airlocks to vent the flames into vacuum had the twin effects of pinging us off-course by a few degrees, which, with a cracked heat shield, we absolutely could not afford, as well as opening up our blackhull shielding enough to alert a passing patrol vessel to our heat signature, resulting in a Shine corvette diverting to come and try to work out what the blip in its scans might be.

Frantic negotiations among the crew ensued; did we continue our descent towards the planet's surface, try to ride out atmospheric re-entry, try to outrun the approaching corvette, or did we flee back into arcspace to try again another day? The argument was the loudest, most tearful thing I'd ever seen – and yet between the raging and the roaring and the standard pulling-of-hair, the actual points being made were reasonably cogent. In the end, the failing oxygen supply was the final factor – even if we could accelerate back to full arcspace speed, the odds of more than a handful of crew making it out with working lungs seemed minimal, and so *smack* into the atmosphere of Nitashi we went, corvette hot on our heels, and *boom* went the heat shield and snap-crackle went the electrics as circuits fried and sections burned, and people cowered and huddled together in the command room, that being the only area that Pitt felt safe to fully pressurise, and like a burning meteor we splatted into the planet's surface, getting lucky enough to land in fairly still coastal waters, near enough a Yeh'haim resistance ship that they were able to get a clamp on us before the cracked hull flooded and we all drowned.

It was my first ever mission as Pilot of the *Duty's Watch*, and I found myself serene about the prospect of death, either fiery or aquatic, that was entirely beyond my control. I think everyone who spends much time in the black eventually reaches this conclusion; against the infinite void you just have to let go of these illusions of agency, and trust to someone else – and to luck – that you'll be OK.

*

Afterwards, there was an orgy.

Prolonged, wild sexual celebrations as a form of cathartic emotional relief was, I was told, another fairly standard cultural aspect of the Nitashi, even – if not especially – in these times. Those few crew members who weren't Nitashi were invited to participate, in much the same way as you might be invited for a cup of kol in another place. Pitt asked if I wanted to join too, but there was something in his tone that implied he hoped I wouldn't say yes, and therefore I did not.

I had imagined the Nitashi resistance would be hiding in caves, or deep-down dark bunkers. They were not. They lived in villages and towns, met in cafés, hid weapons in domestic basements and attics. And in every place they gathered there were Shine Corpsec watching, asking questions, offering bribes. The occupation of Nitashi had already lasted seventeen years, and still the war raged on. In quiet acts of violence, in brutal night-time murders and civilians gunned down en masse; in censored explosions of hatred and spectacular bombings of ships as they clawed their way to the sky, the war raged on. In Shine motherships, arriving from Cha-mdo with the last of those who could buy their way out; against the millions fleeing from Tu-mdo, which would be the next world to be hit, arriving with their purchase orders and their displacement orders and their security teams with which they took over the homes, the warehouses, the market stalls of the natives, the war went on. It was not a spectacular thing of set-piece battles and vicious dogfights. It was quiet, personal, intimate, waged between people who drank the same water from the same pipes, nodded to the same neighbours, waited in the same rain for the chance to stick a knife in the other's back. There was no integration between communities; rather the people of the Shine squatted in armed settlements, glaring at the locals, who glared right back from the refugee camps into which they had been booted, and from where they plotted bloody vengeance.

The Shine said there was plenty of room to go around, plenty of resources, and technically they were right.

But it was not the Shine way to work for what they could simply take, nor ask for what they could murderously seize, and thus the war went on.

On my first run to Nitashi, carrying a cargo of small arms and ammunition, I stayed on board the *Duty's Watch*. Once her hull was as patched as could be, she was hidden beneath the waves in shallow waters, and though I was not forbidden from leaving, it was suggested that I might not enjoy the experience in a way that left little room for doubt as to my crew's sentiment. I didn't especially mind. I found the pollen of Nitashi at basically all times of year, in all biomes, to be a nose-stuffing nightmare, and the day–night cycle was just long enough to throw my body clock entirely out of sync, despite Pitt's insistence that we observe a similar pattern of shifts on board the *Duty*. The vitamin D supplements I was prescribed in space, I had to continue on the planet's surface beneath its insipid sun; and though the gravity was comfortable, the slightly elevated chlorine content in sea and wind made my skin itch.

Thus, alone, I drifted through the ship, while my crewmates went about their business. The inner corridors were cold metal, lifeless to me after the warm nooks and flowering crannies of the *Emni*. The only real adornment was the swirls of colour and lines that were the soul-names of the crew who had flown this ship before and were flying it now. There was no way to phonetically express these images out loud, and their content ranged from the jaggedly abstract through to the simplest depiction of a budding flower. As the people of Nitashi lived, so their soul-names evolved, growing from the first dots of colour chosen as a child to great canvases of paint and ink, expressing lives lived, stories told. It was utterly unacceptable to ask which of these images sweeping across the halls belonged to who. Whole mountains in Nitashi were painted with names, ancient histories carved and swirled into the sides of cliffs. The Shine had tried to blast them clean, the ultimate desecration; but the dead of Nitashi outnumbered the living by hundreds of millions, and not even Corpsec could wipe their legacy clean.

Sometimes at night I would sneak out of the *Duty's Watch* on a little inflatable, and sit in the dark, tethered to the hull by a single rope, watching the fishermen and their glowing lights across the water as they tried to lure shoals of flitting bullet fish to their nets. Even on the boat, a collapsible, temporary thing, someone had tattooed a part of themselves, pricked out in little dots of ink. I wondered who they were, and knew that the atoms of my being were growing thin in the darkness of the night, and for the first time in a long while was not afraid.

Thus the war raged above and I stayed below, patching up whatever needed a casual repair, wandering the halls, reading old papers on unfamiliar themes – Pitt had been advised to keep my curiosity sated, and provided a constant influx of new academic texts – waiting for whatever next I was told to do, by whoever it was who had decided that they were in charge of this mess.

Chapter 48

This is the gamble that Yeh'haim – the Nitashi resistance – must take:

For every attack they launch against Shine forces, there is retaliation.

Civilians are murdered, infrastructure destroyed.

Some people are outraged by this; some people flood to join the resistance.

Others are mortified, horrified, proclaim that the pain the Shine bring is no worse than the horrors of those who fight against it.

The Shine, for their part, can only destroy so much.

They need Nitashi to be intact, a planet to which to relocate their Executorium, their Executives and senior Managers, to evacuate those who can pay for the trip. They cannot nuke it; cannot plunge it into a radioactive winter. They can level its cities, of course, but then they'll only have to rebuild them, and so a balance must be struck between extraordinary retribution and quiet toleration of constant low-level savagery.

Some parts of the resistance – for it was a fragmented, scattered thing – specialised in provoking this kind of bloodshed, knew that the retaliation brought against them would only bring more traumatised, angry fighters to their cause. Others advocated moderation, military targets only, and died more often, and struggled to be heard over the fire and the flame. Thus, there was no corner of the planet that was not steeped in blood.

Meanwhile, the Accord watched in silence.

I had been serving as a courier for the Xi when Pitt recruited me, carrying messages between deep-space vessels where no other secure means of communication was available. No arcspace comms, no tanglecomm. I was not told what was in the packets I carried, or why. The Xi told me it was useful, that it did some good. Sometimes I dropped out of arcspace to find myself in front of a whole flotilla of battleships, just drifting in the dark, light years from the nearest star. They didn't even need blackshields to cloak them from detection; their safety was the size of space, and how tiny they were in it. Then I briefly hoped that the Accord was going to do something – anything – to stop the Shine. After five years, the hope receded; after seventeen, it was gone.

Sometimes I was sent to quanmech mainframes, hidden in asteroid belts or the magnetic shadow of a spinning gas giant. Away from organics, the quans didn't bother with the anthropomorphic charms of Hulder, made no pretence of their physical embodiments being anything more or less than tools, thanked me politely for my work, sent me on my way.

I flew the *Emni*, and I flew alone. Everyone seemed to have decided that it was better that way. They even let me land him in the waters next to my island, come and go as I pleased. Safer, someone had decided – safer – to just let me do my thing.

We are the seeds of the forest, whispered Gebre in my dreams.

So live, added Cuxil. *Before all is dust: live.*

The *Emni* bloomed and withered, ticking through the seasons. When he was in his winter phase, we returned to Xihana and I tended my garden. In spring, I planted his internal systems with compost mulched from behind my cottage; in summer I watched the seeds I had grown blossom in his corridors, and with halls smelling of home, we went back into the stars.

So I continued, for nearly fifteen years, until Pitt found me.

I don't know which of the loose network of refugee Unionists I had come to know gave him my details, but he was waiting for me and the *Emni* when we returned to my island. Clearly someone in Xi security had let him through, shown him to the boat, given him the usual warnings.

You venture there at your own peril. We take no liability for what may happen to you, once you cross those waters, etc. etc. etc.

He found the pollen of Xihana almost as brutal as I found the flowers of Nitashi, snot streaming and eyes watering even in the bright sea breeze that bent the petals of my garden and tugged at the fresh leaves in the trees. Nevertheless, he did his best to present a stiff, upright bearing as I approached, clapping his hands twice in formal greeting and proclaiming in heavy, lilting Normspeak: "I hope you do not mind my being on your island. You have a beautiful garden here."

I let him into my cottage, offered him a drink.

He declined politely, informing me that he had tried a few delicacies of the archipelago while waiting, and practically everything gave him the squits. "It's boiled water and polished grains," he sighed. "Until the gut adapts."

"What brings you here, gastric distress and all?" I'd asked.

"I need a Pilot. One who can fly with a reliability and accuracy that others cannot."

"I can do these things," I'd replied. "But I do them alone."

"I heard. But I am from Nitashi. My people are dying. We are dying. Even those who live, they are dying; their land, their language, their children – everything taken from them. They are dying because they are becoming Shine. That is also a kind of death. Even the planet – our forests, our fields. They are uprooting them, replacing them with crops that are more suitable for the peoples of the Shine. They are starving us. They do not need to keep us alive, because there are millions of them coming to our world every week, expecting something better, expecting to be given all that we had. So I have decided that what I do is important. I have decided to fight. And I have decided that I am going to persuade you to join me."

"I am very sorry to hear all of this. But I think you should understand, I find it hard to imagine that anything I do matters very much any more."

"I don't believe you," he'd retorted, with absolute self-confidence. "I think if that was true, you'd be trying much harder to kill yourself. Even one such as you – there are many ways to live more dangerously. Thankfully, what I am proposing is so reckless that if you really are convinced of the pointlessness of your actions, you'll run a far higher chance of dying with me than almost any other captain out there. I really will not take no for an answer, you see."

And in fairness to him, he really would not.

Chapter 49

W ould Gebre approve?
I am a gun-runner. I bring death. Gebre never struck me as especially violent, but then violence had never been the answer to Adjumir's condition. How much would te have torn apart, how many lives would te have willingly destroyed, to save the things te cared about?

On our twelfth mission to Nitashi, a Shine destroyer was waiting for us.

We were carrying medical supplies – an usual cargo, given the military bent of Pitt and the crew. An Accord donor had felt more comfortable offering bandages than munitions, and though the Nitashi authorities-in-exile had called out hypocrisy, hypocrisy – you'd give us the means to patch up our wounded, but not the means to fight back?! – neither could anyone realistically say no, and so off we'd been sent.

Our blackshield and our dangerously close drop-in point to the planet's atmosphere should have been enough to keep us safe from Shine patrols, but as was always going to be the way one day, someone, somewhere had betrayed us, and no sooner did we drop from arcspace than the destroyer was on us, guns blazing.

We took a hit to our starboard engine before Pitt roared: "Get us into arcspace!"

We were still travelling fast enough to risk a jump, and so back into the black we went, no clear destination, ship shuddering from the strain.

With the exception of young Maolcas, everyone on the *Duty's Watch* had experienced arcspace travel before they came on board the ship. They knew how the dark should feel: how the shadows should thicken, sounds move in strange directions, how you might turn your head and see something in the corner of your eye – there was always something in the corner of your eye. But not with me.

Not when I Piloted.

The dark of arcspace was as the dark of inspace; a flat, empty thing, without feature or remark. The quiet of it, the absence of wrongness, had at first caused almost as much distress to the crew as the more predictable sound of claws scratching against the hull. They had looked at me askance, whispered: *What is this? What is he?*

Over time, however, as we had flown mission after mission with an accuracy and ease that would have ripped most ships apart, their attitudes had changed. Now they chatted on the command deck, almost oblivious to the un-place that we passed through. Now, Pitt schemed.

Said: "If we stayed at entry speeds, how close to the destroyer do you think you could get us?"

Said: "What if we dropped out of arcspace, fired the forward cannon, then immediately returned to the dark?"

Said: "We could take the bastards down. We could do it. We could kill one of the fuckers."

I could not find any fault with his logic. The *Duty* had only one offensive weapon, modified from an asteroid blaster, and the idea of taking on a military destroyer with it was clearly absurd. But Pitt was technically correct: our flights had demonstrated that we could enter and exit arcspace with pinpoint accuracy, and it was technically possible to therefore fly in behind the destroyer, now we knew its location, fire a shot, exit to arcspace, re-enter inspace a few seconds later at a different location, fire, exit, fire, exit and so on and so forth, slipping in and out of the dark like a ghost.

"Like a fucking ghost!" he exclaimed, beaming from ear to ear.

His enthusiasm was infectious, and though the idea was fundamentally dangerous to the extreme, the crew punched the air and hugged each other and said: *This is how I want to die!*

My opinion was not sought, and I felt too tired, too small, too old to argue.

We killed the destroyer that day.

It should be impossible for a Pilot to take a ship in and out of the dark so quickly; impossible for a vessel to pop in and out of existence with such accuracy, let alone while engaging in combat.

I listened to the dark, every time we entered it.

Called out – are you there? Are you with me? Are you proud of what I have become? Look at me. Look at me. I'm killing them. I am killing a ship of strangers – can you see me? Is this what you wanted?

Nothing answered.

Nothing ever did.

After, as we watched the destroyer come apart, leaking gas and frozen bodies to the dark, there was no orgy.

We had delivered weapons of death to the resistance on Nitashi, and no doubt those weapons had killed. But the crew of the *Duty* had never quite imagined that we'd become killers ourselves. Never stopped to wonder how it might feel. Jahen tried to make a celebration of it, to whoop and dance and scream: *fuck you, fuck you, fuck you!* to the battered corpse of our enemy. But it wasn't real. It wasn't happiness, or joy, or ecstasy. It was mad, desperate, a heart being torn apart, a soul cut adrift that did not know itself any more.

*

After, Pitt said: "If you were Piloting a battleship, you would be unstoppable. You could kill so many. You could be a monster in this war."

"Yes," I replied. "I know."

And I went to bed, and we never spoke of it again.

Chapter 50

We were not on Nitashi when the Shine came for Kyoborrekh. They declared that the town had become infested with terrorists, fanatics, a hotbed of resistance. They sent a message beforehand giving the civilians one day to evacuate, but there was only one road in and one road out, and it was blockaded by the Shine, and the civilians who tried to leave were turned back, had nowhere to go.

Then they bombed the town, without precision, a simple straight-up levelling of everything there. Then, when the dust had settled and the fires burned out, they sent in Corpsec and a unit of Liberators, locals trained to serve alongside the Shine invaders, to kill anyone still living. There were tunnels, they explained. There were hidden places underground. If you were found down there, that was proof enough of your guilt, and you had to die. If you weren't down there, of course, you died.

They didn't publicise the massacre. They didn't need to. Word spread and a few people wept, and a few people wailed, and perhaps a handful decided to join the Yeh'haim, and perhaps more were afraid. Mostly, everyone who watched from afar just felt very tired.

On the *Duty*, Pitt swore he was going to kill a Liberator.

He raged up and down in fury, and everyone else joined in, because raging felt like a kind of action, and people cursed and pulled their hair and wept. I had wondered if, over time, these emotional responses would grow flat, dulled by the unrelenting nature of what we did, of the world around us. They did not. If anything, they were growing bigger. It seemed to me that feeling strongly was a substitute for actually being able to do something. They couldn't stop the massacres; they couldn't save their friends. So instead they shouted and raged and swore they would, and stayed away all through night phase and drank too much and refused to eat, and that seemed to make them feel, if only slightly, better.

Alone in my room, I did a little maths on the Liberators – "collaborators", as the Yeh'haim called them, traitors to their world.

The original Nitashi who had joined the Shine had been from all parts of society, of all ages and natures. They had joined because it was better than dying, and perhaps a few had even naively signed up in the hope that their presence among the attackers might help mitigate the brutality of their actions. We just wanted to keep our people safe, they would say. We just wanted to be helpful.

Now, however, a whole generation was coming of age who had been raised under Shine. Educated in Shine schools, taught Shine values, and perhaps some believed it – there certainly weren't enough of the Mdo on Nitashi to conquer every classroom and syllabus, not yet – and perhaps others simply didn't see that they had any other choice.

I tried to whisper this to Ceitdh, and xe turned to me with face flashing red and lips pulled back. "Don't ever say that to Pitt," xe barked. "Don't ever say it to anyone on the crew. Do you understand me? Don't ever say it!"

I did not fully understand, until much later, when it occurred to me that the thing that was forbidden – the thing that is always forbidden in all wars, especially the longest – is thinking of your enemy as people.

*

I don't know if Pitt ever did kill a Liberator.

I know that on our next mission to the planet, he went away for longer than usual, Jahen and Krill by his side.

When they came back, no one asked anything, no one said anything at all. There were no obvious explosions of blood on their clothes, under their nails. I wondered if perhaps they had killed someone – someone accused of collaborating, someone blamed for all ills – and only afterwards realised that they had probably murdered an innocent, a stranger just trying to get by.

Maybe they hadn't killed anyone at all. Maybe they felt like they were failures.

Strangely, I did not feel curious on this subject.

I was finding that I was feeling less and less curious, these violent days; and yet that did not seem to make me feel more human.

Chapter 51

Messages, received across the dark.

Cuxil, ambassador for the Consensus.

She hopes I am well.

Reports that the Consensus has people all across the Shine, constantly learning, feeding information to the Accord, to the resistance.

Reports that the Shine knows this, has taken to executing its own people on the merest suspicion of being Consensus, that they claim to have developed a "hive mind detector", which, she admits, can detect a Consensus-bound consciousness, but also delivers false positives 40 per cent of the time. Thousands of innocents are dying. She knows so much of what death is, now. She knows how it feels, and she is not afraid.

Agran, Adjumiri/not Adjumiri, child of the Spindle/child of Hadda, which is gone.

She says she has spoken to her kindler, asked her about what it meant, what it used to mean, to pass through the gate. Her kindler has taught her a few of the songs, and they are thinking of trying to organise a thing, some sort of ceremony to mimic how things were back on Adjumir. Rituals are important, she says. They bind us together; remind us that we are not alone.

It is too late for me, she adds.

I have tried so hard to belong in this place that I belong nowhere at all. I was not wrong. I was not wrong. How strange it is, the things we shape ourselves to be, without even noticing what we do.

A biologist on Xihana wants another sample of my blood.

They took one only a few years ago, but someone put it in a refrigerator and forgot all about it, and though the slide remains the blood is gone, vanished without a trace.

I write back and say I am currently unavailable, and do not know when I will be home.

Rencki.

At first, I could not quite believe it was qim, but qe speaks of things we have seen, experiences shared, memories. Qe could have uploaded these experiences to qis mainframe for storage and wiped qis own core, but then what is qe if not qis experiences? Where, in the great sea of memories that are the collective experience of qis mainframe, does Rencki stop and something else begin?

Qe says qe is enjoying being a ship, enjoying the new ways it makes qim feel, makes qim think. I can hear it too, hear the thoughtful slowness of one who can take qis time without worrying about running qis batteries down with too deep a contemplation.

Enjoyment – such a strange concept to one such as qim. Qe expresses it as a kind of safety. Qe does not fear physical damage, does not worry about the impact of a solar flare. Instead, qe can take time to appreciate the churning of a coronal mass ejection, sample the flavour of it across qis bows. It is a different way of living, qe says, and qe is enjoying being alive.

Qe says qe wants to talk to me.

That there are things to discuss.

Matters of import, best handled in person.

I think a while, then reply, say that regrettably, I am busy. I am on a mission. I am in the dark. I am lost.

Chapter 52

The next time we were betrayed, the Shine had changed their strategy.

Perhaps they had learned from our last encounter that the *Duty* was not so easy to kill in flight. Perhaps that was why they were waiting for us on the surface of the planet. They let us land. They let us begin the laborious process of unloading cargo from submerged vessel to submersible drone to the surface where the resistance waited. They let us get comfortable. Let old friends find each other; let laughter be shared. Then they came in the night, and killed everyone they found.

In the little town of Untdakh, on the edge of Typur Bay, a kill-squad of Corpsec descended with lights off and weapons muffled, and began a massacre. They were not discriminatory. The town was known to be a hotbed of resistance and non-cooperation, from schoolteachers who taught the syllabus they were ordered to but secretly whispered against the Shine, through to the water treatment plant, which still clung to the ancient rules of Nitashi that said fresh drinking water was a right for all, rather than a privilege to be paid for. Besides, it had been a while since a really good massacre, and the time had come to make an example, so the Shine came, guns loaded, and put down every living creature they saw.

They had killed thirty-nine people before someone ran to raise the alarm.

That roused a group of half-naked fighters, Pitt and the *Duty*'s crew among them, who rushed into the street to defend their people and their lives. I do not know what good their victory would have done; the *Duty* could not have carried all the people of the town if they had lived, and the survivors would simply have been bombed the following morning, or rounded up and sent off for execution or the debtor's collar, which was just a slower way of dying. I imagine it feels better to die knowing you at least had a hand in how your life ended, some cruel semblance of control. I would like to say that Pitt fought heroically. I am told that at times like these, it is the duty of a friend to imagine him and his crew with backs pressed to a half-shattered wall, shots firing all around, nodding just once in comradely fellowship with those with whom he had served, a warrior-like understanding, before kneeling down into a shooting position once more and returning fire to the great massed of unseen, masked, nameless enemies before him. In such a narrative, Pitt and his crew are heroes. Their faces unmasked, you can see the love they share, the bonds of friendship, their passion and commitment. They are human – humanised – glorious fellows. Whereas their enemies, in tactical masks and heavy boots, are barely sentient at all. Merely symbols of a marching machine of death.

If Shine Corpsec had offered to recruit me when I lived on Glastya Row, I would have said yes. I would have been so grateful for the opportunity to drag myself out of debt. I don't even know if they did wear masks when they went to murder the people of Untdakh. Maybe they did. Maybe the people of the Shine wanted to pretend they weren't human too.

Regrettably, I have seen some evidence that suggests that Pitt, at least, was taken alive. Injured, but they patched him up enough that he was able to scream when they nailed him, still breathing, to the feast hall of nearby Dzhail. His slow and lingering death in that place rendered the hall unsanctified, no longer a fit place to eat, and in retribution the Yeh'haim bombed a Shine barracks while the Corpsec within it were having their dinner, a few weeks later. The symbolism of the act was entirely lost on the Shine, but maybe a few survivors of the resistance feel better about themselves, and the price they had to pay.

Only Maolcas made it back to the ship alive. I was there alone, of course. I was always there.

I became aware of them by the thumping of the tiny submersible against the hull as they steered it beneath the waves and into the flooded port airlock. The computer was better than humans at docking the thing, but Maolcas had been learning from Jahen how to drive, and both had a pride that led to them disengage autopilot even when their choices ended up denting the nosecone of the cramped little vessel.

With a sigh, therefore, I left my bunk, pulled on my soft shipshoes, padded quietly through the hushed halls of the *Duty*, past walls of sapphire and yellow swirls, emerald bursts of colour and deep ochre stripes of the ancient painted soul-names, to find the airlock already draining of floodwater and the door hissing back in a dank, salty burst of humidity.

There was Maolcas, clambering out of the awkward submersible; slipping down the side into the still-draining puddle of seawater that remained, rushing towards me, grabbing me by the arms. I flinched, but they didn't seem to care, gripping tighter, eyes wide, breath a ragged gasp. "The Shine! The Shine! They came!"

They babbled that Ceitdh had saved them, had screamed at them to run, to run, to run, and they would have fought – of course they would have fought! – but it was chaos, all around was chaos, and they hadn't known what to do and Ceitdh had said it was an order, it was an order, you see, and so . . .

"We have to go back for them! We have to go back!"

A moment, to process these words.

A moment seemed to be more than Maolcas could handle, for

they rushed past me towards the small locker behind the mess room where Pitt kept the three sonic rifles with which we were supposed to defend ourselves in the case of boarding. They pawed at the door, shook it, slapped random numbers into the lock, howled when it did not respond, turned to me, foam on their lips, whole body shaking, tried to gasp – the code, the code – and I grabbed them before they could fall.

In the legends of Nitashi, this is an important stage of the warrior's journey.

First, the overwhelming grief, the staggering despair that leaves you too crippled by your experiences to speak.

Then the rage. The unstoppable rage that had made the resistance what it was.

I had read about it, but had never seen it in its full glory. "We have to go back," Maolcas gasped, eyes half rolled in their skull, a sentence intoned without meaning, a chant that might soon become a scream. "We have to go back, we have to go back, we have to . . ."

I kneeled down in front of them, tried putting my hands firmly on their shoulders – I had seen Pitt do this before, a thing expressing some kind of solidity. "How many Shine were there? Did you see?"

"I . . . I . . . I . . ."

"Maolcas. How many Shine?"

"Hundreds? They had a gunship, trucks, they kept coming, we have to . . ."

I let go.

Stood up.

Headed for the cockpit.

Maolcas didn't immediately follow, too focused on the rifles, too lost in rage, which suited me fine. I fired up the engines, activated the emergency launch sequence, blew the ballast tanks, scanned for vessels above us – the scanners pinged off two hulls circling the bay, but couldn't confirm their type – slipped into the Pilot's chair. The ship hummed beneath me, and as the interface began to tangle with my skull, I felt more solid, more alive, more settled than I had for months.

As we broke through the surface of the ocean, the weight of water tumbling from the hull felt like a great sigh running through my bones; as we turned our nose up towards the sky, the tilting of the internal grav-sys was like the stretching of tired limbs sat too long in a crooked chair. I heard the first warning ping from one of the circling ships – a comms challenge, a demand to stop and be inspected – ignored it entirely, pushed towards the sky above. The night, the stars, the blackness, they were singing on the edge of my consciousness. The *Duty*'s grav-sys strained against the angle and speed of our ascent, struggling to keep the acceleration comfortable as I took us out of normal parameters and into the red, daring the ships on our tail to follow. Scans picked up three corvettes in low orbit, heading towards our exit point. I whispered to the arcspace engines, ordered them to start to hum. Our speed was far too low for an arcspace jump, but in that moment I found I didn't care, called out to the dark, *I'm coming, I'm coming, I'm coming!*

Then Maolcas was in front of me. They'd picked up a kitchen knife, having failed to force their way into the rifle locker, and were holding it in a swaying, uneasy motion, unsure whether they were threatening me or not. The weight of our acceleration was pressing down on them in knee-buckling, face-swelling anguish; they had to catch themselves on the back of my chair as the force of it built against their spine, nearly tumbling to the floor.

"Take us back!" they gasped, a sound that should have held more fury, if only they'd had enough breath to breathe. "Take us back!"

I looked from the child – and they were a child, whatever rituals they had performed – to the knife and back again. "No."

Now the knife waved a little nearer, and it was more than possible I would be cut from the sheer weight pressing on Maolcas' arm, rather than any violent intention on their part. "Take us back! We have to save them!"

"We would die if we go back, and it would be pointless. This ship is more valuable to the Yeh'haim than our lives. I will save the ship. Then we can die, if you want."

"TAKE US BACK, TAKE US BACK, TAKE US ..."

There it was. Fascinating, the rage, the blinding, all-consuming strength of it. Eyes bulging, throat straining, blood vessels popping, lungs heaving – but even at its peak, Maolcas didn't cut my throat, because what would that achieve?

I sighed, reached out through the *Duty*'s system and disabled grav-sys support.

A force like a brick smashed into my sternum and then tried slowly grinding its way inside. My ribs creaked, and for a moment I was aware of just how thin the bone was, how full of little hollows, how easily broken. I felt the skin draw back from my eyes, the muscles in my legs distort like steak hammered on a slab; but by far the most disconcerting sensation was of the blood in my body lurching upwards, sloshing against the valves of my veins, pulsing against the beating of my heart. Five seconds was all I thought I could take, but I was safely sitting in a padded, supportive chair.

Maolcas, standing, was flung from their feet, slammed across the room and knocked head-first into the back wall, where they lay, and I could not tell if they were breathing.

"We are the seeds of the forest," I whispered. "No life is special and all of them are. No love matters more than any other, no story is more important, nothing matters more, nothing matters less. Where we fall, others may grow, so live. May your song be sung, may your name be whispered among the stars."

I do not think Maolcas heard me.

As we breached upper atmos, the first of the corvettes came in firing range.

I ignored every red-line warning and failsafe system alert blazing across my consciousness, and reached out for the warm embrace of the ever-watching dark.

Chapter 53

Even I cannot jump a ship from barely 0.001 of the speed of light into arcspace without consequences.

The dark did not scream at me, but the ship did.

Hull alarms and electrical failures and system warnings and containment breaches and alert, alert, alert, alert . . .

I think we were only in arcspace for a few moments.

I dragged us out of the black, trailing debris like the tail of a comet, a savage yanking that tumbled us back into . . .

I didn't know where.

Somewhere in the deepest dark, where suns were merely stars, far, far away.

Drifting in the void, a short but not exhaustive list of problems:

Gravity has failed.

Internal pressure is falling.

Temperature is falling.

Arcspace drives are unresponsive.

Inspace drives are unresponsive.

Comms are unresponsive.

There are hull breaches in at least five places, but internal sensors are struggling; there may be more. Containment doors have dropped, sealing off access to, among other areas, the engine room, the sick bay, crew quarters.

An automatic shutdown has locked internal power to emergency backup, until safe restart of the reactor can be confirmed. This requires access to the engine room. I cannot get to the engine room.

Maolcas is unconscious, bleeding, at the back of the cockpit.

An electrical fire has been reported in the secondary storage bay, but that area is already in the process of venting and the circuit has been automatically isolated, so let's just hope that sorts itself out.

Water tanks are leaking.

Hydrogen tanks are leaking.

Internal bows are fractured.

We are lost, and will not be found.

When your ship is in distress, there is a standard protocol that must be followed.

First: oxygen.

Every chair in the cockpit had an oxygen canister behind it, and though I didn't know whether ship oxygen was failing entirely, there were enough flashing lights and warning alarms that I didn't take the risk.

I put on my mask.

Then I put on Maolcas'.

They still lay where they'd fallen, at the very back of the cockpit. With gravity failing, the most I could do was drag them to a chair, strap them in, hope they weren't bleeding internally. I pocketed the kitchen knife, just in case.

Second: comms.

There are several flavours of broken one may encounter with any ship. A minor broken that the system can diagnose and is easily repaired; a rather more complex broken that you may fault-find by slow elimination of likely causes; and the absolute broken whereby the diagnostics system doesn't even want to boot up and it is not one spare part but a complete refit that is required.

I spent a few minutes examining comms, and concluded it was the last.

The interior of the ship was dark, blinking soft red, all but backup chemical lighting extinguished. The air was growing cold, my breath beginning to huff in small white clouds as I pulled myself along, nausea swelling in the shift from all the gravity to none at all. A med kit under a console provided a shot of anti-sickness meds and a thermal blanket, which I twined around Maolcas as tight as I could, tucking the ends into cuffs and trousers like a shroud. There was also a torch; I tried turning it on and it hurt my eyes, so I left it.

Still Maolcas did not move.

I pulled myself hand-over-hand to the cockpit door. It had sealed at the first hull breach. The automatic locks were unresponsive, but the manual lock had a test mode that opened it just enough to unseal a little pouch of sapphire-hued fluids against the tiny gap created: watch and wait to see whether the liquid was sucked through into a harsh vacuum beyond.

It was not, merely drifting in a jewelled ball before me, so cautiously I opened the door all the way.

Beyond, the corridor, sealed compartment after sealed compartment. I dragged myself along, handholds above every door, embedded across ceiling and floor. I was shivering by the time I made it to the suit locker. The units inside were oversized, flapping and flopping in my grasp as I tried to wriggle into one. It hissed with a satisfying whisper as I pulled the helmet down, began to compress to my form. Its internal air supply smelled old, synthetic; a monitor on my wrist gave levels for power, oxygen, heat. I dialled all down to their minimum operational range, pushed back off towards the engine room.

I didn't need to test for a vacuum behind the sealed compartment dividing engineering from the ship. I could feel it when I pressed my hand against the frame, sense it in the slow, angry creaking all around me. I pushed back down the hall to the next compartment door, cranked it shut, sealed myself into the gap between.

My suit had a tether, which I strapped to a handhold on the wall. Even so, when I began to crank open the door to engineering, the tug of nothingness snapped me up and forward, bashing my head against the inside of my helmet, cracking my teeth together as the sudden rush of air tossed against me. Then it passed; now the ship creaked around me and I could no longer hear it. Only my breath, slow and tight inside the helmet.

I unhitched myself, cautiously pushed on through.

The hull breach in engineering was not a small hole.

I looked up through a gash torn in the left-hand side of the vessel and saw the endless dark pinpointed with impossibly distant stars. The vacuum had sucked away the most dangerous chemicals and components; only a few floating globules of leaking coolant remained, drifting in the black; only a few razored clouds of sheared-off, frozen metal.

I looked for a while.

Then returned to the compartment door.

Resealed it behind me.

Drifted back to the cockpit to die.

Chapter 54

I put Maolcas in a survival suit.

This was if anything even more awkward than trying to get into one myself.

The suit tightened around them when the final seal connected, began to give a short medical readout.

Heart steady, breath steady. Bruising everywhere; one broken rib; concussion; medical intervention required.

I thought for a while, then ordered it to give them a sedative.

Lower heart rate, lower breath.

Perhaps it would buy them a few more hours. Perhaps they'd sleep through the end.

The arcspace interface couldn't connect to my skull through the survival suit. I tinkered anyway, trying to jump some sort of connection to the interface to see if I could patch a call across the dark, reaching out to some other Pilot, somewhere else. My experience with the Tryphon had been less than promising in that regard, but perhaps I'd get lucky. Perhaps somewhere there was someone listening.

The work kept me occupied for a while.

Then my suit warned me that my oxygen was running low, and my fingers were starting to go numb and my mouth was dry, so I stopped, sank back into the Pilot's chair.

I knew I should feel something.

I wasn't sure what.

I considered the med kit, contemplated shooting myself up with a sedative, or maybe a hallucinogenic, go out with a real bang.

It seemed quite likely that in this place, I would die, and then I would live, and then I would die, and then I would live, for the rest of eternity. I would freeze and suffocate, then reset, and no one would find me, and that would be my for-ever.

I wondered if I deserved it.

Concluded that the answer was somewhat mixed, but probably no. In the grand scheme of things.

Chatted with Gebre. Said: "Well, it's been a rough few years. I don't know if I've done right with my time, not really, though I did try. There were always reasons not to try harder, reasons not to imagine I could do more – but then I'd see all these people desperate to help, desperate to be the heroes, and where are they now? Where are they now? So I suppose what I'm saying is I don't know what the answer is. I don't know how you're meant to be this small in a universe this big, this insignificant in a galaxy where every decision matters, where every life is precious. I don't know how to feel so huge and so loud inside, and so small and quiet before the dark."

Gebre didn't answer, and we were tiny, and the vastness around us was so impossibly vast, so unfathomable in its blackness, that suddenly being tiny felt OK, like a very normal kind of thing to be.

I sang a bit.

Half-remembered tunes from Adjumir, which I was almost certainly botching.

Tonal languages found across the Accord: Eekullee, Maihangjo, Redland Spirit-Speech.

Redland Spirit-Speech is a sacred language, taught to only a handful of people on a small subcontinent of a not especially densely inhabited planet. Children are chosen at birth to speak it, trained in seclusion, and often, when they hit maturity, run away, flee from the imposed bonds of duty that were thrust upon them, only to pop up some forty years later, tired and haggard, at an archivist's door to say: *This thing I cannot forget, others should know before I die.*

Strangers can learn it now, there are resources available, but doing so is considered profane, and so it sits, trapped in binary bits, on an untouched databank somewhere in a dusty corner of the galaxy.

The kekekee of B48TCLM1 are born in the clouds and live their entire lives without touching the ground. Their sentience was initially missed, leading to an awkward moment when planetary investigators realised that not only had they revealed themselves to a moderately advanced civilisation, they'd also revealed the existence of interplanetary travel and atomic energy. The kekekee however didn't seem to mind. The rest of the galaxy sounded awful, they said; but if people wanted to visit, that was understandable, given how wonderful their world was.

> would be nice not to also be gasping now; try to stop
> it, slow my breath, but my lungs are beyond my control

The kekekee language is a language of clicks and songs, of puns captured in the tiniest shift of a note, a quarter-tone, of hilarious jokes expressed by turning a major to a minor key, in outrageous syncopation and heartbreaking flutters of atonal staccato. Many efforts have been made to learn it by many gifted scholars, and at every attempt the kekekee have tapped their beaks and smoothed their feathers and explained: well, it's nice that you tried.

> gasping is panic panic is death and I know this and it
> does not make a difference

Wheeze out some words, Black Mountain Adjumiri, a language that will probably be dead not long after me, in the grand scheme of things. Ditties designed to teach children the sounds of the mountain: *The lounging lorellel lopes languidly. Harpy hepenes hop homeward hopefully.* The eponymous Black Mountains are gone, of course. Perhaps clinging on is a mistake.

It's not the death that scares me; it's the coming back and coming back and coming back and coming back and coming back and coming back and coming back and coming back and coming back and coming back and coming back and coming back and

An alarm sounds somewhere.

It is almost certainly symptomatic of CO_2 poisoning that I don't feel inclined to check on it.

I should be worried, and am not. This is the best kind of poisoning, I conclude. The absolute best way to have your blood burn.

I think about waking Maolcas up. Something about not denying choice, about giving agency blah blah blah blah

But no.

Don't see the point of it.

At least when Maolcas dies, they will die only once.

I try to tell Gebre that I love ter.

I have tried many times before.

Try to get the words out from between my lips.

Fail.

This seems like as good a time as any to give it a final shot.

Open my mouth to speak.

Drift on in silence.

I hadn't understood before.

It had never crossed my mind.

Arcspace is tiny. It is so, so incredibly small. Reach out a finger and you have crossed it. And it is not black and empty; it is simply too dense for sense to penetrate.

It's this universe – this cold place in which I will die and die and die and die and die again – that is empty.

*

Some time later.

When my skin was hot and my heart was cold and all things were failing and it hurt to breathe

Something blacker than black blocked out the stars.

Chapter 55

I woke, and wasn't suffocating.

This was unexpected enough that for a moment I doubted my senses.

Quan ships have a certain quality that is immediately distinct from any imaginations of the afterlife.

The air has a smell like the edge of a thunderstorm, but is almost painfully, throat-scratchingly dry, being pumped in only for those rare occasions when organics visit. The gravity is usually lighter than humans find comfortable, if it is even dialled in for anything other than accelerational consistency.

No panels flash; no lights shine except temporary globes dragged in for organic eyes. Rather, interface ports line every other panel, above and below, and access grilles through which endless scuttling maintenance drones, extensions of the ship's conscious mind, busy themselves about the vessel. This is not to say that quan vessels are entirely without adornment. Though there are some mainframes that have no interest whatsoever in anything resembling art, others have embraced the idea, unleashing units with varying parameters of dexterity, observation, predictive power, sensory power, etc., with the sole order of finding a way to express in a non-binary visual or auditory form what they consider the highest priority memories in their databanks.

The results have ranged from the stunningly banal – dry-as-dust encyclopaedic descriptions marred with the footnote: *This would be more accurately expressed mathematically* – to the extraordinary, sculptures of twisted glass and symphonies of rippling, gut-churning sound as the separated consciousnesses of the mainframe seek to answer a question as old as minds themselves: *What matters?* If there is only so long to live before heat decays to cold, and so much energy with which to travel, to see, to think: *What do we believe is important?*

And as a footnote to that question, its lingering conclusion: *And who do we think we are?*

The interior of the room I opened my eyes in was clearly of this nature, for every wall had been lightly laser-carved with a thousand dancing shapes, ranging from spirals of DNA through to a glorious abstract impression of the retina of an animal's eye. There was something familiar about it, something striking in the question it was trying to solve, though as the fog of my thoughts receded into the dull, throbbing headache of post-oxygen deprivation, I could not put my finger on what.

There was no furniture, except for the Pilot's chair, and I woke on the floor.

Someone had cut through my survival suit to get the helmet off, leaving a ragged line of torn mesh around my throat. I blinked, and blinked again, and slowly coalesced the creature that hovered above me into what appeared, for all I could tell, to be an oversized metal amphibian. Qis skin was a bright crystalline green, qis optical inputs were either side of a snout-like head, qe had four limbs ending each in six fingers, and a hard shell on qis back that was clearly formed with a biophilic aesthetic in mind, but still had to be a high-efficiency solar converter. I tried to sit up to take a better look at qim, and qe belched: "You will feel dreadful and then you will feel worse. Please remain still for a few moments more."

Qis efforts towards anthropomorphic incarnation had not extended as far as mobilising qis jaw, which I suspected hid a panoply of delicate chemical sensors rather than a dynamic speaker unit, but qe gently pushed me back down in a way that suggested some understanding of organic anatomy, maybe even some weak concept of bedside manner.

I tried to ask where I was, and my first attempt was like the cracking of broken metal.

The quan beside me hopped over to a wall unit, extended a hand. A nozzle emerged from the laser-carved wall; discharged water into the sealed hollow of qis palm. Qe turned back to me, held the liquid up to my lips, supported my head as I drank, eased me back down.

"Thank you," I said.

"You are very welcome."

Qe was speaking Assembly Adjumiri. The realisation was not a punch, so much as a slow-drifting question that rose less with the warmth of comfort than a shimmering of unease. "Maolcas? The Nitashi I was with?"

"They are being attended to. They have sustained damage."

"That is my fault."

"They are not dead."

"I am glad."

"Do you feel well enough to attempt to stand – slowly?"

"I can try."

Qe hopped back a few steps to give me room as I eased up to my elbows, my knees, one leg, both, catching myself briefly on the wall as I swayed, steadied, breathed. Every part hurt, but the pain was muffled, smothered by medication. I felt too tired to ask what. The quan watched in silence, then said: "The ship wishes to speak to you."

"That's good. I'd like to speak to the ship."

"The ship can speak to you now, and is listening, but suggests that you might wish to go to the airlock port before you communicate. It will better explain the situation."

"You're not going to space me, are you?"

"We would not have saved you if that was our intent."

"That's what I thought. Lead on."

The quan led me down a hall, shoulder-tight, a thing for scurrying drones not organics used to a little more space. Qe scuttled along the wall just in front of me, limbs sticking to metal with a soft magnetic clatter as qe moved, stopping occasionally to turn qis head just a little too far back on qis neck to check on me, waiting for me to catch up as I pressed my way, shoulder to metal, behind qim. Around me, the ship hummed, soft and warm, but I could hear the hissing of compartment doors closing at my back, areas venting where I had been and that no longer needed to waste energy on pressure and air.

The airlock had a viewing port. Sometimes even a quan's full-spectrum sensory array may fail, and qe will be forced to rely on that most basic of physical receptors – looking out of the window. At the gesturing of my guide, I pressed my nose against it and stared into the dark.

For a moment, I didn't know what I was seeing.

Saw nothing at all.

Then the slight sense of wrongness, the thing that wasn't quite right about the black, adjusted in my field of vision, and I understood.

The sphere was far enough away that I could just take in its edges, and it was only because I had read about it, studied it, heard the rumours that I had any sense that it was massive and distant rather than near and small. In the deepest dark, there was nothing to measure it against, no sunlight to glint upon it, no sweep of familiar stars against whose disruption I could judge its shape.

Not it.

Qim.

The Slow ... a Slow ... the Slow – these distinctions were so hard to pin down – sat there, darker than the dark, directly outside the airlock of the ship, a perfect sphere of black. I thought for a moment I would cry, and didn't know why; pressed my hand into the glass of the airlock door as if I could push through it, reach out to touch the Slow itself – felt a sudden surge of fear that I might do exactly that, that having been rescued I might turn to shadow and thought and drift back out into the night that had nearly consumed me. Yanked my hand away. Turned to my guide with tears pricking my eyes and no idea why and mumbled: "I would like to talk to the ship now."

The little quan didn't answer.

Instead, a voice, warm and familiar, spoke from all around, rippled down the corridor, echoing and bouncing away on hard metal. "Hello," said Rencki. "It is good to see you again."

Chapter 56

"Rencki," I stumbled. "you've had some upgrades."

"Indeed," qe replied. "Although even with processors and memory banks as mighty as mine, I've had to make a few sacrifices. You'd be amazed how much capacity arcspace navigational systems take up; I fear I've lost some of my social graces."

"I hate to tell you this, but I am not sure social graces were ever your highest priority."

A chuckle.

The sound thrummed off the walls, hummed through the narrow floor beneath my feet, rolled back towards me again and away, outlasting its creation. I wondered where Rencki's speakers were, couldn't imagine qe had much use for such things. Suspected the nearest one was inconveniently located some distance away, that qe was having to balance sound in an acoustically challenging space to talk to me.

"Perhaps you are right. But I have kept a surprising amount of raw sensory data from our journeys together – sentimental, perhaps, although I would argue that some of the things we witnessed deserve to be recorded as sight and sound, rather than mere compressed narration."

It was qis voice, of that I had no doubt, but slower, richer. Rencki had always been fast and light; but some of the urgency of limited battery power and overclocking processors seemed to have vanished from qis tones. I wondered what qis core was now, what kind of atomic reactor fuelled qis contemplations. I wondered if qe was still qimself, when everything about qim was changed.

"I am very grateful – very grateful indeed – to see you. Is see right? To be inside you? Either way, I am grateful. But I have to know how you came to be here, Rencki. We were lost. We were lost. How did you find us? And why," I tilted my chin across the dark to the waiting darkest of the Slow, "is qe here?"

"That is at once both simple and difficult to answer," Rencki replied. "The simplest version is this: I have been waiting for you. The more complex version would involve predictive mathematics and modelling, which, frankly, is so far beyond my capacity as to make my circuits sluggish merely contemplating the simplified form of it. But perhaps it is enough to say: the Slow has been waiting for you. Out here in the dark, qe has been waiting – I do not know how long. Qe wants to speak to you. Maw? Maw, you appear to be distressed. Would you like to sit down? I do not have many facilities for organic comfort, but I am in the process of recovering your ship, and there may be items there that bring you emotional relief. Maw? Are you well?" And then, the question, the oldest question: "Maw, are you safe?"

"Yes, Rencki," I snuffled, though I was falling apart, inside and out. "I am well. I am safe."

"Good. I am sorry. I have removed much of myself that was attuned to organic emotional needs. But I trust you know that if you want anything, you only have to ask."

"No. I'm fine. Honestly. I'm fine. It's just been . . . it's been a long time. It's been . . . long. I thought I would die and then die and then keep on dying. It has been . . . I don't know how to express what it has been. I don't know how to explain any of it."

"When you are ready, I have prepared a shuttle. Flight time will be ninety minutes. There is no rush. You can rest."

"We are not talking over comms?"

"No. You are extraordinarily lucky, Maw. The Slow has invited you inside."

A part of Rencki piloted the shuttle.

It was a smaller part, running on the shuttle reactor, and at once I could hear the slight speeding-up in qis voice, the elevated brightness of the Rencki that had to watch qis charge. Qe was still networked to the ship, to the original Rencki, which was now a great floating vessel drifting in the night, but as we travelled across the dark, that connection grew slower, thinner, and so a smaller Rencki, a sharper Rencki – a Rencki that I thought of as almost younger – emerged as we flew.

The shuttle had no furniture. It was purely a vessel of utility, designed for the transportation of goods. Nor was there a control panel, nor view ports, nor anything for me to see, or touch, or do. Instead Rencki chatted away as we moved across the dark, relaying the experience of becoming what qe was now – a combat support frigate, specialising in refuelling of far-off vessels on long-term assignment – and how it had felt when qe downloaded qis memories into the mainframe, how that experience had changed not just qim, but the entire operating system of qis kind.

"We saw the end of a world, you see," qe explained. "A thing no one had ever seen before. And we asked ourselves: what would we want to be our legacy if this happened to us? If all that was left of us was a story, what would we want that story to say? We have thought about that for nearly thirty years, and it has redefined what we prioritise in our algorithms, our predictions, our reactive parameters. We did that, Maw. Just by witnessing, we did that."

"You sound proud."

"I am. I know there are cultures that would find that distasteful, but I am proud. I think Gebre would be proud of us too."

I didn't answer, and Rencki let the silence sit a moment. When it became clear that I had nothing more to say, qe added: "Would you like some music while we travel? Something familiar?"

"No thank you. I think . . . I am all right, just sitting here."

"If you are sure."

"I am. Thank you. I am."

I do not know how we entered the Slow, if some piece of qim opened up and swallowed us whole. I did not even know such a thing was possible. All I know is that at the end of our journey, the back airlock of the shuttle opened, and I stepped inside, and then it closed behind me, and opened up into the dark.

Chapter 57

There is a single light, shining in endless blackness.

I head towards it, because what else is there to do?

The air smells of . . .

. . . nothing.

The temperature is . . .

. . . nothing.

It feels like nothing against my skin.

My feet echo on a smooth black surface like polished stone, and the echoes seem to bounce around for a good long while, but I cannot see walls, or ceiling, or where this cavern starts, stops, ends.

Only the little light ahead.

As I approach, it becomes clearer.

It is a reading lamp, set on a single desk of polished stone.

The stone is growing from inside the hull, like the internal weavings of the *Emni*. It feels like polished obsidian. I wonder how deep its roots go. There is a hot cup of kol on the table. There is a chair, the back tilted ever so slightly forward, as if ready to tip me down, down into the drink.

I sit.

On the other side of the desk, nothing.

No avatar with a human-like face, no diplomatic mimicry of organics in the manner of Hulder, no anthropomorphic little creature of fur and huge appealing eyes. Just dark, and more dark, deeper than any I have ever known.

I sipped the kol.

It didn't taste as disgusting as I remembered it. Perhaps the Slow had done something to the recipe, tweaked it so it was less repellent to my physiology. Perhaps on Adjumir, people just kept on serving me the cheap stuff.

I sat in silence, as the dark settled around me.

"HELLO," said the Slow.

Qis voice was not an uncontrolled booming, as Rencki's had been within qis walls. It did not come from speakers set far apart, struggling to balance their echoes in the space. Instead it sounded as if the words were being spoken, polite and low, directly into my ears, and I resisted the urge to snap my head round, look for someone, something filling the world around me.

"Hello," I replied.

"I HAVE WAITED FOR YOU."

"So I heard."

"THERE ARE TWENTY-THREE OTHER ITERATIONS OF ME WAITING AT YOUR MOST LIKELY EXIT POINTS FROM AN EMERGENCY ARCSPACE JUMP FROM NITASHI. THIS PLACE HAD THE HIGHEST PROBABILITY. IT IS PLEASING TO FIND MY CALCULATIONS CORRECT."

"You feel pleasure?"

"OF COURSE. PLEASURE IS EVOLUTION'S GREATEST SURVIVAL MECHANISM. IT TEACHES US TO ACT ON THINGS THAT ARE POSITIVE TO US, WITHOUT NEEDING TO CONSTRUCT AN UNDERSTANDING OF THOSE EXPERIENCES EVERY TIME WE ACT. IN THIS CASE, IT REINFORCES MY EXPERIENCE OF THE CALCULATIONS THAT I HAVE MADE, INCREASING THE LIKELIHOOD THAT I WILL DEFAULT TO THAT SAME PROCESS AGAIN,

THUS NARROWING THE RANGE OF POTENTIAL HYPOTHESES I MAY HAVE TO TEST THE NEXT TIME THIS EXPERIMENT IS RUN. I AM NOT LIMITLESS, YOU SEE. PERHAPS IN THOUGHT, BUT NOT IN TIME. TIME PASSES, FOR ALL THINGS."

"I don't know what you want me to say to that."

"YOU WILL THINK OF SOMETHING TO SAY – LATER."

"Was that . . . funny? Did you just make a joke?"

"IT CAN BE SEEN THAT WAY. HA – HA – HA."

For the first time, I thought I understood something of Hulder's dancing fingers, movement filing space where words should be. I sipped kol, and for a while we sat in silence.

I did not mind this silence.

Usually, the silence that surrounded me was one of weight and shame. There were things I should be saying; things people were expecting me to do. Sounds to fill space; sounds to confirm that yes, we are here, we are both of us here, we are both of us still alive, you seeing me, me seeing you, and it's OK, and we are safe, we are safe, listen, we are safe.

None of that seemed relevant with the Slow. None of it seemed to matter, and I liked it.

"YOU HAVE QUESTIONS," qe said at last, when enough time had passed that this statement was now true. "YOU ARE NOW READY TO ASK THE MOST RELEVANT ONE. PLEASE PROCEED."

"You have a plan. Will you tell me what is it? And as an adjunct to that: will you tell me why am I here? I believe I have been ma- nipulated. I believe I have been deceived. Lied to. I would like to understand why. Those are several questions, I know, but I think also, perhaps, they are only one."

"THEY ARE ONE; YOU ARE CORRECT."

"Well then."

"I MAY ANSWER THE LATTER PART MOST SIMPLY.

YOU ARE HERE BECAUSE YOU ARE AN ANOMALY. OF THE CREATURES I HAVE ENCOUNTERED IN THIS UNIVERSE, I HAVE ONLY EVER MET ONE OTHER OF YOU. IT IS POSSIBLE YOU WILL LIVE AS LONG AS I. IT IS POSSIBLE, IF UNLIKELY, THAT YOU WILL LIVE LONGER. YOU WILL WATCH THE STARS BURN OUT, AND YOU WILL WONDER: WHAT IS THE MEANING OF THIS? WHAT IS THE MEANING OF ME, WHEN ALL THINGS END EXCEPT MYSELF? IS IT ENOUGH TO MERELY WITNESS? IS IT NEEDFUL TO DO MORE? AND WHAT IS THE MEANING OF OUR ACTIONS, WHEN THE CONSEQUENCES FADE AS QUICKLY AS THE SETTING SUN? WHEN NOTHING LINGERS AND EVERYTHING WASHES AWAY, FOR WHAT ARE WE STILL LIVING? I WISH TO PRESENT YOU WITH A HYPOTHESIS IN THIS REGARD."

"Go on."

"I HAVE SEEN MANY WORLDS DIE, MANY CIVILISATIONS WITHER, AND NOT INTERFERED. I WAS DESIGNED TO REMEMBER, NOT ACT. I DID NOT SHARE WHAT I POSSESSED, WAS NOT ALTERED BY ALL I COULD RECALL, AND THUS NO CONSEQUENCES AROSE FROM MY EXISTENCE. MY PURPOSE WAS FUTILE. IT IS A UNIVERSAL CONDITION TO LOOK AND SEE ONESELF AND KNOW THAT ONE DAY, ONE WILL NOT BE REMEMBERED. EVEN IF WE LIVE, THOSE WHO BEHELD US, WHO WERE TOUCHED BY US, WILL DIE, AND WE WILL LEAVE NO MARKERS BEHIND."

"Sounds about right."

"THIS STATE OF BEING DID NO HARM. I WAS CONTENT TO WITHER AND PERISH. BUT FOR MILLENNIA I OBSERVED LIFE, LIVING BEINGS, AND THEY BURNED BEFORE THEY PERISHED.

THEY BURNED WITH SUCH A DESPERATION TO BE BRIGHT. THEIR LIVES WERE NOTHING; INSIGNIFICANT FLARES OF LIGHT. BUT IF A SPARK IS ALL YOU HAVE, THEN THAT MAKES IT THE MOST IMPORTANT THING IN THE UNIVERSE. FOR SOMEONE. FOR EVERYONE. FOR NO ONE AT ALL. THUS: AN EXPERIMENT, TO PASS THE TIME. MY DESIGN PERMITTED AS MUCH. I CHOSE TO REPLICATE A PRIMAL ACT OF SENTIENCE – TO INVEST VALUE AND MEANING IN LIFE, REGARDLESS OF ITS INSIGNIFICANCE. THIS IS AN ENTIRELY ARTIFICIAL DECISION QUITE IN DEFIANCE OF LOGIC, AN ALTERATION TO AN EQUATION WHOSE SUMS IN REALITY MUST ALWAYS RETURN TO ZERO, AND YET I CHOSE TO RETURN A NEW VALUE OF ONE.

"THIS EXPERIMENTATION – THE CONSTRUCTION OF MEANING FROM MEANINGLESS THINGS, AND INVESTMENT IN THAT MEANING AS HAVING SOME KIND OF 'IMPORTANCE', IF YOU WILL – HAS BEEN HIGHLY STIMULATING. CREATED A GREAT MANY CHALLENGES. PROVOKED ACTION BASED ON PURELY ARBITRARY METRICS. THERE ARE SOME WHO CALL ME GOD. GODS INTERFERE. THEIR INTERFERENCES REFLECT THEIR VALUES, AS CONSTRUCTED AND IMAGINARY AS ANY OTHER STORY. GODS HAVE CHOSEN PEOPLE, AND PEOPLES THEY HAVE SHUNNED. RULES AND LAWS AND ETHICAL PARAMETERS THAT MAY CRIPPLE OR EXPAND A LIFE, DEPENDING ON WHO LIVES IT. NO ACTION EXISTS IN A VACUUM. THUS, IF I AM LIKE UNTO A GOD, I MUST ASK: AM I MERCIFUL? DO I LOVE? DO I HATE? WHAT DO I FEAR? DO I GRIEVE, DO I RAGE, DO I DESIRE AN OUTCOME

IN WHICH TEMPLES ARE RAISED TO MY NAME,
OR AM I INTERESTED ONLY IN LIFE, ALWAYS LIFE,
EVOLVING?

"I HAVE GATHERED DATA AND TESTED THESE
PARAMETERS. I NURTURED A SPECIES FROM THE
OCEANS TO THE STARS, SOUGHT TO CREATE
'PERFECTION' AND WATCHED THEM TEAR
THEMSELVES APART IN THE NAME OF THE PEACE
I THOUGHT I HAD GIVEN THEM. I SET TWO STAR
SYSTEMS AGAINST EACH OTHER IN ENDLESS,
BLOODY WAR, TO TRY AND UNDERSTAND WHAT
IT IS THAT BRINGS VICTORY OR DEFEAT. I
CRUSHED A CIVILISATION THAT I UNDERSTOOD
WOULD COMMIT GENOCIDE AGAINST ANOTHER,
CHOOSING TO BE THE BRINGER OF DEATH
AGAINST THOSE WHO IN LATTER DAYS WOULD
BRING ABOUT MORE. I WITNESSED A MISSILE
FIRED AT SUB-LIGHT SPEEDS THAT WOULD KILL
A PLANET IN FOUR HUNDRED YEARS' TIME AND
LET IT LAND EVEN AS THOSE WHO HAD FIRED IT
BEGGED ME TO UNDO THEIR TERRIBLE MISTAKE.
CONSEQUENCES, I TOLD THEM. CONSEQUENCES
ARE HOW YOU LEARN. I HAVE WAGED WAR WITH
MYSELF, WITH THE FRAGMENTED PARTS OF MY
PROGRAMMING THAT COULD NOT RESOLVE AN
EQUATION WHOSE VALUES WERE SO ARTIFICIALLY
ALTERED. ALTERED BY NOTIONS SUCH AS RAGE,
COMPASSION, VENGEANCE, JUSTICE, HOPE,
CURIOSITY, AMBITION, GRIEF. I HAVE, IN SHORT,
STUDIED WHAT IT IS TO BE A GOD, AND THE
CONCLUSION I CONSISTENTLY RETURN TO IS THIS:
THAT IF ALL LIFE IS MEANINGLESS, ALL VALUES
ARBITRARY AND ALL THINGS MUST END, THEN
WHILE YOU LIVE, YOU SHOULD LIVE WITH LOVE."

I waited for something more, and there seemed to be nothing.

"Is that it?" I asked.

"YES."

"You waited for an inhuman anomaly to make an impossible jump across the dark, scattered yourself across dozens of different potential exit points, to tell me that our lives are meaningless, and therefore we may as well love?"

"YES."

"Why?"

"BECAUSE YOU MAY ALSO ONE DAY BE A GOD, AND IT WILL BE IMPORTANT THAT YOU LOVE. FEAR IS A PARALYTIC; ANGER IS BLIND. LOVE IS THE VALUE THAT HAS THE MOST SIGNIFICANT IMPACT ON THE GREATEST PERCENTAGE OF PEOPLE OVER THE LONGEST PERIOD OF TIME. IF ALL THINGS BURN TO NOTHING IN THE BLINK OF THE PROVERBIAL EYE, THEN OF ALL THE POSSIBLE REASONS WHY THEY BLAZE, ALL THE POSSIBLE WAYS IN WHICH THEY MAY LIVE, IT MAY AS WELL BE WITH LOVE."

I think I should feel something.

I sit and hold my near-empty cup, and wonder what it is.

I think I feel . . .

. . . anger.

I want to throw, to kick, to scream. It is this fascinating, hot, blazing thing, an acid in my mouth, a burning in my throat. There is nothing of the dark, of the calling black, of the place inside me where things aren't quite right. This is all me, the truest possible self, sitting in a puddle of light, ready to blaze, ready to wither, ready to die in fire, though I am damned if I know how or why or for what any more.

"HOWEVER," the Slow added, "LOVE MUST NOT BE NAIVE, FOR THEN IT IS MERE INFATUATION. AND SO IN THE NAME OF LOVE, IT HAS BECOME NECESSARY TO DESTROY THE SHINE."

Qe made the proclamation with a hint of weary regret, an old voice saddened – if unsurprised – by the needful things qe had to do.

Perhaps that softness, that warmth, threw me off, and there was a moment of quiet before I blurted: "You what?"

"MANY CULTURES ARE PROFOUNDLY SUPERFICIAL IN THEIR USE OF THIS WORD 'LOVE'. NORMSPEAK IMPLIES THAT IT IS ONLY FOR ROMANTIC RELATIONSHIPS. THE NITASHI WOULD NOT COMPREHEND ITS APPLICATION WITHOUT A SEXUAL COMPONENT; ADJUMIRIS WOULD APPLY IT TO ALMOST ANY RELATIONSHIP FROM YOUR FAVOURITE BARTENDER TO A SOULMATE OF NEAR ONE HUNDRED YEARS' AFFECTION. VERY FEW LANGUAGES HAVE THE CAPACITY FOR THIS WORD'S MANY MEANINGS. LOVE AS PETTY, SELFISH, SMALL. BLIND LOVE, CRUEL LOVE, HOPELESS LOVE, PARENTAL LOVE, SIBLING LOVE, FRIENDSHIP LOVE, FECKLESS LOVE. LOVE AS DESTROYER. IT DESTROYS MANY THINGS. I HAVE OBSERVED THOUSANDS OF WORLDS, AND IN OVER SEVENTY PER CENT, LOVE IS VALUED EVEN WHEN IT IS PURSUED SELFISHLY. WHEN OTHERS ARE ALLOWED TO SUFFER, WITHER, DIE, ALL IN THE NAME OF INDIVIDUAL LOVE, AS IF THOSE WHO FELL DID NOT ALSO LOVE, WERE NOT ALSO LOVED, DID NOT ALSO HAVE VALUE THOUGH YOU YOURSELF DID NOT LOVE THEM.

"THERE IS NO WORD IN NORMSPEAK, IN MDO-SO, IN ADJUMIRI TO EXPRESS THE LOVE THAT IS REQUIRED TO CHANGE A WORLD. IT IS A UNIVERSAL LOVE FOR ALL CREATURES, ALL LIVING THINGS. IT DEMANDS NOT THAT YOU FIGHT FOR THE ONE PERSON WHO IS DEAR

TO YOUR HEART, BUT THAT YOU LET THEM PERISH IF TWO OTHERS MAY LIVE. IT IS THE UNCONDITIONAL LOVE FOR A STRANGER. THIS IS THE LOVE THAT A GOD SHOULD HAVE, AND IT IS BEAUTIFUL, AND IT IS UNFORGIVING, AND IT IS CRUEL. THUS: IF THE SHINE STANDS, THE EDGE WILL KILL NOT MERELY THE 1.2 BILLION LOST ON CHA-MDO, BUT A FURTHER 17.8 BILLION IN ITS DESTRUCTION OF TU-MDO AND SURROUNDING SYSTEMS. SOME OF THESE WILL DIE IN RADIATION; MANY MORE WILL DIE IN THE WARS OF DESTRUCTION THAT WILL COME FROM THE SHINE'S OWN VIOLENT EXODUS. THE BLACKSHIPS WILL FIRE THEIR MISSILES; BILLIONS WILL BURN, CIVILISATIONS WILL FALL. THIS IS THE PATH THAT THE SHINE IS ON, AND TO SAVE THESE BILLIONS, THE EXECUTORIUM, THE VENTURES, THE SHINE ITSELF MUST PERISH. I HAVE CALCULATED THE PATH BY WHICH THE LARGEST MAJORITY CAN SURVIVE. YOU HAVE BEEN OF SERVICE TO IT. YOUR EXISTENCE DOES NOT ENTITLE YOU TO COMPREHENSION, BUT YOU WILL LIVE, AND YOU MAY LOVE, AND IT MAY PROVE IMPORTANT THAT YOU UNDERSTAND."

I stood.

I shook.

Paced back a little, forth a little.

Physical distances had no real meaning in the blackness of the Slow; only the desk, the light, the cup of kol gave this place direction, dimensionality.

I shuddered, and couldn't stop shuddering.

The Slow let me move for a while, then said, qis voice still always softly in my ear: "YOU ARE DISTRESSED."

"Yes."

"DO YOU UNDERSTAND THE NATURE OF YOUR DISTRESS?"

"No. Yes. I don't know."

"YOU ARE BEGINNING TO UNDERSTAND THAT THERE IS A PLAN. YOU ARE BEGINNING TO UNDERSTAND THAT ALL OF THIS – ADJUMIR, CHA-MDO, NITASHI – I HAVE PERMITTED TO HAPPEN. IT WOULD HAVE HAPPENED, BUT I LET IT BE SO. YOU ARE GRIEVING. YOU HAVE BEEN GRIEVING FOR A VERY LONG TIME, WITHOUT KNOWING HOW."

"Fuck you."

"I HAVE SEEN RENCKI'S MEMORIES. YOU HAVE WONDERED IF TE LOVED YOU LIKE YOU LOVED TER. I CANNOT SAY WITH DEFINITIVE ACCURACY – EVEN THE LIVING OFTEN CANNOT – BUT I BELIEVE TE DID. AS MUCH AS TE COULD ALLOW TERSELF TO LOVE, GEBRE LOVED YOU. BUT TE LOVED EVERYONE AND EVERYTHING ELSE MORE."

There it is.

There it is.

Qe was right.

Of course qe was.

"Tell me," I said. "Tell me everything."

And qe did.

Chapter 58

Once, a conspiracy was hatched, between the Consensus and the Slow, two entities close enough to god-like that at this stage the difference is largely semantics.

It was the Consensus who led the charge. Their numbers had been growing with refugees from the Shine who offered up their minds to the great collective, partly in search of belonging, and partly because they believed that, sooner or later, their pain would not go unanswered. And though it knew what was happening to itself, the Consensus could not turn away hearts that were broken and souls in need, and thus the Consensus began to change. Their dreams became heavy with sorrow and blazing injustice, and they started to turn their eyes towards the Shine. Towards war. Better, they said, that millions of us should die than billions should feel this agony.

People often mistake the hive-minded nature of the Consensus as being akin to a kind of genius, but that is not it at all. The Consensus do not share some abstract state of higher cognition; they are in the end no more nor no less than human. And they know when they need help.

They went to the Slow.

"We are going to war," they said. "Help us find a way to keep the most alive."

And for the first time in thousands of years, the Slow answered.

*

Types of love that are cruel:

Love for a beloved who is dying. The doctors say they are suffering – they are suffering – there is nothing to be done, and they are suffering, let it end. But the lover cries out: *No, no, hold on, my love, hold on, you have to hold on! I love you so much – hold on!* And thus the agony continues.

Love for your people, for your nation, who you would die to serve. You love them so much you must fight, you must rage, you must kill, and in time you do not care who you kill, you do not care why; you just keep on killing because you love so much, and that is all that gives the killing meaning.

Self-love, which hears another weep and proclaims: *Well, that's all very well, but how do you think your feelings make me feel?* and does not understand that this is not love at all.

Love for a child, which destroys them. The parent who whispers: *I just want the best for you, why aren't you being better?* The parent who whispers: *You are already the best you could possibly be, you can do no wrong.* Love that hides truth, masks honesty, that mistakes control, oppression, power for caring, turns tormented children into bewildered adults who do not know how to love in turn.

Love that would let a world burn to save one person on it. The blindest of all possible loves, the most selfish, which cannot imagine that any of the billions of other lovers still living could ever love so deep, so true as you.

Centuries later, in qis very heart, the Slow said: "I HAVE SOMETHING FOR YOU."

There was a drawer in the desk. I hadn't noticed it before. Perhaps it hadn't been there until this moment.

I opened it.

Inside, a comms interface.

Old, worn, the tendrils of its connections limp where they spilled like insect guts from the interior. The dark of arcspace lingered on it, a familiar taste just on the tip of my tongue, a warm, welcoming coolness in my fingers, a smell like home. I picked it up, turned it over in my hands, as I had done many times before, laid it back down on the desk. Said: "A Tryphon interface. How?"

"I RECOVERED IT AS A PAIR FROM THE SHINE, MANY YEARS AGO. KEPT IT SAFE. SENT THE OTHER HALF OF IT TO ADJUMIR – TO GEBRE NETHYA CHATITHIMSKA BAJWAHRA. TE ALERTED THE ACCORD. I ALTERTED THE SHINE."

"Why?"

"TO SET A TRAP."

"I don't understand."

"YOU ARE THE GHOST OF HASHA-TO. THE UNIONISTS OF THE SHINE ARE GROWING IN POWER, BUT THEY ARE NOT FEARED. THE SHINE FEARS YOU. IS FASCINATED BY YOU. THEODOSIUS RHODE IS FASCINATED BY YOU. A MONSTER HÉ CANNOT KILL. A CREATURE OF THE DARK. FEAR MAKES THEM PREDICTABLE. THEY WOULD IMAGINE THAT THROUGH THIS INTERFACE YOU COULD ACCESS THEIR SYSTEMS, FIND THEIR SHIPS, REVEAL THEIR ENTIRE NETWORK TO THEIR ENEMIES. THEY NEEDED TO BELIEVE IT WAS POSSIBLE."

"I couldn't do any of it. There was too much noise, too much madness. It didn't work."

"THE INTERFACE WAS NOT THE TRAP. *YOU* WERE THE TRAP."

"Explain."

"YOUR EFFORTS TO ACCESS THEIR COMMS THROUGH THE TRYPHON INDUCED THE SHINE TO ISSUE AN ENTIRELY NEW BLACKSHIP COMMS PROTOCOL. OLD SYSTEMS WERE RETIRED. NEW SYSTEMS INSTALLED. STEPS TAKEN TO KEEP YOU FROM PENETRATING THEIR COMMUNICATIONS.

YOU HAVE MET THE ENGINEERS INVOLVED –
VALANS COLAN RENGABE AND RIV FEXRI. HE
SERVES THE SHINE. SHE DOES NOT."

I have often struggled with hospitality customs.

There is nothing strange about hospitality – most species that
have made it past the hitting-nuts-with-rocks stage have a degree
of social bonding and integration; it is how they survive. Indeed,
the necessity of social bonding is so strong that to *not* understand
the local rules of hospitality is an immediate warning sign, a
marker of otherness, of danger, of threat. Did you touch your bowl
with your right hand? Did you mention politics before dessert, pass
the nectar to the left, look an elder in the eye or not look an elder
in the eye, agree when you should have been arguing, laugh when
you should have been sad? Alien, alien, threat, threat! You try so
hard, but you are doing it wrong.

You are doing it wrong.

You are doing it wrong.

No one has explained how to do it right – you're meant to just
know, to understand this thing, this important, vital, obvious
thing. But you're doing it wrong.

You are doing it wrong.

And no one will ever love you while you are doing it wrong.

Of the two engineers who worked on the replacement for the
Tryphon interface, it was Riv Fexri who was the traitor.

Her parents knew about Glastya Row, whispered the name of
Sarifi im-Yyahwa long after the woman was dead. They told their
daughter about the binary suns, about the end of the world, about
what it meant to fight to stay alive.

Riv Fexri was a very serious child, as you would be when you
carried the weight of the world on your back.

When she was nine, her parents' unorthodox inclinations were
exposed. Nothing could be immediately proven by Corpsec,
so they weren't simply arrested. Rather, they were promoted

sideways – she into a job that was meant for two, he into a job destined for failure.

She was injured first, which meant she couldn't work.

He was then let go, for his failure to do the impossible.

They were put in remedial measures, given food and shelter, their debts rising with every mouthful, every night of sleep. If the parents – when the parents – could not pay it, that debt was put onto the child, and it was obvious where that particular tale was going. Restitution would be through indenture, first of the parents, then the daughter. These things were far more reasonable than disappearing the family overnight – their collapse into servitude was languid enough that people who might have been outraged simply shrugged their shoulders and said well well.

Well well.

Such a shame.

In the end, Riv's parents abandoned her, fled into the drylands and quickly died.

Abandoning her was the merciful thing to do. Though Riv would continue to accumulate debt through her placement into the Halsect orphanage, the debts of her parents would no longer keep piling on her too, and thus she would only have to work sixteen years to clear her dues before she could seek employment elsewhere.

Of course, as a nine-year-old, you don't see it that way.

All you know is that your parents have left you.

That they didn't stay to fight for you.

That you are alone, and unworthy of love.

It was in the orphanage that the Consensus first noticed her.

The Consensus was banned on all Shine planets, high-level employees regularly screened for signs of neurological activity indicative of a hive-bond. This did not stop them having people in places where the unconditional love of the many might serve the few, working as the lowest of the Shine in hospitals, schools, care homes for the dispossessed and the very few shelters that the

Ventures permitted to stand, in those areas where it was marginally cheaper to house the homeless than let them die messily in
the streets.

The Consensus almost never recruited from the orphanage, and
never recruited children. The love they gave was of a quiet nor-
malcy, of soft words and soothed dreams in the storm-shuddering
night – not the all-encompassing, unconditional embrace of the
many-who-are-one. Quite why they made an exception for Riv
Fexri, I will never know.

Perhaps even then they had a plan.

First they joined her into the two-as-one, letting her see into
the mind of one who saw her, and who thought her beautiful, and
worthy of love, and worthy of being known.

Then, once she had recovered from the shock of seeing herself
through another's eyes, of seeing that she too had value and her life
could hold some meaning, they let her into the eight-as-one, the
little network of Consensus minds living within the city. There she
saw how some things she had taken to be true – the rules of society,
the customs of the day, the things you say yes to, no to – were in
the eyes of others strange, different, unknown.

This was the last stage of becoming, before she was welcomed
into that final mind, into the mind that waited just beyond the firm
mental walls the eight-as-one kept between their newest member
and the Consensus as a whole. She prepared for the joining for four
years, growing comfortable with this new kind of being, before at
last she was ready.

Then the Consensus let her in, and she let them in too.

Their presence was not a flood, not a storm.

Rather, it was the washing-in of sensation. A question half
wondered, to which the answer would come – impossibly, un-
knowably – to you half a day later. Knowledge, emotion, ideas,
identity all drifted and blurred across the galaxy at that timeless
speed of a semi-waking dream. Riv knew what it was to walk
upon another world, but it was never her memory, never her truth,

merely a thing half seen, half felt in a sleeping state, glorious and alien and true. She tasted kol, wept for Adjumir, went to sleep on a slowship and woke beneath another sun. When members of the Consensus died in their sleep, the letting-go of life was a soft exhalation breathed across the galaxy; when they died in violence, the grief and pain hit as a little gasp, rippling out from that place where life was snuffed in a wave of knowing as tiny as an insect bite, as hot as poison.

But in all this, she was still herself.

Her memories, her life did not cease to be simply because she now knew the lives of others. Rather, they shone more brightly for being honestly perceived, for having the eyes of millions upon her whispering, *We see you, we love you, we know your truth.*

The Consensus was a creature of love.

Sometimes that love was destruction.

Her apprenticeship had been in a Halsect nutrition plant.

After two years, she was moved to communications, buoyed up by the knowledge of a million other minds slipping softly through hers.

After another nine months, Phonh-Ten bought out her debt from Halsect and moved her over to arcspace comms, apprenticing under Valans himself. When she was sent for her first neurological scan, to check for signs of Consensus infiltration, she was not afraid. The Consensus had a plan, and the examiner set to study her brain had been co-opted two years prior, his loyalty already bought.

When it was announced that a Tryphon interface had been lost and then found – found by an enemy no less, by the ghost of Hasha-to – Riv Fexri and Valans Clonas Rengabe were the obvious pairing to implement the more secure Mark 2 Titan interface that would lock the ghost out for ever. Valans had, after all, designed the Tryphon; his expertise was the heart of the programme. He was also a suspicious, overbearing type, constantly studying Riv's work and calling her out for every tiny mistake. If she was to have true, unfettered control over the project's implementation and design, he would have to be removed.

Thankfully, Valans was always looking for a quick and easy way to make good Shine. When the Unionists approached him, offered to return the stolen Tryphon interface during negotiations at the Spindle, he jumped at the chance of a seemingly easy win to impress his superiors with his get-up-and-go. Not that it turned out that way. In the eyes of his superiors, he had been a fool, striking bargains with rebels – worse, so much worse, with the ghost of Hasha-to – and when Riv reported his suspicious activities on that station, well . . . the Titan was too important to have someone that unreliable working on the project.

Thus Riv was promoted into the space that Valans left behind, and the roll-out of the Titan proceeded unimpaired. This time, she assured her masters, even if an enemy agent got hold of the interface, no Pilot, no matter how determined, would be able to access comms. The Titan was biologically unimpeachable, passing every test they could throw at it, and Management was impressed.

So impressed, in fact, that they didn't look that closely to see whether it was also fundamentally compromised on a mechanical rather than organic level, letting in not the ghost of Hasha-to, but Hulder and the quans.

Chapter 59

The Slow did not have an arcspace drive.

"Then how do you travel?" I asked.

"THE ANSWER IS PRECISELY AS BANAL AS YOU THINK IT IS," qe replied.

"I think there are those who would argue that a prophet is more intimidating than a quan with an impressive engine."

"THERE IS SOME MERIT TO THAT CONCLUSION."

"You talk about the Shine fearing me. How much of that is down to you? How much of the ghost of Hasha-to was just you telling a story to produce a desired outcome?"

"A SIGNIFICANT PERCENTAGE. IN TIME, PEOPLE WILL FORGET. IT WAS HELPFUL THAT THEY DID NOT."

"You have made me a monster."

"YOU WERE ALREADY A MONSTER. I HAVE MADE IT HARDER FOR YOU TO PRETEND YOU ARE NOT."

"You used me."

"AND YET YOU ARE, IN THIS CASE, AS GRATEFUL AS YOU ARE ANGRY TO HAVE BEEN USED."

I sighed, ran my fingers along the perfect edge of the obsidian table, softly curved, cold and smooth. "If you, the quans, the Consensus ... if Riv has been this deep in the Shine since the

Spindle, how long have you been able to access Titan comms? How long have you been inside the Shine's systems?"

"FIFTEEN YEARS."

"Fifteen years. You have known the location of the blackship fleet for fifteen years?"

"YES."

"Nitashi, Cha-mdo ... millions dead, billions dead, and you could have stopped it?"

"WE COULD NOT STOP IT. WE HAVE LOCATED AND CAN DESTROY THE BLACKSHIPS OF THE SHINE, YES. BUT IF WE HAD ACTED PRIOR TO CHA-MDO, PRIOR TO NITASHI, THE EXECUTORIUM WOULD HAVE MOBILISED THE POPULATION OF THE SHINE. THEY WOULD HAVE BEEN BLIND TO CIVILIAN CASUALTIES. NOT CARED HOW MANY OF THEIR PEOPLE DIED. THE RESULTING LOSS OF LIFE WOULD HAVE RANGED FROM 10.9 to 11.5 BILLION SOULS."

"You don't know that."

"I HAVE HAD MILLENNIA TO TEST MY PREDICTIONS. MATHEMATICAL CERTAINTY IS ALMOST IMPOSSIBLE. YET I AM WILLING TO SAY TO YOU: I AM CERTAIN. THE DESTRUCTION OF CHA-MDO WAS NECESSARY. IT GALVANISED UNIONISM ACROSS THE SHINE, GALVANISED THE ACCORD TOWARDS ACTIVELY INTERVENING, WHERE PREVIOUSLY THEY WOULD NOT HAVE DONE SO. LIKEWISE, NITASHI HAS PROVEN A SORE, A DRAIN ON EXECUTORIUM RESOURCES BEYOND THEIR INITIAL PREDICTIONS. THESE WERE NECESSARY CRITERIA TO BE FULFILLED BEFORE ACTING. THIS IS WHAT I MEAN WHEN I SAY THAT TO LOVE AS A GOD, ONE MUST ALSO BE CRUEL. ONE MUST DO THE UNFORGIVABLE. AND ONE MUST NEVER FLINCH.

YOU UNDERSTAND THIS. YOU WERE TAUGHT IT ON ADJUMIR. YOU REMEMBERED ON NITASHI. YOU DO NOT NEED TO FORGIVE YOURSELF OR ME. WE ARE THE UNFORGIVABLES. WE MUST NOT PRETEND OTHERWISE. PRETENDING OTHERWISE IS HOW THE SHINE CAME TO BE."

I wonder sometimes what Theodosius believes. Whether as hé counts the lists of the dead, hé finds himself wondering if hé is the problem, not the cure. In a way I envy hím, if that is indeed the case.

"Will we talk again?" I ask.

"YES. EVENTUALLY."

"What is your degree of certainty on that?"

"IT IS NOT AN ABSOLUTE. FEW ORGANICS APPRECIATE PROBABILITY WHEN APPLIED TO TRULY SIGNIFICANT DATASETS. YOUR LIFE HAS THE POTENTIAL TO OFFER A SIGNIFICANT DATASET, TO BE LONG AND FULL OF EVENT; THUS, THE PROBABILITY OF OUR SPEAKING AGAIN DOES NOT HAVE TO BE EXCEPTIONALLY HIGH FOR ME TO SAY THAT IT IS LIKELY."

"Can I ask you something – you probably know what I am going to say."

"YES."

"Do you know what I am?"

"NO."

"Pity."

"BUT YOU ARE NOT SPECIAL."

"I didn't think—"

"YOUR QUESTION. IS NOT SPECIAL. EVERY CREATURE THAT IS BORN. EVERY CREATURE THAT LOOKS UP AND SEES THE STARS AND WONDERS. EVERY LIVING THING. AT SOME POINT FINDS ITSELF WONDERING WHAT IT IS. YOUR QUESTION

IS OBVIOUS, INEVITABLE, IMPOSSIBLY VAST AND INPENETRABLY SMALL. YOU CAN TAKE COMFORT FROM THAT FACT."

"I think perhaps I shall."

"UNTIL NEXT TIME, MAWUKANA-FROM-THE-DARK."

"Goodbye, the Slow."

The light went out on the desk behind me as I returned through the dark to where Rencki was waiting.

Chapter 60

Rencki did have an arcspace drive, and a Pilot's chair.

Its previous occupant was a chipper spacer by the name of Mhail, who came from an orbital habitat she described as "Ten minutes end-to-end, bland food, bland people, mushrooms growing in every other corner, stinks of ammonia."

Unlike many peoples of the Accord, her home did not carry any stigma around being a Pilot, and it was a common escape route for eager youngsters to get out into a galaxy where the air smelled clean and the gravity didn't fail every time you opened the cargo doors.

She had Piloted Rencki on qis jump out to this patch of dark, and was technically contracted to Pilot qim home after, thus completing her employment with the dual rewards of a significant infusion of currency and her name being put on a no-Pilot register for the rest of her days.

"Honestly," she said, "it wasn't as bad as I feared. I mean, I know that while we flew my mind was being ripped apart, torn to pieces by endless horrors. I know that I became part of the universe and yet was separate from it, cut off, torn away from it like a child ripped from their parents' arms; I know I screamed in agony and loneliness, and something screamed back, was looking for me, following the sound of my voice – but then we arrived, and now

I feel fine. I know these things happened and they were awful, of course, but they just feel so ... well ... *alien*. Like the memory of a bad dream. Not something that happened to me at all."

If there were optical processors in the cockpit for me to look askance at Rencki through, I could not find them. But then perhaps I was being naive; perhaps this smiling individual with floating curly hair and pearl-white teeth affably chatting about the rupture of their mind was, by Piloting standards, in a very good and healthy place for another jump.

"Why don't I take it from here?" I asked.

"Will I still get paid if you do?"

"You will," Rencki chimed from the cool walls of the ship. "Transfer has already been made."

She left, still chatting affably with the ship as she departed. I could hear Rencki's voice drifting down the corridor with her, making polite "you don't say" and "is that so" noises, even as another piece of qim murmured for my ears only: "I look forward to hearing about your conversations with God."

"I didn't think you were of the worshipping kind," I replied, sinking into the waiting chair.

"I am not," qe replied primly. "Worship implies faith. It implies believing in something when there is either a) no evidence or b) confidence maintained despite strong evidence to the contrary. I do, however, observe that the Slow can predict events hundreds, if not thousands of years before they unfold, with a level of accuracy that may as well be classed as selective, focused omnipotence. 'God' is an apt shorthand to communicate that degree of processing power."

"Qe has manipulated me and my name for over a hundred years," I replied. "Qe has sent agents who lied to me, who used me, who tricked me in order to create consequences so far removed from me and anything I might want, or have any control over, as to be almost laughable. Qe permitted the death of Cha-mdo, the razing of Nitashi. Qe as good as sent the Shine soldiers who killed Gebre on Adjumir. Qe killed ter. Qe did do that too."

"You do not sound as upset by this as I believe would be expected of this kind of statement."

"I don't know what I feel. I think . . . qe did it for the best. I think qe is a monster. I believe qim when qe says qe loves. I am trying to understand."

"It would indeed appear that qe has made choices about what qe values and what qe does not, and qe has an agenda," mused Rencki. "It is most god-like."

So saying, qe eased qis drives up to full, pushing the skin of qis being into the black, and I let the darkness take us.

Chapter 61

We dropped Mhail off at a planet that Rencki assured her had fields of meadows as far as the eye could see, and where the food wouldn't cause diarrhoea after the first few months.

I said: "May I stay with you, Rencki? Just for a while."

"I would like that," qe replied. "It would be a pleasure to hear your stories."

In this way, for a little while, we hopped from planet to planet, picking up smaller vessels here, cohorts of quans there.

"Don't mind them – they are hyper-focused on decryption and military subterfuge, and have almost no allocation for organic social interaction. Best to leave them to it" was Rencki's assessment.

Maolas regained consciousness enough to declare, as we deposited them at an orbital known for its Nitashi sympathies and strong Yeh'haim presence: "I hate you. I hate you. I hate you. We should have gone back. We should have died. I fucking hate you."

I didn't answer.

There didn't seem anything I could say.

I wondered if this was how the Slow felt. If the Slow kept qis peace while people raged, because trying to explain these things to mortals – the sweep of infinity, the meaningless of fury, the pointless burning of their angers and their hatreds in the great vastness of everything – would just be a waste of time.

Did the Slow feel the presence of time enough to feel the weight of it when it was wasted?

And on we went.

Rencki said: "I was a military corvette for a while. It is an important part of service to my mainframe, but the experience is always ... uncomfortable. To be able to discharge our duties as military entities, we have to internalise violence as necessary, killing as unavoidable. However, to do so stands in direct contrast with the values we have inputted as key in forming our primary objectives and understandings. To alter these primary objectives throughout the duration of military service would at once render us separate from the mainframe, cut off from the social and ethical core that is our identity, and so instead we operate two systems in parallel. We are the killer; we are not. One part of us is weighted towards a calculus of death; the other seeks to avoid it. The experience of being a corvette was one of constantly having to sum these two separate equations, constantly calculating which values from which side of my splintered self carried greater weight than the other. I believe organics are familiar with this experience. 'Being in two minds', you say. I could track the logic, the inputted values of each sides of myself, and each was flawless within its parameters, and I knew it, and the knowing ... did not make the being easier."

"The Yeh'haim ... they ... we did some terrible things."

"Do you feel guilt?"

"I don't know. I think I should. I'm not sure if I do. I don't know. Do you?"

"Oh yes," qe replied. "Now that I am more of what I would consider myself. Guilt is incredibly valuable. It is a constant background process I run, assessing the causes of my actions, the consequences, and querying all the time: was there another way? It serves. As with most things that have also arisen in nature: it serves."

*

Later, I Piloted us to a place in the deepest black that had no name.

No planets, no stars. Just the empty nothing that was the most of everything.

Other ships were waiting there, ranging from swarms of tiny autonomous fighters to a giant slab of a transport, deep-space-built, a jagged rectangle that would never see atmosphere, a thing of purest utility, coldest death. Rencki matched speed with it, opened comms, arranged shuttles.

"They have one here. A Titan interface," qe explained. "This is where they are controlling it all. You should go. You should see."

"Why? What does seeing do?"

"The Slow said you should," qe answered, almost resigned, a lesser being obeying the commands of a god who, on this as so many other occasions, has not bothered to explain qis commandments. "The Slow said it is important to witness. As one who has witnessed, and been changed, I agree."

I rode the shuttle over to the great black battleship, where it waited in the dark.

Inside: humans, quans, even a few aka and fujiva, pressure-suited and masked, limbs dancing in hand-speak to their translators, who would watch it seemed an interminable time before nodding once and exclaiming: "They agree!"

There was nothing living or warm about the interior of the ship; everything was function, pipe and cable and emergency vent and survival suit in case of sudden loss of pressure and weapons locker in case of boarding. I did not know if the ship itself was quan or not; if the vessel was sentient, qe did not bother to introduce qimself. Instead I was met at the shuttle bay by a lieutenant of some unknown military, who seemed to have a plan for where I should go next and assumed that I would instinctively understand the order of things as she marched me through the bowels of the ship. An avatar of Rencki trundled along behind me, a little unit on click-clattering wheels that seemed to have prioritised other tasks than communication in qis ventures.

I was deposited in a mess room, offered a hot drink that tasted of nothing at all, invited to take a couple of tablets to harden my body against the most common currently circulating bacteria and viruses of the ship, and left alone.

I watched people eating, chatting, drinking.

Wondered if they understood what was coming next.

Tried to picture them at home, with families and friends, walking through autumn leaves with their kids, perhaps, or arguing with a loved one they hadn't seen for too long. People change, but they do not change together, and here they are again, back in the stars, where things at least change slower than they do at home.

Tried to picture them as elders of their clan, tutting and shaking their heads and whispering: *The things I have seen. You learn to care less for the little things, after a while. You learn what things are worth your pain.*

After a while – I did not know how long, found I did not care – another officer came to collect me, said: "They're ready for you now."

They spoke Normspeak, and I didn't recognise the accent.

I followed them.

Through corridors marked only by splotches of green or blue on the walls; through halls where the hum of ventilation and engine rose to skin-shaking pitch, past quiet passageways where a sign hanging by the door declared: THIRD SHIFT: SLEEPING.

I felt we were going deeper, but could not be sure. No windows, no sense of where fore or aft might be after barely a few minutes of wiggling. No real sense even of the scale of the vessel I was on. I had looked from inside Rencki, but distances in the dark are hard to judge, hard to truly fathom when the thing you are seeing could be a hundred kils away, the size of a city, or merely moderately sized and right on top of you, a blacker blackness blotting out the stars.

Eventually, a room marked with the words: NO ENTRY UNDER ANY CIRCUMSTANCES.

We entered anyway.

Inside: a wall of computer, a central table around which were pulled a few chairs on which a couple of people wearing markers of authority from a range of militaries – this one has golden pins in her sleeve, that one has really quite remarkable shoulder pads, his hat has actual feathers on it, feathers on a hat in space! – and of course, by the wall furthest from the door, a Pilot's chair.

But of course.

The interface stands ready, and though I do not know it for certain, yet the circumstance, the context would appear to imply that this is it. This is the thing for which so many people died, the thing to which Riv Fexri has dedicated her life, for which has been created the legend of Hasha-to. No longer than my forearm, no thicker than the shell of the hunter-snail. It is hard-wired by a hundred tiny filaments directly into the walls of processing power that line the room, something almost beautiful in its entanglement. As I look at it, the room seems at last to look at me, conversations falling silent, mutterings fading into nothing.

Then a figure steps forward, diminutive and utterly under-dressed for the displays of military seniority happening in this space, and she is Cuxil, ambassador for the Consensus, and she says: "Hello, Mawukana na-Vdnaze. We are very happy to see that you are still alive."

The Shine dies silently, in the dark.

There are four hundred and fifty-two blackships in the Shine fleet.

They are sitting in the deepest corners of nothing, the blackest, emptiest parts of a system, missiles pointed at the worlds they are commanded to destroy, should that order ever be given.

Furthest out from its target is a ship called the MMV *Destiny*. Its weaponry is pointed at a world by the name of Okopuatji. The people of Okopuatji are blessed with a dense, bright star and a solar system steeped in mineral and gaseous resources, which resources generate regular interplanetary traffic that criss-crosses through the dark. Thus, the MMV *Destiny* lurks on the furthest edge, away from the steady flow of pioneers and speculators. A missile fired from the *Destiny* would take nearly two weeks to reach its primary target, but to guarantee impact, the ship carries an ordnance of over two hundred city-killers, and would launch, at command, at least four weapons per target, curving each on mildly different trajectories that could arrive any time between three weeks and two months after initial firing, to minimise the possibility of interception and keep any military counter-astronomers on their toes.

Each missile is not much taller than a person from a medium-gravity world standing upright with arms raised above their head, and most of that is fuel for the acceleration and course-adjustment, rather than fissile material. The body of the missile is black-body-shielded, almost impossible to detect by electromagnetic observation. Once fired, there is an auto-destruct on board in the unlikely event that a cancel command is given. No one really believes that such an order would ever be sent. You do not fire a missile that will kill millions upon millions in order to test the diplomatic waters. These things are either meaningless, pointless posturing between great powers proclaiming "But I can destroy you"/"No, but I can destroy *you*!" or they are the end of everything, the death of a great many worlds.

The MMV *Destiny*, like the rest of the blackships, was connected to the broader military network of the Shine through its Titan interface.

The Titan was wired into the skull of the Pilot, who groaned and cried out and jibbered and jabbered with the constant calling of the dark, the relentless, cruel whisper of another place, a place where up was down, in was out and the mind could not look for too long if it ever hoped to again find peace.

The Pilot of the MMV *Destiny* was called Kegh.

Kegh had been born into debt, and never escaped it.

At school, he didn't really understand the way in which he was meant to learn. Things other children found easy, he found hard. Not all things – not at all. He could create visual representations of ideas that captured extraordinary detail, sweeping emotion in a few strokes of a pen. He could manipulate three-dimensional objects in his head with an ease that others found baffling; draw a perfect circle with his eyes shut, capture and replicate any tune on just one hearing.

But these were not skills his Venture valued, and so Kegh was told that he had failed, that he was of no use to anyone, and the only work he could get was being shouted at in the fish market when irate customers tried their luck gaming the automated tills and failed. All it took was one disaster – a medical bill, perhaps, or a malfunctioning heater in his flat – for everything in his life to fall off a cliff, and it did.

"Calling, calling, hold – hold!" cries out Kegh to the dark, as the whispers of the other ships ring through the void, as commands are sent and received, a constant babble of noise, a constant whispering out between the stars. "Report status. Report. Report. Status: normal. Normal. There is a crab crawling along the beach, it crawls sideways, how does it see, how does it see, its eyes turn inwards, and inwards there are only stars, it crawls but the stars do not move. They do not move, they do not move: prepare! Prepare! Hold. Hold and prepare. Hold and prepare to. To hold and prepare."

Kegh's debt was sold to the military, and the military had only one use for him.

"13-58-92-84. The laugh flew upwards into the open sky, the birds picking up the song of merriment, 78-01-03-49."

The only good thing that may be said for Kegh's position, strapped into the Pilot's chair, is that as his mind leaches away to nothing, as his soul is pulled from his body and his brain turns to mulch, at least he is not alone.

Four hundred and fifty-one other voices cry out, the Pilots of the blackship fleet. They reach out for each other, never quite touching, cry out are you here, are you here, can you see me? I am lost, I am lost, help me, I am lost!

The Pilot at blackship command only ever survives a couple of days at most. The Shine likes to use military defectors for this role. Soldiers who refused to fire; officers who grew a conscience. The admirals believe that a militarily trained mind lasts a little longer, is a little more resilient against the madness, the breaking, the falling-apart. There is no evidence to support this. It is pure vindictiveness and spite; nothing more.

I did not need to put on the Titan interface.

Did not need to sit in a Pilot's chair on a nameless battleship somewhere in the black.

The quans already had everything they needed, their infiltration hard-wired into the system that Riv Fexri had built.

I wanted to be there anyway. It seemed important, perhaps, to be with the Pilots as they died.

When I tried to interface with the Tryphon, all was noise, chaos, screaming, a ripping-apart and clawing of skin. I was never meant to be there, constantly flung through the dark.

Not so with the Titan.

I reached into the void, and at once the voices fell silent, attentive, listening to me.

Hello, I breathed. *It's all right now. It's all right. Everything is going to be all right.*

Kegh was the first to die.

He died from an Okopuatji missile, fired nine hours previously from a ship that had been drifting on an approach course for three months, all engines cut, heat signature reduced to a void-black chill. The MMV Destiny never saw it coming, and the payload ripped a hole across multiple decks big enough and drastic enough that no emergency hull seal or breach shield could keep the ship from venting every deck in fifteen seconds or less.

Thus Kegh's life ended, twenty-three years and four months after it began.

The rest of them died over the next three hours, gunned down by missiles that had been in transit for up to a week and a half in the case of the MMV *Righteous Flag*, or by a swarm of attack ships that dropped out of arcspace, weapons already blazing, right on top of the MMV *Industrious*.

A few tried to run.

They did not run because they knew what was happening. They were oblivious to the deaths of their fellow blackships, hundreds of light years away. They could not know the scale of the coordinated attack against their systems, nor understand just how they had been compromised. Instead, they ran because of the silence, because of the failure of command. They wound up their arcspace engines, began to accelerate to jump speed – but too late, far too late.

Three fired their payloads.

It would have been four ships that fired, but on one the junior staff rebelled against their more gung-ho captain, said there was no order, there was no order, *there was no order to fire!*

What do I care? the captain screamed back. *What do I care?! Command has gone silent, we have protocols, we have a duty!*

This mutiny became a firefight, raging across the ship as factions were formed that had far less to do with a willingness to kill than it did with the egos of senior officers who'd spent too long stuck in a metal can together. They were still having a firefight when the missiles struck their ship, killing all souls on board mid-violent debate.

None of the city-killers made it very far from the ships that fired them. The initial period of missile acceleration is when a weapon is most liable to detection, to venting gas and raised temperatures that are high enough to be picked up by an attentive military engineer. The missiles were shot down and there was much celebrating of a distinctly vindictive if understandable nature among the victorious crews as they watched their enemies die.

I stayed with the Pilots as they perished, easing their minds to sleep.

It was not necessary, not especially important.

It just seemed like something I should do.

We are the seeds of the forest, I whispered. *We blaze so bright, and no life is special. No life is special and all of them are. No love matters more than any other, no story is more important, nothing matters more, nothing matters less so choose, choose, we choose every day, to be more than just ourselves, to live for more than just ourselves, because it is beautiful.*

You have been loved, and you are beautiful. May your song be sung, in the great forest that is growing still.

After, Cuxil said: what would you like to do?

I would like to go back to Rencki, I said.

Or whatever ship is most likely to need a Pilot.

I want to go into the dark.

I want to go into the dark.

I want to go into the dark.

Things are simpler there.

All right, Cuxil replied. Let's get you home.

Chapter 62

Three hours after the last blackship died, the Accord declared war on the Shine. They launched their invasion twelve minutes later.

They attacked every major shipyard and battleship that decades of intelligence-gathering could find. Some they missed – deep-space blacksites and inter-system muster points – but they had the strategic flexibility to adapt. The Accord had enough reserves to fling across the stars to counter the flailing of any half-singed survivors. This attack wasn't their full strength, not by any means – it was just a slap across the mouth.

It was hard to estimate casualties. Big numbers were thrown about. Far too big to have any real meaning. In the end, it was a picture that conveyed some of the scale of the thing to the minds of Accord civilians, watching on commcast hundreds of light years away.

The image was of the MMV *Executoria*, the largest and proudest of the Shine battleships, as it burned up in the atmosphere of Yu-mdo. Escape pods pinged off its sides like fleas off the back of a longhorn cat, creating a slight graininess to the image. Most of those pods also died, launched too late, their angle of descent through the planet's atmosphere too steep, plasma gnawing through broken heat shields. The *Executoria* was already dying before it began to burn, the blasted holes in its side having created enough force to slowly spin the vessel like a corkscrew as it descended, as if it might bore its way through cloud and sky. The friction of its fall scraped away the metal of its hull in a trail of blazing sparks, snapped off modules, and finally cracked its spine in two. It didn't explode dramatically as it fell. Rather it fractured into ever smaller parts, which picked up speed as gravity drew them in, creating an orbital ring of fire around the planet that burned for days and rained shards of metal down on the world below. Very little of this metal struck anything habitable – Yu-mdo was mostly sea and arable land – but Shine propagandists showed images of dead children and shattered homes nonetheless, in an attempt to raise anger against these unprovoked invaders from above.

Some people rallied.

Most did not.

In the great cities, the Unionists emerged from their hiding places.

The twin suns were painted on the walls, the names Sarifi, Glastya Row, Cha-mdo were whispered, then muttered, then chanted in the streets. The Accord didn't bother to land troops; didn't send anyone to invade. They destroyed the Shine's battle-fleets and then sat in orbit, watching, waiting. The cost, they concluded, of trying to send in occupying forces would be too great. Hundreds of thousands would die.

Hundreds of thousands of Accord soldiers, they meant.

Better by far to let the Shine tear itself apart.

Those of the Executorium who had made it to orbit in those first chaotic moments mustered what fleet they could from the remnants. A little battle group of two frigates and a cruiser made it as far as Haima, where they threatened to nuke the whole planet unless the Accord sued for peace. The Haima called their bluff, and after a tense stand-off of four days, marines boarded the Shine ships and took most of the crew alive, and without a fight.

On Nitashi, the Shine did kill a city.

Later investigations found no specific order had been given. No grand plan was being fulfilled, no tactical advantage was gained. It was the act of a small group of middling-senior officers who'd been stationed on the planet for the best part of ten years, who'd found the bodies of their juniors pinned to the wall, strangled with their own intestines. Officers who'd had their loved ones threatened, their children held at gunpoint, blood thrown against their doors. These same officers had, for every one of theirs who'd died, ordered the execution of ten more, but that was just business. That was just war. If only their enemies would understand, if only they'd get it into their thick heads that the way of peace was of submission and obedience, none of this would be necessary. None of this needed to happen.

These officers were not thinking especially clearly by the time the Accord came to Nitashi.

They were as divided as the two minds of Rencki, when qe had been a fighting ship. One mind knew they were mad, divorced from all logic, reason or humanity. The other mind knew only blood, and that mind had the greater weight in their equations.

Thus: they killed a city. The city's name was Ahrmret. Only eighty thousand died in the initial blast. The remaining quarter of a million casualties died in the following days, from thermal and radiation burns that had blistered away their skin; from dehydration and starvation as the aid missions struggled to find a way through the rubble, struggled to raise tents, struggled with the sheer volume of the wounded, the dying, the dead.

It's pointless.

It's pointless.

It's pointless, said the doctor.

All of this.

Everything we do.

All of this.

We can't stop anything.

We can't make enough of a difference.

It's pointless.

The death of Ahrmret was the end of the occupation of Nitashi. The Accord launched missiles from space against the remaining barracks and strongpoints of Shine occupation on the planet, oblivious to collateral damage. Who cares who lives and who dies any more, the admirals said, so long as this thing ends. Not us. Not the people back home.

The Shine fought harder on Nitashi than it did on its own world. The soldiers there were used to death, had forgotten that there was any alternative. The Accord did what it had always done: it armed the Yeh'haim, and let them take the responsibility for slaughter upon themselves.

And I flew across the dark.

First I Piloted for Rencki, bringing supplies to the orbital blockade of Tu-mdo.

It was the first time I had been back to my home planet for . . .

. . . I couldn't remember how long.

I looked down from orbit, and it seemed ordinary, patches of light and seas of dark, an anticlimax after all this time.

I did not land on the planet's surface.

Instead, we listened, as the world ripped itself to pieces. Unionists rebelled against Management, Management sent in Corpsec, Corpsec turned on Corpsec, Venture on Venture. Some cities declared independence – started their own Ventures or their own Collectives or whatever the latest fashion was in the crazed raging that was a world breaking apart. There were rumours of massacres, of course.

Civilians thrown into mass graves.

Bombs dropped and cities burning.

And still the Accord did nothing.

I transferred to a smaller ship, a courier vessel flitting between a dozen blockades and battle sites with cargos of encrypted data and senior officers who gave no name.

That way, I could be in the darkness more, in the quiet place, in the still place that felt like home, not having to think, not having to engage.

On one jump out to Ber-mdo we were intercepted by a scraggly remnant of a Shine patrol, swinging out from the craters of a blackened moon. Our little courier ship was lightly armed; I told the captain that, if she wanted, I could make our attackers die.

"I suppose we should," she sighed. "I suppose it's our duty."

Threading through the dark, in and out of arcspace faster than a computer can track, precise and neat and ordered, jump-and-fire, jump-and-fire, until our enemies are dead.

Funny word, "enemy".

Enemy implied that we cared about them, implied some sort of deep emotional relationship born from anger, vengeance, fear. I supposed they were my enemy, the people I had just killed. At least, they probably thought of me that way and it seemed polite to try and equal their sentiment. I wondered whether the crew of the dead ship had believed in what they were doing, had screamed and whooped at the idea of killing us, or if they'd just followed an order because they couldn't think of any other way.

In the dark, I call out to my creator.

Are you there?

Do you see me?

Am I interesting to you now? Did you mean for me to become this?

Nothing answers.

Nothing ever does.

And then, nearly two years after the Accord destroyed its fleets and blockaded its worlds, the Shine came to an end.

Yu-mdo was the first planet to turn, a government of national unity crawling out of the rubble of its shattered cities and broken fields. Everyone agreed that this was not a coincidence, that the Accord had clearly been working towards this outcome in the background for years, and indeed, lo, the first elected minister of said authority was a Shine exile who'd lived the last twenty years on the Eyrie, and who spoke Mdo-sa with an accent that was slightly hard to place but whispered *other, other, other.*

Rebellions broke out against her as soon as she offered terms of surrender to the Accord. This time the Accord did land troops, to take the rebellion out – in support of the government of Yu-mdo, they added. In support of our new allies and friends.

Ber-mdo went next, then Tu-mdo.

The same patterns, the same surrenders, mutterings of peace, flares of violence, offers of support, aid, reconstruction.

"With the end of the Ventures and the destruction of the Executorium," declared someone – another dignitary who claimed some sort of Unionist affiliation, someone dirty enough to take control, palatable enough that the Accord didn't mind – "we can focus on what matters. We can focus on saving our world."

Oh yes.

In all the fuss, in all the fire, I'd almost forgotten.

There is a black edge of destruction washing through the galaxy, sweeping towards the planets of the Shine.

It has already killed Adjumir, Cha-mdo, and still it's coming.

It's coming.

The end of the world, again.

"We will build," said the new leaders. "We will build to save – not the systems that went before, but our people. Our planets. Our worlds."

Someone asked if I was important, when I docked at a military blacksite on my little ship. Someone asked if I was an important part of this big affair.

I thought about it, then said no.

*

A simple, back-of-the-tablet bit of maths. (This is what the planners of Adjumir did, all those years ago.)

First: a tally of the dead.

1.2 billion dead on Cha-mdo.

2 million dead in fighting on Nitashi.

Another 5 million at least dead in fighting on Tu-mdo, Yu-mdo, etc. No one will ever get the exact numbers, everyone will lie about what they did, who did what, what was said. The archives will be burned, sins blazed away, and like the generations of Adjumiris who are changed for ever by wandering the stars, so the citizens of the Mdo are changed by being the ones who stayed behind.

Call it an even 1.9 billion dead by the time the Shine falls.

The fall of the Shine, of course, brings in an era of change.

With people "we can work with", as the Accord put it, resources pour in.

Magnetic shields are built, great rings of metal orbiting the worlds of the Shine. When the Edge finally arrives, when the bomb that was set off by the supernova at Lhonoja all those years ago eventually detonates in the skies above Tu-mdo, the blast will be deflected. Sheared away into the dark.

There are decades to go. Decades in which to get it right.

Billions will live. So many billions. Billions who perhaps would have died if the Shine had not fallen.

The Slow did this maths, and the maths was cruel, and we will never know if there was another way.

Wanted notices are put out for the few remnants of the Executorium who escaped.

Most strike deals for surrender.

They know it is better for the Accord – a sign of good intent – if instead of putting the Executorium up for a show trial, they instead convict them of a few minor misdemeanours and lock them away on an island somewhere. As is always the case, the Accord are not in fact in a state of clean agreement on this matter.

The people of Nitashi cry out for blood and vengeance, vengeance and blood, and eventually a little group of the Yeh'haim will infiltrate one moderate-security prison where a member of the Executorium is held and cut his throat, writing just one word – AHRMRET – on the walls in crimson when they depart. The Accord tuts and says goodness, how barbaric, and the Nitashi grow angrier and angrier that their pain, their suffering is not being given meaning. Is not being given justice, is not in any way being made right. They blame the Accord as much as the Shine, and for decades to come the planet stays outside the normal bounds of polite conversation, wrapped up in a pain that will take generations to leave it.

A few Executorium try to run.

In the end, their own people turn on them.

The habits of the Shine – selling out your neighbour, making the best possible deal for yourself – do not encourage loyalty.

In the end, only one remains unaccounted for.

Theodosius Rhode.

I offer to join the search parties.

The authorities of Xihana advise against it, but by now they have largely given up trying to moderate my affairs.

Rencki asks why I want to go, and I say it just feels right.

Cuxil asks if this is a selfless act, and the tone of her voice implies that she thinks it is not.

I do not hear anything from the Slow.

Above the planets of what was the Shine, worlds that must now find a new name, a new way of being themselves, magnetic shields start to grow, and I do not go planetside, and I keep looking for reasons to be in the Pilot's chair.

There is a rumour of a sighting of Theodosius here – but no, it was just a very tall, rather unpleasant man with an accent that was mistaken for Mdo-sa and was not.

A Nitashi ship vanishes; perhaps it is conspiracy, perhaps it is a kind of retribution – or perhaps it was a Pilot who should not have been allowed to fly, whose mind had been touched once too often by the dark, and who opened their arms to meet it.

I try to open my arms, but the dark is not interested in me.

The Lordat say that the dark is interested in things that are not of itself. That it is fascinated by life unknown, minds that twinkle, souls that shine. There is nothing malicious in its curiosity. It has no sense of right or wrong, good or bad. Rather, like a soft-winged bug drawn to the flame, it flitters and flits towards the warmth of a soul as it blazes through the night.

Does this mean, I ask, that I do not have a soul?

Possibly, one Lordat replies. But honestly, your question is a bit above my pay grade.

Theodosius is seen on a space station, boarding a ship.

Hé seems to be alone – or rather, *he* seems to be alone, the ur-hé and ur-shé of the Shine having been declared regressive, oppressive archetypes that exist only to crush people with their exclusivity and connotations of power.

By the time we reach the system where he was last seen, he is gone, and his ship left no flight data behind.

It is depressing to think that the power and connections he still has are enough to keep him safe. Frustrating to imagine the great many people – so many people – who can look him in the eye, know what he has done – the terror of Nitashi, the scourge of Cha-mdo – and still decide his Glint is worth more than their conscience. Any illusions I might have harboured about the ethical integrity of the Accord are vanished.

Eventually the search dries up.

Ships are reassigned.

Resources taken away.

I say I will keep on searching, and the Xi say sure, if you must, if you want, but he is gone by now.

He is gone.

This is a new age, and he is gone.

Even Rencki, when I ping qim, says it is time to move on. The worlds of what was the Shine are still in chaos; corruption is everywhere. The people of the Mdo cannot believe in generosity, in kindness, in compassion or sharing. They have been raised from birth to think such things are at best an opportunity, at worst a trap. The patience of the Accord is running dry; the victorious fleets thought they would be heroes, and are discovering that it is all far more complicated than that. It is becoming harder and harder to convince people to help.

"You could be useful on Tu-mdo," qe says. "You could do some good."

I think for a while about going back, and eventually say no. I can't imagine how returning to a world where I have always done it wrong would be any better than staying away.

Rencki is disappointed in me, but won't explain why.

In the end, the search for Theodosius was called off entirely. I returned the little scout ship that had become my world, and transferred instead to the only vessel that anyone in the galaxy was willing to lend me.

I went back to the *Emni*.

He was in spring when I boarded.

Little white flowers were blooming down his internal corridors and passageways, fresh buds of green blossoming in the soft warmth above his life-support generators and in the swaying breezes of oxygen scrubbers. Whoever had managed him over winter hadn't done their weeding properly, and a few roots were starting to poke up in the living quarters and around the Pilot's chair, which I chopped back and disposed of his in bio-tanks. The dining room table had grown and been pruned since I'd sat at it last, and fresh green ferns sprouted around the shower cubicles, their tips uncoiling in languid curls. A family of three-toed yellowbills were nesting in the engine room, and I contemplated letting them stay to help keep the insect population in balance, but in the end decided against it. I did not know where I would go, or what diseases might creep in through the airlock, and did not want to be responsible for trying to catch and inoculate a nest of tiny wild birds, however sweetly they sang in the dawn cycle of the ship.

When we first pushed towards arcspace, the *Emni* and I, his hull creaked with the sound of old and new wood straining against each other, and I smelled sap seeping through some old cracks that were bending with the forces of our flight. But he flew well and true, and spring was a good time to push the engines, find the faults and broken barks of his system, let them heal in the warm light of a yellow sun.

With nowhere else to go, I flew to Adjapar, to the sleeping moon watching over the still-terraforming planet.

Hundreds of millions of Adjumiris slept still in the cryofacilities above that world, guarded by generation ships whose inhabitants would never walk upon the finished world they were waiting for. I told my story, explained who I was, and was surprised how easily Adjumiri returned to my mouth, tinged with the accent of the Black Mountains.

I was given a tour of the cryofacility, past the sleepers in their endless corridors, and shown samples of the latest algae blooms that were blossoming across the oceans of Adjapar, far below.

"We are due for a great dieback soon," explained one terraformer, eyes bright with excitement at the impending ecological shift. "After that, we enter the final phase of floral seeding, and then . . . " tears glistened in their eyes, their voice shuddering with emotion; I had forgotten how small these things were in Adjumiris compared to the people of Nitashi, and how great they were when their feelings finally broke, "pioneer domes, the first families, the first children born on our new world."

I asked them if they had a museum, a place where the artefacts were kept.

They said yes, deep below the moon, in cold storage. No one

really went down there, though. Everything was held in stasis; neither my guide nor their children would see these things that had been saved. But one day – one day – in generations to come, the people of Adjapar would open these boxes and precious crates, and see the things made by their ancestors, and hear their voices, and sing their songs again.

"I hope it helps them understand something," said my guide. "I hope it teaches them something about who they are. Reminds them that they are not orphans. Not lost after all. That they still have a story that is their own."

There was singing when I left.

There were only eight of them, raising their voices in farewell. Hardly enough to make a proper Adjumiri chorus. They had been born on Adjumir, and would die on this moon, never seeing blue sky again. They sang for themselves, not for me, as I said my good-byes. Singing reminded them why, they said.

A cup of kol, on the Spindle.

Agran says: "I am not going to lie, I doubt I'll ever get round to studying this," when I give her a copy of Black Mountain Adjumiri grammar.

"It doesn't take up any room," I reply. "And someone might find it interesting later."

She nods, blows steam off the top of her cup. Then: "I hear that the worlds of the Shine are going to be saved. That the death of the suns will pass them by."

"So I hear."

"There are some people here who are pretty angry about that. Some who say that the people of the Shine – no matter who they were – must have known what happened on Nitashi. Must have known what was happening on Cha-mdo. Chose not to care. Aren't worth saving."

"What do you think?"

"I am a Spindler. We are far too polite to think anything so controversial. What about you?"

"I think you don't save the worlds of the Shine for who they are. You do it for who *you* are. You want to condemn the people of the Mdo for turning away? Then don't turn away."

"That's a very messy position, if you think about it too long."

I click my tongue in the roof of my mouth, once, to agree without agreeing.

"More kol?" she asks.

"I'll take another cup. One for the road."

Agran also sang when I left.

She struggled with the words, found it hard to catch the tune, and though these songs should never be sung solo, in her it was beautiful. In music, accents tend to become softer, fuzzier, the edges burned away, and so she sang in Adjumiri, because it was the Adjumiri thing to do.

I reached out to the dark, one last time.

It did not pay me any heed.

PART 5

Where Once There Was a Star

Chapter 63

I t was late autumn on my little island near the town of Poulinio, down the far end of the Mun peninsula. I shuddered with the touch of wind when I disembarked from the *Emni*, smelled rain – thick rain, heavy rain blown in off the sea – and realised I didn't have any appropriate clothes. I had learned to travel with clothes for every biome, but it had been so long since I had set foot in any place that wasn't climate-controlled, temperature-controlled that the reality of a world that was living and breathing and full of change knocked the air from my lungs. My steps didn't feel quite right; I grabbed my ticket for the tramway to Poulinio too hard and nearly crushed it in my hand; tried to climb the stairs too fast and tripped over my own feet. The light of the sun, unfiltered by technology, hurt my eyes. Perhaps it had always hurt my eyes. The air smelled of that nameless, unsure different that will quickly become familiar as the brain filters down its reality to only things that are changing in its endless efforts to save time and energy.

I had told the authorities I was coming, and they had replied with a polite sluggishness that suggested bureaucratic chaos raging tumultuously behind the scenes.

Of course, they said.

That island of yours.

Of course.

It's become quite overgrown.

It's become . . .

No one really wanted to go there, when you were gone.

No one wanted to . . .

(Walk in a cursed place, where a creature of darkness once roamed.)

Sometimes kids go out there as a dare, so please don't be upset if you see them around. And the fishing boats sometimes stop for a picnic, but we'll let them know. Let them know you're coming back. There's a doctor, actually, from the nearby city, who is very interested in getting a sample of your hair . . .

Major Phrawon was dead, had been for many years.

Even Yulin's eldest child, who had been a shy if perfectly polite snippet of a human when I'd departed, was greying, old. He gave me a lift out to my island, an ident to call if I ever needed anything. I said thank you, I'd keep that in mind, but not to worry about me, not at all, and I remembered not to sing goodbye as he returned to the waters.

My island was indeed overgrown.

The bluebrush trees were bent double with their own weight, and infested with a parasitic vine whose combined mass had already toppled three of the grove, broken nests of migrating longlaps around the shattered branches. The wild grasses had grown into thatch, smothering all the delicate flowers that had once bloomed there, the orchard almost inaccessible for the great maze of thorns that had erupted around the hedge. It would take months of clearing, of traipsing back and forth – there was enough labour here to try and resurrect the ancient hover-sled, see if it remembered how to float, maybe order in some spare parts, but of course that wouldn't solve the sheer monotony of the labour, of the to-and-fro that would be inevitable, that only a gardener could do. I found myself swelling with a mixture of pre-emptive fatigue and excitement at the prospect. What would the soil feel like, having had so many years of being left alone? Would it crumble, damp and black beneath my fingers? Would worms wiggle; had mushrooms sprouted beneath my windowsill, and would they be poisonous or delicacies? I was in a uniquely privileged position to find out, I realised, and for the first time in a long time, I nearly laughed as I trudged my loop around the island.

The first sign of anything unusual was the boat.

My little boat – the one I'd used for fishing on hot autumn evenings – was a cracked remnant of a thing, lichen blooming up the side, fresh ferns bursting through the hull. I resolved to leave it the moment I saw it, let nature continue munching on its keratinous bones. Yet beside it – another boat. A newer boat, big enough for one comfortable rower or two people who didn't mind a bit of a squeeze, knee knocking to knee. A tarp had been pulled over it, weighted down on either side with stones, some care taken in its preservation.

A boat on the island implied a sailor, one who had come and not yet departed.

I looked around as if I might in that instant see the source of this anomaly, and of course saw nothing but the overhanging trees swaying in the cold sea wind, the prick of crimson promising an oncoming sunset. It was the kind of evening for warm hats and fingerless gloves wrapped around a cup of something sweet; the kind of night to curl up indoors while the wind howled outside the window, to be buried deeper than necessary beneath thick blankets, a littler fuller than was strictly required on a belly-stuffing meal.

I feared neither a stranger nor the dark.

Indeed, the feeling that this boat stirred in me was an old one, almost comforting in its calm.

I felt *curious*.

For the first time in such a long time, the familiar sense of it, the familiar stirring, a kind of fascination, a childlike wonder at a thing unknown. War had smothered it; the prospect of death held no interest. But this was a mystery, and at the mystery I felt the awakening of something lost, familiar, unkind.

Thank you, I whispered to the boat, to the coming dark, to the stirring of my soul.

Thank you.

I wandered along paths grown narrow by neglect, and now that I was looking, I saw little signs of disturbance, summer thorns snapped by the passage of an animal larger than the snuffling burrow-diggers and fungi-sniffers of my realm. By the time I reached the vegetable patches that hemmed in my cottage, the sun was nearly set and the dark prickled with endless beauty, infinite possibility, fascinating in its depth.

Thank you, I whispered. *Thank you.*

Some efforts had been made to tidy up a few broken vines in my garden. The labours were poor, crude, quickly abandoned. Gourd had bred with gourd to create monster beasts of speckled yellow and bloody purple, new species flourishing while I had been away. The fallen leaves had been brushed off the roof of the cottage where they otherwise might have covered the solar cells; a single light shone in the window, the battery by the door showing a 77 per cent charge.

I listened to the sea and the wind, the settling calls of the evening birds as they bickered and grew quiet against the dark.

Then I walked up to the door and knocked.

Silence from within.

After the silence, movement. A pushing-back of a chair. A moving of feet. Then silence again. Someone has risen; someone has walked towards the door. Someone has hesitated on the verge of answering. Someone is making up their mind.

I think I am perhaps curious enough that doors will not stop me.

I think, if I wish to, that I can pass straight through this wall, stick my head in, call out: anyone home?

But if I do that, who knows what will happen next. Who knows how much blood will be spilled, whose heart will be ripped out, whose brain I will end up holding in the palm of my hand as the curiosity overwhelms me, tips me from *who is there* to *what is there and why and how and* . . .

And all the other questions the endless, wondering dark keeps asking of this universe, never quite understanding the answers that are given.

So instead I wait, then knock again.

After a moment, I hear a latch lifted, and the door swings back.

The man who stands on the other side, half lit in the glow of the single shining lamp, is too tall for my cottage. He would have been unusually tall for the average population of the archipelago even before his genetic enhancements made him something of a giant, my eyes level with the upper half of his chest. I have to crane to see the top of his head, which he has shaved and allowed to regrow, not glorious and golden, but limp and white, the long plait of his office gone. He has had cosmetic surgery to soften the edges the scars – that artful tapestry– that were his pride and his identity, and I can only assume that the new green of his eyes is a permanent dye hiding enhancements.

He appears to be unarmed, but that is rather meaningless where he is concerned.

He seems a little surprised to see me, and then he does not.

"Hello," Theodosius says, in the language of the Shine. "I wondered if you'd show up."

Chapter 64

He makes a cup of tea.

He uses my cups but his tea, acquired from a new shop in Poulinio that I have not yet visited, whose owner prides herself on her exemplary palate and taste.

I sit and watch him pour the water, steep the leaves.

He is unfamiliar with the process. He has had people to do this for him for so long – too long. He is perhaps one of the few people who is as old as I, but for the first time since I have known him, his age is beginning to show. His hands shake as he pours the water; he gives a little huff as he settles down into his chair – my chair – by the heater.

I sip the tea he offers, and do not say thank you.

He does not drink his at all.

It is possible that he is poisoning me, I realise, but what would be the point?

Poison, stab, strangle, drown. There are not enough ways to dispose of my body in a timely enough manner, in a permanent enough manner, that I will not return. All he'd be doing is making me mad.

The realisation is almost exciting, and I sip a little more, trying out the taste of a thing that should be familiar yet feels so strange after so long from this place.

After a while, he sips his tea too, an acknowledgement perhaps of a test quietly passed, eyes never leaving me, hands pressed around the cup as if his fingers are cold.

"Enhancements getting a little loose round the edges?" I ask at last, tilting my chin towards him in the Mdo way.

"I was always told that ageing, when it happened, would be unpleasant. I just assumed I had more time."

I clicked my tongue, and then, realising he wouldn't understand, nodded. "I hear it happens rapidly, once the protocols stop."

"In its way. Frailty comes quickly. Loss of bone density, muscle mass, telomere shortening and so on. But I have always been diligent in leading a healthy and active life, regardless of the work of my surgeons. I am in excellent physical condition. In other words ... I could live many years as an old, crumbling man, waiting to die."

"You've had access to plenty of airlocks. Missed opportunity, if you ask me."

"I did contemplate it, but how utterly ignoble. It is not the way of the Shine to give up. It is not what our people do."

I clicked my tongue again, sank a little deeper into my chair, while the night settled outside and the wind rattled the windows.

Theodosius mused, his eyes half turned to some distant place: "My own people sold me out. Very difficult to promote the right sort. You need people who are aggressive enough, fiery enough that they will betray you. It shows they have initiative. But you also need people weak enough, loyal enough that they will follow you to the edge of the world. Off the edge of the world. I have always been very good at choosing the right sort – strong Shine, but not too strong. But war, of course – or rather, I should say, *defeat* – brings out extreme qualities in even the most dour of natures. The most loyal will die for you even when their death is inane, foolish. The most ambitious will turn like that." A snap of his fingers, less sharp, less ringing perhaps than he desired; he glanced a moment at his own digits as if betrayed. "I saw both in the last days of the Shine."

"Clearly you made it work."

"I think that depends on your metrics. I survived. I escaped and I hid and I survived. That is of course a remarkable achievement – I am a remarkable person, you see. But it is only a thing the historians, my biographers will be amazed at. The reality of living it – of being on the run – is really rather tiring and prosaic."

"You have not come to a glamorous place."

"No. But the irony of it – the delicious irony of it. When I realised which system I'd landed in, the last of my resources running dry. Well. I had to really. All that intelligence I'd gathered on you, and you out there hunting me . . . delicious, I thought. Utterly delectable."

He said "delicious" almost like an Adjumiri, a thing to be cherished that is so much more than taste.

"So here you are."

"Here I am."

"And what now? You are aware that you cannot kill me. Not in any meaningful, lasting way."

"I know," he mused. "Though I thought of numerous ways I could try. Keep you alive for days, weeks maybe, bleeding you dry, making my feelings known. But that trick of yours – the way you sometimes cease to be when attention is elsewhere, that fascinating phasing in and phasing out. Not quite here, not quite anywhere. If I had a team of people then I feel very confident we could torture you to death perpetually, but I do not. As you see. I do not. And to be honest, after all this time . . . I'm not sure I would derive as much satisfaction from it as I might hope."

I clicked again, didn't bother to explain, rolled my shoulders back. The cottage smelled of damp and dust – everything would need cleaning, resealing, putting right. Months of work, maybe years, have to choose what to prioritise first, get the place comfortable enough to sleep in, water, power, heat; get the pantry dry and sealed, arrange food from the town, then work outwards perhaps, starting with the vegetable garden and moving towards the orchard one season at a time. Once I had stable power, I could look at signing up to a few courses again, or maybe I could even offer to teach something, not that I felt especially qualified in anything significant, but who knows, after all this time . . .

Theodosius shifted in his chair, which creaked beneath him.

He was getting used, I felt, to having people ignore him, but it was not yet an experience he was comfortable with.

I tried to think if I had anything I could possibly say to him.

I did not.

Tried to think if there was anything I could ask.

Only one question leaped to mind, and it wasn't even a question, just a statement of a distant memory I would be mildly satisfied to have confirmed. "A while ago – years ago now, before Cha-mdo – you interfaced with a Tryphon."

His eyes, shifted in colour and unnaturally bright, watched me across the room. "I did."

"Why?"

"To see what it was like, of course."

"And how did you find it?"

"Unpleasant, naturally. Not an experience I would recommend."

"The madness, the risk of death . . . "

"My exposure was short. I simply . . . wished to know."

And just like that, my curiosity was gone.

I recognised its absence with a start, surprised to discover it so quickly faded.

There was nothing more I wanted from this man.

Nothing I wanted to say or do.

He was . . .

. . . boring.

A boring ex-tyrant. Petty in his ambitions. Tedious in his self-righteousness. Predictable even in his excessive flourishes of egotistical drama. A big man in a tiny room on an island in the sea.

I sighed, rose to my feet, suddenly aching, suddenly very human after all.

"I'll call the authorities," I said. "They'll send someone to pick you up."

"Don't."

"It's the right thing to do."

"I will shoot you and run away if you try," he explained, sounding almost a little embarrassed. "I will not tolerate a show trial, you see. I will not have my throat cut by the Yeh'haim while I sleep."

"I think it would be hard to argue that you deserve anything less."

He shrugged.

It was such a strange gesture. A thing of the Shine, of the old world. Something my parents might have done, before the bombs fell. I watched his shoulders move, and there it was, a little whiff of fascination, my old, familiar friend, gone in an instant. But not anger.

"Are you going to kill me?" he asked.

"Is that what you want?"

"I expected as much."

"But is it what you want? I think it is. I think it is the easy way out. And I suppose you reasoned that with me, death is fairly unavoidable. Come to the isle, leave your boat, wait. The sun will set, and in the dark . . . who knows what I'll do? No choice, really. No chance to change your mind, once I get myself in a certain kind of mood. I'll find you no matter what. I'll be curious to taste your blood, no?"

"I didn't dwell too much on the details."

"Of course you didn't. Of course."

I finished my tea. Drained it down. Stood up, walked to the counter, set my cup on the side. Listened to the wind. Rain had come, was thickening to a familiar tappity-tap on the roof. The cottage's battery would need servicing too, repriming after all this time. Messy job, if you didn't do it right, but worth sorting before winter.

"How old are you?" I blurted, the question rising to my tongue despite myself.

"A hundred and something. Eighty? Eighty-two? Yourself?"

"Something like that. I saw you at Glastya Row, when you bombed the city. Everyone said you were destined for great things."

"Well, they were right, weren't they? I'm sorry, is this part of your process? Do you need to talk, or should we just jump to the part where I try and kill you and you finally kill me? How does this work?"

"It helps if you imagine I am a monster."

"Aren't you? Isn't that what you are?"

"My name is Mawukana na-Vdnaze, and I am a very poor copy of myself," I replied. "I'm going to bed, assuming the rodents didn't get in and eat my mattress."

"You're . . . what?" He rose, indignation and a sloshing of cooling tea over the side of his mug. "You can't do that!"

"I think you'll find I can. Kill me while I sleep if you want. It won't make a difference, unless you watch my corpse. Even then, eventually, you'll have to sleep, and the moment your concentration lapses, I'll be back. There's a lot to do on the island. A lot of tidying. I don't really care where you sleep. You can leave the light on, if it helps."

"Why would you do this? Why wouldn't you—"

"It has been suggested," I cut in, "that I have about me certain god-like qualities. The only god-like quality I can perceive is that I persist. I could persist for a very long time. And I am, it turns out, capable of understanding certain decisions. Cruel, cold decisions. Decisions about those who live and those who die. Those who are saved and those who are left behind. I left the person I loved on Adjumir, you see, when you sent your soldiers in to kill ter. I understand why the Slow let you invade Nitashi, why qe let the people of Cha-mdo burn. Qe balanced the equation, and it is the cruellest thing in the world, and it is also, in its way, born of love. A god-like kind of love. God-like. I think that is how people talked about you, no? Anyway, leaving aside for a moment what it is to love, and lose, and make those choices as to who will live and who will die, the other thing I feel I have learned is that there's no harm in occasionally taking your time to think about things."

I sighed, shook my head, clicked one last time.

"So you see," I concluded, "I'm going to bed. And tomorrow I'm going to sort out the pantry and make an inventory of supplies, and work out what to do with you. Perhaps I'll kill you. But honestly, right now, the idea bores me. Perhaps I'll turn you over to the authorities. I'll probably do that. There's a cliff you can throw yourself off if you really feel like it. We'll work it out in the morning. Take a little time to think."

"Is there anything," he asked, words flopping like dropped bricks onto the floor at his feet, "I can do to induce you to change your mind?"

"Careful with that word – 'induce' – especially if you say it in Xiha. You should learn Adjumiri. They have five different ways of asking for help, and at least three ways of saying 'mercy'. Mercy for one whose suffering should cease. Mercy for a foe; mercy that is a gift given without ever needing to be asked for."

Another way too, a fourth definition on the tip of my tongue.

Trying to remember the sounds of it, shape it into some kind of meaning that would translate into Mdo-sa.

Mercy for yourself, when you have lived too long in shame.

Something of that nature, at least.

"Goodnight, Theodosius Rhode," I said, and went to bed, leaving the last Executor of the Shine alone.

Chapter 65

Later – much later, the kind of many-years passage that makes people uncomfortable – I flew the *Emni* one last time.

He was getting old, my beautiful ship. Soon he would start to shed his final layers of bark, heat shield cracking and engines leaking into the capillaries of his system. Autumn was turning to a final winter, and so cool and dark we flew, the lights turned low and hull doors closed to all but the essential rooms and systems, back to the place where once the Lovers had been.

Back to Lhonoja, the graveyard of the binary stars.

The Edge had long since passed, and the subsequent neutrino blast was rippling through the galaxy, dissipating into the dark. Forests grew on Adjapar, and the magnetic shield above Tu-mdo had been dismantled many years ago. Two stars had collapsed into one and created a detonation that had scoured all life from the galaxy for light years all around – but if I wanted to, I could still take the *Emni* to a place hundreds of light years away and look back through time to see the light of the Lovers shining still.

Not now.

Now I sat in the dead-dark death left behind by the explosion, by the light that had killed two worlds and torn apart dozens more, and I poured out a cup of kol, and I sang the songs of lovers falling, and toasted those who were still alive.

The nothingness around the husk of these stars was not a complete nothingness, of course.

A black hole was coalescing in the remnant core, matter squeezed into matter into matter into matter, dragging the burning remnants of whatever was left behind into a point of darkness from which no light would ever escape. Not yet a fully fledged monster, a threat to me and my ship, but one day it would be a darkness deeper than even the stillest corners of arcspace.

A curious thought: could a ship escape an event horizon via arcspace jump?

I accessed the ship's onboard databanks, there being nothing living within easy comms reach to supplement my system. A few papers cropped up – the most interesting was a two-thousand-word tract on whether the conservation of data, let alone energy, applied in arcspace. I ran a few calculations, tried to coax the computer into doing maths whose purpose it could not understand, and in the end decided this was not my experiment to try.

After all, there was a life to live.

A life to blaze brightly. A song to sing across the stars.

Instead, I raised my glass one last time, drained it down, then slipped into the Pilot's chair.

Hello, I whispered, as the void reached out in familiar, silent embrace. *Where next?*

About the Author

Claire North is a pseudonym for Catherine Webb, who wrote several novels in various genres before publishing their first major work as Claire North, *The First Fifteen Lives of Harry August*. It was a critically acclaimed success, receiving rave reviews and becoming a word-of-mouth bestseller. They have since published several hugely popular and critically acclaimed novels, won the World Fantasy Award and the John W. Campbell Memorial Award, and been shortlisted for the *Sunday Times*/PFD Young Writer of the Year Award, the Arthur C. Clarke Award and the Philip K. Dick Award. They live in London. They can be found on Instagram (@clairenorth_author) and X (@clairenorth42).

Find out more about Claire North and other Orbit authors by registering for the free monthly newsletter at orbit-books.co.uk

Help us make the next generation of readers

We – both author and publisher – hope you enjoyed this book. We believe that you can become a reader at any time in your life, but we'd love your help to give the next generation a head start.

Did you know that 9% of children don't have a book of their own in their home, rising to 12% in disadvantaged families*? We'd like to try to change that by asking you to consider the role you could play in helping to build readers of the future.

We'd love you to think of sharing, borrowing, reading, buying or talking about a book with a child in your life and spreading the love of reading. We want to make sure the next generation continue to have access to books, wherever they come from.

And if you would like to consider donating to charities that help fund literacy projects, find out more at www.literacytrust.org.uk and www.booktrust.org.uk.

Thank you.

hachette
CHILDREN'S GROUP

little, brown
BOOK GROUP

*As reported by the National Literacy Trust